Echoes of Guilt

Echoes of Guilt

Rob Sinclair

CANELO

First published in the United Kingdom in 2020 by Canelo

Canelo Digital Publishing Limited
31 Helen Road
Oxford OX2 0DF
United Kingdom

Print ISBN 978 1 78863 901 9
Ebook ISBN 978 1 78863 900 2

Look for more great books at www.canelo.co

Printed and bound in Great Britain by Clays Ltd, Elcograf S.p.A.

For my Gran

Prologue

Hope? No, there was no hope left inside him now. Not after so long. Not after what he'd already been through.

Guilt? No. Not that either. He didn't deserve any of this, even if it was inescapable that his own choices and mistakes had led him to be here.

Fear? At one point, yes. In fact, before fear, there had even been courage, back when his initial fight was still burning strong. His confidence, charisma, arrogance even, had seen him through the first stages of this ordeal. He'd firmly believed back then that there'd be a way out. A way to turn things on his captor. A way to make *him* pay.

Such optimism was nothing but a blurred memory. Fear had soon taken over, but he wasn't sure there was even any of that left any more. His tormented mind had moved to a different place altogether. A grim and dark place from where he knew there was no chance of a return.

So what was this emotion that so consumed him now?

He heard the footsteps outside. Hard. Slow. Deliberate. His tired and pain-wracked body instinctively tensed. The throb of his weak heart, which had miraculously kept him going through all of this, ramped up to a soft thud – the most dramatic response it could now muster.

He struggled against the restraints – a thick metal chain, wrapped around his midriff and chest – that dug into his skin and kept his arms pinned to his sides, and also kept him pinned to the metal workbench he was lying on. His legs were similarly tethered, and with the patchwork of open wounds across his flesh he'd long ago realised that the less he moved, the more he was able to push the persistent agony he was in deep into his troubled mind.

What was that? The well in the pit of his stomach.

If not fear then what?

The thick key turned in the lock and the sturdy metal door heaved open with a whoosh of fresh but cold air that sent his hacked skin prickling.

The man walked in and a switch was flipped and the darkened room became bathed in a sinister orange glow.

Could light from a flickering overhead bulb really be sinister? It seemed ridiculous to think so. Yet in this dank and depressing room, he had no doubt it was true, even if it was more to do with *what* the light illuminated rather than the light itself.

The door closed with a hefty *thunk*.

His eyes were moving rapidly now, his gaze flicking around the room, looking anywhere but at the man who was slowly taking off his overcoat as if eking out every last millisecond of tension.

He glanced over to the ghoulish array of items on the shelves to his left. The tidbits – souvenirs – were the little that remained of the countless lives that had ended within this room.

Next his eyes settled on the bench across the way, upon which sat the tubes and the vials and jars that had been used to force-feed him after he'd refused to eat for so long. The paltry liquid nourishment had done its job – just – of keeping him alive when he would otherwise have been dead.

Just looking at the equipment made his throat ache. And yet that was nowhere near the worst of it. On the adjacent bench sat the nightmarish collection of metal tools. Instruments that had already been used to inflict the most horrific pain and injuries that he wasn't sure could ever properly heal. That bench was where his eyes now remained fixed.

The man stepped over to him... Picked up a scalpel that he twisted in his fingers. The tormentor caught the eye of his captive. No words were needed. Both men knew what was coming next.

And that was when he finally put his finger on what the emotion was that now swelled inside him, nearly bursting from every pore.

Desperation.

That was all he had left. More than anything, he was simply desperate for this trauma to be over. Desperate to be given the chance to breathe his last undignified breath. He wanted... no, he *needed* to die. Today. Here. Now. This had to end.

And so he mustered every ounce of strength to do the only thing he could think of doing.

He begged.

Over and over. He pleaded desperately, horribly. Seconds passed. Minutes? He couldn't tell, as the garbled words fell from his mouth one after the other.

All to no purpose.

Soon he was spent. He had nothing left to give. Nothing left to say. The man still held his eye. Still held the scalpel between his twisted fingers. His eyes burned brightly in the electric light.

'No,' he said. Calm. No amusement, no anger or hostility. Absolute calm and detachment from the hideous actions he'd already undertaken. 'I'm not even close to finishing with you yet.'

Then he stepped forward, blade in hand.

Chapter 1

Five years later

Dani rolled her eyes when the door to the house finally opened and DS Easton tumbled out, doing up the top buttons of his shirt as he went, his winter coat draped over one arm as he shuffled along the path to her car.

He sank down into the passenger seat, shivering away, but then it was only one degree outside and his coat was uselessly dumped on his lap. When he caught Dani's eye, she couldn't resist an accusatory glance at the clock on the dashboard.

'Sorry,' he said.

'Let me guess,' Dani said. 'The kids?'

Easton nodded. Not that they were his kids. Aaron was unmarried, didn't even have a girlfriend right now. Unfortunately Dani believed it was increasingly likely things would stay that way for some time, with his sister and her kids having apparently moved into his cramped two bed house for good. What had started as them seeking shelter for a few days after his sister had walked out on her last down-and-out boyfriend over the summer, had turned into a six-month stay. So far. The kids had even been enrolled in a local school three months ago, much to Easton's dismay.

Dani had seen the girl and boy – Jasmin, eleven; Carl, nine – leaving the house ten minutes earlier, all bright and breezy.

'I don't know how anybody does it,' Easton said as Dani pulled the car back onto the road. The rear tyres slipped on a patch of black ice but Dani soon found traction again, though she'd keep her speed steady until they were on roads that the council had actually bothered to grit. The cold snap was already a few days in, and cars and homes and trees and gardens were covered in a thick layer of silvery frost that the low winter sun would struggle to shift. 'Getting those two ready and out the house... I've been up since six.'

It was now eight thirty.

'So where's Sis?' Dani asked, sounding about as unsympathetic as she felt. Perhaps not an uncommon position for Dani, given her continuing battle to overcome the after effects of the TBI – traumatic brain injury – that had nearly ended her life a little over four years ago, though in the case of the Easton domestic situation, she really believed it was a mess he should have sorted by now. At least his police work was far more organised and far less calamitous than his home life.

'She never came back last night,' he said. 'Who bloody knows where she's ended up this time.'

'You never sound too bothered by—'

'She's fine,' he said. 'She texted me to say she'd be back to pick the kids up from school. She's not laying in a ditch somewhere.'

Dani knew he was glad about that, even if he didn't sound it.

'So, we're off to court, eh?' Easton said.

Dani nodded.

'What exactly are we expecting to get out of this morning?'

The way he asked the question made it seem as if he thought they were wasting their time. Easton was the closest thing to a partner that Dani had ever had in the police force. As a DI she was his superior, and technically on any case there could be a whole team of Sergeants and Constables working with her, but she trusted Easton more than any of them and regular had him by her side. Yet on more than one occasion recently he'd expressed his doubt about the amount of time she continued to spend on the Damian Curtis case. But then the case remained far more personal for her than it was for anyone else. She wouldn't give up, even if the trial was already underway, and the CPS, in theory, already had everything they wanted from the police.

'I want to hear what this new psychiatrist has to say for himself on the stand,' Dani said.

'Everett?'

'Yeah.'

'Probably the same as he said the last time we went to see him at Rampton.'

Rampton Secure Hospital, where Sheldon Everett's patient, Damian Curtis, was being held; Curtis, who'd murdered six people over the summer and was now on trial for his crimes. His defence team were doing everything they could to argue that he hadn't the mental capacity to kill. That his hands had taken those lives, but that he couldn't be held culpable. But this wasn't a simple case of diminished responsibility – a mentally ill person taking the lives of others, their actions caused by their mental issues. Curtis's defence were arguing that, in fact, his actions had been very clearly and carefully directed by another party, with Curtis nothing more than a puppet in a sick and twisted charade.

The prosecution had robustly rebuffed those claims so far, instead setting their sights on Curtis and Curtis alone. They wanted a murder conviction. Curiously Dani found herself on the defence's side. Her serious issue, and one that had caused her to lose many nights of sleep over the last few months, was that she disagreed with *who* the defence team were claiming to be Curtis's directing influence. Both in the courtroom, and throughout the UK press, Curtis's now dead ex-psychiatrist was being blamed. Dani, on the other hand, seemed to be the only person in the world who thought the culprit to be someone else entirely.

Her twin brother.

The public gallery in the courtroom inside the unnecessarily square and bland-looking Crown Court in Birmingham city centre was only half full, despite the large media focus that the trial had garnered in its build up. In a way Dani was glad about that. She and Easton took seats at the front of the gallery where nothing but a wooden barrier and low tinted glass separated them from the prosecution and defence teams.

Despite it being his first appearance at the trial, Sheldon Everett looked tired and dishevelled, both in his clothing and his appearance, as he headed up to the stand. His thinning mucky grey-brown hair was a flopping mess, his glasses hung lopsidedly across his face and his cream shirt was rapidly untucking itself and spilling out around his low-riding trousers. He looked like he'd been dragged through a hedge backwards, but Dani knew from her previous interactions with him that he was both intelligent and articulate. He was also strangely charismatic, though Dani had never mentioned that fact to anyone else for fear of ridicule.

Damian Curtis's lawyer, Iona O'Hare, a heavyset woman in her forties, warmed Everett up with a series of open questions which did little other than give the judge and jury and every other person in the courtroom a potted history of Curtis's recent past: his actions a number of years ago which had led to the deaths of his girlfriend and young son and for which he'd been convicted of their manslaughter; the years he'd since spent in Long Lartin prison – though it was conveniently omitted that for much of that time Curtis had been sharing a cell with Dani's brother, Ben, who himself was serving a life sentence for murder – and the fact that Curtis had been released on parole earlier in the year, having served a little more than half of his sentence, and how, after just a few weeks of freedom, he'd gone AWOL and his killing spree had started.

There were six victims to that spree, all of them people involved, one way or another, in Curtis's previous manslaughter trial: judge, lawyer, witnesses; even Dani and her boyfriend Jason had been targets of Curtis – Jason, when he'd still been with the police, having been Curtis's arresting officer all those years ago. Jason, had remained in hospital as he battled to recover both physically and mentally from his near-death experience at the hands of Damian Curtis during his rampage of violence.

But what was the truth about why Curtis had snapped?

'And the final victim of the defendant's alleged killing spree was Dr Helen Collins,' O'Hare said, a statement rather than a question. 'She'd been the defendant's psychiatrist for much of his time in incarceration.'

'So I'm led to believe,' Everett responded.

'And can you explain, based on your knowledge of criminal psychiatry, what the nature of her work with the defendant would have entailed?'

'In fact, I've had open access to her records,' Everett said. 'So I've the benefit of a great deal of information as to her relationship with Damian Curtis.'

'And?'

'And her initial appointment came while Curtis was being held on remand over the deaths of his girlfriend, Charmaine Dillon, and her son. Collins was an expert witness at Curtis's first trial, testifying as to his mental health issues.'

'And what issues were those?'

'Collins attested that Curtis suffered an array of mental health problems. Severe manic depression, psychosis. Her conclusion, which she shared with the court, was that Curtis acted with diminished responsibility the night he killed Ms Dillon and her son. He pleaded guilty to their manslaughter and was sent to Long Lartin prison, which I'd argue was unlikely to be the best place for him.'

'Could you explain that?'

'Damian Curtis is a very damaged and disturbed man. He needs constant medical supervision and intervention, and a highly secure mental institution, such as Rampton where he is now being held, is by far the most appropriate facility for such a person.'

Dani looked from Everett over to Lloyd Barker, the CPS barrister who remained seated, eyes cast down at the folder he had on his lap. Was he even listening to this? Why wasn't he interjecting? Not that Dani knew exactly what he should be objecting to, but currently Everett was being given free rein, it seemed.

The conversation went on with Everett describing, in his own opinion, the work that Collins had carried out with Curtis while he was in prison: the number of meetings the two of them had held, the contents of the many written notes Collins had kept of their sessions, together with audio recordings, all of it pointing to the ongoing belief that Curtis remained a seriously troubled man, although not necessarily one who had ever displayed sociopathy.

At least not until his release.

'Which leads us to the defendant's parole in May of this year,' O'Hare said. 'Weeks after his release, he is alleged to have killed his first victim, Oscar Redfearne.'

Alleged. Why was O'Hare even bothering to stick with using that word all the time? Everyone knew Curtis had killed those people – at least in a physical sense. The only real question was *why*, and whether he could be held responsible.

Still nothing from Barker.

'According to the charges put against him, yes,' Everett said.

'And in the days that followed, it is alleged that he took another five lives.'

'Again, that's not a proven fact, but that's why we're here, I guess.'

Everett looked nervously over to Barker, as though he too was expecting an objection. Barker still said nothing.

'Was there anything in Dr Collins's records to suggest the defendant was a threat to the public, prior to his parole?'

'Absolutely not. Otherwise he wouldn't have been released.'

'Collins never noted that the defendant displayed any indications of sociopathy?'

'No.'

'So this violent spree was somewhat out of the blue, would you say?'

'It didn't fit with his previous behaviour.'

'Objection,' Barker said, suddenly rising to his feet. 'This witness had no direct contact with the defendant until some time after the alleged crimes, so his view as to the defendant's *previous* behaviour is without grounds and irrelevant.'

The judge concurred. O'Hare didn't look in the least perturbed. In fact she looked faintly amused for some reason.

'Mr Everett,' she said. 'Was the defendant's alleged violent behaviour, that is the subject of this trial, at odds with the evidence you have seen of his behaviour and mental health issues through what you know of Dr Collins's work?'

'Yes,' Everett said.

'Thank you. And so, in your professional capacity, what explanation is there for the defendant to have carried out these horrific acts he is alleged to have committed?'

'I didn't have the benefit of analysing Curtis until after these crimes took place, but what I can tell you is that his mental health problems are all consuming. He's a very, very disturbed man, in many different ways. But, perhaps most pertinently, his fragmented mind also makes him highly susceptible to coercion.'

'You believe it's possible that the defendant was coerced into killing?'

'I think it's a highly likely explanation. In fact, my own experiences with him show that his psychosis manifests itself, in one respect, in him hearing voices in his mind, and having discussed this issue at length with Curtis, it's entirely plausible that at least one of those voices has been… implanted.'

There were a few questioning murmurs around the courtroom now, though Barker was head down again.

'Implanted?' O'Hare said.

'What I mean is, it's my view that at least one of the voices that Damian Curtis has heard could be there as the result of someone deliberately manipulating his fragile mind.'

'And what would it take to achieve such a feat?'

'It's not a heavily researched area, but this wouldn't be a simple task. Most likely, in my opinion, such manipulation could only be carried out by someone with extensive knowledge of mental health.'

'A psychologist or psychiatrist?'

'Someone medically trained in mental health, yes.'

'And, remind me, which people with such qualifications was the defendant exposed to during his time in Long Lartin prison?'

'Records show he had brief interventions and check-ups from various medical professionals during his time in prison, though these were all routine in nature, and were procedures carried out with other corroborating witnesses present. The only person who meets the professional criteria, and who also had, in effect, unfettered access to Damian Curtis, was Dr Helen Collins.'

'Is it your view, therefore, that the only person who could have coerced the defendant into committing these crimes, was, in fact, Dr Helen Collins?'

'Yes.'

Even more murmurs now. Dani clenched her fists to channel her rising frustration. What the hell was Barker doing, just sitting there?

'Thank you, Mr Everett,' O'Hare said.

She took her seat and the judge prompted Barker, who after a couple of seconds of delay finally decided to look up from his folder. He apologised to the judge in his typically foppish manner, then rose to his feet.

'Mr Everett, do you have any direct evidence that Dr Helen Collins manipulated Damian Curtis in the way you have suggested?'

'I mean, there was of course no physical record of this. She had no notes describing such a procedure, there were no audio or video recordings, or—'

'I think your answer is "no" correct?'

Everett paused.

'Mr Everett, yes or no, do you have any direct evidence that Dr Helen Collins manipulated Damian Curtis in the way you have suggested?'

'No.'

'Do you have any direct evidence that any other person or persons manipulated Damian Curtis in the way you have suggested.'

A short pause. 'No.'

'And so the belief you have just expressed, that Damian Curtis was coerced into killing, is in fact a belief that is not corroborated by any direct physical evidence whatsoever.'

Everett said nothing.

'Mr Everett?'

'Sorry, I didn't realise that was a question. I'm here to give my expert opinion which is based on my expertise in this field. Expert opinion is in fact considered evidence, is it not?'

'Noted. But other than your *opinion*, there is no direct evidence either that Damian Curtis was manipulated into killing, or that if he was, who that manipulator may have been. Is that correct?'

'Well… if you're only talking about physical evidence—'

'Yes, I was.'

'Then yes.'

'Thank you. Likewise, do you have any evidence of a *motive* for such manipulation? Either in relation to Dr Helen Collins or any other party?'

'Motive?'

'Why would Dr Helen Collins have manipulated Damian Curtis into killing people? Herself included.'

'I… I… that's not what—'

'Do you have any evidence of a motive for why Dr Helen Collins, or any other party, would manipulate Damian Curtis in the way you have stated on the stand here today? A simple yes or no will suffice.'

'I've seen it suggested that Dr Collins was having an aff—'

'I'm not asking for hearsay, or for what you've read in the press. I'm asking about evidence which you have directly seen. Is it yes or no?'

'No.'

'Thank you. No more questions.'

—

The first recess of the day soon arrived and as everyone in the courtroom rose to leave, Dani had to hold back from storming out. Barker stood and turned and did a double take, eventually catching Dani's eye. His lips turned ever so slightly in an awkward smile of acknowledgement, before he looked away again and began a conversation with his underling.

Was that it? Dani wondered. A little look and a smile? Or a smirk, was it? After all of the time and effort Dani had put into this case. After all of the interviews with Curtis and his lawyer, with her brother Ben, with Barker himself, and now when the big day came he was simply going to gloss over the entire theory of there being another party playing Curtis, as though it was some batshit crazy story whipped up by a struggling defence team.

Dani moved off to try and intercept him.

'What about Ben?' Dani said, not shouting, but loud enough to get his attention.

Barker turned, now looking less than impressed.

'DI Stephens, good of you to come along.'

'Don't patronise me. So that's it? You're disregarding everything we talked about? Everything I worked on.'

He stepped closer to her, looked around him as though nervous someone might overhear, but there was barely a soul inside the room now except a couple of clerks.

'DI Stephens, this is not the time or the place.'

'For what? Exploring the truth? I thought that was kind of the point of this place, actually.'

'Damian Curtis is on trial today. Not Dr Collins, and not your brother.'

With that he turned and marched off.

Dani remained where she was, her brain rumbling, her anger bubbling. She felt like going after him and having it out with him. Would it even make a difference?

'Come on,' Easton said, coming over to her side, his tone conciliatory. 'You ready to go? I think we've seen enough here, don't you?'

Dani agreed.

Outside the court building, the centre of Birmingham was bathed in low winter sunlight that cast long shadows between the city's tall buildings. Swathes of tarmac intermittently glistened wetly where the warming rays had started to melt the frost, but there were large corners where icy white remained untouched. Those cold and bleak areas drew Dani in as she headed down the steps onto the street.

'He's got a point,' Easton said, breaking their silence and Dani's line of thought.

'Barker?'

She practically spat the word.

'Curtis is on trial here, Dani. He killed those people. Everyone knows that.'

'But we both know that's not the whole story.'

'We *believe* it's not.'

Why was nobody listening to her about Ben? He'd been Curtis's cellmate. He was himself a murderer, was known to be cunning and manipulative. Just look at what he'd done to Dani who still suffered, mentally and physically, after he'd tried to bludgeon her to death. Although perhaps that was it. No one was listening to her for that very reason. She was *too* connected to Ben for anyone else to take it seriously.

Dani huffed. 'Don't you get it?' she said. 'This is the only chance the CPS have to cement the theory of a third party onto the record. The defence are handing it to them on a platter, even if it is Collins they're pinning and not Ben. Curtis took those lives, I know that, but someone else made him. So why is Barker trying to bury that? How will they ever convict anyone else if they've already rubbished the notion during Curtis's trial?'

'Like I said, I agree with you, but this trial really isn't going to determine that.'

'Isn't it? So if the CPS push and get a murder conviction for Curtis, quashing the theory of a third party coercing him, what then?'

'You're saying that'd be a bad thing? To get Curtis for murder? Even after what he did to you and Jas—'

'Of course it's a bad thing, if it means that the CPS pat themselves on the back and walk away like it's job done. If the CPS go down this route now they're basically rubber-stamping an automatic defence for Ben. There wouldn't even be any point in pursuing it to trial.'

Easton shrugged as though he was OK with that; as though there wasn't any prospect of such a trial, regardless of what happened here.

'I'll see you later,' Dani said.

She stormed off towards Corporation Street, further away from HQ.

'Where are you going?' Easton shouted.

Dani didn't answer, just huddled her head into her coat as she strode away.

She'd only made it ten yards when her phone buzzed in her pocket. She stopped walking and lifted it out. Someone from HQ was calling.

'DI Stephens?' she said.

She turned back to the courthouse. Easton was still standing there watching her. Dani listened without saying a word. Perhaps something about the look on her face told Easton what he needed to know, because he started to edge towards her.

'OK. We're going now,' she said, before hanging up.

'Not good news, I'm guessing,' Easton said.

'No. We've got a body.'

Chapter 2

It was nearing midday by the time Dani and Easton arrived in Oldbury, a small market town within the Black Country, a few miles west of Birmingham. Like most towns within the area, Oldbury remained scarred by the remnants of its industrialised past. At least for this town retail dynamics had taken over, perhaps due to its proximity to major road networks – the M5 included – which had seen the opening of a number of modern retail parks over the last couple of decades that now encircled the town like a corrugated steel exoskeleton.

The address Dani and Easton arrived at was a few streets away from the old high street, where traditional shops and businesses sat with stoic dignity next to numerous abandoned units, a continuous struggle to remain trading.

The street they were on was straight as an arrow with two rows of identical terraces opposite each other. Each unit was narrow with just a door and single window taking up the ground floor, and tiny front yards that were used mainly for storing wheelie bins, it seemed.

With cars parked on both sides, bumper to bumper, Dani found a space several doors away from where they needed to be, though as they headed onto the pavement, it was clear which house they were aiming for because of the uniformed copper standing outside with a bright yellow hi-vis jacket on.

At least during the week the kids and teenagers were still at school, and parents at work, limiting the gawkers somewhat.

Dani took out her warrant card as she ducked under the blue and white police tape which had been rolled across the front

17

gate. She held it up for the PC at the door, who she didn't recognise at all.

'Bathroom, downstairs,' was all the grumpy sod said as he stepped out of the way of the door.

A downstairs bathroom, in a two up, two down home: a strange quirk that remained prevalent all over the country in houses of a certain age. When these terraces were built at the start of the twentieth century, there was no bathroom inside at all, just an outside toilet. Modern plumbing had brought those toilets inside, though the cheapest and simplest solution was to tack the toilet to the back of the house at ground-floor level. Modern central heating had soon brought modern bathrooms into homes, but with such limited space, once again the cheapest and simplest solution prevailed: a bathroom at ground level, at the back of the house, beyond the kitchen.

Dani put plastic gloves on her hands and covers over her feet before she stepped inside.

She heard sobbing coming from inside the front downstairs room. Dani moved to the doorway and peeped into the modest lounge to see a female PC sat on a sofa next to a teary woman. The woman looked to be in her forties and was wearing jeans and a zipped-up hoodie. Her carefully manicured fingers were scrunched around a tissue.

'Detectives,' the PC said as she got to her feet. 'If you head into the back room, the FSIs are in there.'

'Thank you,' Dani said. 'And this is?'

'Bianca Neita,' the PC said. 'A friend. She found Ms Doyle's body.'

At the mention of the victim, Bianca sobbed even more loudly.

'OK, thank you,' Dani said. 'We'll come back to speak to Mrs Neita shortly.'

Dani stepped back out and she and Easton carried on through the narrow corridor into a galley kitchen. Much like the hallway and the front room, the furnishings in here were modern enough, but clearly cheap. There was little that was homely about the place at all, everything bland. Dani envisaged a landlord with a well-oiled routine of turning modest but outmoded dwellings into modern but affordable rental units, devoid of any real character.

They moved through the kitchen to a small utility area; off to their right the door to the back yard, in front of them a door open to a bathroom where two white-suited forensic investigators were hunched down by the bathtub. Beyond them Dani spotted the dark matted hair draped across the white of the bath.

The FSIs both stood and turned. Dani recognised the man who stepped forward as Saad Tariq, one of the more senior and personable of the team of FSIs she dealt with.

'Morning, Detectives,' Tariq said.

'What have we got?'

Tariq moved out of the way and Dani stared down as she swallowed hard. The water had by now been drained from the bath, leaving the woman's body slumped. Her dull skin was white as a sheet, her lips blue. Her glassy eyes were open, staring across to the wall. Her slim body was blemish free, Dani noted, with no obvious sign of external injury.

'PC Rowden in there said she's found the victim's driving licence,' Tariq said. 'Clara Doyle. Thirty-eight.'

'Any idea what's happened?' Easton asked.

'No. This is going to need a PM.' Post-mortems were carried out by a pathologist. The FSIs were trained to deal with crime scenes, rather than specifically dead bodies themselves, though their experience of scenes was often useful in gaining an initial insight. 'No sign of abrasions or contusions to the body, as you can see. When we got here the water was still in the bath, but cold. No idea how long she'd been submerged for.'

'Her head was submerged?' Dani said.

'Not fully, about up to her nostrils.'

'So she could have drowned?'

'Possible. But she was moved by the friend, who initially pulled her up to check her breathing, so you'd have to figure out with her exactly what it looked like before we arrived. We're not going to know what's happened to her until we take her out of here.'

'What's in there?' Dani said, pointing to the half-finished tumbler by the side of the bath.

'We'll get it taken back to the lab, but smells like vodka to me.'

'And there's these,' Easton said.

Dani turned to him. He was by the cabinet above the sink, the mirrored door open to reveal a whole swathe of toiletries and pill bottles. A lot of pill bottles. It reminded Dani of her own bathroom cabinet and her constant struggle to ease herself off the medication that had become such a big part of her life in her struggle to overcome her TBI.

'Diazepam,' Easton said, holding the bottle out to Dani. She didn't take it. Instead she stepped over to the cabinet and glanced across the other labels.

Diazepam, also known as Valium, was a classic anti-depressant, Naproxen, a high-strength pain reliever and anti-inflammatory and Mirtazapine, Amitriptyline were two other types of anti-depressant.

Together with the alcohol by the side of the bath, and the lack of external injuries, Dani was already quickly coming to a conclusion as to how Clara Doyle's life had come to an end. So why had the Homicide team received the call?

Dani turned to Easton. 'You go upstairs, take a look around, I'll go and speak to the friend.'

Easton nodded and headed off, and Dani was soon seated in an uncomfortably hard armchair in the cramped living room.

'Mrs Neita, can you tell me what happened here?'

She snuffled into her tissue for a few seconds, then began to twist the wedding band on her finger around – anxiety? – as she turned her reddened eyes to Dani.

'She didn't turn up to work this morning. She wasn't answering her phone.'

'Work?'

'Hatty's Coffee Shop. It's a few minutes' walk from here. It's not like her at all.'

'So you came over?'

'I knocked on the door. She didn't answer. I was really worried, you know?'

She paused now, letting those last words hang. Why was that? Some sort of justification? But for what?

'I tried the door. It wasn't even locked. When I pushed it open, that was when it happened.'

She paused. Dani looked to PC Rowden and back to Bianca again.

'What happened?' Dani asked.

'The back door. It slammed shut.'

Dani's eyes narrowed. 'Did you see someone?'

'I… I just… I think… maybe. No, not really. But the door slammed shut. Why was the back door open if it wasn't because someone was there?'

A good question.

'I rushed through into the kitchen. I thought it was a burglar. I went right up to the back window. Then I saw the gate crash shut too.'

'Did you see someone *that* time?'

A pause. 'No, but the gate. It wouldn't close itself, would it?'

She sounded more defensive now.

'Anything you saw, however small, would be really helpful,' Dani said.

'I'm sorry, I… I *know* someone was here, but…'

Dani gave her the time, but she didn't finish the sentence.

'What next?' Dani said when she realised Bianca needed the prompt.

'I was standing in the kitchen. I called to Clara. I got no answer. I was about to go back towards the front, I already had my phone out to call 999 because I thought she'd been broken into… Then I pushed the bathroom door open. I don't even know why.'

She hung her head and sobbed again and Dani gave her the time to compose herself. Of course, Dani had to keep an open mind to what Bianca was saying. In fact, could Bianca even be a suspect? Dani couldn't rule out such a possibility, but right now she didn't believe that to be the case. This woman was genuinely shocked and traumatised.

'I screamed,' Bianca said. 'I ran to the bath. I grabbed her head and tried to pull her back up—'

'So she was under the water?'

'What? Y–yes? Her mouth, her nose, eyes. I didn't know what to do. She wasn't breathing. I thought about giving CPR.'

'Did you?'

'No. I was so confused. I ran out and called an ambulance then I went back and… oh God.'

She buried her face in her hands now.

'Mrs Neita, was the water hot?'

She looked up at Dani as though it was a ridiculous question.

'Of course it was. Well, not hot, but warm.'

It might have seemed obvious to Bianca, but it wasn't to Dani. She stewed on that response for a few moments.

'The police got here first,' Bianca said. 'It took… I don't even know. Maybe not even two minutes. I was still by her side, still talking to her, trying to get her to wake up.'

The room fell silent for a few moments. Dani waited to see if Bianca would add anything unprompted. She didn't.

'How did you know Clara?' Dani asked.

Bianca stared at Dani as though unsure about the change of direction.

'I… we met at the coffee shop. She's been around here a couple of years, I think. But… I don't know that much about her really.'

'She lives alone?'

'I think so.'

'No kids.'

'No.'

'Husband, boyfriend?'

'She never talked about one.'

Nor were there any pictures suggesting she had a partner. In fact there were barely any personal items in the house at all.

'Had she ever missed a shift before?'

'Not that I remember. That's why it was odd. Especially to not answer her phone either.'

'We found a lot of pills in the bathroom. Anti-depressants mostly. Did you know she was taking those?'

'Why would I know what medication she's on?'

The way she said it was as though it was a horrible question to ask.

'So you didn't know?'

'I didn't know. Why would I? She was just a… wait. Are you saying…'

She didn't finish the question.

'I'm saying there's a partly drunk glass of vodka by the bath,' Dani said. 'And a medicine cabinet filled with medication of various sorts—'

'You think she killed herself?'

'Would that surprise you?'

Bianca huffed as though the question wasn't worthy of a response. 'I already told you, there was someone else here.'

Dani nodded as she processed all of the conflicting things she was seeing and hearing. She could understand why the PCs who'd attended the 999 call had phoned the Homicide team, not least because of the as-yet-unexplained death, but particularly with a witness account of a potential intruder. But did that really explain any of what Dani was seeing here?

'Er, Dani.'

She turned to Easton who was standing in the doorway.

'Can I have a word?' he asked.

'Sorry, Mrs Neita, please excuse me for a moment.'

'Do you know how long you'll need me for?' Bianca said as Dani got to her feet. 'The shop's still closed. We can't lose a whole day's takings.'

'If you let my colleague take your details, and a brief statement, you can go. We'll be in touch if we need anything more.'

Bianca nodded mournfully.

'I'm really sorry you had to see this,' Dani said before she stepped out into the corridor.

'I overheard what she said about someone being here,' Easton said, just louder than a whisper.

'And?'

He pursed his lips and shook his head. 'No sign of a boyfriend or anything. No clothes, that sort of thing.'

'A girlfriend?'

Easton initially looked puzzled, as if that thought had never crossed his mind. 'I mean, no, I don't think so. No extra toothbrush either. But more to the point, I can't see any evidence of an intruder either. No obvious forced entry, no sign of anything having been disturbed. TV, laptop, tablet, purse all still here.'

Dani thought for a moment. What were they not seeing?

Or perhaps they were seeing everything. A severely depressed woman, living alone, who'd taken a morning bath with a cocktail of pills and a glass of vodka. Back door left open because of the steam from the bath? Gate swinging in the wind. Death by suicide or misadventure, whichever it was, it was the same result for poor Clara Doyle.

'But there is something,' Easton said.

'Yeah?'

'Follow me.'

Dani followed Easton up the stairs, the coarse-weave brown carpet scrunching under her feet. The upstairs of the house had just three doors off the landing: a small toilet, a box room that was used as some sort of dumping ground for clothes and suitcases and unused furniture, and a slightly larger bedroom at the front that was clearly Clara Doyle's space. The double bed had sumptuous sheets, ruffled from recent use. There was a small dressing table with perfume and make-up messily arranged, a bedside table, but no other furniture, though there was another internal door in one corner. Dani's immediate thought was that perhaps it was a fitted wardrobe, or even a tiny corner en-suite, but as she looked to the handle and saw the small padlock she realised that this was the reason Easton had called her up.

'What do you think?' he said.

'Let's try and find a key. If not, we break it off.'

Easton nodded and they set about on their search. There weren't that many places to look, and Dani was the one who found it, stuffed beneath underwear in the bottom bedside drawer.

She held the key aloft, and Easton looked over at her victoriously, though Dani was feeling quite different. What were they about to stumble on here?

She moved to the door and with a rise of tension pushed the small key into the lock. She unclasped the padlock, then held her breath as she opened the door.

She was left staring into a darkened space. She reached around the inside wall and found a corded switch which she tugged down. A soft yellow light flickered on.

Neither of them said a word. Dani took a halfstep in, her eyes darting left, right, up and down as she took in the patchwork of photos, handwritten notes, newspaper clippings that adorned the wall. Like a crime scene board, or the work of a raving conspiracy theorist. There were scribbled notes, red and black lines drawn all over them, linking the various bits of information in some unknown way.

'What is this?' Easton said.

Dani said nothing as she continued to look. One thing was for sure. There was a theme here. Two men in particular, whose faces appeared several times over.

'Go and get Mrs Neita.'

Easton hurried off. Dani continued to try to take in what she could. What was Clara Doyle doing with all this?

Easton was soon back, both PC Rowden and Bianca with him. Bianca now looked both scared and seriously uncomfortable.

'This is horrible,' Bianca said as Dani stepped back out of the cupboard, or whatever it was. 'I'm in her bedroom. She's dead downstairs and we're all in her room going through her things.'

'I know it's not nice to do, but we have to do it,' Dani said. 'Please, can you come and take a look in here.'

Bianca hesitated but was soon by Dani's side within the small space, staring aghast at the picture wall, much in the same way as Dani had moments before.

'Do you recognise any of these people?' Dani asked.

No response. Bianca's eyes flicked across the wall.

'Are they her family? Friends?'

'I… I just don't know.'

Except one thing was clear: she wasn't paying any attention to the older guy. One of the pictures was a press cutting and gave his name as Nicolae Popescu. Bianca was looking all over, anywhere except at his pictures.

Dani reached forward and grabbed the largest, most clear photo she could of Popescu. With a round but lined face, receding hair, large Slavic nose, he looked mean and vicious.

'Do you know this man?' Dani said. Bianca quickly looked away from the photo, catching Dani's gaze. 'Nicolae Popescu. Who is he?'

'I've no idea,' Bianca said, her words quavering slightly.

Dani stared at her, but Bianca didn't say anything more.

'OK, you can go,' Dani said.

Dani realised she sounded pissed off now, but only because she was certain Bianca was holding back on something. Why?

Bianca and PC Rowden retreated and Dani waited until she was sure they were out of earshot.

'Who is this guy?' she said to Easton, holding the photo up.

He shrugged sheepishly. 'I honestly don't know either, but I agree her reaction was off.'

'Then let's find out.'

Easton was soon beside Dani in the cramped space, scanning the photos on the wall. 'And this younger guy?' he said. 'What's the deal, do you think?'

Dani really had no clue. Like Popescu, the younger man appeared in several of the pictures, though his name wasn't clear as there were several other names written on the pictures or next to them: Michael Marin, Patrick Beatty, James Alden. Dani's eyes flicked across the pictures, the clippings, the notes, the jumble of names and words – coded? – that adorned it all. How could anyone make sense of this…

Then her eyes settled. She felt a sickly feeling in the pit of her stomach. A shiver ran right through her and she whipped her eyes back into the bedroom as though she was expecting to see a ghoul there.

There was nothing. Nobody at all.

Her eyes soon found the picture again. Her heart rattled away in her chest.

'What is it?' Easton said, clearly picking up on her edginess.

Dani said nothing as she reached forwards with the tip of a blue plastic-covered finger.

'What the—' were the only words she could muster.

It made no sense to her, it made no sense to him, but there was no doubt whatsoever that the man her finger had rested on – the man standing with a wide smile in a group of five, alongside the young man who appeared in several of the other photos – was her brother, Ben.

Chapter 3

'This isn't right,' Dani said, closing down the pop-up screen with an agitated press of the mouse.

'What?' Easton said from across the open-plan office space of the Homicide team at HQ. A few other eyes peeped up over their low dividers to look in Dani's direction, but she ignored the questioning looks.

Easton was soon by her side, hovering over her screen.

'Clara Doyle doesn't exist,' Dani said.

No response.

'No national insurance number,' she said. 'No marriage records, passport, driving licence—'

'So—'

'So the licence found in her purse is a fake.'

'Fingerprints?'

'No match.'

Easton sighed. 'We'll have to send a team back to her house. Search everywhere. There must be a clue as to who she really is. A bank account, something.'

'Good idea. But the bigger question is why? Why the fake identity at all?'

Easton said nothing again.

'We'll get the search done,' Dani said after a few moments of silence. 'Check with her landlord. Does she pay him from a bank account? What ID checks did he do? Let's arrange another meeting with her friend, Bianca, too, plus whoever employed her at that coffee shop.'

'What about the men in the pictures?'

Dani sighed. 'All we've got to go on are their names and their faces.'

'We can narrow down their ages at least to match to other records.'

'To a certain extent. Except we don't even know when most of those pictures were taken. And it's not quite that straightforward.'

Dani clicked away with her mouse, pulling up the other search results.

'James Alden, Patrick Beatty, Michael Marin,' Dani said. 'Those were the three names that appeared by the photos on that board that all seemed to relate to the younger man. So which one was he really, and why the aliases? And from first glance there are tens of results just in the West Midlands for those names.'

'Social media?' Easton said.

'Already tried. Briefly, anyway. Nothing that looks like our guy. The only option we have left to identify this man is to dig into every single person with one of these names until we find the match.'

'Yet we don't even know why we'd be doing that.'

Dani glanced up at Easton, not sure what to make of his statement.

'No,' she said. 'But I think we have to. If only to help figure out who our dead woman really is.'

'What about the other guy? Popescu.'

'Well, that's where this all gets even more murky.'

Easton raised an eyebrow.

'Nicolae Popescu,' Dani said, pointing to the onscreen profile once she'd brought it up. 'Take a look.'

Easton leaned forward and took control of the mouse as he scrolled down, his eyes flicking from left to right and back again at speed.

'It's definitely him,' Easton said. 'The same guy as in the pictures.'

'Romanian national,' Dani said. 'Arrived in the UK 2008.'

'Convicted of... bloody hell.'

'GBH. Attempted murder. He spent three years in prison before he was deported.'

'Which was in 2013. So he's been out of the country for seven years?'

'According to Border Force's records, at least.'

'What do we do with this?'

Dani stood up from her chair, and peered over to DCI McNair's office. She could just make out her boss through the small window next to the closed door.

'Let's go and ask.'

'So you've got a Jane Doe, who may or may not have died in suspicious circumstances,' McNair said, glancing over the top of her glasses to Dani, the way she often did. Kind of like a stereotypical school headmistress from days gone by. Was that the look McNair intended? In her fifties and with her ever formal appearance perhaps it was.

'No, I'd say there's no doubt right now that her death is absolutely suspicious,' Dani said. 'Even disregarding the nature of her death, we have a witness reporting that she believed someone else had been in the house—'

'But she didn't actually see anyone, you said.'

'She didn't. But there are CCTV cameras on the streets around there, and we have a pretty good idea of time. We might find someone if they were hang—'

'Who said any intruder came on foot?'

'No one, but—'

'Then you're going to have a hard time tracking down a mystery person of unknown description, travelling by unknown means, in an unknown direction.'

Dani slumped a little. It was a fair point. But that didn't mean it wasn't necessarily still worth a try.

'What else?' McNair said, sitting back in her chair now. She didn't look uninterested exactly, but she did look like she wasn't sure why one of her senior detectives was so over-excited. Not that Dani believed she was.

'We did a brief search of the house,' Dani said. 'The only alcohol we found was a half-empty bottle of vodka. All those pills we found... none of them were properly labelled. They weren't dispensed from an official pharmacy, and the dates had all expired.'

'So you're suggesting?'

'I'm suggesting our Jane Doe wasn't a regular drinker, and it's possible she wasn't even regularly on that medication. Perhaps it wasn't hers at all.'

'So you're telling me you don't think this was an accidental overdose?'

'I'm telling you at least that a lot of elements here don't add up.'

'Suicide then?'

'There was no note, but... it's possible.'

'As possible as any other outcome right now,' McNair said. 'One bottle of vodka? Out of date pills? So perhaps our victim got hold of those things for the very reason of killing herself.'

'I agree that's a theory that fits,' Dani said, even though she didn't believe it at all. 'But at the very least there are a lot of factors here we need to look at more closely. A possible intruder. False identity, perhaps an unscrupulous landlord who's failed to carry out proper checks on his tenant, same for her employer. And even if she killed herself, someone still supplied her with grey market medication...'

'And then there's those pictures. And your brother.' McNair said the last three words with a strange sneer. Almost accusatory. But towards Dani rather than Ben.

'We've no idea what Clara Doyle, or whatever she's really called, was aiming for with that picture board,' Easton said, 'but it's worth a deeper look into who those men are so we can try to figure it out. What links them to each other? What links them to our dead woman?'

'I agree,' McNair said. 'There is enough here to raise suspicion of foul play, although quite what the nature of that foul play is I have no idea. This isn't a drop-all-cases inquiry, but I'm happy for you to go ahead and do what you can to identify this poor woman, and determine what happened to her.'

Dani waited for McNair to say something else, though she really wasn't sure what more she wanted from her boss, who'd essentially just given Dani carte blanche. The best possible position she could be in, really.

'I heard you were in court this morning,' McNair said, casting her eye to Dani.

The out-of-the-blue comment knocked Dani for a few seconds.

'We both were,' Easton said.

The curious look on McNair's face suggested she hadn't known that.

'I understand why the trial is important to you,' McNair said, her gaze now firmly back on Dani, 'but I don't want you letting those proceedings distract you from your job.'

'Noted,' Dani said.

'And if you do go back there… try not to get into any more disputes with our CPS barrister inside the courtroom. The last thing I need is for one of my detectives to be hauled into the slammer for contempt.'

Dani bit her tongue; the best thing to do with her anger on the rise. It wasn't the warning from McNair that had her riled, but rather the fact that someone had reported her exchange with Barker. Who? And why? It had hardly been a big deal.

Had it?

'It was nothing, really, Ma'am,' Easton said. 'Just a brief discussion.'

McNair didn't look convinced, but Dani was at least glad for Easton's support.

'OK, don't let me keep you any longer,' McNair said.

'Thank you,' Dani said. 'We'll keep you updated.'

McNair nodded then turned back to her computer screen as Dani and Easton made their way out.

Dani closed the door behind her and let out a sigh. She looked over to Easton who pursed his lips and shrugged.

'Thank you,' she said.

'So what now?'

'Let's get some of the team set up.' Dani looked at her watch. Nearly four p.m. 'Then I know exactly where we should go to next.'

–

When Dani and Easton exited HQ not long after, it was already dark outside, the streetlights were on and the temperature was steadily dropping from its paltry daytime high. Shivering as she huddled down in her coat, Dani's feet crunched on the newly gritted pavements as they headed along Colmore Row towards Victoria Square. Off to her left, recently erected Christmas lights twinkled invitingly in the trees that encircled St Philip's Cathedral. As atmospheric as it looked, it left Dani with a sorrowful feeling, knowing that Christmas was around the corner and Jason was still stuck in hospital rather than at home with her.

'I know seeing Ben in that picture has set your brain off,' Easton said. 'But shouldn't our priority be in finding out who Clara Doyle really is?'

'That's what we are doing,' Dani responded.

'Yeah. But is it?'

Dani glared at him, but he took it on the chin despite her response to him being far more snarky than his to her. But why was he doubting her now when minutes earlier he'd been so quick to defend her in front of McNair?

'It's coming to the end of the day,' Dani said. 'The team are all set up to get stuck into Jane Doe. But we can still push

33

forward with this other guy tonight.' Although who really was the younger man from the pictures? James Alden? Or Patrick Beatty? Michael Marin?

Easton said nothing, as though he was content that his point had already been made. And Dani did get his point, even if she didn't agree with him. Ben being in that picture had sidetracked her thoughts, but she was determined to get to the bottom of it sooner rather than later. Was his picture being there, in Clara Doyle's house, nothing more than pure coincidence?

'I never pictured Ben as a management consultant,' Easton said.

Dani looked at him quizzically.

'Sorry. You know what I mean, though? I didn't know your brother before... I've only ever known him as a convicted murderer. It's just strange to realise that before all that he was just... a normal guy.'

Dani said nothing, but Easton's word struck a nerve. Yes, Ben had *appeared* normal. To everyone, Dani included. But had that ever really been the case?

Heading through the thoroughfare of the International Convention Centre, they were soon walking across one of the many ornate iron bridges that were scattered over the city's canal waterways: trendy Brindleyplace with its array of modern bars, restaurants and office spaces rising in front of them. During warmer weather the paved terraces were filled with people eating and drinking at all hours of the day. This afternoon the terraces of the bars, fairy lights shimmering, had a congregation of gas heaters burning away expectantly, but the only souls brave enough to stay out in the chill were small gaggles of smokers.

'Fancy a pint after?' Easton said.

Dani wasn't sure whether he was joking or not.

'You're not entertaining the kids and your sister tonight?' she said.

He rolled his eyes at that. 'I can't wait to go home. How can you not tell?'

'Let's get this done first,' Dani said. 'Then maybe.'

The offices of Ellis Associates took up the top two floors of a glass-fronted office block with 360-degree views across the city. Dani and Easton explained to the receptionist who they were, and who they were there to see, and were left to wait, twiddling their thumbs, by a cluster of black leather sofas and armchairs.

'You been here before?' Easton asked.

'No. They used to be over by Snow Hill.'

Easton huffed. 'Would have saved us the walk.'

Seconds later the security doors beyond the reception area opened and a short, stocky man in tight-fitting blue trousers and an open-necked salmon pink shirt strode out. With a snide sneer on his tanned face, Dani knew immediately who it was, even if she'd never met him face to face before.

'Detective Stephens,' he said, giving a wide but disingenuous white-toothed smile to go along with his bone-crushing handshake. 'I'm Harvey Forster.'

He looked at Dani with obvious recognition. She hated that. The way strangers knew her for all the wrong reasons. It reminded her of those darkest of days, after Ben had attacked her, when her face was all over the papers because of what he'd done. Would she ever fully regain her sense of privacy again?

Yet another thing Ben had taken from her.

'Good to meet you,' Dani said, 'and this is DS Easton.'

Another handshake.

Harvey Forster. Not the name Dani was most familiar with. When Ben had worked for Ellis Associates, a lifetime ago, he had always referred to Forster as Rottweiler, and Dani could already understand why.

Forster escorted them through the security doors, along a corridor lined with glass-fronted meeting rooms, most of them empty now the working day was drawing to a close. They ended up in a small corner room that was by far the least salubrious they'd passed, with a cramped table for four and just a thin strip of a window, as though Forster was making a point that the detectives didn't deserve anything better.

Already seated in the room was a stoic-looking woman in a pin-stripe jacket who was introduced as Mary Philips from HR.

No offer of a tea or coffee or even water. Not for two coppers who weren't on the client list.

'So, Detectives, fire away,' Forster said, trying extra hard to express his nonchalance.

Easton shuffled in his satchel and pulled out a copy of the photograph from the wall in Clara Doyle's house.

'Can you tell us about this picture?' Easton said as he pushed the paper across the desk.

Forster frowned and looked to his colleague first before picking the picture up and squinting as he stared at it.

'Well, I'm sure you know the basics,' Forster said, putting the picture back down. 'There's a caption right there underneath saying it's the Project Reflow team from Ellis Associates.'

'Yes, we can read, thank you, Mr Forster,' Easton said and Dani glowed inside at his blunt tone. Apparently, he'd already decided what kind of a man Forster was too.

'Is this about Ben Stephens?' Forster said, now fixing his hard glare on Dani. 'I do find it odd that his sister is investigating, if it is. Whatever it *is* you're investigating. I would have thought the police had procedures to avoid conflicts like that.'

'Mr Forster, thank you for your insight,' Dani said. 'But if you could please explain to us a little more about the circumstances behind this picture.'

'I was told on the phone this was an inquiry into one of our ex-employees,' Forster said. 'I'm sensing it might be a bit more than that. Do I need someone from our legal team here?'

Dani turned out her hands. 'I can't make that call for you. Unless you're telling me you think you need legal advice before you can speak to us?'

He squirmed uncomfortably in his chair, his arrogance absent for a second or two. 'But what are you investigating exactly?'

'A murder,' Easton said.

Another squirm.

'Mr Forster. Please, can you just tell us what you can about this picture. A little context.'

'It might have made it more straightforward if *you* gave *me* some context, but… OK.' He sighed, as if for dramatic effect. 'Reflow was a project we undertook on behalf of Birmingham City Council, in relation to the redevelopment of an old gasworks site in Perry Barr. I led the project. The other people in the picture were my core team. The *Birmingham Mail* carried a small story about it once we'd completed.'

'And this man here,' Easton said, putting his finger onto the face of the man that appeared all over the picture board in Clara Doyle's home. 'You know him? We have three potential names for him. Michael Marin. Patrick Beatty. James Alden.'

Forster stared at the picture again, his face now creasing. Concern? Or was he just deep in thought? Mary Philips was typing away on her laptop.

'He looks familiar,' Forster said. 'But honestly?'

'Here he is,' Philips said. 'James Alden. He did work here.'

'Mr Forster? Do you recognise that name?' Dani said.

He nodded, though was still frowning. 'I do, but it's not sparking much. I'm not sure if you'd said the name to me without this picture that I'd have recalled him at all.'

'So he doesn't work here any more?'

'Certainly not on my team.'

'Mrs Philips?' Dani said.

'Just give me a minute,' she said without looking up from her screen.

'You didn't know James Alden well then?' Easton asked Forster.

'Obviously not.'

'You've no idea how long he worked here for? When he stopped?'

'I'm sure my colleague is about to tell us all the answer to that.'

The room went silent for a few moments as all eyes turned to Philips as she busily typed. She seemed to sense this and her cheeks reddened a few seconds before she stopped typing. She looked first to Forster then to Dani.

'James Alden,' she said. 'He joined the firm in 2013 as an associate. That's our graduate entry level, although he was actually twenty-six at that point. Well, at least according to his CV.'

'*According* to?' Dani questioned.

'It seems he was only with us for a little over twelve months,' Philips said. 'I don't understand exactly what happened from these details, I only joined three years ago, but there was a disciplinary hearing by the look of it. He lied about his qualifications. He was fired for gross misconduct.'

Dani's brain was now firing.

'None of this is familiar to you?' Dani said to Forster.

She could tell her suspicious tone riled him. 'No, it is not. Otherwise I would have already said. You realise we're a global firm? We have ten thousand people in this country alone. I don't know every associate who comes and goes, nor the reasons why.'

'So who led the disciplinary?' Easton asked Philips.

'It's not all here,' she replied. 'I'd have to do some digging.'

'The fact his CV was bogus only came out months after he joined?' Dani said.

'I'm sorry. Again, I'd have to look into why. You have to understand we don't routinely check every single item on a candidate's CV for factual accuracy. I'm not sure any employer does?'

'But you do identity checks?' Dani said.

'Of course,' Philips said, like it was a ridiculous question.

'We'll need to see exactly what checks you performed then,' Dani said. 'And we'll need a copy of his CV, plus any other personal details you can give us: addresses, emergency contacts, bank details, payroll records.'

Philips opened her mouth but said nothing. She looked over to Forster.

'You'll have to make a request through official channels,' Forster said. 'I'm sure you understand.'

Dani and Easton shared a look. 'That's fine,' Dani said.

'I can only assume that you being here therefore has something to do with James Alden?' Forster said. 'Rather than any of the other people in the picture.'

Of course he was fishing about the fact that Ben was also in the picture. 'That's correct,' Dani said. 'We'll need that information as soon as possible, so please have it ready to go when we get the formal request in.'

Dani got to her feet. Easton followed.

'We'll be in touch.'

–

'You OK?' Easton asked as they traipsed back towards the canal.

'Yeah,' Dani said.

'I've never much liked those in-your-face corporate types.'

'No. Me neither.'

But really she wasn't thinking about Forster at all, but about what on earth they were stumbling over with Clara Doyle and James Alden. And what the hell did Ben have to do with any of this? She still couldn't escape that glaring unknown.

'So do you fancy that pint?' Easton said.

Dani stopped and thought for a moment. It was barely five o'clock. There were plenty of useful things she could still do in the office. Plus she wanted to go to the hospital later to see Jason before she headed home. But she also really wanted something, anything to take her mind off her still swirling thoughts about her brother and all the shit that forever hung around him. And her.

'Yeah. Why not.'

'Six pounds for a pint!' Easton stammered, holding a tenner out to the indignant barman. He looked to Dani. Pure disgust. 'I should have taken you for a coffee.'

He dug in his pocket for the extra coins to cover their two pints.

'It's fine,' Dani said, whipping out her card which she pressed against the contactless machine. 'On me.'

Easton looked even more sheepish now. They grabbed their drinks and found a table by the window, looking out to the shivering smokers huddled there.

'Life choices, eh?' Easton said as he took a huge gulp from his glass.

'Something like that.'

'What's on your mind?'

Dani took a lengthy sip. She wasn't a big beer drinker at all, but it did taste damn good today. As it should for the price.

'Clara Doyle. James Alden,' she said, which was true, even if it wasn't the whole truth.

'You heard from Barker?'

Dani quickly re-checked her messages and emails. No, there was still nothing from him, even though court was in recess now until the morning. But then, what was she expecting him to contact her about?

'You ask me, this case could be exactly what you need to take your mind off that trial.'

'Yeah. I'm so pleased Clara Doyle is dead. What a great service she's done for me to take my mind off Curtis's trial. I'll have to thank her next time I see her.'

Easton's cheeks flushed. 'I didn't mean it like that. Just, you've got to stop beating yourself up over the past. Over Ben. It's only the thought of him that torments you. You need to get him out of your head.'

She agreed with Easton absolutely on that. Yet what he'd said was an impossible task.

Easton's phone vibrated in his pocket. He lifted it out.

'Yeah?'

Dani's eyes pinched as she listened to the one-sided conversation. Her heart steadily drummed in her chest with anticipation, because she could tell, even from the meagre words Easton was using in response, that the call was work related.

After a couple of minutes he put the phone back down on the table.

'News?'

He shook his head as if in disbelief.

'James Alden,' he said. 'Grayling thinks she's found him.'

They'd set DC Grayling up looking into Alden and his aliases, trying to find a solid ID that matched.

'Found him physically?' Dani said, hopefully.

'Unfortunately not. And that's the problem. James Alden isn't his real name at all. Liam Dunne is.'

The name meant nothing to Dani. 'OK?'

'Dunne was reported missing five years ago. He's not been seen since.'

'What the—'

'There's more. He was reported missing by his sister: Clara Dunne. Her details, date of birth, match to—'

'Clara Doyle,' she said.

Easton simply nodded in response.

Chapter 4

Two hours later, realizing there was little more she could usefully do that night, Dani arrived at the hospital which, despite it being gone seven p.m., was swarming both inside and out; cars in the car park, and patients, visitors, doctors and nurses filling the waiting areas and corridors. Organised chaos was a kind way to describe it, utter confusion another. Not that Dani begrudged any of the staff here. They were, on the whole, incredible people, yet the institution they worked for was forever constrained by growing demand set against dwindling resources, making the lives of the professionals there near impossible.

With Christmas a little over three weeks away, the overworked staff had somehow found the time to put up decorations and twisted plastic Christmas trees. It didn't look much, but Dani knew it would mean the world to the patients who'd be stuck here through the festive season. She herself had spent two Christmases on a ward not dissimilar to this one, back when she was first recovering from her TBI; a recovery that would never fully be over, even if she had long since left behind those dark days in hospital.

By now all of the regular staff on the rehab ward recognised Dani, and even though she'd only been here the previous evening, it took her several minutes of hellos and chit-chat before she finally came to Jason's room.

When she stepped inside, the familiar smell – what was that hospital smell? – and sound of the room filled her head and sent her mind spinning with almost entirely miserable memories.

She noticed the staff hadn't yet been in here with their glittering decorations. Was that because there was still hope that Jason could be back home before then?

Dani was disappointed to see that Jason was asleep in the bed, and she tiptoed over to him. She took the seat next to the bed and put her hand onto his, hoping her gentle touch would rouse him. Jason had been in this hospital, albeit not in this room, or this ward, since the summer. Since Damian Curtis had turned up at their house and tried to tear Jason apart with an axe and knife. Although he was now heavily scarred, Jason's surface wounds had healed while he was still in a coma. The most serious of his injuries were internal; in particular, the damage to his brain from cracking his skull on the floor, and the knife wound to the back which had wreaked havoc with his nervous system.

When he'd first woken from his coma nearly six weeks ago, he had been paralysed from the neck down. That had come as more of a shock and trauma to him than it had to Dani, who'd already been prepared for the painful fact. The days since then had been gruelling for everyone, but Jason in particular as he mustered every ounce of resolve to try to get his body and his brain working again.

He'd made massive progress too. He could now speak more or less normally, and his mind was improving daily. The doctors expected him to make a full mental recovery, and he was unlikely to be blighted by the same issues that Dani still suffered from as a result of her own head trauma, which had irreparably damaged her frontal lobes – the part of the brain that controls emotion and personality. As for the rest of Jason's body... he could now use his arms and hands almost freely, including eating on his own, although his stamina was non-existent and his dexterity remained shot, causing him to seriously struggle with seemingly simple tasks such as writing his own name. Much of his time these last couple of weeks had been spent trying to get himself on his feet again. A task which largely ended in frustration and tears.

But Dani was sure he'd pull through. Hell, she had, from her own ordeal at the hands of her brother, and she had no doubt Jason was a stronger person than she was. The worst of it, certainly from the outside in, was the pain he was still in. Jason's nervous system remained in pieces and his body, his limbs and his head, were riddled with pain every second of every day due to misfiring nerve responses. The only way for him to gain relief was through drugs, which meant he spent much of his time asleep.

Dani squeezed his hand a little harder and this time he responded, his hand twitching before his body shuffled. Eventually his eyelids fluttered open. Dani didn't say anything as she waited for him to come around.

It took him a couple of minutes before he sat up in the bed. He winced in pain as he did so and squeezed his eyes shut for a few seconds.

'What time is it?' he said.

'Just gone seven.'

'You've finished work?'

'Kind of.'

More than likely she'd be straight onto the computer when she arrived home. She briefly explained about her day. Strangely she focused on the couple of hours she'd spent at court that morning, rather than the new case. Why was that?

Probably it was because she was terrified about the implications of the link to Ben.

Jason took it all in. Didn't say a word. Not that she needed him to. She just needed to rant. She hoped his silence was due to the fact that he understood that, and not because he didn't have the heart or the strength to tell her she was wrong.

'It's not too late,' he said, after a few moments of silence.

'To get Ben?'

'To get whoever. It's never too late.'

'Anyway,' Dani said, waving away that ambiguous remark. 'Tell me about your day. How many steps did you manage earlier?'

Jason started talking, though Dani knew she was only half listening.

Steps. Not real steps. Not yet. Most of his body weight was taken by his arms on the parallel bars, but still it was a start, and a horrifically difficult process she herself had once gone through.

She often wondered whether it helped or hindered the position she and Jason now found themselves in that she too had come back from the brink of death; had had to relearn so many basic activities like eating, talking, walking, just as Jason now was. Or did her experience somehow compound the problems, and add a layer of resentment to it all, particularly given how she'd been a terrible patient herself. Not necessarily all her fault, as the damage to her brain, and by extension her personality, was beyond her control, even if she and others didn't always get that. Jason had at least been spared that affliction.

She couldn't count the number of arguments she'd had with him back when she was recovering. The number of times she'd flipped at him, at others, for no real reason. She'd screamed for Jason to leave her alone. She'd pushed everyone away, him included, partly because of some sort of shame, but mostly because that was just the way her brain had rewired itself. She was angry, impatient now, and struggled with empathy far more than before.

Jason had been so much more upbeat, basically his old self. But was a part of that because he was simply determined not to follow Dani's dark path? Was it all a front?

Either way, Dani felt downright miserable about the whole thing whenever she thought about it.

'Dani, are you even listening?'

Jason's face was screwed up in concern now. Or was it just the pain?

'I'm sorry,' she said. 'It's just been a really tough day.'

'Yeah,' he said.

He looked at her as though to say, 'I get it.'

Perhaps he did, but it didn't really make her feel much better.

'I'm really tired,' he said. 'And I can sense you've plenty on your mind. If you need to go…'

She squeezed his hand and he squeezed back as firmly as he could.

'I love you,' she said as she leaned forward and kissed him on the lips. 'I'll be back tomorrow.'

'I love you too,' he said.

She got up and headed for the door.

Chapter 5

Despite the cold and the dark, the streets in the centre of Liverpool were busy when Ana emerged from the revolving doors of the office block. A fierce wind whipped across the street from the nearby Mersey, as it so often did here, but today the blast of air was bitingly chilly too, stinging Ana's cheeks as she walked. Still, she had on the woolly hat and gloves that her friend Cat had bought for her birthday a couple of weeks ago, and she was plenty used to cold winters anyway, though this would be her first in the Northwest of England.

Walking through the revamped shopping streets surrounding the trendy Liverpool ONE development, Ana was soon heading away from the eager crowds of commuters on their way home, and Christmas shoppers out spending more money than they could afford on gifts that people hadn't asked for, and onto much quieter streets. In the near distance was the city campus of Liverpool John Moores University, which was encircled by a swathe of modern but affordable apartment blocks, many exclusively housing students, but plenty of others, used by young professionals and the like.

As 'affordable' as those apartments were, Ana wasn't quite flush enough just yet to afford one, not after only six months of her new job. Her new life, really. Not long ago she would never have imagined living such a relaxed and free life as this, even if she was earning little more than the minimum wage. For now.

Perhaps sometime next year she'd be able to upgrade accommodation, once the initial twelve-month rental period on her low-grade ground-floor room in the shared house she was now living in was up.

A shared house, but actually there were only three bedrooms in the 1960s semi. It was on a stretch of two dozen identical properties that were otherwise surrounded and dwarfed by much larger and grander blocks. Only one of the other bedrooms was currently occupied, by a young Chinese PhD student who'd taken on the Western first name Meghan to try to fit in to her new environment. As pleasant as Meghan was, she was rarely around. In fact, Ana hadn't seen her at all in the last few days, and wondered whether perhaps she'd already gone back to China during the university's Christmas break – the students seemed to be forever on a holiday of some description.

Ana dug in her pocket for the key as she walked on down the street, her eyes busy working over the space in front of her and across the road. However safe this place felt, the whole city really, she would always feel on edge walking alone at night.

The only people about were a couple across the road, walking a little dog, and they passed on, mid-chat, without even looking in Ana's direction.

She headed up to the front door, unlocked and opened it. The hallway was dark. So Meghan still wasn't around. Ana flicked on the lights, glanced briefly down the hallway to the open doorways for kitchen and lounge – no sign of anyone – before she shut the door behind her. She stripped off her gloves, hat and coat as she headed to the locked door which was first on her right. Her bedroom. The other two bedrooms were both upstairs, where it remained pitch black. Ana shivered at the thought as she looked up. Even though she and Meghan didn't socialise together much, it was at least comforting when someone else was in the house. But was this how it would be now for the next few weeks? Just Ana on her own each and every night?

Perhaps she should ask Cat to come and stay with her, though with her new boyfriend, she had become more and more busy recently.

Ana turned the key in the lock then pushed open the bedroom door. She was instinctively reaching for the light switch when she knew something was wrong. Yet she could see nothing inside the room. Could hear nothing untoward either.

What hit her was the smell.

His smell.

She'd never forget it.

Her fingers completed the journey to the switch, even though she wished they hadn't, because as soon as the cramped space beyond was lit up, she was left staring into Victor's menacing eyes.

'Nice to see you, Ana,' he said in their native tongue, the words dripping from his mouth with unspoken hate.

Ana was already turning, but as she did so she spotted the shadow moving behind her, out in the hall, and she could only shrink down and flinch uselessly as the thick arms wrapped around her and crushed her, lifting her off her feet. She let out a stifled scream before a gloved hand clamped over her mouth. She wriggled and writhed but was no match for the man's strength. He carried her into the room and threw her down onto the bed.

Her hair flopping in front of her eyes, Ana gasped for breath as she propped herself up on the hard mattress. She could scream. She could charge for the door. But what good would it do? Victor had found her. There was no escape.

She blew the hair from her face. Set her cold stare on Victor who was sitting on the worn Ikea sofa in the corner of the room.

'You're doing well for yourself,' Victor said, looking around the room as though he was impressed. 'Clever girl.'

'I'm not a girl.'

'But you are clever. At least you think you are. Running from me like you did. To here?'

'I didn't run.'

'But you didn't tell me where you were going.'

That was true enough.

'Did you think I'd just forget about you?' he asked.

'Why are you here?'

Victor chuckled. Ana's insides boiled with hatred at the mocking sound.

'I missed you,' he said. 'I always told you, Ana, you're special to me.'

'You say that to every woman.'

'No,' he said, shaking his head, a beastly smile on his face. 'Only those that I control.'

The goon by the door – Ana didn't even know his name – scooped up Ana's coat and threw it onto her. She angrily swiped it away.

'You're going to need that,' Victor said. 'It's cold outside.'

'I'm not going anywhere with you,' she spat.

Victor got to his feet. He moved over to the bed and Ana squirmed back.

'Oh, yes you are,' Victor said. 'You're coming home.'

She only saw his balled fist a second before it smashed into her face. Seconds later, she was out.

Chapter 6

Dani wasn't sure whether to feel happy with the little time she'd had, or disappointed that she'd not managed to spend more than the grand total of ten minutes with her niece and nephew before they'd headed out to school with Harry's friend's mum. She got to see them so rarely that even ten minutes was a bonus, though it was never long enough. It felt even more strange that she saw them so irregularly now that Dani was living only a couple of miles from them, but the relationship between her and Ben's ex-wife, Gemma, was never going to improve beyond its current level – a level of acceptance of each other – and Dani had stopped even trying to figure a way to make it anything more than that.

Not that Dani didn't like Gemma. There was nothing particularly offensive about her; she was kind, caring towards her kids, amenable – generally, at least. And outsiders might have thought that their shared trauma, the fact that Ben had tried, and failed, to kill them both, would be something that brought them closer together. Unfortunately, it was the opposite. Ben's crimes, his very existence, had ultimately put a huge wedge between the two of them, and Dani couldn't erase the feeling that Gemma, in some way, blamed Dani for what had happened – simply because she shared DNA with Ben.

'How's the new place?' Gemma said, coming back into the lounge which was, as ever, messy with kids' toys and clothes. She handed Dani a steaming mug of coffee.

Dani leaned forward and manoeuvred a pile of football comics and Lego pieces out of the way to make space for the mug on the coffee table.

'It's fine,' Dani said. 'A bit lonely, but...'

She didn't know how to finish the sentence.

For a few weeks after Damian Curtis's bloody attack at Dani and Jason's home in Harborne, on the other side of the city, Dani had stayed in the house alone. Those had been among the worst weeks of her life. An old, creaky house, haunted by its recent bloodshed. Jason, still in hospital in a coma. Dani, her own demons amplified by it all, had been in a nosedive and on the brink of teetering back into a normality of pills and alcohol to see her through. But she'd soon realised there was no solace there, and so, even before Jason had woken from his coma, Dani had not only forcibly weaned herself off the medication – at least back to prescribed levels – but she'd moved herself and all of their things out of their Harborne home and rented a three-bed semi in a leafy part of Sutton Coldfield. It was not only near to where Gemma lived, but also Easton. Not that their proximity had a direct bearing on the choice. It had been suggested to her by more than one person that perhaps a three-bed semi – a traditional family home – was overkill for her living on her own. But it wasn't just for her. It was for her and Jason, even if he wasn't yet there by her side.

'Jason'll be out soon, though, won't he?' Gemma asked.

'I'm sure he will.'

'You're going to stick around here then?'

'I really don't know. But it's certainly more convenient for coming to see Harry and Chloe.'

Gemma went silent at that and Dani had to push her embarrassment and disappointment to one side. She got that she wasn't the ideal aunt. Not just because of her history, but because of her hectic, unpredictable and often macabre workload. Yet she really would push the boat out to be a bigger part of the kids' lives if Gemma would just let her. It wasn't as though

Gemma had a big family in the local area that she put ahead of Dani.

'So come on then, spit it out,' Gemma said.

Dani raised an eyebrow.

'We've done the chit-chat,' Gemma said. 'You've asked about my job, my crappy love life. I've caught up on the perils of being a murder detective. So now we can get to it. What's Ben done now?'

Dani didn't know whether to be angry or amused by that, though it was true that the interactions between the two of them usually came back down to Ben eventually, one way or another. An incredibly depressing predicament as far as Dani was concerned.

'Possibly nothing actually,' Dani said as she fished in her bag for the picture.

'Really? Last I heard you thought he'd set that Damian Curtis guy up for several murders.'

Dani winced at that comment. 'Kind of,' she said.

'What happened to that then? I read in the paper the other week that Ben's lawyer—'

'Daley?'

'Yeah, that arsehole, he's suggesting Curtis's psychiatrist did it.'

'Dr Collins? We don't know for sure.'

'Daley seems to know. Apparently he's preparing an appeal to have Ben's sentence overturned, because her evidence is so tainted.'

'It's not quite as straightforward as that. Ben isn't innocent, they won't get away from that. The point is that if Collins is proven to have coerced Curtis, then all of her work is irrevocably tarnished. She stood on the stand at Ben's trial. They'll say the outcome of his trial was compromised because of her now-tarnished testimony. It gives them scope to enter new evidence as to Ben's mental state at the appeal. If that happens then, in theory, it's possible Ben's murder conviction could be reduced to manslaughter by reason of diminished responsibility.'

Gemma's eyes were glazed over. 'But he could get out? That's what you're saying?'

'That's never going to happen,' Dani said. 'I promise you.'

Despite forcefully saying the words, she was petrified that she was wrong. What would it take for Daley to create enough doubt in a judge's mind for them to downgrade the original murder conviction?

Dani slipped the picture across the table. A close-up of Liam Dunne, aka James Alden. Not the one taken of the Ellis Associates team, with Ben alongside. Dani wanted to test Gemma's memory unbiased.

'We're dealing with a new case, and this man is a person of interest.'

Gemma looked confused by that, as though she couldn't understand why a new case would have anything to do with her. She picked up the picture as Dani reached for her mug and took a sip of the too-milky mixture. She set it back down again.

Initially, Gemma stared at the picture with that same unconvinced frown, but after a few moments there was a flash of something else.

'Wait a sec. Yeah, I think...'

Then her face changed to one of concern.

'His real name is Liam Dunne,' Dani said. 'But he also went by James A—'

'Alden. James Alden,' Gemma said. The look of concern remained, though the tension in her muscles suggested she was trying to hide it.

'That's the one,' Dani said. 'He worked for Ellis Associates, for about a year, back in 2013.'

Gemma replaced the picture on the table, sat back on the sofa and held Dani's gaze. Dani kept the silence going, waiting to see if Gemma would offer up anything else.

'You said he's a person of interest,' Gemma said. 'In a murder?'

'An unexplained death. How did you know him?'

'You just said. He worked at Ellis Associates. Same as Ben. I'm presuming that's why you're here? Although I really don't see what it has to do with me.'

'Yesterday we found his sister. Dead. Their parents and grandparents are all dead too, their only living relatives are all in Ireland or elsewhere, so James is her only obvious kin, and we're struggling to find him. To find out much about him at all, to be honest. So when I said person of interest, I was perhaps being a bit strong.'

Gemma's face relaxed just a little at that.

'Honestly? I really didn't know him that well,' Gemma said. 'I must have met him… I don't know, two or three times, tops. Just social occasions. Ben's office party. Team dinner. And I didn't know his sister at all. Wouldn't even have known he had a sister, to be honest.'

'What was he like?'

Gemma looked put out by that. 'How do you mean?'

'Was he a nice guy? A dickhead? A drunk? A womaniser?'

'He was single, I think. He was… fine. Unremarkable, I'd say.'

'But you remembered him?'

Gemma frowned. 'You showed me a picture and reminded me of his name. What's your point?'

'Did Ben get on with him?'

'So this does have something to do with Ben?'

'Indirectly, I guess so, but it's complicated and there's only so much I can say at this stage.'

Gemma scoffed and rolled her eyes. 'Of course. I don't know what Ben thought of him. You'll have to ask him. I don't think they were particularly pally, and I don't remember the two of them ever doing anything together outside of the work crowd.'

'Any animosity between the two of them?'

'No. What are you reaching for, exactly?'

'Do you have any idea where he lived. Anything like that?'

'I think we've already established how little I know of him, haven't we?'

'Yeah. I guess we have.'

Though Dani was sure there was a little more to the story than Gemma was letting on. Her caginess was unfortunately a normal occurrence when Dani was around, but there was something else underneath here too.

Dani took another sip from her coffee, then glanced at her watch.

'I really do need to get going,' she said. Gemma remained where she was. 'If you do think of anything more about him, names of friends, girlfriend, where he lived, anything at all, just give me a call.'

'I will.'

'And… it was nice to see the kids earlier. You know I'm always happy to help out, if you need me.'

Gemma said nothing to that. Just gave a forced smile as Dani got to her feet to leave.

Chapter 7

The West Midlands Police's Missing Persons team was housed in Harborne Police Station – a 1980s redbrick building not far from the neighbourhood's high street, and only a few miles south of the centre of Birmingham. Dani knew the area well. Not more than a couple of hundred yards away, the other side of the high street, was the Victorian terrace that she and Jason had bought together less than twelve months ago. Not home. Not any more. Not after Damian Curtis had so horrifically invaded that space.

The Harborne house – Dani and Jason's first together, a place that should have helped cement their commitment to each other, a place where they had wanted to start a life together – was now rented out to a South African professor at the nearby university, and her husband and son. Dani had no intention of ever going back there. Today was the first time Dani had even been back to Harborne since she'd moved out, and there was a sickly sensation in her stomach as she stepped from her car, the earlier conversation with Gemma for now a distant memory.

'I'm getting bored of this cold,' Easton said as he shut the passenger door and cupped his hands to his mouth.

The temperature on the car's thermometer had peaked at minus two on the journey over. They were certainly experiencing a stark welcome to winter.

'It's only early December,' Dani said. 'We've a way to go yet.'

'Tell me about it.'

'And aren't you glad you'll be enjoying Christmas surrounded by your family this year?'

Easton shot her an unamused look and she had to hold back her smile. They edgily traipsed across the frozen pavement to the police station.

'Having the kids around will be nice, actually,' Easton said, shrugging. 'Brings back memories.'

Dani said nothing to that. She'd not experienced a Christmas with kids since she herself had been one. While she could imagine it added extra wonder and excitement to the day, and while it was true those years at home with Ben and her mum and dad still evoked a huge fondness in her mind, it simply remained impossible to reconcile those memories of Ben, the boy she'd grown up alongside, with the man who was now behind bars. And it also seriously grated on her that she'd never been invited to spend a Christmas with Gemma and the kids. Would she ever?

–

A few minutes later they were seated in an ageing office space that housed four detectives from the Missing Persons team. Hot tea and coffee was steaming away on the table and would, hopefully, do the job of warming Dani through.

'I have to be honest with you, this case isn't familiar to me at all,' DS Carr said.

In her early thirties, with long, straight red hair and a face that was dominated by freckles, Dani knew Jane Carr to be an eager and competent detective. Her boss, sitting next to her, DI Gregory, was a portly man in his forties, nearly bald on top but with an ever-thickening goatee.

'And you know I wasn't on the team that long ago,' Gregory said, his words sounding like a lame excuse. Dani didn't know Gregory well, but what she did know of him was that he was always happy to push responsibility away from himself.

'But you were here then, DS Carr?' Easton said.

'I was,' she said, 'but I was only a fresh-faced DC. Liam Dunne's case was run by DI Calvert.'

'She left before I joined,' Gregory said.

'Then what can you tell us from the records?' Dani asked, even though it was likely to be little more than she or Easton could have gleaned themselves from the HOLMES 2 system.

Carr shuffled the papers in front of her for a few moments as her eyes flicked across the pages.

'Liam Dunne. Thirty-three years old. Went missing sixth of June 2015. He was born in southern Ireland, but held dual UK citizenship due to his mother. He first moved to the UK to attend university at Loughborough, studying economics.'

She frowned now as she stared at the information.

'To be honest, there are some oddities here. His history after university is very patchy, in terms of jobs, taxes, addresses.'

'We think that's because he was using aliases,' Easton said.

Carr raised an eyebrow. 'I don't see anything about that in here,' she said.

'So it's not in his profile that he worked for Ellis Associates?' Dani said. He'd used the alias James Alden for that job and had very possibly lost the job because of the false name and history.

Carr shrugged. 'Doesn't seem to be.'

'What about the circumstances of him going missing?' Dani asked.

'There was very little to go on, by the look of things. His sister, Clara Dunne, reported him missing. That was the sixth of June, but actually it seems we never pinpointed the actual date he disappeared. She'd not had contact with him for a couple of weeks by that point.'

'A couple of weeks?' Easton said, as though it was unusual for siblings to not talk for that long. He would surely wish to be in that position right now.

'What about family?' Dani asked.

'They have no other family alive in the UK. Their mother lives, or lived, at least, outside Cork, but the extended family weren't close. It looks like we did get help from the Garda to check for proof of life in Ireland, but it didn't turn up anything.'

'And no proof of life in the UK either?' Dani asked.

'Nothing when we last did our checks,' Carr said. 'But it's not an everyday thing when someone has been missing for five years.'

'And it's going to be seriously clouded if you're suggesting this man potentially used different identities,' Gregory said.

Which was a fair point.

'We can give you what we have of his profile. Addresses, the like,' Carr said.

'Please,' Dani responded. 'But do you actually know anything concrete about when or how he went missing?'

'Honestly, no. His last recorded employment, at least in his real name, was way back in 2009. He had only one bank account, which was last used twenty days before his sister contacted police. We were told he regularly changed his phone number, likely because he was using prepaid SIMS.'

Dani and Easton shared a look. Why would Liam do that?

'And when was the final phone number last used?'

'Again, it was a few days before Clara contacted police, from what I can see. We also did searches on CCTV around his home. The address we were given as his home, that is. But we never managed to pick up anything of him at all, never mind pinpointing his last whereabouts. Neighbours didn't know him. Landlord had no contact with him. The last and only person found who'd had anything at all to do with him for months before his disappearance was his sister.'

Which altogether was painting a picture of a very strange life indeed.

'Maybe he was James Bond,' Easton said. 'Secret lives and all that.'

His quip elicited a chuckle from Gregory, though a similar thought had already crossed Dani's mind. Could he have been a deep undercover policeman even? But then surely his disappearance would have by now been clarified.

Regardless, it looked like there was a lot more work to do in order to figure out what had happened to Liam Dunne. Would more thorough searches for James Alden, Michael Marin and Patrick Beatty turn up any clues?

But then was it even the job of the Homicide team to do those searches? There was no body for Liam. No evidence at all that he had been murdered. Clara Dunne was Dani's case, but her brother was still just a missing person.

'If we give you the details of the aliases, we'd really appreciate your help in trying to track any proof of life,' Dani said.

Gregory looked a little uncertain, like he thought it was a waste of time. She'd had similar conversations with him in the past along these lines. She could understand there was only so much his team could do to trace people who had simply disappeared, but sometimes it seemed like he wasn't even that bothered about trying. Like he'd already made his mind up that there was nothing he could do to help certain people.

'We can do that,' Carr said. 'You said this had something to do with his sister?'

'Clara Dunne,' Dani said. 'Her body was found yesterday.'

The curious look Carr now gave her boss suggested she hadn't known that.

'Her death set us onto Liam because we think she was here, in the area, looking for him,' Easton said. 'It's also notable that, like her brother, she was using an alias.'

'So she was killed?' Gregory asked.

'Well, that's what we're trying to figure out.'

Chapter 8

'This is just getting weirder and weirder,' Easton said as Dani pulled her car back onto the road.

'Tell me about it.'

'So Liam goes missing in mysterious circumstances, five years ago, after years spent living under false names.'

'Living *and* working under false names, apparently.'

'But why?'

Dani really didn't know.

'Then at some point, Clara becomes obsessed with his disappearance,' Easton said.

'Perhaps only because the disappearance was so weird to start with.'

'Perhaps. Then she starts using an alias as well. Clara Doyle? Fake driving licence, the works.'

'And now she's dead.'

Dani glanced over to see Easton shaking his head, confused. She felt the same way. There were so many answers they didn't have.

They drove on in silence for a few moments. Dani could tell Easton was still deep in thought.

'We're not going back to the city centre?' he said, as if finally coming out of his trance.

'No,' Dani said.

'No court today either then?'

'No point is there?'

Easton didn't answer that, though Dani certainly wasn't finished yet with Damian Curtis. Still, it was far more healthy for her state of mind to concentrate on events she could control, rather than dwelling on her past. Even if it was someone else's past she was dwelling on.

'So where are we going then?'

'You'll see.'

—

On the outskirts of Tipton, the 1950s semi was on a twisty cul-de-sac that led to the entrance of a primary school. Like so many other towns in the Black Country area, Tipton had been at the heart of the nineteenth-century Industrial Revolution, though following the closure of most heavy industry from the 1970s onwards, was now increasingly a commuter town to other areas within the region.

As Dani shut down the engine and stepped from the car the sound of the young kids playing in the nearby school caught her ears. She looked over to the tall green metal fences of the school, beyond which was a blur of movement as the pupils raced around haphazardly, giggling and shouting and squealing.

'Is that before or after their lunchtime sugar rush?' Easton asked.

'You would know better than me,' she said.

He rolled his eyes.

Dani locked the car and glanced up and down the street and then along the short drive to the house they were standing by. The houses here were modest but far from downtrodden, though some had clearly been loved and cared for more than others, with neatly trimmed gardens, new windows and doors and faultless tiling on the roofs. A few others were in need of a good dose of TLC, though the one Dani and Easton were standing outside fell somewhere in between. That wasn't what stood out about the house to Dani. The thing that stood out most was that every window at the front of the house had thick curtains drawn across them, both downstairs and upstairs, and there was no car on the poky drive.

'Anyone home, you reckon?' Easton asked.

'Let's find out,' Dani said.

They headed up the drive. The pockmarked tarmac had been gritted and there were indentations in the sandy mixture from thick-soled boots. Possibly just the postman, but possibly from someone else coming or going recently.

Dani pressed the bell then knocked loudly three times.

After thirty seconds there was still no response. Dani tried again.

'Maybe we should have called in advance,' Easton said.

But Dani could hear faint movement from the inside now. The click of locks. Then the door edged open a couple of inches, until it caught on a chain. Two yellowy eyes poked out from the darkened interior, barely five feet from the floor.

'Yes?' said the woman in a croaky voice.

'Mrs Popescu?' Dani asked. She showed her ID and introduced herself and Easton. 'We'd like to talk to you about your grandson, Nicolae.'

Brigitta Popescu said nothing as she stared at Dani. A moment later her eyes disappeared and the door was pushed closed.

Ten seconds passed. Twenty.

'Weird,' Easton said.

Dani was thinking the same. She was about to knock again when the door reopened, without the chain this time, though only just enough to reveal the homeowner. Hunched over, shakily holding a walking stick, Brigitta had a withered face, and even with her cardigan and long skirt it was clear she was a bag of bones by the way jagged joints poked out against the fabric.

'Please. Come in,' Brigitta said, and it was already clear from her thick accent that English wasn't her first language.

Dani and Easton followed into the house. Easton shut the door behind them, and they were plunged into near darkness. There were no lights on in the hall, and just a faint glow of orange and yellow coming from the back room. Dani couldn't even see the end of the stairs in front of her because the top floor was pitch black.

'Please,' Brigitta said, as she continued to shuffle through the darkness towards the rear of the house.

Dani and Easton followed. As she passed by the front room, Dani peeked in and realised the gloomy space beyond was being used as a bedroom. Brigitta certainly looked too frail to be getting up and down those stairs. So was the top floor used at all?

They were soon inside a cramped sitting room at the back of the house. Long thick curtains were pulled across the windows, just slivers of light coming into the room around the top edge of the blackouts.

Brigitta rummaged through the dark and groaned painfully as she lowered herself into an armchair.

'Please,' she said, indicating the adjacent sofa.

Dani and Easton both took a seat. Dani's eyes worked across the room. No sign of a TV. A table lamp on a unit in the corner glowed orange, but its low-power bulb was doing a lousy job of lighting the space. By Brigitta's side was another unit where a series of candles burned away, their short flames flickering.

Beyond the flames was a dull painting on the wall – Jesus on a cross? – though it was hard to tell in the dim light. Around the candles were various photos, cast in shadow, though Dani was sure each of them showed the same young woman.

'You live here alone, Mrs Popescu?' Easton asked.

'What?'

Easton repeated the question more loudly and clearly.

'Yes. Yes. This is my home.'

She said those words forcefully as though the house was perfectly suitable for a frail woman in her late eighties.

'Mrs Popescu, we'd like to talk to you about your grandson,' Dani said.

A nod in response. Apparently she didn't find it unusual that two police officers were here asking about him.

'Are you happy for us to speak to you alone? Or do you—'

'You're here about Nic?'

'Yes. Have you spoken to him recently?' Dani asked.

'Heh?'

Brigitta cupped her ear. Dani repeated the question, louder and more clearly, much like Easton had moments before. She could sense him smirking beside her.

'Nic? No. He doesn't call me for weeks.'

'He's still in—'

'My birthday. He called then. I'm eighty-six. No card, just phone call. He's a busy man.'

'Can you—'

'But he did send flowers.'

She sat forward and looked around the room, as though searching for them, then mumbled under her breath, 'They died, I think.'

'Is there a reason you've got all the curtains closed?' Easton asked.

Dani had wondered the exact same thing, though she wasn't sure if it was appropriate to ask or not.

'How I like it.'

'Mrs Popescu, the reason we're asking about Nic is that—'

'You want tea?'

Dani paused.

'Heh?' Brigitta said, cupping her ear again. 'Coffee?'

'No, I'm fine, thank—'

'In the kitchen. Please. Tea. Milk only.'

Dani looked at Easton and saw the amused grin on his face.

'I'll go,' Easton said, just beating Dani to it.

She sighed as he got up and headed out.

'Mrs Popescu, I need to ask you about two people I think your grandson knows.'

'Nic?'

'That's right.'

'Ah, he's not such a bad boy. His heart is good. He used to live here. Did you know?'

Dani smiled and got to her feet as she pulled her phone out. She picked out a picture each of Clara and Liam Dunne as she moved over to Brigitta and knelt down by her side. The smell of musky oldness filled Dani's nostrils.

'This man is Liam Dunne. But he might also have called himself Patrick, or James. I think your grandson may know him.'

Brigitta was staring at the picture but she gave no reaction at all.

'Do you remember ever seeing him? Or hearing about him?'

'Him?'

Brigitta pointed a shaky finger at the photo.

'Yes. Him. Do you know him?'

Her weary eyes found Dani's now. She looked seriously surprised by the question.

'No. I don't know this man.'

'How about this woman? Her name was Clara.'

Brigitta focused on the screen again, this time only for only a second before she looked away and slumped back down in the armchair.

'So that's why you're here.'

'You know her?'

'Her? No. I don't. But now I know why you're here.'

'You do?'

'Another one,' Brigitta said.

'Sorry?'

'She's dead,' she said, shaking her head mournfully.

Dani's skin prickled, then she jumped when she heard the footsteps behind her.

It was just Easton, carrying two mugs. He paused. 'Sorry, did I—'

'Don't worry,' Dani said, focusing back on Brigitta. 'Mrs Popescu, what do you mean? Did you know Clara?'

Brigitta shook her head.

'Are you sure? You just said she's dead.'

'Isn't she?'

'She is. But… You also said *another one*. What does that mean?'

Brigitta looked away now, to her right, to the series of photos in among the flickering candles.

'There's always another one.'

Dani looked around to Easton who was still on his feet. In the darkness she could just make out the concerned look on his face.

'Sorry, Mrs Popescu, can you explain that?' Dani said.

Brigitta shuffled in her seat and reached out and grasped the nearest of the pictures. As Brigitta brought it closer Dani could see it was a black and white photo of a young woman, probably late teens or early twenties, with dark but pretty eyes and long dark hair.

'Is that your daughter?' Dani asked.

Brigitta remained focused on the picture.

'She was twenty years old. A baby, really.'

'What happened to her?'

'She was taken. Just like all the others.'

'Taken by who?'

Dani's heart was racing in her chest now. And when Brigitta finally looked away from the photo and caught Dani's eye, it sent a chill right into her bones. Dani shivered and was sure she felt a rush of cold against her right side. The flames from the candles flickered more ferociously and Dani whipped her head around to the doorway.

Easton was already back on the sofa, and there was no one else there. When she turned back, the candles were calming again.

'Mrs Popescu, what do you mean she was taken? By who?'

She leaned forwards and whispered fearfully. 'The Strigoi. Sooner or later, they come for us all.'

Dani shivered again, a split second before there was a crash from out in the hallway.

Chapter 9

Dani's heart nearly erupted out of her chest. She jumped up and spun around. Easton too was on his feet and looking sheepish as he darted forwards to the doorway.

'*Bună ziua!*'

Dani relaxed a little at the soft and untroubled female voice. She was soon out in the hallway with Easton where a young woman, in jeans and white tracksuit top, was by the now closed front door, just scooping up some bags from the floor, her puffer jacket hanging off her arm. She flinched when she looked up at the two coppers.

'It's OK, we're with the police,' Easton said, holding out his warrant card for the woman to see.

'I thought I saw a car,' she said, straightening up and hanging her coat over the banister. 'What do you want?'

Like Brigitta, her accent was strong, though her grasp of English far more natural.

'We were just asking Mrs Popescu a few questions about her grandson, Nicolae,' Dani said.

The woman said nothing now as she stared.

'Your name is?' Easton prompted.

'Stef. I'm her niece. Great niece, actually.'

'Do you think we could talk?' Dani said.

'If this is about Nic, then I really don't have much to say, but you can try.'

The woman squeezed past and into the lounge. She took a sharp inhale of breath and then a jumbled flow of vowels and consonants rolled from her tongue at lightning speed as she moved over to the curtains and yanked them open.

When she was done she turned to Dani and Easton in the doorway.

'Sorry for this,' Stef said. 'I keep telling her not to live in the darkness, but she insists.'

With the winter sunlight reaching into the room, Dani could make it out properly for the first time. Her eyes instinctively fell upon the candles and pictures next to Brigitta. Now properly visible, it was clear the arrangement was a long-standing shrine, and the pictures there included those of at least two different young women. Not Stef, though.

Brigitta squirmed in her seat, her eyes squinting as she looked away from the glare and down to the floor. Stef berated the old woman once again though this time Brigitta bit back with her own Romanian tirade. Stef waved it off with an angry flick then looked over to Dani and Easton.

'Could you tell me what this is about?' Stef said, her tone bordering on hostile.

'Perhaps we could speak with you alone for a few moments?' Dani asked.

Stef looked unsure but then relented and she led the way into the kitchen where she quickly rolled up the blinds and turned on the overhead spotlights to reveal a dated but well-equipped space.

'So?' she said.

'Your aunt mentioned Strigoi just now,' Dani said. 'Do you know what she means?'

Stef sighed and rolled her eyes. 'She's eighty-six, and her brain is barely there. Take no notice of her fairy stories.'

'So what happened to her daughter?'

'Claudia?' Stef said and she looked a little unsettled now, but also suspicious.

'Is that her name?' Dani said. 'The young woman in the pictures?'

'Yes. A lot of those are Claudia.' Stef looked down to the lino-covered floor. 'She disappeared a long, long time ago. Before I was even born. When Brigitta still lived in Romania.'

'What happened?'

'Nobody knows.'

'They never found her?' Dani asked.

Stef shook her head.

'How long has Brigitta lived here?'

'More than twenty years.'

'And you?' Easton asked.

Stef glared at him. 'About four.'

She sounded almost accusatory, as though waiting for a retort from Easton as to whether that was a sufficiently long time.

'How well do you know Nicolae?' Dani asked.

'He's technically my uncle, but I don't know him well at all. Is that why you're here?'

'Kind of,' Dani said. 'Are you in contact with him?'

'Me personally? No.'

'But Brigitta is?'

'It's more that he's in contact with her. When he wants to be. There's no phone number to call him on. No address to send him letters. He just gets in touch sometimes.'

'So he's living—'

'In Romania. In the mountains near Brasov. It's where our family comes from.'

She took her phone from her pocket and typed away.

'What do you do here?' Easton asked.

Stef looked up from her phone with a scowl on her face. 'Here at my aunt's home? Or here in *your* country?'

Easton raised an eyebrow, perhaps questioning her snottily put together response. 'You can answer both if you like. Not that I'm judging, just interested.'

'Why?'

'We're following up on the death of a young woman,' Dani said. 'An unexplained death.'

72

'A Romanian woman?' Stef asked.

'Actually, no.'

That seemed to throw her. Dani took out her own phone and pulled up the same two pictures that she'd earlier showed to Brigitta.

'Her name was Clara Dunne, though she also went by Clara Doyle. We're also enquiring about her brother, Liam Dunne.'

'He's dead too?'

'Missing,' Dani said.

Stef took the phone and studied the pictures for a few seconds.

'I'm sorry. I don't know them.'

'You're sure?' Easton asked.

'Why would I lie?'

'Clara lived not too far from here, in Oldbury,' Dani said. 'She had pictures of your uncle in her room, alongside her brother.'

'Pictures? Like—'

'Clippings. Not framed photos. Not personal pictures. Clippings, pinned on the wall.'

Stef looked truly puzzled now.

'I'm really sorry, but I have no idea what you're talking about.' She looked at her watch then shook her head impatiently. 'Look, I'm behind already. I need to wash and change Brigitta, make her lunch, then I need to get back to work.'

'And work is?' Easton asked.

She gave him that same snotty look. 'I'm a cleaner.'

'That's fine,' Dani said. 'We'll get out of your hair.'

She pulled out a card and handed it over to Stef who looked at it suspiciously for a few seconds before taking it.

'If you do think of anything, about Nicolae, or Liam, or Clara, just give me a call. Anything at all.'

Stef didn't say anything more.

Dani and Easton turned to leave. As they passed by the lounge, Dani stuck her head inside to thank Brigitta and to say goodbye. The old lady was slumped in the armchair, eyes closed, snoring loudly. The black and white picture of Claudia remained held close to her chest.

Dani looked over to the shrine one more time, tried to push away the creepy feeling that continued to build, then turned and headed for the door.

Chapter 10

Banging and clattering from somewhere down below woke Ana from her alcohol and drug-fuelled sleep. She winced in pain and held a hand up to her throbbing head, squeezed her eyes shut, hoping the pain would subside.

It did, at least enough for her to keep her eyes open for more than two seconds, though as she focused on the room in front of her, she wished she was still asleep. At least when she was asleep, passed out, unconscious, whichever, she was some place other than here.

She reached across the armchair to the side table that was crammed with empty vodka bottles and plastic cups. She picked up one of the cups then groaned as she got to her feet and plodded barefoot across the sticky carpet to the 'bar' – a corner of the bachelor pad room that Victor had set up and which comprised of a shoddily built wooden bar, mirrors and stools, and a wall filled with bottles and optics; though the usual course of events for a party was that the bottles all ended up being passed around the room and tossed aside when empty, like they had last night.

Ana's welcome home party, so Victor had called it. The party, for his and his friends' exclusive benefit, had consisted of Ana and three young women she'd never met before plus Victor and ten other seedy men. Plus enough alcohol and cocaine to… to what?

Just thinking about that made her groin and her insides ache.

Ana filled her glass with water. Downed it. Did the same thing twice more then turned back to the room. It was a mess.

The space – about thirty feet by thirty feet – wasn't only used by Victor as a party centre, but as some sort of office for the warehouse below. There was no bed here. Anybody who stayed long enough to need sleep crashed out – or passed out – on the carpet or whatever item of furniture they fancied. This sleazy and sordid room was, in Victor's mind, an impressive introduction to the new women he added to his roster.

That was the other reason they had stayed here last night. There were new women arriving soon, he'd told Ana.

She gulped at the thought of that and felt another knot in her stomach that she knew from past experience would rarely leave her as long as she stayed under Victor's watch.

Another crash from down below. Shouting now. And dogs barking.

That was odd.

Ana moved across the room and grabbed a silk robe to cover her semi-naked and cold-to-the-touch skin. There was no one else in the room with her. She wracked her mind but could remember little of the night before. Just how Victor liked it. Though she could remember his gurning face on top of her, the smell of his alcohol breath as he thrust back and forth.

Ana rushed over to the sink and threw up the meagre contents of her stomach, then dry heaved a few times as she tried to erase the memories.

No, those memories would never fade.

A scream from below now. A man's scream.

What the hell was going on down there?

Ana walked over to the door. Tried it. Unlocked. Likely because Victor was still here, downstairs somewhere. He wouldn't have left her unattended and unsecured if he'd gone out. The bathroom and kitchen to what had perhaps originally been nothing but a regular office space above a bog-standard commercial property, were both along the corridor here, and Ana was given relatively free access to them while Victor or his men were around – even if they would question her movements if they saw her hanging about outside the office.

She peered out. No one else in sight along the corridor. She carried on out, hunched down, moving slow, her feet soft and quiet on the cheap laminate wood floor. She moved over to the closed door to a small storage room. This door, too, was unlocked. She opened it, as quietly as she could, and glanced up and down the corridor again before she stepped into the dark space, leaving the door ajar, to listen for sounds from outside.

Ana crept into the corner and crouched down by the metal shelving unit, then carefully pulled away the dusty boxes underneath that sat on top of a large MDF board and contained who knew what. She pulled the board aside, too, to reveal a gouge in the suspended floor that had a one-inch hole driven right through the plasterboard ceiling below, and gave a glimpse into the smaller of the warehouse areas on the ground floor.

After all this time Ana still had no idea how this hole had first come about. She imagined perhaps at one point in time there'd been a light fitting suspended there, and when it was removed the warehouse owner – whoever it had been at that time – simply hadn't bothered to patch the ceiling over.

Ana liked to think that the story was a little more rebellious than that. That at some point in the past, one of the women had snuck in here and deliberately made that hole for the very purpose of spying. After all, Ana had been shown this place by Iulia, so it was something of a little secret among the oppressed.

What on earth had happened to Iulia?

Ana moved closer to the floor and supported her torso on her forearm as she pushed her face and her eye closer to the hole. She squirmed around a little to spy around the space below.

There he was. Victor. On his feet. Arms folded. Eyes pinched. He was staring across the room to…

Ana moved a little more, pushing her head right up against the dirty wall in the far corner so she could see the other side of the room below.

Ana held back a gasp. A man on a chair. A man Ana didn't recognise. At least not from this angle. That was no surprise.

Victor had so many people under his control. The man was naked. His hands were tied behind his back with rope. The skin on his neck and shoulders glistened red from blood.

'Get him off the chair,' Victor snarled.

Three men came forward from behind Victor. The bound man moaned and pleaded as the oafs untied him and rough-handled him onto the mottled concrete. Ana watched, aghast. The man's hands remained bound together, and one of Victor's men took those while the others grabbed a leg each. They twisted to pull his legs open and prevent resistance, though despite the man's pleading and begging, he was barely struggling, Ana thought. Had they already beaten the fight out of him, or was he drugged?

'Last chance,' Victor said. 'Tell me.'

'I don't know!' the man shouted.

'OK, do it,' Victor said.

Another man came forward now. Where did Victor find these brutes? Why did they all follow his word so absolutely, like he was some sort of deity?

Ah yes, of course. Ana knew the answer. Money.

The man who came forward had a curious-looking jar in his hand. What was that? Food?

He crouched down to the captive and there was a pop as the lid was unscrewed.

At the sound, the barking of dogs became more amplified and expectant. Ana shuffled a little and could just make out one of the animals – a terrier of some kind – its teeth bared, yanking on its chain as it tried in vain to rush forwards.

'Beef paste,' Victor said, moving forward to the man now, his voice calm and considered. 'A little treat for those two. Though nothing beats the taste of real meat.'

The goon spread the paste all around the bound man's groin. The captive writhed pathetically, his cries now little more than a murmur.

'Do you know, I first saw this in my village? It was how the men claimed justice. We had no police. No courts with lawyers.

78

The village, the people, we upheld the law. That man's name was... shit... Who gives a damn? But I was only twelve years old. I remember it so well. This man, he'd raped a teenage girl. Raped her over and over. She was so damaged no man wanted her after that. The villagers beat him, they dragged him naked through the streets, while everyone else looked on and hurled abuse and spat. Then they smeared pig's blood over his... you know what. That pathetic little sprout you have there. Now, blood isn't as effective as paste, I'll tell you that from experience, but we were so poor... Then they set the dog on him. Just one dog.'

Ana was quivering with fear now, she realised. Though still she couldn't take her eyes off the ghastly sight.

What the hell should she do?

'Twelve years old,' Victor said. 'I'll admit, I was physically sick.' Victor put his hand on his heart. 'There was nothing pleasant about watching that, about seeing that man's flesh being torn open, sinews pulled and stretched and snapped like if you or I were chewing chicken from a bone.'

There was a tiny scraping sound behind Ana and her heart lurched as she whipped her head around.

She held her breath.

There was no one there.

She looked across to her feet and realised her toes had caught the edge of the flap of a cardboard box. She slowly exhaled, then put her eye back to the hole. Though why was she even watching this?

'Do you know what happened to that man?' Victor asked.

There was no answer. The man continued to plead.

'He survived. Can you believe it? As a boy I thought there was no way a human could live after something like that. He had a hole between his legs the size of a football. But a doctor stitched him up. Gave him a tube and a bag for the piss and the shit to fall into. The man survived. But what kind of life do you expect he had after that?'

Again the man didn't respond – at least not with any coherence. He was barely even moving now. Paralysed by fear?

'That's going to be *you*,' Victor said. 'Unless you tell me what you know.'

No, he wasn't paralysed. As Victor straightened up, the man found a sudden strength and was writhing around and bucking as he screamed and called and shouted and begged with everything he had.

A tear escaped Ana's eye. She was petrified, mortified, horrified.

'Release the dogs,' Victor said as he turned away.

But then a split second later, 'No! No! I'll tell you! Please!'

A dog rushed forward, mouth open, teeth bared, saliva flying. Victor held up his hand and the dog was all of a yard from its meal when it was yanked back again by the chain still around its neck.

When Victor turned back to face the prisoner, he had a wicked smile on his face. He opened his mouth to say something but then his second-in-command, Alex, came rushing over, phone pressed to his ear.

'Vic, you need to look at this,' he said, his growly voice hushed but still audible from a distance, such was his style. 'It's Stef.'

He pushed the phone towards Victor who glared daggers at his friend. He snatched the phone away and stared at the screen.

'Police?' Victor said, disgusted. 'OK. Let's go.'

He slammed the phone into Alex's hand and looked down at the meat-paste-covered man.

'I'll deal with you later,' Victor said, showing true anger for the first time. Anger because his plans had been abruptly halted? 'You're coming with me,' he said to Alex.

Then he stormed off…

Not in the direction of the exit. But in the direction of the stairs.

Shit.

Ana jumped up. Grimaced in pain when her head smacked off the metal racking right above her. She saw stars and fought to get her focus back. She couldn't lose consciousness now. If Victor found her in here... she imagined herself tied up, covered in meat paste, the dogs barking and salivating with predatory greed as they raced towards her.

No. No. No.

She fought through it. Shook her head. Slid the MDF back into place. Heaved the boxes across. Was up on her feet as, out in the corridor, she heard the *clunk-clunking* as Victor and Alex strode up the metal stairs.

Ana smoothed her robe down, straightened her hair to remove the dust, then stepped out into the corridor. With shaking hands she pulled the door closed, then rushed on wobbly legs the few steps to the bathroom door; spinning on her heel when she reached it, she saw the boot of Victor emerging from the top of the stairs.

'Hey,' he said.

Ana stopped and turned back to face him, trying her best to appear calm as she – apparently – exited the bathroom.

'You're up,' Victor said, his face not hiding his suspicion.

Ana forced a smile and nodded.

'What were you doing?' Alex said, moving past Victor and up to the bathroom door. He stared inside the empty space.

'What do you think?' Ana said, surprised at how snarky she sounded. Better than fearful. 'I went to the toilet.'

'I didn't hear it flush.'

'You walk through life listening for toilets flushing?'

He scowled and glared. 'You didn't wash your hands.'

'Wanna smell to make sure?'

She lifted her hand towards his face but Victor stepped forward and grabbed her wrist and squeezed hard enough to make her wince.

'Enough,' he said. 'Back inside. Now.'

Victor released her wrist and spun her around by the shoulders.

'Party time already?' Ana said, as she started to walk back.

'No,' Victor said.

And that was all that he said to her before they were back inside the unkempt space.

'You didn't call her back?' Victor said to Alex as he rummaged about the place. Wallet. Keys. Coat.

'She didn't answer,' Alex said. 'Maybe they're still there.'

'Why the fuck are the police talking to Brigitta?'

'About Nic. But not just about Nic, apparently.'

Victor scoffed.

'Right, let's move.' Victor looked over to Ana. 'Tidy this place up. It looks like a dump.'

Ana said nothing.

Victor and Alex moved for the door. Alex headed out first. Victor turned back to Ana as he grabbed the handle to pull it closed.

'This time you'll stay put,' he said with that usual smile-cum-sneer. He lifted up the key in his hand to show her, then slammed the door shut. Ana rushed forward as the lock clicked into place. She heard them padding away. Rattled the handle. No. It was locked tight. And now she was trapped.

Victor and Alex's footsteps faded away.

Downstairs was strangely subdued now too.

What had happened to the man? To the dogs?

Still, at least those animals hadn't had their feed of fresh meat. Yet.

At the thought, Ana's insides stirred uneasily and she had to hold back the urge to dry heave again.

There was a clunk and a bang somewhere in the distance below. Victor and Alex heading out?

After that everything was quiet, except for Ana's uneven breaths, and the constant throb of her jittery heart.

Chapter 11

Dani started up the car but didn't drive off, instead waiting for the heat to kick in, and the mist to clear from the windscreen. Next to her Easton blew into his hands then stared back up to Brigitta Popescu's home.

'Is it just me, or was that place seriously—'

'Weird?' Dani suggested.

'I was going to say spooky.'

'Spooky? I didn't think you were the type to scare easily.'

'Neither did I.' He shivered theatrically. 'Though did I ever tell you about the time I went to the haunted house at Drayton Manor when I was a kid?'

'No, but you should.'

He seemed to dwell on that. 'Nah, no point in opening myself up for abuse.'

He actually looked genuinely contemplative now, only adding both to Dani's intrigue and her amusement. Easton dug in his pocket and pulled out his phone and Dani realised she wouldn't be hearing the story today.

She pulled the car onto the road, turned it around and headed back the way they'd come. She was approaching the T-junction at the end of the street when another car turned in and pulled to a stop on the kerb. A battered Vauxhall Insignia, two men sitting in the front, hard glares on their faces. Dani caught the eye of the driver as she passed.

'What's that all about?' she said.

Easton was paying no attention.

Dani glanced in her rear-view mirror as they moved on, and made a mental note of the registration.

'What's got you so engrossed?' she said to Easton after a few seconds of silence.

'Strigoi,' he said, eyes glued to his phone screen.

Dani waited for him to expand on his answer. He didn't.

'And?' she said.

'You heard of them before?'

'No.'

'Me neither. But I thought, when Brigitta said it, that it was going to be some sort of gang or something. Like the Mafia.'

Which had been Dani's first thought too.

'So what is it?'

She glanced at Easton and caught his eye. He looked genuinely puzzled.

'Bloody vampires.'

Dani laughed. 'Seriously?'

'Seriously. Well, kind of. When I say bloody vampires, I don't mean literally suck-your-blood bloody.'

'You've lost me.'

His eyes were back on his screen as he scrolled.

'Strigoi,' he said. 'Romanian folklore. They're believed to be the origin of all modern vampire stories. Werewolves too, in a way. Though they're not blood-sucking bat-loving immortals or anything like that. They're basically evil spirits that terrorise the living, that can transform into animals and all sorts.'

Dani wanted to find the revelation ludicrous — because it was — and make light of it, yet as she thought back to that dark house, to Brigitta, the eerie shrine by her side, the cold breeze on her neck, there was no doubt something had left her feeling hugely unsettled.

'So Brigitta Popescu thinks vampires took her daughter,' Dani said.

'Not just her daughter, apparently.'

That was true. Brigitta had intimated there were 'others'. Other what, though? Other mysterious deaths, like Clara Dunne's? Or other unexplained missing persons, like Clara's brother Liam? And like Brigitta's own daughter.

'What on earth are we supposed to do with this?' Easton said, sounding as flummoxed as he looked.

'An exorcist? Or maybe we just need to stock up on silver bullets.'

'And stakes. And garlic.'

'S-t-a-k-e-s or s-t-e-a-k-s?'

'Too early for s-t-e-a-k.'

Although they were both smiling, the mood soon turned contemplative during the silence that followed. Yes, they were making light of the ramblings of an old woman, but there was little that was funny about what they were stumbling over here, Dani realised.

'Let's get back to HQ,' Dani said. 'I want you to dig further into Nicolae Popescu. His crimes. What he's been up to since he was sent back to Romania. Make sure we can pinpoint his whereabouts.'

'You don't believe he's really there?'

'I really don't know. But I do think there's an obvious link between all these people, and what's happening. Liam, Clara, Nicolae. We're just not seeing it yet.'

Another silence followed. Dani could feel Easton staring at her. When she next stopped at some red lights she looked over at him. She couldn't read the look on his face. Suspicion? Disbelief?

'You think there are more, don't you?' he said.

'More what?'

'More deaths. More bodies. Dead bodies.'

Dani said nothing. But based on past experience, she certainly wouldn't rule it out.

'I'm getting lost in all this,' Dani said, sticking her head up over the divider to grab Easton's attention.

'Which bit?'

'All of it.' Dani sat back in her chair, away from her screen, sighed. 'I just can't find anything that links the Doyles to the Popescus. I mean, at one point Liam lived within a couple of miles, but so did thousands of other people, but that's the closest thing I've got. There's no commonality in employment records, no links I can see on social media—'

'We could always ask him,' Easton said. He got up from his seat and moved over to Dani.

'Who? Nicolae?'

'Yeah. Why not?'

'Except for the fact he's in Romania and probably would rather cut his own eyes out than help the UK police.'

'A bit of a leap.'

'Maybe, but certainly if there is anything untoward happening here—'

'Which I think is what you're trying to tell me, right?'

'Right. So why would Popescu ever tell us anything if that's the case. And it's not like we can haul him in to make him sweat when he's across the far side of the next continent.'

'Unless he isn't even there.'

A sudden flash of hope washed over Dani as she looked up to Easton, but it was dashed even before he spoke when she saw the apologetic look in his eyes.

'Sorry, I didn't mean I'd found anything to confirm that,' he said. 'In fact, I did find a Facebook profile that I'm pretty damn sure is him, and it shows him posting pictures back in Romania as recently as three weeks ago.'

'Pictures of what?'

'A walk in a forest.'

'How do you know it was in Romania then?'

He rubbed the back of his neck nervously. 'I don't, but—'

'For God's sake. Social media posts are just a tiny aspect of what we need to cover here, Easton,' Dani said, her agitation rising, even though it wasn't really directed at him. A voice in her head warned her to soften her tone a little. A self-awareness she'd developed recently to try and keep her TBI-enhanced brusqueness in check. 'What I mean is, he could be there on holiday. Someone else could be posting on his account. The pictures could be Photoshopped or not even of Romania in the first place.'

'Fair enough.'

'We need real evidence before we rule him out.'

'Rule him out of what?'

A good question. But one Dani didn't know the answer to. Which was why she ignored it.

'I'll speak to McNair,' she said. 'We'll look to get a request put out to the Romanian authorities. We need to know an address, details of employment, taxes, phone records, whatever. Hard proof to show Nicolae Popescu is really in Romania. And if he is, we need to know what links he still has to people in the UK.'

'Why are you even doubting his whereabouts?'

Again, Dani didn't answer. 'There is this, too,' she said.

She clicked away and pulled up the details she'd found earlier.

'That car I spotted at the end of Brigitta's street.'

'What car?'

Dani rolled her eyes. Of course, he'd been too engrossed in his vampire search to have spotted the car.

'A Vauxhall Insignia. Two rough-looking guys inside. Except the car is registered to Brigitta Popescu.'

'She doesn't strike me as much of a driver.'

'Certainly doesn't. She's also the main driver listed on the car's insurance.'

Easton huffed. 'So who was the chap driving, then?'

'Which is the question we're going to need to get to the bottom of.'

'Am I sensing another trip to Tipton?'

Dani sighed and looked at her watch. 'I'd rather avoid it, if we can.'

'But at the very least we've got some guy driving Brigitta's car, uninsured.'

'Looks like it.'

'If you're looking for someone to sweat out...'

'Agreed. Make a call to the local station. Let them know the deal. If they can get a PC in a car to sit on that street and wait then great, but at least make them aware we need to find that vehicle, pronto. When they find it, tell them to arrest the driver if it's anyone other than Brigitta Popescu.'

'On what grounds?'

'You said it yourself. Driving while uninsured.'

'But you think there's more going on than that?'

'I'm absolutely certain of it.'

She just didn't have a clue what.

–

Dani was tired and seriously frustrated by the time she made it home. Having first stopped at the hospital to see Jason, it was nearly ten p.m., and the house was unexpectedly frigid. It turned out the heating hadn't come on at all during the evening, the pilot light of the ageing boiler having blown out because of the draught coming through the back door. A problem they'd never had at their house in Harborne, where they'd spent thousands on modernising even in the few short months they'd lived there together. This house needed its own dose of TLC, though Dani struggled to bring herself to even think about that while Jason was still in hospital.

After an hour with both the heating on full blast as well as the inadequate gas fire in the lounge, Dani was still ice cold as she sat on the sofa with the laptop, scrolling away.

She'd intended to just quickly catch up on life – social media, the news, emails – before going to bed, but had inadvertently got spectacularly sidetracked. That had started from a simple google of the word 'Strigoi'. Which had turned into a deep dive research of Romanian folklore, evil spirits, vampires and werewolves. Not to mention the history of Vlad the Impaler, the brutal fifteenth century Wallachian ruler, best known for his horrific methods of torture, but also the inspiration for Bram Stoker's infamous character who revolutionised vampire folklore: Count Dracula.

All of which only added to Dani's chill, and the feeling of creepy isolation as she sat alone.

Dani cupped her hand to her mouth as the gory accounts of Vlad's brutality transformed into grotesque images in her mind.

She nearly jumped out of her skin when there was an unexpected bang from somewhere outside the room.

Heart thudding, Dani stared across to the partially open doorway. No other sounds came, but she was soon silently slipping the computer from her lap, onto the seat next to her. Just as quietly she pushed herself onto her feet, just as another thudding sound came, this time causing Dani to flinch anxiously.

Earlier she'd joked with Easton about being easily spooked. And Dani really didn't think that she was normally like that, but there was no doubt she was feeling rattled now. In fact, she'd been on edge all day, ever since that meeting with Brigitta Popescu.

Dani tiptoed to the doorway. The house beyond was all quiet now. Painful memories burned in her mind of the previous occasions she'd been attacked in her own home. Surely it couldn't all be happening again?

As Dani reached the door, she could see the light was on in the hallway. Just as she'd left it. With a rush of adrenaline she jumped out. Spun this way and that.

No one there.

Another thud, and she spun back to face the wall. Rolled her eyes at her own silliness. This time she could place the noise exactly. Though it did help that the bang was followed by muffled arguing. The next-door neighbours. Oh, the joy of a semi-detached house. Dani hadn't lived here long but she'd already figured that the neighbours had an unruly teenage daughter who created havoc for her worn-down parents. The slanging match now taking place next door was a more or less daily occurrence.

There was an even bigger bang and the letterbox on Dani's front door rattled from the force of the vibration. The clip-clop she heard outside confirmed that the daughter was now storming away down the drive. Probably to her boyfriend's car, as was the norm.

At least now the shouting and clattering from the house had stopped.

Though Dani soon realised she took little comfort from the new-found quiet. Out in the hallway the temperature remained uncomfortably low. A gust of wind blasted the house causing a creak and strain somewhere at the back.

No, Dani had had enough of this. She couldn't stay here alone tonight. Not with the horror stories that were now on constant replay in her mind.

Five minutes later, with a hastily packed overnight bag, she was on her way back to the hospital.

Chapter 12

Dani was shocked when the ringing phone woke her and she realised it was gone nine a.m. As expected she'd slept horrendously at the hospital, cramped into the too-hard armchair by Jason's side, and even though he was no longer constantly monitored through the night, the nature of the place meant there was nevertheless a constant stream of noise coming from beyond Jason's closed door. From four till just after seven a.m., Dani had been frustratingly wide awake, and had very nearly bitten the bullet and headed off to HQ early, but apparently tiredness had eventually caught up with her.

Jason wasn't even in the room now. He'd somehow got up and out without her even knowing. What the hell?

She answered the phone. 'Hello?'

'DI Stephens, it's Saad Tariq.'

'Hey. You have something for me?'

'I think so.' He briefly explained the results of tox on Clara Dunne, also the prelims on the various fibres and other samples taken from her home. 'Perhaps it's best if you come down to the lab so I can properly explain it all.'

Dani thought about that one for a moment. 'Have you got the post-mortem results too?'

'I was told they'd be ready this morning. Weren't you planning on going to see Ledford for those?'

'Not if I can avoid it,' Dani said. She never welcomed a trip to the morgue.

'I've got all morning free,' Tariq said, 'if you've time to stop by.'

'No, I've got a better idea,' Dani said.

–

Easton beat Dani to it. He'd already been at HQ when she'd called him, and had headed straight over to Oldbury. She'd needed to take a shower at the hospital and get herself into shape first. She found him standing outside Clara Dunne's home, playing with his phone. Behind him blue and white police tape remained stretched across the front door of the house.

'Let me guess,' Dani said. 'More vampire research.'

He looked at her quizzically, as though it had never crossed his mind. And anyway, wasn't she the one who'd spent all that time yesterday either searching or thinking about Strigoi?

'You look rough,' he said.

Dani snorted. 'Yeah, thanks.'

'Seriously. You have a bad night or something?'

'I was at the hospital.'

Easton looked concerned now. 'Is Jason OK?'

'Oh, he's fine. Just one of those things.'

Easton didn't look convinced but he didn't push further. Likewise, Dani didn't bother to probe into the latest about him and his sister. There was only so much sharing of private grievances she could take.

Tariq soon arrived and Easton did the honours of pulling away the tape and unlocking the front door. With no heating on for the last forty-eight hours, the inside of the house was nearly as cold as outside, and there was a strangely dank and murky smell. Even though Clara Dunne's body had been removed way before any rot had set in, Dani could not just smell, but also sense death in this place now.

A house was just four walls and a roof, but how could any home ever move on from such a thing? The very reason she would have found it impossible to stay in hers and Jason's Harborne home.

'Give us the short version first,' Dani said to Tariq, as the FSI shut the front door behind him. In the hall they each put plastic shoe covers on.

'Certainly,' Tariq said. 'Before I start, I have these for you, hot off the press.'

Tariq took two thin wads of paper from his satchel and handed one each to Dani and Easton.

Dani took the post-mortem report and spent a few seconds quickly flicking through for the vital finds.

'Drowning?' she said, a little surprised.

Tariq held up his hands. 'You know you'll have to go through the details with Ledford, I'm no pathologist.'

'So it wasn't the drugs or alcohol that killed her,' Easton said, a frown on his face as he rifled through the papers.

'Unfortunately, it's nowhere near as conclusive as that,' Dani said. 'Looking at these tox levels, she had easily enough drugs in her system to kill her, plus the alcohol. Was that a deliberate attempt to kill herself? Or was she simply unconscious and slipped under the water?'

Both Tariq and Easton took pause now as they looked over at Dani, as though they were unsure where she'd taken that information from. The sad fact was, as someone who'd relied on alcohol and anti-depressants to get by for years, she knew all too well the potential problems of overdosing on either, or both. She knew the limits, had always stayed within them herself, but what Clara Dunne had in her system was way beyond.

'In fact, you wouldn't even need to be unconscious,' Dani added. 'Just drunk enough to not wake up. You'd be surprised how common it is.'

Neither Easton nor Tariq said anything to that.

'And these bruises,' Dani said, working through the report in her head as she read it. 'On her lower arms, upper arms, around her shoulders.'

'There were no bruises on her body when we were here,' Tariq said. 'It would have been obvious to the eye, never mind in the pictures.'

'Meaning what?' Easton said.

'Meaning they were either inflicted very close to death, or when the body was moved,' Dani said.

Easton now looked seriously baffled.

'You know your stuff, DI Stephens,' Tariq said.

Unfortunately so.

'Bruising can still occur on a dead body,' Dani explained to Easton. 'Bruising is little more than blood pooling beneath the skin, so even when blood isn't flowing, as long as there's sufficient force applied to the flesh of a fresh corpse, then you can get bruises appearing.'

'Most frequently when we move bodies from a scene,' Tariq said.

'But if you're saying these bruises weren't there when you were first called in, but are now, it's also possible the trauma was caused just before death, isn't it?' Easton asked.

'That's one for Ledford, I'm afraid,' Tariq said.

'The logic follows,' Easton said. 'And what about this swelling to the back of the head?'

Tariq was looking more and more uncomfortable now, as though he was being put on the spot.

'Again, it could have been caused when we moved the body. It's not easy taking a sixty-kilo corpse out of a slippery bath.'

'Ledford's saying if the impact that caused that swelling occurred while she was still alive, it likely wasn't sufficient to incapacitate her,' Dani said.

More of a statement than a question, as she was reading the finding direct from Ledford's own words.

'OK,' Dani said, folding the report away. 'Walk us through your scene analysis.'

'Of course,' Tariq said, looking a little relieved.

He produced another report each for Dani and Easton, then got to work explaining.

'First up, I should say we did standard tests with UV light all around the house for bodily fluids, blood, etc. Nothing stood out, but then that was expected as there was nothing about the scene to suggest Clara had been attacked or bled elsewhere within the house.'

Dani made a mental note of that. She'd possibly come back to it later as she wasn't sure it was the most straightforward of conclusions.

'We tested all obvious surfaces for prints,' Tariq continued. 'Around the bathroom, doors and frames, kitchen surfaces, banisters, the like. We found what you'd expect. Plenty of areas with Clara's prints, and one or two areas where we have other unidentified prints, but mostly only partials.'

'Anything that looked unusually print-free?' Dani asked.

'Not really. Kitchen was particularly clean, but that's not unusual as such. A good cloth and a bit of Fairy will take prints off a lot of surfaces.'

'And the partials?'

'There were seven different fragments in total. We've matched five of those, to various degrees of accuracy, to Bianca Neita's prints.'

'And where were they?' Easton said, eyes down, flipping a page as he spoke.

'Front door, on the outside handle. Inside edge of the front door too. Bathroom doorframe. Side of the bath.'

'Which is all consistent with her statement about coming in and finding the body,' Easton said, looking to Dani for confirmation.

'Consistent enough. For now,' Dani said. 'What about the final two partials?'

'This is where it gets a bit more... unclear,' Tariq said. 'One was in the bathroom, on the edge of the cabinet door, and the other was on the top of the baluster at the bottom of the stairs.'

They were standing right by it, and Dani stared over to the dark wood now, as though trying to seek a glimpse back in time.

A thought was building in the back of her mind, but she held on to it for now.

'Let's take a look as we talk,' Dani said.

They moved through to the lounge first, then the kitchen, Tariq regurgitating the procedures his team had undertaken in each room, and the generally bland results that had been returned.

Soon they were in the frighteningly cold bathroom, and Dani felt a wave of sorrow pass over her as she stared at the bleak-looking bath, and the brown tide mark a couple of inches from the top.

'Did you test the water?' Dani asked.

'We took a sample. Not yet tested, though, I don't think.'

'Could you?'

'Certainly.'

Dani looked around the room, from the bath, to the tiled floor where the glass of neat vodka had been found, to the cabinet.

'Nothing on the floors? No footprints, no shoe-prints?'

'The only surfaces you'd get anything useful from were the laminate in the hall and kitchen, and the tiles in here,' Tariq said. 'We found some faint outlines which match to the shoes worn by Bianca Neita, and a few partial foot imprints. We can match some of those to Clara, but some are too smudged to reach a conclusion on.'

'Smudged?' Easton asked. 'As in someone tried to remove them?'

'Unlikely, as it's normally quite obvious when an area has been deliberately cleaned in that manner. I'd say most likely the smudged prints are from Clara walking around in socks. You can still get residue transfer – oils and skin cells – through the material.'

Easton sighed. 'So basically, this all adds up to pretty much nothing. There's nothing I'm seeing here to suggest someone else was in the house. Except for Bianca Neita, that is.'

Was the answer that simple? No, Dani didn't believe so.

'I don't think Neita killed her friend,' Dani said.

'I wasn't suggesting she did,' Easton said.

'I know. I'm just thinking out loud. Bianca Neita's prints are easily explainable. But thinking back to what she said, if we're looking for an explanation of the mysterious figure she claimed to see…'

Dani's brain hit a wall as the thoughts continued to take shape. The bathroom was horribly silent for a few seconds. Dani turned and strode out, heading back for the hall.

'Bianca opens the door. Sees a figure exiting out the back.' Dani turned when she reached the front door, looking back along the way. 'Say an intruder came in, took their shoes off so as to not leave shoe-prints. Gloves on their hands to stop transfer.'

'OK?' Easton said. 'But that doesn't explain the partials then?'

'Actually, it might,' Dani said. 'Shiny leather, as an example, is pretty good at collecting residue. When you put two gloves on you still have to pick the things up bare-handed.'

'Secondary transfer,' Tariq said.

'Exactly.'

'I guess that's possible,' Easton said.

'So going back to shoes,' Dani said, 'when Bianca storms in, the intruder runs. If they'd taken their shoes off to prevent prints, they wouldn't have had time to put their shoes back on before they fled. Nor did we find any obvious footwear left behind, so they didn't scarper in their socks.'

'But they could have had shoe covers on,' Easton said.

'Exactly. But they wouldn't have put those on outside. The ground was damp that day, from frost melt. Wet shoe covers would have left stains on the laminate, which we don't have. So the intruder would have put covers on their feet only when they came inside.'

Dani stared down to the welcome mat by the front door.

'One of my team looked over the mat,' Tariq said. 'We found hair fibres and plenty of dust but nothing much else. We haven't got a clear picture yet on any of the DNA results from the various hair samples, I'm afraid.'

Dani took in the words as she crouched down and took hold of the edge of the mat. She lifted it up slightly to peer underneath. Just as she'd expected.

'It's double-sided,' she said as she flipped the whole thing over. Debris and grit and whatever else was stuck in the thick and coarse pile sifted onto the floor.

'You checked both sides?' Dani asked as her eyes darted across the brown surface.

'I… I'd have to check.'

'No need,' Dani said. She could already see the answer. 'You got any tweezers?'

Tariq did. And they were fine enough to allow Dani to delicately pick off the tiny speck of blue plastic caught in one of the prongs of the mat.

'Bloody hell,' Easton said when Dani held the find up.

'Intruder, gloves already on, breaks in silently,' Dani says. 'Puts on blue plastic shoe covers while on the mat. Kind of like we did, except ours are much better quality. The intruder's were cheap, the type you get at your local swimming pool. Easily snagged. He, or she, turns the mat over for good measure. Then the attack takes place.'

'There's really very little evidence of an attack though,' Easton said. 'Other than the bruising which may or may not have occurred after death.'

It was true, but Dani wasn't finished yet. 'Intruder subdues Clara, one way or another. Puts her in the bath. Drugs her. Drowns her. Wait… no, that doesn't work.'

'Really?' Easton said. 'You almost had me then.'

'Her phone, laptop, everything was still here, wasn't it?'

'Yeah,' Tariq said. 'We bagged it all. The computer forensics team are just waiting on the word before they start processing and searching.'

'That's it,' Dani said.

'It is?' Easton said.

'That could explain the bruises. The intruder was looking for something. Clara was held down. Threatened. Not so forcibly as to cause serious injury, but enough to bruise. Maybe she had a knife to her throat. A gun even. She gave the attacker what they wanted.'

'Which was what?'

'I don't know.' She thought back to the cupboard upstairs. The pictures of Liam Dunne and Nicolae Popescu. 'But they killed her anyway. Then they were disturbed. They had to leave before they were finished. That's why nothing was cleaned down even. The partial prints were a mistake. Which means...'

Dani couldn't quite finish the sentence.

'Which means what?' Easton said.

'Which means as far as I'm concerned, this is now officially a murder investigation. Not only was Clara Dunne killed in her own home, but I believe the reason she was killed was right here, in this house, all along. Now we need to find it.'

Chapter 13

More than two hours later Dani and Easton were still at the scene as Tariq and his FSIs performed an even more deep dive search of the house and its paltry grounds than they had two days previously. They weren't taking any chances this time. Yes, this work could have been covered first time around, but at that point it really had been a matter of conjecture as to what had happened to Clara. As much as Dani would love to have FSIs combing over every inch of every crime scene, that simply wasn't possible, especially in the case of an unexplained death – which is what this scene had been on Monday morning – as opposed to an obvious homicide.

Not any more, though. Dani had already relayed to McNair the initial forensic and post-mortem findings and explained her theory, and the DCI had agreed that it was now prudent to consider Clara's death a murder, and to ensure that as much scene-of-crime evidence was preserved as was possible. No one was to blame for not having taken that step sooner, though Dani was left to think about whether the delay would come back to bite them.

'What are you thinking?' Easton asked.

Dani jumped at the sound of his voice. She spun around and stared out of the bedroom cupboard at her colleague, standing on the other side of Clara Dunne's now stripped bed.

'I didn't hear you come in,' she said.

'You were too engrossed. Literally standing watching a blank wall.'

'Very funny.'

'What's on your mind then?'

'Clara was targeted.' Dani faced back to the wall which two days ago had been covered in photos of Clara's brother and Nicolae Popescu. Now the wall was bare, just faint grimy outlines left where the pictures had previously been. 'This wasn't some random break-in followed by a struggle.'

'Agreed.'

'Her murder took some planning. Someone who knew how to pick a lock, who had a semblance of understanding of crime scene analysis. Who was able to subdue Clara and get her into that bath, barely leaving a mark.'

'Except for those bruises.'

'Which may or may not have been caused by the police. But in any case it was hardly a vicious assault, was it?'

'No,' Easton said, coming around the bed towards Dani.

'It was intricate and well-executed. Without Bianca Neita's intervention, the homicide team may never even have got the call.'

'Where are you going with this then?'

'This feels to me as though Clara was silenced. A murder dressed up to look like suicide. Only the attacker got caught in the act and had to flee.'

'You think it has to do with what we found in here?'

'Makes sense, doesn't it?'

'Not really.'

'You agree Clara was probably trying to find her brother?'

Easton didn't look convinced. 'It's possible. But he's been missing for five years. Why now? And why all the underhand-edness, false IDs and everything?'

'Because she was in danger. She knew that. What if she got too close to the truth? And she was killed because of it?'

'The truth being what? I feel like you're about to come out with some sort of government conspiracy.'

'Well, it is a conspiracy, isn't it? Even if we don't yet know what it's about. But we do have one suspect.'

'Nicolae Popescu?'

Dani nodded, and edged past Easton back into the bedroom and towards the door.

'You mean Nicolae Popescu who was extradited from the UK in 2013?' Easton said as he followed her out and down the stairs. 'Which was two years before Liam Dunne even went missing.'

'Apparently.'

'Which part.'

'Popescu was apparently extradited in 2013,' Dani said. 'Which is why we need to focus on figuring out where he is now, and where he's been for the past seven years.'

Dani stopped in the hallway. In the lounge she could see an FSI on her knees, running a comb over the carpet, picking up various samples of dirt and hair and whatever else.

'I think Clara was on to something,' Dani said. 'About her brother's disappearance. We need to get the computer forensics team to search her electronic equipment. That wall in her room can't have been her only research, so what was her killer trying to find before they killer her?'

'Maybe they found it? Maybe they took it.'

Dani didn't think so. Otherwise the killer would have taken everything they could – the pictures on the wall in the locked cupboard included – in order to leave no clues behind. Though the fact Clara was already dead when the killer was disturbed did perhaps suggest the killer thought they'd got enough out of her.

So had she simply explained where the information was, and the killer was planning on going back and gathering it and destroying it before they were interrupted by Bianca?

Easton looked at his watch. 'Come on, we need to get going, don't we?'

Dani took one last look around, down the hall to the bathroom. She really hoped she'd not have to come back to this wretched place again. 'Yeah. We do.'

The windowless interview room at HQ was warm enough temperature-wise, but there was nothing that could be done to remove the coldness of a place like this: plain floor, plain walls, the only furniture was the plain desk with four plain chairs. One wall was taken up by a large one-way mirror, decoration of a sort, though Dani knew no one was looking in on the other side for this interview.

'Mrs Neita,' Dani said, once Easton and their interviewee had settled themselves into their seats, 'thank you for coming in to speak to us today.'

Bianca Neita nodded in response. She looked petrified and was unable to hold Dani's gaze for more than a second.

'Before we start I'd like to clarify that you are speaking to us voluntarily today,' Dani said. 'You are not under arrest, this interview is not being carried out under caution, and you are free to leave at any time.'

Bianca nodded feebly, looking even more concerned now following Dani's formal words.

'We're not recording this interview on video or audio, though we will be taking notes of what is said today. You were informed that you had the right to bring a companion to this interview, whether friend, family member or lawyer, but you've chosen to come here alone. Is that correct?'

'Y-yes.'

'Please, just relax, we're not trying to trick you here. We only ask that you give us full and honest answers. OK?'

'OK.'

Dani nodded to Easton.

'Please can you describe your relationship with Clara Doyle,' he said. 'By that I mean how and when did you meet. How often did you see each other, socialise together, etc.'

A nice and easy opener for Bianca. And the conversation carried on in that manner for a good twenty minutes as Dani and Easton asked straightforward and not at all probing questions. Largely they were covering old ground, as Bianca had already given a statement to a PC on Monday, but with a witness as jittery as this one, it was absolutely necessary to make her as relaxed as possible before they went too deep.

Dani felt Bianca was finally starting to warm up and relax just as they got to talking about Monday morning – when Bianca had found her friend lying dead in a bathtub. It only took a couple of simple questions about that before pressure and anguish were seeping back into Bianca's demeanour, and Dani took the decision to move things on before they lost their hard work altogether.

'Bianca,' Dani said. 'You'll recall on Monday that, as part of our searches, we found a series of photos in Clara's bedroom, in particular of two males.' Easton pulled a selection of photos from the papers he was holding and arranged them on the desk, facing Bianca. 'We understand this man here is Liam Dunne, Clara's brother.'

Bianca showed no reaction as she stared at the picture.

'Do you know him at all?' Dani asked.

'No.'

'You never met him?'

'No.'

'Clara didn't ever talk about her brother?' Easton asked.

'I didn't even know she had one.'

'And this man, do you know him?' Dani asked, pointing to Nicolae Popescu now.

'No,' Bianca said, though it wasn't nearly as convincing as before.

'His name is Nicolae Popescu,' Easton said. 'He's a Romanian national, but he lived in the area for a few years. We think he left the UK in 2013.'

Bianca said nothing.

'He spent three years in jail for grievous bodily harm and attempted murder. It might have been something you heard about in the local news, even?'

Bianca looked seriously worried again, much like she had when she'd first walked into the room.

'What aren't you telling us?' Easton said, his tone noticeably harder now. 'It's clear to me that you know this man. Or at least know of him.'

Silence from Bianca.

'Did Clara ever mention him?' Dani asked.

'No, she didn't.'

'You have no idea why she'd have pictures of him?'

'No!'

'But you do know who he is?' Easton said. 'I know you do.'

'OK! Look, I don't *know* him,' Bianca said, fixing a hard glare on Easton. 'I know *of* him. That's not a crime, is it?'

'No,' Easton said. 'But withholding potentially relevant information from a murder inquiry is.'

Bianca flicked her gaze from Easton to Dani now. Dani said nothing. She knew the silence, and the insinuation in Easton's words, would become unbearable for Bianca soon enough.

'I don't know him. I swear,' Bianca said, close to tears.

'Then how do you know *of* him?' Dani asked.

'You know how it is?'

'Do we?'

'It's not a big town. I'm not saying I know every face, but... I don't even know how to explain, but everyone's always us versus them these days.'

'Who's us, and who's them?' Easton asked.

'Us. English people. Them, you know? Immigrants.'

She had a hard time saying the last word, as if the word itself was a slur and she was ashamed to be thinking that way.

'Could you be more clear?' Easton asked.

'Romanians, Poles, they're everywhere these days and... I'm not saying this is what I think, and I know not all of them are bad. But some are.'

'So do you or do you not know Nicolae Popescu?' Easton said.

'I already said I know of him.' She was talking with fight now.

'But you haven't really explained how.'

'He's someone who's got a reputation. A local thug. At least he was. People talked about him. I've heard stories. What do you call it? Ext… Ext…?'

'Extortion?'

'Yeah. And there's always young girls hanging around them.'

'Them?'

'The Romanians. So I've heard anyway. They bring them in on vans and… this is just what you hear. It could all be crap.'

'But it's not just what you hear, is it?' Easton said. 'Because you recognised his face too. So it's not just stories about immigrant gangs. You knew his face.'

Bianca shrugged but she looked panicked once more. She knew she was on the spot but was struggling to explain. Was it really so hard, or was it only hard because she was trying desperately to deflect?

'I just know,' she said. 'I saw him before. I've heard the name. And recently people are talking about this sort of thing more and more, aren't they?'

'Are they?'

'Immigrants. It's all anyone ever talks about now.' She laughed, though Dani could tell she was in no way amused by whatever had caused the reaction. 'In a way, it's nice not to be the target of those racist pricks so much any more. We used to get it in the neck because we're Jamaican. Now we're almost accepted as being British too. Muslims and Eastern Europeans are the enemy now, thanks to Brexit and all that.'

'Brexit?' Dani said. 'That wasn't even a thing in 2013.'

'I never said it was.'

'Are you saying Nicolae Popescu is still in the area now?'

'Now? Like today?'

'Bianca, think very carefully here. When did you last see or hear about him? Are we talking days, weeks, months? Or years?'

She took time to think about that one.

'I can't be exact, but it's certainly recently, not years. How'm I supposed to remember that far back? Probably weeks, or something.'

'Weeks? You've seen Nicolae Popescu as recently as the last few weeks?'

She shrugged. 'Yeah. I think so.'

'Do you have any information on where he lives? Other people he knows.'

Bianca looked perplexed. 'No, nothing like that.'

'Now's the time to tell us,' Easton said.

'I said I don't know!'

'But you also said two days ago that you didn't know anything about him at all. So how do we know you're not lying again?'

She hung her head. 'Please. I just...'

'It's OK,' Dani said. 'Just tell us everything you can, you won't be in any trouble with us if you do that.'

'I have told you everything. Honestly. I really don't know anything more.'

Dani waited a few moments, hoping Bianca would add something extra. She didn't.

'OK, I think that's all we need for now,' Dani said.

–

Easton showed Bianca out while Dani waited by the lifts for him to return. She still hadn't finished sifting through emails and messages on her phone, and was attempting to listen to a voicemail, when she spotted him heading over.

'What do we do with this then?' he said to her, as she pulled the phone from her ear, the voice message unplayed.

'We need to find Popescu, don't we?' she said.

'Do we call off the search in Romania then?'

'Definitely not. We need to look everywhere we can. You said yourself there's a social media profile supposedly showing

Popescu in Romania. So if he's not there at all then who's responsible for the subterfuge? Let's try to track his movements both here and over there.'

'You don't think it was him you saw yesterday morning, do you? In that car?'

Dani had asked herself the same question more than once.

'I really don't think so. Not unless his appearance has changed these last few years. But we do need to find those men too.'

Dani pressed the button for the lift and they were soon inside heading up.

'So we're going down the route of Romanian gangs,' Easton said.

'Are we?'

'Extortion, people trafficking. Sounds like that was what Bianca was referring to. And it would explain why Clara was targeted if she was digging into them.'

'That's one explanation,' Dani said. 'Though it doesn't explain anything about Liam Dunne, or why he went missing, does it?'

'Maybe not. Why don't I tap up the Org Crime team? See what they know about Black Country Romanians.'

'It's worth a try,' Dani said with a sigh, though she felt the explanation for what was happening wasn't going to be quite as simple as that.

The lift doors opened and they moved through into the open plan space of the homicide team. The area was buzzing with activity. Dani hadn't made it to her desk before McNair stomped out of her office.

'Stephens, in here.'

Dani glanced to Easton who shrugged apologetically. She followed her boss into the office then shut the door behind her.

'Is there a problem?' Dani said, already a bit perturbed at how het up McNair clearly was. What had Dani done wrong?

'Yes, there's a problem. I left you a message almost an hour ago.'

'I was in an interview.'

'Well, you're not now, are you?'

'I was literally just coming back to my…' Dani paused and decided arguing her case was probably not even worth it. 'What's happened?'

McNair sighed. 'I've been fielding snotty calls from the CPS for the last hour and a half, that's what. And this isn't even my problem, but with you incommunicado who do you think they turn to first?'

The CPS? Which most likely meant this was to do with the Curtis trial. Dani felt a knot in her stomach.

'I'm sorry, I didn't know,' Dani said.

'Yes, well, you're wanted at court.'

'Barker?'

'No. Barker just called to give me an earful. As did his boss. As did the Chief Super. They all want to know what on earth is going on, and why one of our officers – the lead detective on the case, no less – is about to bat for the other side.'

'You've lost me,' Dani said. 'I—'

'Wake up, Dani. It's not rocket science. You've been called as a witness. Not by the CPS, but by the bloody defence.'

Chapter 14

Dani had rarely been as nervous as that Thursday morning when she walked out into the full courtroom, all eyes on her. She shakily moved across to the witness box. Her mind remained in something of a blur as she regurgitated her affirmation.

'I do solemnly and sincerely and truly declare and affirm that the evidence I shall give shall be the truth, the whole truth and nothing but the truth.'

The judge thanked the clerk before turning proceedings over to the defence barrister, Iona O'Hare. She got up from the bench and approached.

Of course this wasn't the first time in her career that Dani had testified in court. It was a matter of routine that investigating officers gave lengthy and very detailed witness statements as to their work on a case going to trial, and so Dani had, by extension, been among the list of potential witnesses from day one, though this was the first time she'd been specifically called by a defence team, as opposed to the prosecution.

She still really didn't know how to react to that at all.

O'Hare had a knowing look in her eyes, and even before she spoke, Dani was sure that she wasn't about to be given an easy ride.

'DI Stephens, we've all had the benefit of your witness statement, but perhaps, in your own words, you can give a brief introduction to your role at West Midlands Police, and in relation to this case in particular.'

Dani kept it short and sweet, and O'Hare was soon asking some bland follow-up questions regarding the chain of events that had led to Damian Curtis's capture and arrest. Nothing contentious, thus far. In fact, much the same tactic Dani and Easton had used with Bianca the previous day, getting her relaxed before they moved to the heart of it. And knowing that only made Dani remain all the more anxious, and sceptical.

'So at what point in the course of the police investigation did you first suspect a third party may have been involved?' O'Hare asked.

'A third party?'

'That the defendant was not acting of his own volition in relation to the crimes he has allegedly committed.'

'It was some way in,' Dani said. 'Either just before or just after the point where we finally managed to find and arrest him, if I recall correctly.'

'You don't recall exactly?'

'No. Not exactly.'

'But it was a line of enquiry that was subsequently followed thoroughly?'

'It was. Arresting Damian Curtis was a big turning point in what had been a gruelling investigation, but it was by no means the end of our work. For weeks, months afterwards we carried on our enquiries to put together our case and to figure out exactly what had happened and why.'

'Which is where our third-party manipulator comes into play, correct?'

'Correct. We did a lot of work to establish whether there was evidence of such a manipulator. A conspirator to the murders, if you like.'

'And what initially prompted you to that line of enquiry?'

'It wasn't one single thing. We were desperately trying to find Curtis before he killed again. One way of achieving that was obviously gaining an understanding of why he was killing people at all.'

'Allegedly killing people.'

Dani shrugged. 'It was apparent to me that a noticeable change had taken place in Curtis during his time in prison.'

'But you had never met him prior to his arrest?'

'No, I hadn't.'

'But you're saying that based on what you knew of him, of his past, of his alleged crimes, you were already beginning to question his guilt. Correct?'

'I never had any doubt that he was responsible, in a physical sense. But... his actions didn't make sense to me. I was seeking an explanation for *why*.'

'Which led you to the theory of someone else manipulating the defendant into committing his alleged crimes.'

'That's right.'

'Objection,' Barker said, though his appeal was half-hearted. 'DI Stephens is not here as an expert witness on psychiatry or psychology.'

'I never suggested such,' O'Hare said. 'I'm merely asking the witness for her thought process and how it guided the police investigation.'

'Objection overruled,' the judge said, grumpily. 'Though please do get to the point soon.'

'Please can you tell us, when this theory was first posed, either formally or informally, who it was you believed most likely to be the person responsible?'

Dani paused. She was slowly beginning to see where this would go. But she felt powerless to stop it. She couldn't exactly lie now, could she? All she could do was to go further down the hole O'Hare had already dug.

'Dr Helen Collins,' Dani said, to murmurs from the room.

'Dr Helen Collins?'

'Yes.'

'Your first instinct – your detective's instinct, if you like, based on all your years investigating murders, and your knowledge of this case, which you were leading – was that Damian Curtis was the person responsible for killing these poor victims, in a physical sense, but that he had been manipulated into doing so by Dr Helen Collins?'

'Correct.'

'Can you explain why?'

'There was no science to it. No great weight of evidence against her at that point, it was simply the most logical and obvious answer to me.'

Dani cringed at her own words. Dig, dig, dig.

'Logical and obvious how?'

'Damian Curtis had been in jail for three years. If someone had put him up to these crimes then it seemed most likely that it was someone who'd spent time with him while he was in jail. He'd had no visits in that time other than from Dr Collins.'

'She was the only person who visited him in those whole three years?'

'According to the prison records, yes. He had no friends or family visits at all.'

'Was that the only reason you considered her?'

'No. Obviously Curtis had interactions with plenty of other people inside jail, from inmates to guards, but Collins was the only one who had regularly scheduled one-on-one meetings with him, and the only one who was trained in psychology.'

'So she was the number one suspect, in your mind.'

'At that stage, yes.'

'So what happened?'

'Excuse me?'

'Why didn't you, the police force, not pursue Collins further?'

'We looked in great detail at her, actually.'

'Really?'

'Yes, really.'

'I understand, from your witness statement, that your *theory* of Dr Collins's involvement lasted all of a few days. In fact, even by the time Curtis was arrested, weren't you already considering an alternative explanation? An alternative suspect?'

Dani paused again, desperately trying to think of any way to deflect where this was going. She had nothing.

'Yes, that's correct,' she said.

'And who was this alternative suspect?'

'Ben Stephens.'

Gasps in the court now.

'Your brother?'

'He is.'

'Your brother, who is a convicted murderer, and was convicted of attempting to murder *you*.'

'The very one. My brother, who also shared a cell with Damian Curtis for—'

'Is your brother trained in psychology or any related subject?'

'Not to my knowledge.'

'Yet you believed he was a more likely suspect than Dr Collins?'

'I did. I still do.'

'You still do?'

'Yes.'

More gasps. Dani looked around the courtroom at the bewildered faces, and the shaking heads. Some were almost sympathetic, as if Dani was a moron spouting nonsense subconsciously.

'But charges haven't been brought against your brother in relation to this?'

'No.'

'Why not?'

'The investigation is still ong—'

'Still ongoing, but no charges brought yet?'

'No. Not yet.'

'Why?'

'Because... because so far we don't have...'

'I think you're trying to say there's a lack of evidence?' O'Hare practically spat the words, like the implication was devastating. 'Despite those many weeks and months of police work.'

Dani said nothing.

'DI Stephens, would you say you always act with objectivity in regard to police investigations?'

'Absolutely.'

'Even when investigations concern your brother? Who tried to murder you.'

'Yes,' Dani said through clenched teeth.

'It would be easy to see how someone could be tainted by such an experience. Would want to *get their own back*, one way or another.'

'Is that a question?'

'Not exactly. The question is, do you believe you acted objectively in this case?'

'Objection,' Barker said. 'DI Stephens is not on trial here, and there is no basis to bring her professionalism into question.'

'But my point, Your Honour,' O'Hare said, unperturbed, 'is that I have to bring DI Stephens' professionalism into question. Because it's my belief that her lack of professionalism has, in all likelihood, jeopardised the defendant's position.'

Dani gritted her teeth but said nothing. The judge thought about O'Hare's claim for a few seconds before sighing. 'I'll allow you to continue. But, please, make your point clearly and succinctly, as it relates to this case and your client's position, and not to DI Stephens' general competence and performance.'

'Understood.' O'Hare turned back to Dani. 'DI Stephens, do you believe that you acted objectively in this case?'

'I already said yes.'

'Some would say it's quite a conflict when a murder investigation involves the brother of the lead detective.'

'Any conflict was discussed internally within the police force, and it was concluded I could remain as SIO. There was no deceit.'

'No deceit? OK, could you briefly explain what procedures were put in place to manage that conflict?'

'It was simple. I was told that for any meetings and interviews with Ben Stephens in relation to the case I'd have to be accompanied by another officer.'

'Basically, you were told not to meet with your brother on your own?'

'In relation to the case.'

'And yet you did?'

Dani clenched her teeth now. 'One time, yes.'

'You broke the safeguarding procedures put in place by your own superiors. Is that correct?'

'On one occasion, yes.'

'Can you explain why?'

'This was before Curtis had even been arrested. Before we were even considering a conspirator. We were desperately trying to catch a killer. I was trying to prevent more deaths. My brother had already made it clear that he knew something about Curtis, something about why he was doing what he was doing, but he was refusing to tell us unless we met his ludicrous demands about immunity. I thought he would be more likely to talk to me, alone.'

'So you circumvented agreed procedure, without prior approval.'

'On that one occasion, yes, but that meeting had no bearing on Curtis's crimes, or this trial, or—'

'But it does, DI Stephens. Because a moment ago you asserted that you always act objectively on investigations, but clearly, you are prepared to break rules, protocol, whatever term you'd like to use, when you see fit.'

'I was trying to catch a killer,' Dani said through gritted teeth.

'Indeed. Hence why we are now here. Can you explain why Dr Collins was not pursued as a person of interest?'

'She was. But she was also dead which limited what we could do somewhat. We pursued the evidence we had, interviewed Curtis countless times, interviewed friends, colleagues, looked through reams of electronic data, trying to ascertain any hard evidence of her involvement.'

'Really?'

'Yes.'

'Or did you simply decide, on a whim, that in fact your brother was the number one target, and went wholeheartedly after him, ins—'

'That's crap—' Dani interrupted.

Barker was on his feet, clearly riled. 'Objection, Your Honour—'

'Sustained,' the judge shouted, his raised voice enough to bring the court to an uneasy silence. 'I've given you the benefit of the doubt until now,' he said, staring down at O'Hare, 'but I will not have you berating a witness like this without any evidence to substantiate your claims, particularly if the behaviour and actions in question are not directly related to this trial.'

'But, Your Honour, this is directly related, I—'

'Do you have any evidence that DI Stephens deliberately swayed the investigation to the detriment of your client?'

'That's what I was hoping to get to.'

'Then do it now. This is your very last chance.'

O'Hare still looked like she was in full control, despite the judge's stark words. 'DI Stephens, this might be a hard question to answer off the top of your head, but your opinion is very relevant here. In all of the hours of interviews — of electronic data searches and other steps that took place after the defendant's arrest, looking for evidence and motive of the so-called third party manipulator — do you have any idea how much time, as a percentage, was dedicated to looking at Dr Collins as a suspect, compared to your brother?'

'That's impossible to answer, it's—'

'Actually, it's not. My team has performed a very painstaking analysis—'

'Objection,' Barker said, on his feet again and sounding severely fed up now. 'We haven't been given any notice of such analysis, or any opportunity to review it for accuracy.'

'I can furnish the analysis, of course,' O'Hare said. 'But it is simply based on records readily available to the CPS. I'd be more than happy for them to reperform the analysis if they don't agree that it's accurate.'

'Carry on,' the judge said.

'Our calculations show that as much as five times the resources, by which I mean investigation time, was targeted at Ben Stephens' involvement as compared to Dr Helen Collins. *Five times*. Does that ring true, DI Stephens?'

'I'd have to review the information.'

'You're more than welcome to do that. Five times the resources, wasted on investigating the involvement of the senior investigating officer's brother – against whom, for very obvious reasons, it could be said she holds a grudge; the senior investigating officer who has been shown to not always act objectively when it comes to matters involving her brother – versus investigating Dr Helen Collins, who DI Stephens has herself admitted was the only person trained in psychiatry who had direct and regular access to the defendant during his time in jail. Yet no charges have been brought against Ben Stephens, suggesting all that effort was wasted. And the point of all this, is who knows what additional evidence might have been found as to Dr Collins's guilt, her motive – while she was still alive even – if the police, under DI Stephens' direction, had carried out their procedures more prudently—'

'Objection,' Barker shouted once more. 'This is pure speculation. I'm very sorry, but the defence counsel is taking huge unsubstantiated leaps—'

'Objection sustained,' the judge said.

O'Hare held her hands up, a horribly smug look on her face. 'That's fine. I'm finished.'

'Does the prosecution have any questions?' the judge asked.

'No, Your Honour,' Barker said.

'Very well. Thank you, DI Stephens.'

The clerk came back over, unable to hold Dani's eye now.

Head down in shame and embarrassment, Dani stepped from the box and trudged solemnly for the exit.

Chapter 15

Ana kept her eyes off Victor as he stepped from the bed and into his boxers and jeans. Just looking at his out-of-shape body was enough to cause revulsion to rise from within her, never mind when his sticky skin was pressed up against hers. She grabbed a cigarette from the bedside table and lit it up and took a huge inhale that sent her brain swimming – pleasantly – and which took just a tiny edge off her mood.

'You remember how to do this?' Victor said to her as he buttoned up his shirt.

She only looked back to him when she was sure he was properly dressed.

'I remember,' she said.

'And no games. You're there to make them feel comfortable. You do anything I don't like... you know how it ends.'

She turned away from him. Yes, she knew what would happen. In the end, it always did.

–

Victor opened the front door and a blast of icy air smacked into Ana's face. She didn't even flinch. The pills dulled pretty much everything. Still, as she stepped outside she found herself pushing her head down into the fake fur collar of her coat – an instinctive reaction, and there was no doubt the soft fabric felt comforting on her skin.

Across the road, the front door of one of the houses opposite opened and the old woman who lived there – old? She was probably in her sixties, which to Ana, at least, was old – came out with her little yappy dog-cum-rat.

'Morning,' Victor shouted over as he and Ana made their way down the drive to his car. The lady – what was her name, anyway? – gave an unfriendly nod in return but said nothing. Her eyes locked with Ana's. She saw nothing but contempt.

'Good morning,' Ana said when the woman reached the end of her drive.

The woman glowered, and muttered a response, then looked away and yanked on her dog's lead. 'Come on, Biffy.'

Ana clenched her teeth. She opened the back door and sat down in the seat. She guessed they'd be picking up Alex on the way and she knew her place.

'Don't let the old bitch bother you,' Victor said as he fired up the engine and pulled out onto the road.

Ana didn't reply.

'She's probably just surprised to see you back here after so long.'

No. It wasn't that. Not exactly, anyway. When Ana had first come here, under Victor's watch, she'd hated the locals. The sly looks, the dubious comments under their breaths. She'd felt unwanted, despised, targeted. But it was never about her, she now knew. It was never even about the fact that she was a Romanian. She'd soon realised this when she'd finally broken free; when she'd started a new life for herself in the North. Even in her short time there she'd found kindness, acceptance. Normality.

No, the ill-feeling here was all down to one thing, and one thing only. Victor.

That old woman… yes, it riled Ana that she still received such a cold reception, but then how many other women had towed behind Victor out of that house these past few years? Ana wasn't the first, and she wouldn't be the last, whatever her fate from here would be.

'Your lack of communication is really starting to annoy me,' Victor said, catching Ana's eye in the rear-view mirror.

'Sometimes I have nothing to say.'

'Then you could at least look at me like I'm a normal person, and not some monster.'

But he was a monster. Did he really not see that?

'I'm sorry for upsetting you,' she said.

'I never brought a girl back before.'

Ana was looking out of the window now as they drove along, the endless rows of featureless bricks and mortar passing by in a blur.

'But then, I never had a girl before who I was actually happy to set free.'

Set free? Like she was a wild animal in captivity. And it wasn't as if he'd open the door and let her leave. There'd been a bit more to it than that when she'd packed her bag and jumped on a train and somehow ended up in Liverpool. She'd begged and pleaded with him for weeks for a chance to lead her own life. When she'd first arrived in England, she'd just been another of Victor's playthings. That had lasted for more than two years: Ana passed around like a piece of meat. But she'd become more than that. Victor had seen something in her. She'd become his girlfriend. Or at least his vision of a girlfriend. Because of what he called her savviness she'd even begun to help him organise the other girls. Not entirely against her will, either. Part of her hated herself for that, but being his sidekick was little more than self-preservation.

But he had let her go. After she'd caught him fucking other women for the... no, Ana couldn't remember how many times. Too many times. She'd used that against him. He'd claimed he loved her, that he would do anything to keep her. She said if he truly loved her he'd let her be happy.

Eventually she'd left for Liverpool, not with a blessing but with some sort of acceptance.

At least for a few months.

'I was never truly free.' She could feel him, always. 'You tracked me down and brought me back.'

'I tried, Ana. I really tried. For you. I tried to give you what I knew you wanted.' Victor pulled the car to the side of the road and Alex stepped from his house and headed towards them. 'But I couldn't do this without you, Ana. You belong with me.'

–

Victor held Ana's arm so her heels didn't slip on the icy tarmac as they walked from the car towards the front of the warehouse. When they stepped into the warm interior she saw that the large and mostly empty space was all set, with four of Victor's men already hanging about, each standing casually by a parked car.

'They're only a minute away,' one of the men called over. Ana didn't know him. Other than Alex she didn't know any of their names, even if some of the faces were vaguely recognizable. Quite frankly, she didn't want to know, and actively sought to pay them as little attention as she could.

'Come and stand with me,' Victor said to Ana and the two of them set themselves up alongside Alex in the middle of the warehouse floor, facing towards the still closed loading doors.

Moments later Ana heard the rumble of a clattering diesel engine, and then there was a knock on the metal doors, hard enough to make the material rattle, the echo carrying around the large space.

The doors were pulled open and the minibus drove in, parking side on, facing towards Ana and Victor. The driver and front passenger both stepped out. The driver slid open the side door and one by one the bewildered-looking young women were shepherded out, huddling together.

Twelve in total. Ana looked over their faces. There wasn't any real sign of fear yet. They were too young, too naïve, and had seen nothing to be fearful of thus far in their journey, though it was clear they were starting to question just what was happening.

Ana stepped forwards, tottering gracefully on her heels, hips swaying, her overcoat still on, but opened up to show off her long, slender body.

'Welcome to England!' she said, beaming a smile. That was enough to get the girls' attention and they all turned towards her. 'If you straighten yourselves into a line, we'll take a look through your details and get you to your final destinations as soon as we can. My friends here will bring you a drink and a snack while you wait.'

As if on cue, two women who could well have stepped from a minibus like this one just a few days ago, came from the stairs carrying trays of juice and biscuits. A few of the women refused, most didn't.

'As you know we've already matched you to a job to suit each of you, and we've arranged your accommodation,' Ana said. 'From you now, we'll need your passport and your mobile phones. I'm sorry, I don't know what you were told, but your phones will be useless here.'

She gave the women the usual bullshit about how their phones from home would be cripplingly expensive. How the prepaid phones they would soon be given would be charge-free for them, as part of their work. A lie.

Ana went along the line with a big plastic box, and one by one took the phones, while alongside her the two women who'd brought the refreshments took passports and crossed the names off the bogus job lists in their hands.

With each phone Ana took, her heart rate ramped up a little more. Her eyes darted left, right. She risked a sneaky peek over her shoulder, too. There were plenty of eyes looking in her direction, but were Victor and the others really paying attention to Ana? No, she didn't believe so.

Ana was standing in front of the third to last woman when she finally worked up the courage. She took the phone from the woman's hand and clanked it down against the other phones in the box. But she didn't release it. Instead she quickly scooped her hand out as she moved along to the next woman, and then sank it, and the phone, into the inside pocket of her coat.

She reached the next woman and their eyes met.

Had she seen?

Ana tried her hardest not to but she couldn't resist looking behind her again. Victor was glaring at her coldly. But he said nothing, and was soon laughing at something Alex said to him.

Ana carried on with the remaining two girls then took the box of phones away and set it down on a table at the side of the warehouse. She walked back over to the women; they were looking far more apprehensive now, but wouldn't do anything about it. Not so soon. They never did.

It was time to give them the biggest lie of them all. The one designed to make them forget all about the fact they'd just handed their freedom over to people they'd never met before.

'As you know, you'll be starting your new jobs very soon, but we don't want you to have to worry about a thing here. That's why each of you is getting a welcome bonus… one *thousand* pounds.'

The women looked stunned by that. They were muttering and chattering to each other as Ana carried on her patter and the wads of cash were handed out. Of course, the bonus was a smokescreen too. A sweetener to keep them onside, at least until they reached their final destinations. The money was real enough. What they didn't know was that virtually every penny would be siphoned from them within the next twenty-four hours – accommodation, taxes, food, electricity. From then and thereafter, they'd never be left with more than a few paltry notes to their name. Within days they'd be desperately poor, even more so than they'd ever been back home, and entirely dependent on their handlers, but right now they still genuinely bought into the idea that they'd just arrived in some sort of paradise.

The whole process took less than thirty minutes. Ana continued as the perfect hostess, chatting individually to some of the newcomers, talking about why they'd come, where they'd come from, what they wanted to be when they were older. And giving in return an almost entirely fabricated version of her own life in the six years she'd been in England.

Before long, the by now even more nervous-looking women had been split into four groups, and each was with their chaperone by one of the parked cars.

Minutes later the warehouse was empty except for Ana, Alex and Victor.

Within a couple of hours the new women would all be at their new 'homes'. Within a few more hours the reality of their new life would finally be sinking in, along with the first of the drugs, the first of the alcohol, and the first of the men.

Within a few days the women would wish they were dead.

'You were amazing,' Victor said to Ana with a devilish look in his eye.

'That's why I'm here after all,' she said to him with a coy smile, and even though her words had sounded confident and playful, she felt nothing but wretched emptiness inside.

Chapter 16

'You've got to stop beating yourself up,' Jason said.

Dani continued to stare out of the window to the busy street below, where the main road outside the hospital was in rush-hour gridlock.

'It's a murder trial,' he said. 'O'Hare's got nothing personal against you.'

'Nothing personal?' Dani spun around and glared at Jason, prone and vulnerable in his wheelchair, and he looked a little taken aback by her ferociousness. That little voice in her head sounded out but she took no notice. 'It's nothing *but* personal. She was basically accusing me of scuppering the Curtis investigation. Of sidelining our searches into Collins in order to dig up dirt on Ben.'

'Which is exactly what happened,' Jason said, not rising at all to Dani's anger. 'It's only the motive for that course of events that she got wrong. Of course there was more weight to the investigation into Ben. Because it was quickly concluded that Collins wasn't involved.'

'I'm not even so sure myself any more.' Dani pushed her fingers into her temple to try and stop the throbbing in her brain. She'd hoped the extra pills she'd taken earlier at home would lift it, but apparently not.

The problem was, the more she thought about it, the more O'Hare's words, her accusations, rang true. Dani *was* desperate to find evidence of Ben's guilt, even now. Even with the Dunne case she was busy trying to figure out what Ben's involvement could be.

Was it just because she was so scared that one day he would be released from prison unless she could convince the world he was a monster? Or was it out of pure spite? Or just plain and simple obsession?

One thing she did know: she'd hold off making another trip to Long Lartin to see him as long as she possibly could, but eventually, if she wanted answers, she knew she'd have to go back.

'Dani?' Jason said. She realised he'd been talking to her but she'd not heard a word.

'Sorry.' She hung her head and headed over to him. 'What were you saying?'

'Give me a hand into the bed, will you?'

They were both soon out of breath from the effort, and Jason looked pained as he pulled his body into position on the mattress and propped himself upright. Dani took the seat next to the bed.

'I was speaking to Dr Shah yesterday,' he said, 'and... well, do you want the good news or the bad?'

'I'm not sure I can take any bad.'

His face dropped at that. Perhaps he'd sensed the genuine dismay in her words.

'It wouldn't be the worst thing to go back to see Dr Schulz again, you know. Get yourself back on the anti-depressants, even if it's just a low dose.'

Ha, yeah. About that, she thought.

'What was the good news?' she said.

He smiled and took her hand. 'You won't have to bother bringing me any presents over here for Christmas.'

It took a second for her jumbled brain to make sense of that. When she did, she suddenly felt weak inside. Though it was in a good way. Kind of.

'And the bad?' she said.

'You're going to need a bigger turkey.'

She had no clue what to say. So she leaned forwards and sank her head into his chest and didn't even try to stop the welling tears from rolling free. Jason wrapped his arms around her and squeezed – at least as tightly as his still frail body would allow.

'Though you're going to have to figure a way to get the wheelchair up the steps and through the door,' he said. 'Unless you want to just winch me in through the window.'

'Jason, I'll carry you home over my shoulder all the way from here if I have to.'

His grip soon became even weaker, she knew it was a struggle for him, though he held on. Dani stayed nestled into him for several minutes, barely another word spoken between them until her phone rang.

'You'd better get that,' Jason said, taking his arms away.

Dani really didn't want to, but she did.

She got up from the bed and went back to the window.

'DI Stephens, it's Sergeant Lyle from Tipton. I was asked to give you a call about a Vauxhall Insignia?'

'You found it?'

'We stopped it not even a mile from the station just a few minutes ago. Two occupants, both of them currently in our cells. But... what do you want us to—'

'Do you have their names?'

'Yeah. What they've given us anyway: Victor Nistor, the driver, and Ana Crisan, or something like that.'

She'd been hoping he was going to say Nicolae Popescu. The two names meant nothing to her.

'You've seen IDs?'

'Only the fella had ID. But he gave us a home address too, for them both.'

Lyle told Dani the address, which likewise was unfamiliar. Not Brigitta Popescu's address, even though Victor Nistor was driving her car.

'OK. Hold them. I'll be there as soon as I can.'

It was three hours later when Dani and Easton finally made it to Tipton. Not because the journey was long, but because Dani had stopped at HQ to first do some digging into the two people she was about to meet.

Dani had never been before, but Tipton Police Station looked more like a small yet modern office block than a police station – the kind of office a start-up tech company might occupy – and the building was curiously located with a crumbling trading estate on one side, and an expansive new housing estate on the other. Dani parked up and they were greeted inside the carpeted reception area by Sergeant Lyle, who was tall and well built, though had a youthful face that Dani found was at odds with the rest of him. The youthful face didn't look too happy.

'I didn't realise you'd be so long,' he said.

Dani and Easton looked at each other but didn't bother to respond.

'We've only got four cells here,' Lyle said. 'We've just had to take someone else ten miles away because we've no more space, and I don't even know why your two are in here.'

'It's part of a murder investigation,' Dani said. 'So we're very grateful for your assistance.'

Though the way she said it, she didn't sound too grateful.

'You might want to tell your prisoners that,' Lyle said. 'The chap was arrested for driving uninsured, and we bagged the woman for suspicion of immigration offences. The best my PCs could come up with on the spot. But the longer we hold them on potentially false pretences, the more chance there is that I get it in the neck.'

'There's no false pretences here,' Easton said, and Dani could tell his hackles were raised too.

'Why don't you go and get them and we'll get this moving?' Dani said.

'Both of them at once?'

'Have you got a spare PC who can help us?'

'Yeah.'

'Two interview rooms?'

'Three, actually.'

'Then we'll interview them both at the same time, in different rooms, if you can help too. That way we'll get on our way even more quickly.'

Lyle huffed at that, though Dani really didn't know why it was such a big problem.

'Which one do you want?' Easton said to Dani when Lyle skulked off to find a helper.

'I'll take Ana first,' Dani said. 'Chances are the woman, if she knows anything at all, will open up to me more readily than you. You get Victor warmed up for me though.'

'My pleasure.'

The interview room was a bland affair, as all police interview rooms were, though the relative newness of this one was at least evident, with blemish-free light blue walls and floor, modern lighting, and functional chairs and table.

Dani was sitting next to Lyle's colleague, PC Nawaz. Ana was opposite, eyes down, hands folded on her lap. She looked a little older than her supposed twenty-four years of age, though she had a naturally pretty face and smooth skin that Dani hadn't had herself since her late teens.

'Do you know why you're here, Ana?' Dani said.

Ana held her eye for a second, but was soon looking down again. 'Not really. The officer said something about immigration, but I'm an EU national. I don't know why there'd be a problem.'

Her English was excellent. Far more anglicised than Stef and Brigitta's, though with just enough of a twang to show her origins.

'I'm afraid there's a bit more going on here than problems with immigration, Ana. But I'm sure you know that, don't you?'

Dani let the question hang. It was a basic fishing attempt, but she'd already decided from the couple of hours of research into Victor Nistor and Ana Crisan, that she and Easton had undertaken at HQ before coming here, that there were a number of oddities about the two prisoners, to say the least.

'How long have you been in England for?' Dani asked.

'Over six years.'

'So you came here when you were...'

'Eighteen. There was nothing illegal. I came on the Eurotunnel, with my passport.'

'You've not left the UK since?'

'No.'

'What's your relationship with Mr Nistor?'

There was a small but perceptible twitch in her face. 'He's my boyfriend.'

Nistor was forty-two years old. The age difference was big, but not implausible.

'You live with him?' Dani asked.

'Yes.'

'For how long?'

'I don't remember. I've known Victor a long time.'

'This is where I'm getting a little confused. Because you say you came here six years ago.'

'Yes.'

'But you didn't register with HMRC, to work here, until...' Dani looked at the paper in her hand, for effect mostly, '...earlier this year, in fact. The only record I have of employment for you is with Janx Publicity Ltd, a media agency based in Liverpool. Which again, was this year.'

'I didn't need to work before that,' Ana said.

'Didn't need to? You had a lot of savings? Or was it just that you didn't bother to register to pay taxes?'

Ana was looking a little riled now. That was fine.

'Is that it?' Dani said. 'So what were you working as? A waitress? Cleaner? Fruit picker? Taking cash and pocketing it. It's not uncommon. But it is illegal.'

'How dare you,' Ana said, her face twisted in anger. 'I didn't come here to work slave labour. I have a good education, I...'

She seemed to lose the trail of thought, or perhaps just decided that what she was about to say actually wasn't going to help her.

'You're what?' Dani said. 'Too good for jobs like that? I mean, looking at this...' Dani wafted the paper in the air, '...at what I can see about Janx, I'd agree. Nice-looking job that. A hundred and thirty miles from here. So what are you doing back in Tipton?'

'I came to see Victor.'

'Your boyfriend.'

'Yes.'

'Just visiting?'

'Yes.'

'You also gave the officers your home address as the same address as Victor.'

'We live together.'

'You live together? But you work in Liverpool. And also rent a room in a house there.'

Ana looked shocked now. As though she couldn't understand how Dani had figured out so much of her background already.

'The other interesting thing is that my colleagues up north had a quick word with your landlord. Your housemate. Your employer too. Apparently, you didn't show up for work the last three days. Your boss has been calling you non-stop.'

Ana was clenching her teeth.

'I lost my phone,' she said.

'Which explains why we didn't find one on you when you were arrested, I suppose. But you probably still could have told your boss that. Probably not the smartest way to climb the corporate ladder. Why *aren't* you in Liverpool, at work, anyway?'

'I missed Victor too much,' Ana said, though it was even less convincing than her previous answers.

'Yeah, I'm sure he's a real charmer. What does Victor do for work, again?'

'He owns a transport company.'

'Good for him. So what do you know of Brigitta Popescu?'

Ana flinched again.

'You do know her?'

'She's a family friend of Victor's.'

'A family friend. Is that why he drives her car?'

A confused look now. Dani wasn't sure if that was genuine or not.

'You didn't know it was her car?'

Ana didn't say anything.

'I've met Brigitta,' Dani said. 'She doesn't really seem like the driving type.'

'Maybe Victor bought it off her.'

'Maybe. Or maybe they're just such close friends that she doesn't mind him using it. Permanently.'

'Is that a crime?'

'Not at all. I'm just trying to figure out the dynamic. So how well do you know Brigitta and her family?'

'A little.'

'You've known Victor for… how long?'

'Years.'

'Since before you came here.'

'No.'

'And you've been living with him, but you only know a little about a family who have gifted your boyfriend a car?'

'So this is all about his car?' She looked genuinely confused now.

'No, Ana. I'm afraid it's about a *lot* more than that. But you must know that?'

Ana said nothing, though her façade was wearing down bit by bit. Dani felt a little bad now. Even without having met Victor, she had a pretty good idea of what she thought the dynamic between him and Ana was, and Dani wasn't here to heap more pressure onto someone who was more likely victim than suspect, but she had to be hard first, to show Ana the reality of the predicament she was in.

'Do you know Nicolae Popescu?' Dani asked.

If she did, Ana now hid it remarkably well.

'Ana?'

'I've heard of him. I've never met him.'

'He's still around here, though, right?'

Ana's eyes pinched a little. 'I don't think so.'

'You haven't seen him recently?'

'I'm not sure I've ever seen him. I just know who he is. Brigitta's grandson. I've certainly heard the name.'

'In what context?'

'I don't remember.'

Dani paused, but Ana offered up nothing more. It was time for the photographs. Dani dug two out. One of Liam, one of Clara.

'Do you recognise either of these two people?'

Ana spent a few seconds studying the pictures. There was no flash of recognition, or of unease now. 'No,' she said.

'You're sure? The man is Liam Dunne, the woman is Clara Dunne. They're brother and sister.'

Ana shrugged and shook her head.

'Clara's dead. Liam is missing.'

Ana looked perplexed, but also increasingly fragile. Was that simply because she was slowly realizing that her being here was more serious than she'd previously thought?

'I really don't know what you think this has to do with me,' she said.

Dani said nothing.

'I don't know these people!'

'What about Victor?'

'I have no idea.'

Dani leaned forwards now. She put her hand onto the desk, on top of Ana's. Ana didn't flinch at all, didn't make any kind of move to take her hand away.

'Ana, if you need help, just tell me. I will help you. But don't hold back on me. I need to know what's really happening here. With Victor. With Popescu. With the Dunnes.'

Ana still didn't move her hand. She held Dani's eye. Then opened her mouth to speak, just as there was a knock on the door.

Now Ana did whip her hand away, and Dani clenched her fist in frustration as she turned to Nawaz and indicated for her to get the door.

She'd only opened it a few inches when a suited man barged into the room.

'This interview is over,' he shouted, glaring angrily at Dani.

'And you are?' she said, getting to her feet.

'Ms Crisan's lawyer.'

No name, apparently. Dani looked to Ana who appeared as surprised as Dani was.

'Ana informed us she didn't have a lawyer,' Dani said. 'And told us she was happy to talk to us without one.'

'Well, now she does have a lawyer. Ana, come on.'

The man made a move towards Ana and Dani stepped in front of him.

'Excuse me, but Ms Crisan is here under caution. You don't get to decide when we release her.'

'Under caution? For what offence? And be very specific, Detective, because I will make a very clear note of everything you say to me.'

Dani's brain whirred, but what could she say? The reality was they really had no grounds whatsoever to hold Ana any further. The checks Dani herself had carried out before coming to Tipton had shown Ana's immigration status was bona fide.

Tax offences perhaps? But there was no actual clear evidence of that. In theory they were entitled to hold her for twenty-four hours without formal charge, but was there any sort of charge even on the horizon?

'OK, Ana, you're free to go,' Dani said.

'Wise decision, Detective,' the man said.

Ana got to her feet.

'But Ana,' Dani said. 'Have a think about what I said. If you want to discuss anything at all—'

'Yes, yes, Detective, we'll be in touch.'

The man shoved past Dani and ushered Ana towards the door.

'A pleasure to meet you, Mr...'

'Green.'

That was all he said as he and Ana left the room. Dani followed them out, along the corridor. When they exited into the reception area, Dani had to hold her nerve when she saw Victor Nistor already waiting there, near the exit, arms folded, looking smug.

He beamed a smile to Ana and she somewhat reluctantly moved over to him. He held out his arms and embraced her, his eyes finding Dani's as Easton approached looking sheepish.

'Nothing I could do,' he said.

Dani said nothing to him. She got it. They'd arrested Victor for driving without insurance, based on the instruction she'd given to the local police, and even though they could easily pin that on Victor, it wasn't really a serious enough offence to warrant arrest on its own. Without other aggravating circumstances, a fixed penalty notice would have sufficed. Victor might not have known that when his car was first stopped, but his lawyer certainly did.

'Did you at least get onto Dunne and Popescu before you were shut down?' Dani asked Easton quietly.

'Barely. Learned nothing.'

Ana, Victor and Green were all now moving for the exit.

'We'll be seeing you,' Dani shouted out.

Green turned around and shook his head, as though disappointed by Dani's need for a parting comment. Victor didn't turn around at all.

But Ana did. A meek glance over her shoulder. Fear in her eyes now.

A moment later she was out of sight.

'What a bloody balls-up,' Easton said.

'Not at all,' Dani said.

'How?'

'Because whatever Victor is up to, the Popescus too, they're at least properly on our radar now. We know who they are, and they know we're looking into them. Now we just need to figure out what the hell is really going on.'

Chapter 17

'What exactly are you asking for?' McNair said, looking over her desk at Dani, somewhat suspiciously.

Dani sighed. She thought she'd been clear enough. It had almost got to the point in their relationship now where Dani felt McNair had to be initially obstructive whenever Dani asked for something, or updated her boss on something, purely out of habit.

'I think we've got enough here to suggest that Nicolae Popescu is somehow involved in Clara Dunne's death,' Dani said.

'Enough? You have nothing!'

'No, Ma'am, I don't believe that at all. Popescu is a known violent criminal. We have a witness statement saying he's still in the UK, despite having been officially deported several years ago. Pictures of him were all over Clara Dunne's wall. And I've seen the way people react when his name his mentioned.'

Dani expected a bite back from that last comment. Something along the lines of *someone's facial expression isn't evidence of murder*, but actually McNair didn't say anything at all for a good while.

'But it's not Popescu you're suggesting we set up surveillance for,' was McNair's eventual response.

'Only because we don't know where he is,' Easton said.

'Which is a big flaw, don't you think?'

'Not really,' Dani said. 'We could set up surveillance at his grandmother's house. At Victor Nistor's house, his place of work too. Eyes and ears. I think we'll soon figure out what these people are up to, and whether and how they're involved in Clara Dunne's death.'

McNair rolled her eyes. 'Dani, this is all just so… limp. You must see that?'

'That's what I'm trying to rectify. We need to know more.'

'Have you spoken to DCI Fairclough?' McNair asked.

Fairclough being McNair's equivalent within the Organised Crime team.

'I spoke to him briefly,' Easton said. 'Before we went to Tipton to interview Nistor and Crisan.'

'A trip which sounds like a complete mess all on its own,' McNair said, holding Dani's eye as she spoke.

'Fairclough knew of Popescu,' Easton said, 'and agreed that back in the day he'd been involved in a gang who had something of a racket going. Drugs, prostitution, extortion. Popescu's jail sentence was for attacking the leader of a rival gang from Poland. But Fairclough said they weren't big players back then. Just a bunch of local thugs, and they haven't had an active investigation in the Tipton area for years. He'd never even heard of Victor Nistor.'

'Which could be for a very good reason,' McNair said. 'There's nothing for us to be interested in.'

'Or it could be because nobody has bothered to look properly until now,' Dani said. 'Nistor's record is clean, but I've spoken to people on the streets around where he lives, around where his business is located…'

McNair looked incredulous now, as though what Dani and Easton had been doing was ridiculous.

'Do you know how many people claimed they knew Popescu? Knew Nistor?'

'Tell me.'

'Not a single one. But it was the way they said it. And yes, I know I can't use something so basic as evidence, but – Easton will back me up on this – based on the reactions we've seen again and again today, people are scared of these guys. Scared enough that they won't even acknowledge they know of them.'

McNair was still staring at Dani. No one spoke for several seconds. Which was good, Dani realised, because it meant McNair was giving the idea serious consideration now.

'Let me speak to Fairclough directly,' McNair said. 'I find it hard to believe his team have completely missed Nistor if he really is what I think you're saying he is. I'll put a call into Baxter too.'

Chief Superintendent Baxter was both Fairclough's and McNair's boss.

'But it's four p.m. on Friday night,' McNair added, 'so even if they agree to anything at all, it's unlikely to be concluded and in place until next week.'

'I can live with that,' Dani said.

'And I won't make any promises about what level of surveillance they'll agree to, if any at all. I can tell you now, it's highly unlikely to be covert eavesdropping GCHQ style. More likely a copper in a car nearby each of the addresses you've given, and a bit of a more thorough background check than you've already done yourselves.'

'Every little helps,' Dani said.

'Something like that. Is there anything else?'

'Not for today. Thank you.'

'I suggest you both go home and take a break and enjoy your weekend.'

Dani and Easton both got to their feet and thanked McNair again before they headed out of the office. Dani closed the door behind her and let out a big sigh.

'You're beginning to make a habit out of this,' Easton said.

'What's that?'

'Getting McNair to actually agree with you and give you what you ask for.'

'Tell me about it. It's almost as if she trusts my instincts these days.'

'Even if you are going to completely ignore her advice.'

'I am?' Dani said, eyebrow raised.

'She suggested relaxing and enjoying your weekend. Only I can't imagine you spending the next two days with your feet up and the TV on.'

'Sounds like hell,' Dani said with a wry smile.

And he was absolutely right, she had zero intention of taking the next two days off.

Not while there was still a killer out there.

And one way or another, there always was.

Chapter 18

Saturday was already turning out to be as busy as Dani had expected. She'd built up the courage to spend Friday night at home though, as tired as she was, it had still been a restless night, and first thing Saturday morning she'd been back into hospital to see Jason, and also to discuss with the doctor the arrangements for Jason coming home. It had been agreed that they'd need some trial days beforehand: taking Jason back home just for the day, then for a day and night, and with Dani in the midst of an all-consuming investigation, it already felt like time was fast running out before Christmas. Dani really wasn't sure how she was going to fit everything in.

She'd have to.

But she'd figure that out later. She still had plenty on her plate today. Already this morning she'd tracked down two of James Alden's – aka Liam Dunne's – old work colleagues. People who knew him when he'd worked for Ellis Associates. And it wasn't just because of the link to Ben that Dani was so determined to follow that line of enquiry. More than that, Dunne's short-lived job with Ellis Associates was the only tangible evidence she had of his recent history.

The two house calls that Dani had made had proved fruitless. One of the ex-colleagues, a woman named Caroline, said she'd barely ever spoken to Alden in his time at Ellis Associates, as she'd been out of the country for more than six months that year on a project. The other, Henry Welter, hadn't been home. Dani would make a point of a second visit to him, not least because she vaguely remembered him herself from a random occasion when she'd bumped into Ben and his work pals one Friday night in central Birmingham. She'd sensed then that he was a nervous, nerdy type – the type that would usually be far easier to pressure into divulging information, if he knew anything at all.

Dani was now on the M6 from Solihull to Tipton, at least two more destinations in mind for today, though it felt almost uncomfortably unusual to be doing this alone, given the professional twosome she and Easton had become recently. And so, after several minutes of internal debate as to what she was up to, she bit the bullet and decided to give her colleague a call.

He sounded harried when he eventually answered.

'Are you at home?' Dani asked. The background noise sounded more like he was stuck in the middle of a wild tornado.

'Yeah, but… just give me a second.'

There was clattering and shuffling and static until a few moments later the line went quiet.

'Can you hear me now?'

'Yeah.'

'I'm in the shed.'

Dani smirked. 'Lucky you.'

'It's the only bloody place I can get any peace and quiet. Those kids… they're like that Tasmanian Devil.'

'Looking after boisterous kids. The best form of contraception.'

'Tell me about it. I mean, I love them, but… I feel like I've aged a decade recently.'

'I thought you were looking more grey.'

'Thanks. What are you up to anyway?'

'Just out and about.'

'I figured. Anything interesting?'

'Not yet. But there's a couple of things you can help me with.'

'Dani, I would, but I'm stuck here—'

'In the shed?'

'No, not stuck in the bloody shed—'

'I was joking. And it's something you can do from home, if you've got time?'

A sigh. She wasn't going to pressure him if he really couldn't, but she was hoping he'd see it as something of a break from childminding.

'What is it?' he said.

She smiled. 'I was digging into Liam Dunne's file this morning. Did you know he's got his own house?'

'No. Why's that—'

'He bought it outright in 2012. Cash. Seventy thousand pounds for a two-bed terrace in Walsall.'

'OK?'

'From what I understand of his finances, it was paid for through an inheritance sum he received a year before that. That was nearly two hundred grand in total.'

Easton whistled.

'From what I could see, he never did anything with it, other than stick it into his bank account. He bought that house, then was living off the rest. That's where it gets odd.'

'How?'

'He had that job at Ellis Associates, in 2013, under a false name. I still have no reason why he did that, but it was a decent job. The start of a career really.'

So why had he lied?

'Except he got turfed out,' Easton said.

'He did. And we still need to find out exactly why.'

They were still waiting on release of the personnel records to confirm that.

'But he'd already got all this money a couple of years before that job,' Dani said. 'From the death of his maternal grandma, I believe.'

'Presumably Clara Dunne got the same?'

'It's one thing you can follow up for me?'

'Sure.'

'Then in 2014, he gets the boot from Ellis Associates. He's still got some of the cash left in his bank at that point, though, which potentially explains why we don't see him going out for another job.'

'How much was there when he disappeared?'

'A little over twenty thousand.'

'So he still spent about another hundred grand, between 2011 and 2015,' Easton said. 'On what?'

'Good question, right? If you get into HOLMES, perhaps you can take a deeper look at his financial records? Any big one-offs? Or was he just taking small amounts out regularly?'

'Could have been a gambler?'

'Could have been. Gambler, drugs, partying, who knows.'

'Plenty of activities which also could have got him into trouble.'

'That's one of the things I'm thinking.'

'But then surely Missing Persons would have checked that out already?'

'Check in their files, but I wouldn't presume so. And if they haven't, I think we should.'

'OK. I'll get onto it.'

'Thanks. And one more thing.'

'Yeah?'

'This house in Walsall. I drove past it earlier. It's... abandoned. The thing is, he still owns it. Liam Dunne has been missing for five years, but he's not been declared dead, so his finances, his house, his whole life, is just in indefinite hiatus.'

'Creepy.'

Dani agreed. How could someone's whole life, their existence, become stuck in some sort of a time-warp?

'I think we should go and take a look,' Dani said.

'Inside his house?'

'Yeah. Obviously our colleagues already went there back in 2015. It's routine, not just to check for clues as to why someone is missing, but to check if the poor sod is simply lying dead in their own home.'

'But he wasn't.'

'No. Nor did they find any clues as to where he went. But they did have to break in to check that, and then resecure the property after. We literally have the key to his house already.'

'You want me to get it?'

'Arrange to, yeah. But also just check to make sure we're following protocol. If we need to renew a warrant, then do it.'

The truth was, Dani had no clue what the exact protocol was for revisiting someone's home five years after they'd gone missing, because it was a genuinely unusual case. When one party in a relationship went missing, for example, the house was still occupied by the other partner. Many single people who went missing were in rented accommodation or mortgaged, so their homes would soon become repossessed and resold or re-rented. Liam Dunne was in the more unusual position of living alone in a home he owned outright when he went missing, and his home had simply been left to rot, all of his belongings included, for more than five years.

Dani could only imagine the state of the place now. But she was certain it was worth taking the time to look around.

'OK, I'm on it,' Easton said. 'Anything else?'

'Yeah. Don't give the kids any more sugar.'

'Very funny.'

Dani ended the call just as she pulled her car through the open gates at the entrance to the warehouse. There were no marked bays in the forecourt so she parked up next to the only other vehicle there – a rusted white van. She gathered her thoughts then stepped out into the cold.

The building in front of her was clearly occupied. For starters she could see lights were on inside because of the glow emanating from the gaps between the large loading doors and their frames, though the warehouse had certainly seen better days. The corrugated steel shell that stretched up from the brick base was intact, though heavily corroded around some of the edges. Plastic panels in the roof – presumably to let natural light in – were covered in green sludge. The signage above the loading doors was faded beyond comprehension, and it wasn't clear if that was due to years of natural erosion, or if the current occupiers had yet to put up their own fascia.

In fact there was no indication at all, either along the outer barbed-wire-topped metal fence, or on the building itself, who the current occupier was.

Dani stuffed her hands into her pockets and scrunched her head down into her scarf and headed towards the basic entrance door to the side of the much larger loading doors. She looked around her as she went. The street beyond was mostly made up of 1920s terraces, with small commercial units like this one interspersed here and there. The street was quiet, though traffic noise carried over from the parallel main road a hundred yards further east.

Dani knocked on the door and rang the service buzzer. As she awaited a response she looked up and spotted the small CCTV camera fixed overhead, pointing down to cover the entrance.

Was someone inside looking at her now?

Several moments passed and Dani was about to knock again, more loudly, when she heard grumbling from the other side of the door, which edged open and the glowering face of a man Dani didn't recognise poked out.

'Hi, is Victor around?' Dani asked.

'No, he's not,' the man said, his face not hiding his suspicion. His accent was strong, English clearly not his native tongue.

'He does work here though, doesn't he?' Dani said.

'He went out.'

'Do you know when he'll be back?'

'Who are you?'

Dani explained. The man's face turned even more sour.

'You have warrant?'

'I didn't come to search this place. Just to speak to him. You don't need a warrant for that.'

'Speak to him about what?'

The noise of a car engine caught Dani's attention and she turned to see the Vauxhall Insignia that belonged to Brigitta Popescu drive into the lot and park up next to Dani's car. Good timing.

Victor Nistor was alone in the car. He stepped out, hauling a large brown bag from KFC in one hand, and a tray of three drinks in the other.

'You?' he said when he clocked Dani. He didn't look particularly perturbed, more surprised. He idled over.

'Mr Nistor. I was hoping we could talk.'

'You want something hauling?'

Dani looked around the near empty forecourt. 'If I did, I don't see much choice of vehicle around here.'

'Because we're busy. So you don't want to use my business then. So why are you here?'

'I didn't get the chance to talk to you yesterday. I'd like to ask you a few questions.'

'About my car? Insurance all properly paid for now. It was just my error. I can show you the receipt if you'd like?'

'No need,' Dani said. 'I'm not interested in your car, or your insurance status.'

'Huh. Not today, eh? Then what?'

'Can I come inside? I'm freezing.'

He seemed to weigh that one up. He let out a deep sigh.

'Before your food gets cold,' Dani added.

He rolled his eyes. 'OK. But you'll have to watch me eat.'

Victor's friend, who remained to be introduced, stepped out of the way and Victor ushered Dani through.

One word adequately described the inside of the warehouse. Sparse. The whole centre of the warehouse floor was bare. Along some of the walls was steel racking, though it was mostly empty too, with just some simple tools and a few card-board and plastic boxes containing goods of an indeterminate nature. It was chilly, too, with the only heat source being two amber-glowing electrical filament heaters plugged into the wall, though it was at least a few degrees warmer than outside. The fact Victor's friend had been working in here with his thick overcoat on showed just how cold it was, even if it wasn't at all clear what type of 'work' he'd been doing.

Victor headed off to the far corner of the space, where a door led into a basic office, though Dani also noticed that there was a staircase next to it which led up to a mezzanine level. Up above, the windows to that space were all blacked out. So what was up there then?

Inside the office that contained two basic-looking desks and a clutter of filing cabinets but not much else, Victor's friend helped himself to two of the KFC meals before leaving Dani and Victor to it.

'Take a seat,' Victor said.

Dani did so and Victor unwrapped and took a huge bite from his chicken burger.

'So business is good?' Dani said.

Victor nodded as he chewed. 'Booming. Can't you tell?' he said when he'd partially swallowed the mouthful. 'But I'm sure that's not why you're here, Detective. You investigate murders, yes?'

'Now, where did you hear something like that?' Dani said.

A casual shrug. 'I googled you. You're quite famous, aren't you?'

His eyes flicked up to above Dani's ear now. An almost imperceptible glance, it was so quick, and possibly not even fully conscious, but Dani recognised it clear as day. It was the same look she'd received who-knew-how-many times following the day Ben had tried to cave her skull in – the focus on her a result of the media furore which had followed up to and during Ben's trial. The scar remained – an ugly lumpy bald patch of skin –

though Dani had become an expert at keeping it covered. Still, people couldn't resist looking.

'Famous for all the wrong reasons,' Dani said. 'Never a good thing.'

'No? But I'm confused why a murder detective is interested in me.'

And truthfully Dani was confused as to why Victor was even entertaining her, given it was clear what her agenda was. Yesterday Victor had been quick to hide behind his lawyer, yet here he was openly inviting Dani into his supposed place of business, ready to answer whatever question she threw at him related to murder.

Was that purely down to his obvious arrogance, or did he really have nothing to hide? At least as far as murder was concerned?

'Then let me ease your confusion,' Dani said. She pulled out the increasingly worn photographs. 'This is Clara Dunne. She was found dead, we believe murdered, in her home in Oldbury early last week.'

'Poor girl.'

'She wasn't a girl, she was thirty-two.'

Victor glowered, as if it was a distinction that meant nothing to him.

'Did you know her?' Dani asked.

'Never seen her before,' Victor replied.

Dani said nothing but continued to stare at him, trying to tease out anything unspoken. But he was as cool as could be as he chowed down on a handful of fries, before taking a long slurp of his drink through the straw.

'How about this man?' Dani said, revealing the picture of Liam Dunne.

Victor shrugged. 'Don't know him. He dead too?'

'Good question. That's Clara's brother, Liam. He's been missing for five years.'

'Sounds pretty dead to me then.'

'You'd know from experience?'

Another petulant shrug.

'But you don't know him?' Dani said.

'No. Though it seems you think I should?'

Dani ignored that comment. 'So how do you know Nicolae Popescu?'

Victor thought about that one, chewing through another large mouthful of burger. Soon he'd be done and he'd have to think of an alternative delaying tactic.

'Our families are close,' he said. 'Back home.'

'So you knew him growing up?'

'A little.'

'How long ago was that?'

'Nicolae was older than me, about ten years older, I think. And I've been here ten years. He came here before that.'

'What brought you here?'

'Money.'

'Money?'

'Isn't it obvious?'

'Perhaps you could explain?'

'Have you ever been to Romania?'

'No.'

He huffed. 'It's a different country now to when I was a child. Under the communists… you people are lucky.'

'*You people?*'

'English. Westerners. Whatever. You've never known real conflict, not on your home soil.'

'Perhaps not in my generation, no.'

'When I was a child, an adult too, it wasn't just that we were poor, the regime was… ruthless. Can you imagine what it's like when people from your village – people you've grown up with, whole families – simply disappear in the night?'

Dani shook her head, though she genuinely was trying to imagine.

'That was normal to us, even if it was always terrible. As children we were frightened, all the time, petrified of the police. One wrong word against Ceaușescu and you'd be on the list. Can you imagine living like that? Every miserable day in fear for your life?'

'I can't.'

'No money, no jobs, and potential death every day.'

'But that was a long time ago. A long time before you came here.'

'You know about the revolution?'

'I know it happened.'

'In 1989.'

He took a pause as he finished his burger. Dani waited.

'I was only a child back then,' he said. 'Living in Bucharest. I was there the night Ceaușescu spoke to the crowds. Over one hundred thousand people, protesting the regime. I'll never forget the look on his face, to know that his entire life was crumbling before him. The only reason he didn't have his army execute every single one of us was because his top general refused. Do you know about this night?'

Dani could vaguely recall some of the story, but not really. She certainly hadn't lived through it, and had been only a child then.

'That general was shot. Still, not all the army was so kind. More than a thousand of us died in the fighting that night. Ceaușescu fled in a helicopter. We watched him flying away. He thought he could do what he wanted. But when he landed, his own army took him prisoner. He was executed by them. Christmas Day, 1989. More than thirty years ago.'

Victor gritted his teeth now and slowly shook his head – remembering?

'It's some story,' Dani said, not at all sarcastically. In a way she was actually interested to find out more. 'But I'm not sure of the relevance?'

'The relevance is you asked why I came here. The answer is, why wouldn't I want to come to a country that has lived through so many decades of peace, is rich and prosperous, rather than a country which is still scarred by that recent bloodshed?'

'Fair point. So what about Nicolae Popescu?'

'What about him?'

'Why'd he come here?'

'I don't know. There's nothing more to tell. I knew him at one time. I know his family. I look after his grandmother. She's an old lady who can't take care of herself.'

'Very generous of you. And Nicolae is… where?'

'I don't know.'

'In England?'

'I doubt it. He was deported. Surely you know this already?'

'So you've had no contact with him recently?'

'Not for years.'

'And you have no information as to where he now is?'

Victor turned his hands outwards. 'I'm very sorry.'

Dani sighed as her brain rumbled. Victor made a big deal of checking his watch.

'I have a call to make in three minutes,' he said. 'If you don't mind?'

'That's fine,' Dani said, getting to her feet.

'Let me show you out.' Victor got up too.

'Of course,' Dani said. 'You wouldn't want me roaming around, would you?'

Victor said nothing.

As Dani walked back out into the main room, she glanced up the staircase but could make out little of what was up there. All was quiet on the warehouse floor. No sign of Victor's colleague now.

'Where's Ana today?' Dani asked as they headed for the exit.

'At home, I think.'

'She's not here?' Dani asked.

'Why would she be here?'

'So who was the third meal for?' Dani said, glancing behind her and up to the blacked-out windows of the mezzanine level.

Victor looked put out by that question. 'Another colleague.'

'Can I speak to him?'

'I don't even know if he's in now.' Victor looked at his watch again. 'It's Saturday afternoon, you know?'

Dani wasn't sure she did, but she decided not to push the point.

Victor stopped a few steps from the door.

'It was nice to meet you,' he said, as Dani reached for the handle. 'Though hopefully it won't be necessary again.'

'I guess we'll have to wait and see about that.'

Chapter 19

'Who's down there?' Ana asked as she stared across to Alex on the opposite sofa.

He didn't even attempt to reply as he dove into his meal. She even hated the way he ate a damn fast food meal. Was there anything redeeming about this worm of a man?

Ana's food remained untouched on the coffee table.

'I heard talking down there,' Ana said. 'It sounded like a woman.'

A sly smile from Alex. 'Maybe it is. You know Victor.'

Ana clenched her teeth. Alex was trying to rile her, like always. But, actually, would she really be that bothered if Victor was fucking some slut down there? It certainly wouldn't be surprising given past form, and she was long past caring about being the one and only object of his affections.

Wasn't she?

'So?' Ana said. 'Who is it?'

Alex said nothing this time, just continued to bite and chew and slurp.

Earlier, when Ana had heard the buzzer downstairs, she'd almost immediately crept out into the hallway, and was halfway to the broom cupboard to begin spying when she'd realised Alex wasn't staying around to entertain whoever it was, and was coming up the stairs. She'd had to quickly dart back into the upstairs office and pretend she was napping.

Alex, the dumb idiot, had no clue.

But Ana was intrigued. If it was someone important down there, business-wise, then why wasn't Alex there too? And if it was someone important, or even some woman Victor was 'entertaining', then why had he only showed them into the shitty admin office downstairs, rather than to party central or whatever this shit space was?

'You're not eating your food,' Alex said.

'Wow, you're so smart.'

'You don't want it? I'll have it.' He grabbed the paper bag from the table and made a big deal of taking a handful of her fries and stuffing them into his mouth. Ana was hungry, but she wouldn't give him the pleasure of showing him she cared.

'You really need to get laid,' she said.

'Is that an offer?'

'Alex, the only way you could ever get someone like me is—'

'If you weren't Victor's I'd fuck you anytime I wanted. And there's nothing you could do about it.'

Her insides curdled at the thought, though the natural venom with which he spoke only made Ana all the more angry.

'Spoken like an expert, Alex,' she said. 'The only way you get a woman is through raping her.'

Alex slammed his food down onto the table and was on his feet in a flash. He took an angry step towards Ana. She was smiling, egging him on, even if she did cower back on the sofa as he towered over her.

'Well, go on then,' Ana said, purring. 'You know you want to.'

'One day. You just wait.'

'One day what?'

Ana and Alex both whipped their heads to the door. To Victor. He looked pissed off. How much had he heard?

Would he even care much if he'd heard everything? Ana genuinely had no clue whose side Victor would take.

'Alex was just telling me how he'd like to—'

'Teach that bitch detective a lesson.'

Ana glared at Alex, but he wasn't looking in her direction at all, his eyes fixed on his master like the good little dog he was.

Victor sniffed. 'Is that right?' he said to Alex. 'You think that would get the police off my back?'

'No. But it's still something I'd like to do.'

'Yeah, well, it's good that I'm in charge then. Because that's about the dumbest possible thing we could do now.'

Alex deflated. Ana wanted to beam a smile but she held it in. No point in drawing Victor's attention to her glee.

So the visitor had been a policewoman? Ana pictured Detective Stephens, who'd interviewed her all of twenty-four hours ago. Why was she hanging around again?

'Anyway, we need to go,' Victor said to Alex.

'I was just eating my—'

'No time. Come on.'

'Don't worry,' Ana said. 'I might save you some.'

OK. So she couldn't help herself. Alex glared at her but said nothing. Moments later he followed Victor out of the room and slammed the door shut behind him. Ana heard the lock clicking into place.

'Bastards,' she muttered under her breath.

She grabbed the now cold chicken burger from the bag, unwrapped it and took a bite, her belly grumbling in anticipation. She'd not eaten since breakfast. As she was chewing she moved across the room to her coat, which she'd folded away and placed neatly under the desk, out of sight. She waited a few seconds until she heard the bang downstairs as Victor and Alex left, on their unexplained quest.

When she was sure they were gone, she unfolded her coat and felt around the inside seam. She found the small fold with the three-inch tear and dug two fingers in to remove the phone. She held it in her hands for several seconds, just staring at the black screen.

It was only yesterday that she'd stolen the phone, though its presence seemed to have been a burden for an age. A burden? It was, but the shiny plastic device in her hand also offered some sort of solace.

The first chance she'd had yesterday, she'd turned the phone off, to save its battery. It had only had forty-four per cent then, and Ana had no charger for it, and no way to get one. When she and Victor had been stopped by the police yesterday she'd had the forethought to hide the phone under her car seat, and luckily the police hadn't found it. She was sure Victor still had no clue she had it.

So here she was again. Alone. Staring at this thing, wondering what the hell she was doing.

The phone had a little over ten pounds worth of credit, although it was in Romanian leu. But who would Ana even call? Her family back home?

Detective Stephens?

She'd said she'd help Ana.

Ana switched the phone on. It took several seconds for the low-res screen to flicker to life.

Thirty-nine percent. Shit. No. She had to save this. She had to be sure of her plan before she used it even once.

A bang downstairs.

That was enough to make her mind up. Ana quickly turned the phone off and stuffed it away again.

Then, misery and helplessness taking hold, she shuffled back over to finish the soggy, cold food.

Chapter 20

Dani was feeling increasingly frustrated as she headed the short distance across Tipton to the cul-de-sac where Brigitta Popescu lived. Had she learned anything at all from the day's events? Not really. Other than that Victor Nistor was up to something. But was it something related to Clara Dunne's murder? Liam Dunne's disappearance? Dani really had no clue, and certainly no direct evidence to back up that theory.

But she wasn't giving up on Victor, nor was she giving up on today yet. She was in the area, so she may as well cover every base she could.

Just over a week before the winter solstice, night-time was coming earlier and earlier each day, and with four p.m. still several minutes away, it was already dusk when Dani parked up outside Brigitta's house. Streetlights were flickering to life as Dani stepped onto the pavement. The street here, outside of school times, was deathly quiet. No pedestrians, no cars – other than those parked up and steadily frosting over – and barely any sounds coming from the homes that were largely cloaked in darkness.

Already feeling just a little uneasy, particularly being here alone, Dani sent a brief text to Easton updating him on her fruitless meeting with Victor, and telling him where she now was. She moved up the driveway to the front door and knocked, then rang the bell.

She waited for several seconds. Then several seconds more to give Brigitta the benefit of the doubt. It wasn't as though she was nimble. Obviously no Stef helping out right now, though?

That reminded Dani. She did want to speak to Stef more formally at some point.

Dani knocked again. Waited even longer this time, but there was still no answer.

Had someone taken Brigitta out? Dani could hardly imagine someone as frail as she was heading out by herself. Particularly in this cold. And when it was dark.

Dani crouched down, pushed open the letterbox and peered inside. The space beyond was dark, just as it had been the last time Dani and Easton had been here in the daytime, though Dani could definitely see a glow of orange coming from the lounge doorway. She held her breath to listen for sounds, and she was sure she could hear faint mumbling from somewhere within.

Eyes still peering in, Dani reached up and pressed the bell again.

The mumbling stopped. Dani waited. And waited. No sign of Brigitta coming to the door. Then came that same sound again.

Was it mumbling or something else entirely?

Thoughts flashed through Dani's mind. What if Brigitta was hurt? Had fallen and couldn't get up?

Dani tried the door.

It opened.

Dani sucked in cold air until her lungs were full, then nervously stepped inside. She closed the door softly behind her.

'Mrs Popescu?' she shouted out.

The house was warm inside. Almost too warm. Particularly with the thick coat and scarf that Dani was wearing. Not just warm, but stuffy and uncomfortably humid too.

'Mrs Popescu?' Dani shouted again.

No response. Though Dani could hear that mumbling again – chanting?

Dani stepped slowly along the dark and eerily quiet hallway.

'Mrs Popescu, it's Detective Stephens. Your door was unlocked.'

The chanting stopped. Dani froze on the spot. Waited in the silence for a few seconds. Then the jumbled words started up once more.

What the hell?

Dani moved forward, reached the doorway to the lounge. Orange light crept out from the room, though as before large swathes remained in darkness. The inadequate lighting created long, sinister shadows that snaked and weaved across the furniture and the walls. The more Dani stared, the more the shadows twisted and flowed.

'Mrs Popescu?'

Dani stepped into the room, her eyes still not yet fully adjusted to the dark. She didn't know whether to gasp or heave a sigh of relief when she spotted Brigitta, now silent, sunken into the armchair in the far corner.

Light flickered all around her from the shrine-like display by her side, though the outline of her body could barely be made out in the dark, her features almost imperceptible except for her wide open and glassy eyes.

She was staring over at Dani.

'I thought you would be back,' she said, her words slow yet strangely assured.

'Mrs Popescu, are you OK?'

Then she began to chant again. Slow, rhythmic words that meant nothing to Dani. Eyes now almost accustomed to the darkness, Dani stepped further forward, her gaze fixed on Brigitta's chest where her hands were clasped around a six-inch cross.

Dani had no clue what to say or do. Brigitta was trance-like, her body unmoving as she chattered away, her stare as intense as her words were indecipherable.

Then Brigitta stopped talking and squeezed her eyes shut.

Dani just stood there like an idiot.

'Brigitta?'

'Bones,' Brigitta said, the word coming out as a solemn moan. Her eyes remained closed.

'Sorry?'

'Bones… So many bones.'

Dani was sure a tear rolled down Brigitta's cheek, though in the dark she couldn't be sure of anything she was seeing.

'Bones?'

'So many. Have you seen them yet?'

Her eyes sprang open, gaze fixed on Dani, whose heart thudded against her ribs. She stumbled back a step, such was the force of Brigitta's look.

'They're coming for you,' Brigitta said, voice loud and clear. Instructive, decisive. Almost as though the words had been spoken by a different person than the frail woman Dani had met before. 'They know everything. And they're coming for you.'

'Who?' Dani said, trying her best to keep her cool. 'The Stirgoi? Is that what you mean?'

Why was Dani even doing this? Evil spirits? Vampires? It was ridiculous.

Yet standing in this room, in front of Brigitta in this trance, or whatever it was… Dani had never been so petrified or so freaked out in her life.

Brigitta said nothing now. The long, spindly shadows swirled around and reached out towards Dani. She took another nervous half step back – glanced over her shoulder to the dark empty space beyond. But was it empty? How could she even tell?

'Have you seen yet?' Brigitta asked, the words shaky, almost a sorrowful sob. 'Have you seen the bones?'

'Brigitta, what are you saying? Where?' Dani said, not realizing until she'd spoken how rattled she was. 'Whose bones?'

Brigitta leaned forwards in her chair. As she did so her face caught in a swathe of light, the deep ridges and lines of her aged features accentuated, and made all the more menacing.

Her cracked and withered lips moved into a sort of pout. She reached out a finger.

'Yours.'

There was a clank, and the room was plunged into blackness.

Chapter 21

Dani's heart exploded in her chest. At least that's what the moment of panic felt like as she stepped back in terror. She crashed into the sofa arm, then the coffee table, until finally her back thumped against the wall. She pushed both her hands onto the cold surface, as though checking it was really a wall and nothing more. Some sort of comfort at least to know there was only bricks and plaster behind her now.

But she could see nothing in front of her at all.

'Brigitta?' Dani shouted, terror in her voice. 'Brigitta!'

Nothing. No chanting, not even any sounds of the old woman breathing. All Dani could hear was her own uneven breaths and the whistle of wind as it forced its way into house. From where, Dani had no clue, though she was sure she could feel its chill.

She fumbled in her purse for her phone. Took it out with shaky fingers.

'Brigitta, can you hear me?' Then muttered under her breath, 'It's just a power cut. That's all.'

Dani held her breath as she clumsily tried to find the torch on her phone. Brigitta still hadn't made a sound. Was she even there any more?

The torch light finally flicked on, though its white arc of light was pathetic and barely touched the edges of black.

Dani twisted the phone around and shone the meagre light into the corner.

Brigitta's chair was empty.

'Mrs Popescu?' Dani croaked, her voice almost giving in she was so scared.

There was a rush of air right next to her. Dani screamed in horror and bolted to the side. She whipped the phone in that direction.

The light reflected off two bloodshot eyes. Two bloodshot eyes that were all of a yard away from Dani.

Angry eyes.

'Who are you?'

Brigitta. Standing right in front of Dani. She wanted to feel relief, but she wouldn't just yet.

'Mrs Popescu, it's me, Detective Stephens.'

'Why are you in my house?'

She sounded confused, and more than a little scared now. Completely different to moments earlier. What was this woman on?

'I think there was a power cut,' Dani said, briefly glancing over her shoulder to the hallway which remained pitch black. 'Do you know where your fusebox is?'

Brigitta said nothing as she stared coldly at Dani.

'You wait there,' Dani said. She turned and moved out of the room. As soon as she stepped into the hallway it was like walking into a different realm. All of the tension, all of the terror of the lounge evaporated.

'Come on, Dani,' she said to herself under her breath.

She stepped into the kitchen, and to the door that led under the stairs. She opened it up and shone the torch into the cramped cupboard beyond.

At least there wasn't a basement leading down in here. Dani really wasn't sure how she'd cope having to go down there.

Sure enough, behind the stack of hanging coats, was the fusebox, and Dani saw the tripped switch straight away. She flipped it back into place and there was another clunk as the system came back to life. Not that the house was exactly bathed in light in that moment.

Dani moved back out of the cupboard and closed the door, then, out in the hall, she flicked on the lights.

'No! Why did you do that?' Brigitta said, standing in the lounge doorway, a hand up to shield her angry and sullen face as though the light was burning her. 'I hate it like this.'

'I just want to make sure everything is OK,' Dani said.

'Who are you?' Brigitta said, shooting Dani a cold glare, though her hesitation and confusion remained.

'Mrs Popescu, I'm Detective Stephens. We met the other day. Do you remember?'

She didn't say anything, but she didn't look convinced.

'We were talking in the lounge a few moments ago? You were telling me about bones?'

'Bones. What are you talking about? I'm phoning Victor.'

Brigitta turned and shuffled out of sight into the lounge.

'That's probably a good idea,' Dani said.

Though she didn't want to be here when he arrived. She'd had enough of this place, of Brigitta and Victor for one day.

She moved back into the lounge to see Brigitta with a cordless phone in her hand, heading back to her chair in the corner. The phone was shaking in her hand. Fear or just old age?

'Vic. Yes.' Then she babbled on for a few moments in lightning-speed Romanian. The only word that Dani made out was *politie*. Police. Brigitta put the phone down and glared back at Dani.

'He's coming now.'

'Mrs Popescu, are you sure you don't remember what you were saying to me? It was only moments ago?'

'How did you get in here?'

Dani sighed.

'I knocked a few times. You didn't answer, but the door was open.'

'Yes, well. Victor is coming now.'

She nodded. Didn't stop. Her eyes moved from Dani to a spot somewhere on the far wall. She continued to nod.

'I'm glad,' Dani said. 'He'll be able to take care of you.'

Dani turned. She just wanted to go.

'It's not me that needs taking care of.'

Dani said nothing, just shuddered as she walked out and made for the front door.

Chapter 22

Ana sat shivering in the car. She'd been here, in the dark, for twenty minutes now. With the engine and the air-conditioning off, her warm breath had quickly fogged up the cold windows, so she'd now wound down the one next to her, making the interior of the cabin as cold as it was outside.

At least she had her thick coat on, the stolen phone hidden within.

She stared out at the block-like detached house beyond the car. She knew nothing about architecture, but the bland, grey three-storey buildings on this street, with their uniform proportions and flat roofs, looked as if they'd been designed by a bored child.

Ana had never been to this particular house before. Had never been to this downtrodden street before, though she knew exactly what she was looking at. Victor ran several properties like this in the area. Ana didn't know the exact number – it wasn't like she was a business partner of his – but she knew from the number of young women who passed through that Victor – along with his 'associates' spread through the region and beyond – had something of a mini empire.

What was Ana even doing here? All Victor had said when he came back into the warehouse, two hours after he and Alex had left, was that there was a problem. That he needed Ana to help him sort it out.

But so far she'd just been left in the car.

The unlocked car. She didn't have the key. She couldn't drive off. But she could step out if she wanted to.

She could run.

Why hadn't she already?

A banging door wrenched Ana from those hopeful thoughts, and a moment later Victor came striding along the poorly lit path to the car. Ana took a large drag from her cigarette then stubbed it out and flicked the butt out of the window as Victor reached it.

'You're needed,' he growled.

—

Ana said nothing as she stared. Felt nothing, really, which was quite surprising to her. And it wasn't that she wasn't shocked. She was numb.

She'd never seen so much blood. In fact she could scarcely believe it possible that a human body could contain so much.

Red splashes streaked the walls, the ceiling, the floor, which also had a large puddle growing beneath the grotty single bed.

The bed. Upon which lay the lifeless crimson-soaked body of Maria.

Even with all of the red that covered her, Ana recognised the young face. The woman – a teenager, really – had arrived in England all of twenty-four hours ago. Ana had been the one who'd basically stolen her freedom from her, and sent her on her way to this place.

Ana couldn't explain why, but she'd looked through each and every one of the confiscated passports from yesterday. As though knowing the names and birthdays of these young women somehow brought Ana closer to them, somehow gave her more of a justification for the things she was doing. The things she was doing for Victor.

Ana jumped when he stormed back into the room, Alex in tow.

'I don't fucking believe this,' he shouted. 'One day she's been here. All of that effort for nothing.'

Ana felt sick at that. She knew exactly what Victor was thinking. Money. He didn't care one bit about poor Maria, what she'd been through in this room, the life that had been forever torn away from her. He only cared about himself. The hassle he'd had in bringing Maria here, which was now all to waste.

'Ana, stop staring into space like a damn statue. Clean this place up.'

Ana nodded then picked up the rubber gloves that lay on the edge of the bucket that was filled with frothy water.

As though water and soap was going to make this scene disappear.

'Who was he?' Alex asked Victor.

'A regular. Jim, is all these idiots know. They've told me what he looks like, but they know fuck all else.'

'Somehow we'll find him.'

Ana had already gleaned a little of what had happened. Jim was apparently a regular user of Victor's girls. A not at all uncommon type, sadly. The type who couldn't get a girlfriend through the normal means, basically because he was an obscene and violent drunk. So he resorted to paying for sex. Only he knew, just like everyone else did, that he was an obscene and violent drunk, so he was made to pay more, and was generally happy to do so. And he was made to pay more for good reason, because every now and then the women he used would end up with black eyes, or cut lips or bleeding genitalia, when he took his life's frustrations out on them.

Extra money. Not for the victims, but for Victor, for the hassle of him having banged-up prostitutes rather than pristine ones.

'She was only eighteen,' Ana said, unable to take her eyes off Maria's body.

'Forever young,' Alex said.

That comment got him a glower from Victor. It really should have got him a boot down his throat. Ana would have kindly put it there herself.

'You put her here,' Ana said. She glared at Victor, who ignored her.

'Watch your fucking mouth,' Alex said.

'Or what?' Ana said. 'You're going to call Jim out to get me? Beat the crap out of me? Cut me to pieces?'

'Ana, you're upset,' Victor said, sounding way more calm than anyone else in the room. 'But we will catch this guy. And we'll make him pay.'

'Make him pay? How much? Two hundred pounds? How much was Maria's life worth to you?'

Victor shot over like a rocket, snarling. He grabbed Ana by the throat, took her off her feet and launched her up against the wall with a painful thud.

She grimaced in pain and gasped for breath.

'Remember who you're talking to,' he said. 'Remember where I dragged you from. You want to be back in a place like this instead? Being fucked every day by God knows who?'

Ana couldn't have answered the question even if she'd wanted to.

'Well, do you?' Victor roared.

Ana shook her head, at least as best she could.

'Now clean up this mess. I don't want to hear another word from you.'

Victor let go and Ana clattered down into a heap on the blood-soaked floor. She glanced up to see Alex staring at her, a ghastly smile on his ghastly face.

'I'm going to find him,' Victor said. 'And when I do...'

There was a knock on the front door downstairs. Ana heard chatter. Victor disappeared off to see who it was.

Ana pulled herself onto her knees.

'Back where you belong,' Alex said to her.

She ignored the jibe. She had nothing left to say to this man.

Moments later Victor arrived back in the room, trailed by two burly men, who Ana thought she vaguely recognised. Both were dressed in black, with thick leather boots covered in silly blue plastic covers, and leather gloves.

One of them whistled when he saw the sight, as though he was impressed with the gory scene.

Ana felt like launching herself at him and tearing a hole in his neck.

One of the men unrolled some thick plastic sheeting and he and the other grunted as they hauled Maria's limp body off the bed. It clattered onto the sheet and the floor with a sickening thud and squelch. They rolled the body tight, casual as can be.

'You know who did this?' one of them asked.

'Yeah,' Victor said. 'And you can be sure you'll soon be rolling that bastard up too.'

'If you can find him,' Ana reminded him. She didn't get any response.

Having finished wrapping, the two men casually hauled the plastic bundle up like it was nothing more than a rug. Like there wasn't a young woman's body in there.

'Where to?' one of them said to Victor.

'Same place as the others,' was Victor's chilling reply.

Chapter 23

Just days ago Ana had been in Liverpool. Supposedly the start of her new life. Full of hope, even if that hope had been as brittle as glass. That time in the North, however fragile, had been six glorious months, out from under Victor's sight and living her life as a free, 'normal' woman in another country, working in a job that utilised her intelligence and her skills.

Now look at where she was. Back by his side. In some ways she wished she was eighteen-year-old Ana again. The Ana who'd been duped into coming to England on the promise of a better life. That life had been a nightmare, but at least, even as she'd been abused, her conscience had been clear. Now she was nothing more than Victor's wretched accomplice, actively responsible for the misery of others.

She watched from the window as the two men outside heaved Maria's wrapped body into the back of their waiting van. Moments later they drove off silently into the night. To where, Ana had no clue, though Victor's haunting words continued to swirl in her mind as she got to work.

Alex hadn't stayed in the house much longer after that, though Victor remained somewhere – Ana could hear his raised voice below. He'd said he'd go to get some help for Ana in cleaning up the mess, but so far she was alone, on her hands and knees scrubbing away at the wall. The carpet was beyond saving, she'd already decided. She'd told Victor that, though so far he wasn't listening.

'You only need to do the basics,' he'd said to her. 'Surface clean while I arrange the proper job.'

Spoken like a true expert. Which was all the more horri-fying.

And that was the main reason why, after several minutes alone, she stood up, took off the rubber gloves, and moved over to the chair in the corner – the blood-free corner – where her coat was neatly folded.

She performed the by now almost ritual-like process of unfolding the coat, finding the seam and tentatively and expec-tantly reaching in with her two fingers to draw the device out. She powered it up. Held her breath as she did so. Continued to listen to the voices and other sounds from below and above.

The door behind her was closed. She got up and moved over to it and peeked out into the hallway.

Noone there.

Then she delicately typed in three numbers as her heart raced in her chest.

Could she really do this?

She only let out the held-in-breath when the operator answered the call.

Too late. She'd couldn't hang up now.

'Police,' Ana said, as quietly as she possibly could.

Then she gave the details, as blandly as she could. Body in a van. The registration number. Two men. Dangerous.

'And please, let Detective Stephens know. West Midlands Police.'

Then she hung up.

Her chest heaved as adrenaline surged at her act of treachery. She turned the phone off. Footsteps thudded outside the room. Two sets, Ana thought, coming up the stairs.

She jumped up,put the phone away and refolded her coat and was just pulling the second rubber glove on when Victor pushed open the door and stepped inside.

He stopped and glared at Ana, then around the room, as though unimpressed with what he saw.

Ana looked to the man who walked in with Victor. He was short, plump, and carried a large plastic suitcase. He had plastic shoe covers on his feet, a large white plastic overall covered his body, gloves on his hands, something like a shower cap on his head, face mask over his mouth and nose. The only skin visible – tanned but heavily lined – was the narrow strip above and below his hollow and dark eyes.

For some reason Ana almost laughed at the sight. Almost. He looked... ridiculous. But also intensely creepy.

'Come on,' Victor said to her. 'We're done here.'

He reached out and grabbed Ana's wrist.

The man with Victor took a deep inhale of breath as he looked around the room. Ana could tell by the rise of his cheeks behind his mask that he was actually smiling.

'Let me know when you're finished,' Victor said to him.

'Oh, I will,' the man said in a jolly English accent. 'But what a pickle, Mr Nistor. What a pickle indeed.'

Ana pulled away from Victor to grab her coat, then left the room in tow with him, feeling immediate relief as soon as she was out in the hallway, away from the sight and the smell of Maria's blood.

But the relief was short-lived, because her mind was already tumbling with dark thoughts as she descended the stairs. The phone call she'd just made echoed in her mind.

She had no clue what would happen from here.

Had she just sealed her own painful fate?

Chapter 24

The chirping phone woke Dani from an unusually deep sleep. It took her brain several seconds to calibrate and remember where she was. Not at home. Home? The house in Sutton Coldfield had felt less and less like home every day recently. On the earlier drive back from the bizarre visit to Brigitta Popescu's house, Dani had firmly decided that there was absolutely no way she was staying anywhere alone tonight. She couldn't remember ever being so freaked out in all her life, even if it had all seemed like nonsense soon after she'd been away from there.

Regardless, she'd still needed to go back to the house to collect a change of clothes to take to the hospital. There she'd once again struggled to get any real rest on the hard and awkward armchair next to Jason, but apparently at some point tiredness had still got the better of her.

Only to be rudely interrupted by her phone.

Which was still ringing. Had she fallen asleep again, just thinking about answering it?

She shook her head and pulled herself up in the chair and reached out for the phone. Jason was snoring loudly next to her, the drugs he continued to take to hold the pain at bay enough to keep him in a deep sleep.

The call went to voicemail just as Dani grasped the phone. She stared at the screen. Three missed calls, from a withheld number, all within the last two minutes. The time was a little after one a.m.

The phone screen lit up again with another call and the device vibrated in her hand. Dani hit the green button and pulled the phone to her ear.

'Hello.'

She listened intently to the voice on the other end. Her attention and alertness increased almost exponentially with each word spoken.

'I'm on my way,' she said, already halfway across the room for her coat and bag as she ended the call.

–

Dani travelled alone the few miles towards the town of Brownhills, at the very northern tip of the West Midlands Police boundary with Staffordshire. She'd managed to rouse Easton from sleep at the first attempt, but he was housebound, looking after his sister's children, while she remained out and about who-knew-where – most likely spending the night with one of the many men she had on some sort of drunken roster.

Back in central Birmingham, and every other large town or city up and down the country, the streets would no doubt be thriving with drinkers and club-goers at this time on a Saturday night – or was it Sunday morning yet? – but in the relatively far-flung, small town of Brownhills, the streets were dead, and as Dani drove on along the high street, where every unit was closed up, shutters down for the night, it was almost like a ghost town.

Until she passed over a roundabout on the nearby A5, where the flashing blue lights up ahead were like a beacon of activity, drawing her in.

She counted six police cars as she approached. One ambulance. Overhead she could see the far-reaching searchlight of a helicopter, sweeping the area all around. As she parked up and shut down her engine, she heard the helicopter for the first time, too, could even feel the vibrations from its whirring rotors.

The dashboard thermometer read minus five. Dani braced herself for the blistering cold as she stepped out of the car.

Even without the blue strobes of light, the road – a major east-to-west route – was well lit, though it was flanked by tall and dense evergreens either side that gave little clue as to what lay beyond. A tall and stocky officer in a bright yellow jacket wandered over to intercept Dani as she approached the cordon that was blocking the road in both directions.

The officer introduced himself as Talbot. He'd been expecting Dani.

'What happened?' she asked.

The last she'd heard, the van the police were searching for had been pulled over and the two drivers apprehended, but she could already sense tonight wouldn't be quite as straightforward as that.

The officer shook his head, disappointment. 'The traffic officers were waiting for back-up. We heard the rumour about a body inside the van. They couldn't leave the scene with the perps until help arrived. But...'

He scratched his head like he wasn't sure exactly how or why whatever had happened had indeed happened.

'The bastards fought back. Knocked one of our guys clean out, the other one... he's in a bad way.'

He looked quite disturbed by that fact.

'The perps are still running?' Dani asked.

A rub on the back of his neck this time, another nervous, almost apologetic reaction. 'Chopper lost them about five minutes ago.'

Which perhaps explained why the helicopter was now circling almost randomly, the searchlight sweeping all over rather than honed on one spot.

'And the van?' Dani said.

'Come and take a look. We haven't opened it up yet. Obviously it's not been our priority, and it's locked, and I really wasn't sure on protocol.'

Which was perhaps understandable, given the ever-changing nature of the scene, though Dani had a flash of worry that perhaps the delay in opening up that van could be a huge mistake. The mystery caller had claimed there was a body in there, but what if the person inside was alive? Or at least had been when the van was first stopped.

Dani headed into the mix of police cars and uniformed officers, warm breath swirling into the air all around. The paintwork and glass of the vehicles glistened with ever-thickening frost. By the open back doors of the ambulance was a copper, face bloodied, holding gauze up to the side of his head.

'Ahmed's the one that got off lucky,' Talbot said. 'Wyatt's been rushed off to A&E already.'

Dani nodded. She'd try to catch up with Ahmed soon enough, but he wasn't the priority for now. Catching the two runners was. And opening that van, even if Dani was massively apprehensive about what they would find.

'You've got dogs out?' Dani asked as they approached the closed back doors of the van. The front of the vehicle was off the road, sunk into a ditch, a patrol car right alongside it. Dani could imagine the scene as the arresting officers had closed in and forced the van to a stop.

'Yeah, but they lost the trail already. We've got farms dotted all around here, and there's a lot of water in the fields, pools, streams too. Whether the two perps know a few tricks about how to lose dogs or not, it seems the landscape's helped them out here.'

'But fields also means there's not many places to hide, surely? From the eye in the sky?'

Talbot shrugged. 'There's plenty of villages around, though. Honestly, I don't know. But for now, they're gone.'

And while Dani wasn't going to apportion blame for that, at least not yet, it was a bitter pill to swallow. The police had actually done a sterling job to begin with. Only minutes after the 999 call handler had put the alert out, the van had been tracked using ANPR and then traffic officers had quickly picked up the trail just the other side of Brownhills. That initial flurry, up to the point where the van had been stopped, had shown a well-oiled machine in operation.

After that…

'Any idea who the mystery caller was?' Talbot said.

'No idea.'

'Or why they asked for you specifically?'

Dani did have an inkling, but she didn't want to say it just yet.

'I recognise your name,' Talbot said.

And there was that glance to go along with his words. Dani avoided an eye-roll. Just.

'Let's get these doors open,' Dani said, nodding over to the van.

'They're locked,' he reminded her.

'Then get a crowbar or whatever.'

Talbot looked unsure for a moment but then nodded and headed away. As he did so he grabbed the radio from his chest, though he was too far away for Dani to hear what was said. He disappeared out of sight for a few moments and Dani looked around the scene, trying to sort out her thoughts which were all the more jumbled given the time of night and the lack of sleep.

Dani looked up to the sky. The helicopter was over in the distance to the north, perhaps a mile or two away. Then the searchlight turned off. The chopper circled around and turned to head back south.

Dani was sure she knew what that meant.

Talbot, another yellow-jacketed officer by his side, was back with Dani just as the helicopter hurtled by overhead.

'Nothing we could do,' Talbot said, his face apologetic. 'They'll come back out if we get a sniff, but for now…' He shrugged. A lame gesture.

'We'll catch up with them,' Dani said, trying to remain positive. 'We've got the van, and whatever trace evidence we can find.'

'We haven't called Forensics yet,' Talbot said. 'We didn't really know what we were looking at here. But we do know the van reg is bogus. Or at least, it doesn't belong to this vehicle.'

'Let's just get this thing opened up,' Dani said.

Talbot nodded to his colleague who stepped forwards with the crowbar. He clanked the prongs into the gap between the back doors and grunted as he heaved. The lock snapped and the left-hand door swung open a couple of inches.

Dani reached forward and pulled both doors wide. She stared at the thick roll of black plastic inside. Talbot pulled back the ends of the plastic a few inches. Just enough to reveal strands of light blonde hair, stained with dark smudges. The other officer shone his torch onto the bundle as Talbot tore through the layers to expose the first foot or so of plastic.

They were left staring into the deathly eyes of a young woman.

'Shit,' Talbot said.

Dani said nothing.

'Do you know her?' Talbot said after a few moments of ghastly silence.

'No,' Dani said. 'But we'll do everything we can to figure out who she is. Call Forensics in.'

Talbot brought his radio back up as Dani continued to stare. The woman was all of twenty years old, and even judging by the little Dani could see of her, there was no doubt she had suffered a horrible and violent death.

No, Dani had no clue who this woman was, though she had a very clear idea who would.

Chapter 25

Monday morning came around far quicker than Dani expected it would. Having left the crime scene at Brownhills at just gone eight a.m. on Sunday morning, Dani had had every intention of taking only a quick rest before carrying on working through the day.

That had never happened. Having called and given Easton the lowdown on what had happened in Brownhills, she'd crashed out at the hospital for several hours, only waking in the early afternoon, at which point, despite her impassioned protests, Jason had persuaded her to take what he'd described as a much-needed break. And the break *was* much needed, even if it wasn't entirely welcome. Dani had spent most of the rest of the day wishing the hours away, and had even managed to do some bits and pieces from afar when Jason was otherwise engaged.

Which was why, come nine a.m. on Monday morning, she walked into a meeting room at HQ which was already filled with a dozen other officers for the team briefing she'd managed to set up.

Most of the participants were from Homicide, but there were also three less familiar faces from the Organised Crime team. Snow was falling outside the large windows which ran along one side of the long room. The first snow of the season. In typical British fashion, the roads around central Birmingham were already in chaos, and Dani had to hope the inclement weather didn't have an adverse effect on their work.

The room hushed as Dani and Easton got themselves ready. McNair was sitting up front too, though it was Dani who took the lead and opened up.

'We have two murder victims which we are treating as linked,' Dani said, pointing to the photos of the bodies of Clara Dunne and the Jane Doe from the van. Dani briefly explained the circumstances of how each body had been found. 'We're light on direct physical evidence that connect these two crimes, but we do have some commonalities between the two.

'Firstly, we believe this man, Nicolae Popescu, may have had some involvement in Clara Dunne's death.' She pointed to the picture of him. 'Popescu was deported from the UK in 2013, though his whereabouts since then are up for debate, and evidence is sketchy to say the least – however, we are still in discussion with the Romanian authorities on that front. Regardless, we're keeping an open mind. He may be in the UK, and if he is, he's here illegally at the very least.

'We also have this man. Victor Nistor. Another Romanian national who's lived here for several years. He owns a haulage business in Tipton. There's a direct link between him and Popescu.'

Dani explained about Brigitta's car, and the fact Nistor was apparently some sort of carer to Brigitta.

'And lastly, we have the 999 call that was made in the early hours of Sunday morning, which provided the police with details about the van in which we found Jane Doe's body. We know the call was made from a handset with a Romanian number, though we've had confirmation it's a prepaid device which isn't registered. That call was from an anonymous female. I've listened to the call myself several times, and it's evident the caller is not a native English speaker. Possibly Romanian, possibly not, but as far as I'm concerned it's another piece of evidence pointing towards Nistor and Popescu. We're still waiting on confirmation of triangulation of that call to pinpoint where it was made from.'

A hand went up at the back of the room. DC Constable, one of the Homicide team.

'Yes?'

'Sorry, are you saying the only link between Jane Doe and those two suspects is the fact the phone was Romanian, and the accent of the 999 caller?'

Dani thought about that one for a second. Was that true? It felt like there was so much more than that.

'Do we have enough to bring Nistor in?' Constable then asked, giving Dani a bit of leeway to ignore the first question.

'I don't think so,' Dani said. She explained about his previous arrest and Nistor's tough lawyer who surely wouldn't stand the police interrogating their client without a clear charge. An arrest would get them another twenty-four hours to interview him formally, but Dani would rather have something more concrete against him before they did that. 'We do have the go-ahead for surveillance against Nistor, though. At his home address, business address, and also at Brigitta Popescu's address. That surveillance is getting underway as we speak.'

'What about the Jane Doe?' DC Grayling shouted out. 'Any idea who she is?'

'Her prints don't match anything on file,' Easton said. 'So she doesn't have a criminal record, and nor has she come through immigration, if indeed she's not a British national, which is one possible theory.'

'There was no ID for her in the van,' Dani said, 'so at the moment she remains unidentified. Similarly, there was no ID for the males, but we have had Forensics do a thorough sweep of the van and we're hoping to see some results of that today. The post-mortem of Jane Doe will also be taking place soon.'

Although Dani wasn't really expecting that to give them much more than they already knew, which was that the young woman had died in a brutal attack.

'So what's the theory here?' piped up a voice from the back of the room.

The gruff DI Ricard was part of the Organised Crime team, and the most senior member of that team in the room. Dani knew of him but had never worked alongside him.

'The theory is that Victor Nistor is running an illegal operation out of his business address in Tipton. Whether prostitution, drugs, extortion, or whatever, we don't know yet. We do need to find out. The working theory is that Clara Dunne was investigating the disappearance of her brother, Liam, who hasn't been seen for more than five years. We don't know what linked him to Nistor or Popescu, but we believe they know what happened to Liam. Nistor, or people close to him also knew Clara was digging, and they silenced her. The very fact she herself was living and working under an alias shows she was making progress in finding what had happened to Liam, and was concerned for her safety.'

Ricard sniffed at that, as though it sounded ridiculous, though it was he who'd asked for the theory. Theories were just that. Unproven. And they were fluid and changeable. There to give an investigation a direction.

'And what about your Jane Doe?' he asked. 'Why was she killed?'

'I really don't know,' Dani said, trying to sound confident. 'But I do think that the two men transporting her were likely in the process of disposing of her remains, given how we found her body. So this does once again point to an organised operation, rather than some random killing, particularly when paired with the 999 call.'

'DI Stephens,' McNair said, getting to her feet. 'Perhaps you could concentrate on the most important strands of investigation that we'll be following.'

Dani wasn't sure whether the prompt was for her benefit or not.

'Of course,' she said. 'I already mentioned the surveillance which is in operation as of this morning. Secondly, we'll have a dedicated CCTV team led by DC Constable, who will be trawling records on various fronts. Liam Dunne's disappearance. Clara Dunne's murder. The van we intercepted on Sunday morning – we'll scour records for other sightings of it – to see if we can pinpoint either where it was likely to have come from, or where it was going to. We need to keep digging into Nistor's background, and also Popescu's. Where is he now? Then we have forensic findings to consider and cross-refer.'

Dani looked at her watch. She still had a couple of minutes before she needed to scarper.

'Are there any more questions?' she asked.

'Are we making a public announcement?' asked a young female officer Dani didn't recognise.

McNair got to her feet again to answer that one.

'Not yet,' McNair said. 'We've decided it would be prejudicial to make a public announcement linking the two deaths at this stage. The two perps who escaped custody yesterday know we have Jane Doe's body, and that we're looking for them, but we have to assume they don't know how we came across the information about that van. The point is, we may well have an ally somewhere within Nistor and Popescu's circle, and we need to both work on identifying that person while not jeopardising their safety.'

'But you don't have any information on who the insider is?' Ricard asked.

McNair turned to Dani.

'No. Not at this stage,' Dani said.

And she didn't feel even slightly bad for the lie.

Chapter 26

With the snow still falling, thick and lusciously white, and the temperature low enough to ensure the flakes stuck wherever they fell, the city centre streets were already looking like a winter wonderland as Dani gingerly walked along the pavements. Even if she had changed into winter boots before leaving HQ, the surface remained treacherous.

One issue dominated Dani's mind as she walked. Ana Crisan. Why hadn't she told the team about her suspicion that Ana was the anonymous caller? Dani really wasn't sure, but it felt like the right thing to do, not just to protect Ana, but to protect Dani too. She knew there was a lot of doubt in the air – aimed at her – from the hastily pulled together investigation team, and throwing more unsubstantiated beliefs at them would only further alienate Dani, and open her up to more abuse and rebuke if it turned out she was wrong.

Regardless, the team had plenty else to be doing to further the investigation, and before she revealed her hand, Dani would continue to ponder how best to reach out to Ana.

Satisfied that the team – whipped by McNair and Easton – were in good shape, Dani was determined not to lose touch with proceedings at court. It was only last Thursday, all of four days ago, when she'd been up on the witness stand, but so much had happened – to her, at least – since then, even if she'd only missed one day of the trial.

Wanting to remain as inconspicuous as she could, following the grilling she'd received from O'Hare while on the stand, Dani took a seat in a quiet spot in the public gallery. She'd heard news that the two sides were expected to give their closing statements today, and it was possible a verdict could be delivered soon after.

No one else in the public gallery paid Dani any attention, and as the court filled and then rose for the judge, Dani was glad that neither O'Hare nor Barker had clocked she was there.

Yet proceedings had only just got underway when O'Hare dropped her latest bombshell. Would anyone really have expected anything less at this stage? She really was a first-class sneak.

'Your Honour, we have one further witness who we'd like heard. This relates to evidence that has only come to light during the course of the trial.'

Barker was understandably unimpressed with this, given how far into proceedings they already were, and the judge ordered both barristers over to the front where a heated though muted back-and-forth exchange ensued between the three. From where Dani was sitting she couldn't make out any of the conversation properly.

The judge soon sent the two barristers back to their benches and announced the decision to the court.

'We will hear the defence's witness, who must be heard by video-link, for reasons that will soon become apparent. The court will recess for thirty minutes to prepare.'

–

Thirty and a half minutes later, Dani was back in the same seat in the public gallery and the court was soon full once more, albeit with one noticeable addition. A large TV screen on a stand right in front of the witness box.

Dani already had a sickly feeling as to where this could be going. The judge opened the session and handed over to O'Hare. A clerk headed over to the TV and seconds later the screen flickered to life and Dani was left staring at a live link of a painfully familiar-looking interview room.

Seated in the middle of the room was her brother.

Her brother, who seemed to be staring straight at her. Could he actually see her? She'd never live-linked in court herself, but she presumed the witness could see the court just as clearly as the court could see the witness. But could Ben make out Dani?

O'Hare completed the formalities, introducing Ben, his background, and some other crap Dani barely heard because she was too shocked and too angry to properly listen. All she could do was to stare at him. Despite being in a drab room and in his prison garb, he looked confident and in control and Dani was sure he even had a snide grin on his resting face.

'Mr Stephens,' O'Hare said, 'we're particularly interested in the time you spent sharing a cell with the defendant. Is it true that you, too, like the defendant, were a patient of Dr Helen Collins?'

'Correct.'

Ben went on to explain his own relationship with Collins. How she'd been part of his defence team during his murder trial, attesting, as she had for Curtis, that Ben had acted with diminished responsibility when he'd killed. The jury hadn't bought it in his case.

'But you didn't carry on seeing Collins, in a professional capacity, after your trial concluded?' O'Hare asked.

'No,' Ben said.

'But you were aware that the defendant did?'

'Yes. Damian...' Ben sighed. 'He can be just as normal as anyone else. In fact, most of the time he was. We chatted together – just chatted like anyone else would – so yeah, we talked about Collins. It's not like we get to do much in prison, is it? So him heading off to talk to his shrink was... a thing. Something.'

He looked a little embarrassed by his own lack of eloquence. He never used to speak like that. Had prison worn him down that much or was it all part of the Ben Stephens show?

'And how would you describe the defendant following these sessions?' O'Hare said. 'By that I mean, did his character, his manner, usually change from when he left to see Dr Collins, to when he returned to his cell?'

Ben nodded. 'Sometimes, yes.' He sighed again. 'You have to remember – and this is me talking from an uneducated standpoint – that Damian was pretty messed up. I mean, I said you could have a normal conversation with him, but it wasn't always like that. There were times when he completely zoned out. Times when he mumbled away to himself. Argued to himself, and I know there were times when he was talking to other people in his head. Like, actually talking out loud, but to people who weren't in the room.'

'Real people? As in people he knew, like family members?'

'I really don't know. But coming back to your question, Damian definitely changed.'

'Changed how?'

Ben regurgitated what Dani took to be a well-rehearsed spiel. He'd made similar comments to her before, when she was actively investigating Curtis and trying to track him down to prevent him from killing again. Ben had claimed that a new voice in Curtis's head had taken hold. A female voice, who Curtis was battling with and trying his best to eliminate from his mind. Of course there were already statements in the police files related to all of this. So why was Ben here? Virtually, at least. O'Hare must have something new, a revelation that she intended to use as one last throw of the dice.

'And this voice,' O'Hare said, 'did she have a name?'

Ben shrugged. 'I've no idea. The conversations he had with whatever or whoever he heard weren't like that, and it wasn't as though I felt I could ask. Honestly? I was scared.' Though he didn't seem scared at all as he retold the story. 'But I definitely noticed him becoming more and more agitated following his sessions with Dr Collins.'

Dani clenched her teeth and her fists as she waited for the revelation she was sure would come.

'More agitated, how?' O'Hare asked.

'There was one time in particular, and I do have a record of the date, when he came back to the cell… to put it mildly, he was a gibbering mess. He was begging, begging *me*, to help him. He kept on saying things like, *why is she doing this to me*, and, *I can't do what she's asking*. Then he'd scream at the top of his voice, *she's put her inside me. Get her out!*'

A strange silence fell over the courtroom, as if no one knew how to take Ben's theatrical performance. Dani's eyes flicked to Barker, who was slowly shaking his head – disgust? – but he hadn't jumped up to protest at Ben's accusatory, yet so far baseless, claims.

'You said you remember the date of one particular episode?' O'Hare asked.

'Of course. Not one particular episode, but *the* episode. Eighth of April, last year.'

Barker was now deep in conversation with his assistant. What were they saying?

'And why specifically do you recall this date?'

'My understanding is that it was the anniversary of the car crash that saw Curtis put in prison in the first place. When he came back from his session with Collins that day he was ranting like a lunatic. *She wants me to kill them, she wants me to kill them.* Things like that, over and over. He got… not physical with me, but he was aggressive and out of control. It felt like it would only take a spark for him to snap completely and tear me to pieces.'

'What happened to calm him? Did he indeed calm down?'

'Obviously when someone goes nuts like that, it doesn't go unnoticed. People in the other cells must have thought he was murdering me, or murdering someone, at least. There was shouting, banging everywhere. Eventually two guards had to come in and restrain him, which wasn't easy, to say the least. Eventually they dragged him out of the cell still kicking and screaming. I didn't see him for two days after that. When he came back it was like nothing had happened.'

'Did you ask him about that episode?'

Ben looked put out by the question. 'Of course I didn't. I couldn't risk a repeat, could I? Calm Damian was always better, for me, than the alternative.'

'Do you believe, based on these experiences, that the defendant, when he said, *she wants me to kill them*, was referring to Dr Collins?'

'Yes, I b—'

'Objection!' Barker shouted, rising to his feet. 'The question is intrusively leading.'

'Sustained,' the judge said.

'Sorry, Your Honour,' O'Hare said. Though she didn't look sorry at all. The question didn't stand, and nor did Ben's interrupted answer, but the jury had still heard it. 'I'll rephrase the question. When the defendant uttered phrases such as *she wants me to kill them*, who did you believe he was referring to when he said *she*.'

'Objection, the witness is not a medically trained professional able to give such an opinion.'

'He's more than entitled to give an opinion,' O'Hare said, 'and no reference was made to it being an expert opinion.'

'The witness may answer,' the judge said.

'I thought he was referring to Dr Helen Collins,' Ben said to murmurs around the courtroom.

'No more questions,' O'Hare said, 'but before I pass over to my learned friend, I'd like to point out for the record, that we've looked specifically into the witness's account of these events, which took place on the eighth of April last year. It is correct that the defendant spent time with Dr Helen Collins that morning. From just after nine a.m. to almost twelve p.m., which I note, based on our review of data, was the third longest session she ever held with him at Long Lartin. Also, the two guards in question that day were Hamza Khan and Graham Molten. Unfortunately, Molten passed earlier this year from a heart attack, but we do have his written record of Damian Curtis's outburst from that day. Guards are required to file such reports whenever there is a breach of the peace of this nature. We also have a sworn statement from Khan confirming his recollection of events from that day, together with his assertion that he too heard the defendant calling out, *she wants me to kill them.*'

O'Hare moved forwards and handed a piece of paper first to the judge, and then to Barker who took it and almost immediately handed it to his assistant.

'Are you finished with the witness?' the judge asked after taking a few seconds to read the paper in his hand.

'Yes, Your Honour.'

'Does the prosecution wish to ask any questions?'

Barker leaned in to his assistant who was rabbiting away in his ear, pointing to the statement in his hand and shrugging and other such like confused gestures.

'Your Honour, we have no questions,' Barker said. He sounded dejected.

'Then the witness is excused,' the judge said.

A clerk wandered over to the TV. A split second before the screen went blank, Dani was sure Ben caught her eye and smirked.

Chapter 27

Minutes later, the judge adjourned the session. Closing statements would be given when they reconvened. O'Hare had dropped her final and most explosive bombshell, and Dani was livid. New evidence that had come to light? No, O'Hare had played everyone with that. So why had Barker, yet again, pretty much let her get away with it?

Just as she had done numerous times before, Dani made a point of intercepting Barker outside the courtroom to try and figure out exactly that.

'Why are you letting them do this?' she asked, not holding back on her clear agitation.

Barker huffed and rolled his eyes like Dani was nothing but an unrepentant and troublesome teen.

'I'm not letting anyone do anything,' Barker said. 'But even I have to be cognisant of the fact that sometimes the weight of evidence swings against us. I have to say, DI Stephens, I find it most worrying that the defence team have time and time again found a way to pour doubt on Collins's role here. Her death noted, I'm beginning to wonder why the police haven't more fully investigated her role, particularly as not having done so is harming this trial.'

'Are you serious? Collins didn't do it! Ben's evidence was a complete fabrication.'

A raised eyebrow now, in Barker's continued show of indignant nonchalance. 'Fabrication? A fabrication that involved approved contemporaneous records of a now deceased prison guard? Plus a sworn statement from another. Are you saying they're all involved in a conspiracy?'

Was she saying that?

'I don't know about them, but I do know Ben is lying. I *know* him. Even if Curtis did say... whatever it was. *She wants me to kill them.* So what? Ben could have made him say that. He wouldn't exactly create a voice in Curtis's head called Ben Stephens now, would he? It's no more likely that it was Collins than Ben—'

'I'm sorry, but I really don't see your point of view. Taking your heart out of this situation – which I appreciate is really difficult for you to do, for reasons I sympathise with greatly – which scenario do you think is more believable?'

Dani was stumped by that.

Faced with the evidence, and the testimonies of the guards, why wasn't she even willing to entertain the notion that maybe she had got it wrong? Was she so desperate for Ben to be punished that she'd let it cloud her judgement?

'But that doesn't mean I'm wrong,' was all she could come back with.

'No, perhaps not. But unfortunately in a trial I can only work with what I have. Please, if you'll excuse me, I need to make sure I'm ready for this.'

He turned and walked off.

-

'Aren't you going to tell me what happened?' Easton asked.

The car in front swung into her lane without warning and Dani slammed on the brakes. The back tyres skidded on the slushy surface and Dani fought for control.

'Fucking idiot!' she screamed, thumping the horn.

'You might want to calm it a bit,' Easton said, not at all friendly.

Dani glanced to him and saw the unimpressed look on his face. She didn't bother to respond.

'I get the trial is hard for you,' Easton said. 'But you're best just trying to forget about it. You can't influence the outcome now. Let it run its course, and do what you need to do on your active cases.'

Let it run its course? Let Ben smear a dead woman who did nothing wrong, just so he can then play the whole situation to his own advantage? How could she possibly sit by and let that run its course?

Though she did get Easton's point, to a degree. What she really needed to do was to push Ben out of her mind, concentrate on Clara Dunne and Jane Doe's murders. She'd felt in the zone earlier during the team briefing, now she couldn't have been further from the zone if she tried.

They travelled on in silence for a couple of minutes and Dani's tension eased, if only a little.

'I was doing some reading over the weekend,' Easton said, his change of subject welcome and Dani really did try to push away any further thoughts of Ben.

'Your talents never cease to amaze me,' she said.

'Ha bloody ha, very funny. It was nice to have some peace and quiet and a few moments to myself, to be honest. Anyway, I was reading up on vampires.'

'*Twilight?* I bet you read them all, didn't you?'

'Wow, Dani, your inner comedy is something else today. No, not *Twilight*. Want to know what I found?'

'Knock me out,'

'So, what we think we know as vampires, or Strigoi in Romanian, weren't these fanged things with blood dripping from their mouths, living in the dark, blah blah. They were basically undead corpses that come about when someone dies in sin – or for some other reason the soul doesn't leave the body in death.'

'OK?'

'Did you know people used to black out mirrors in the homes of dead people, because they were scared that if the soul, when it left its body, saw its reflection, it would become trapped? They also smeared garlic on doors and windows to stop vampires entering. It's amazing how many of the tropes we know are centuries old now, but things that people really did do to ward off these spirits.'

'There's truth in every legend, as they say.'

'And babies were particularly vulnerable to being converted, at least until they were christened.'

'Ah, it makes sense now. So this was just a way for the church to control its people? Scare stories to make sure everyone went to pray, everyone was christened, lived sin free, etc., etc. And made their donations every Sunday, of course.'

'So cynical.'

Dani huffed.

'But once you're a Strigoi, you're immortal,' Easton said. 'A walking corpse, roaming the earth, not just killing people but converting others too.'

'So they're more like zombies then,' Dani said.

Easton seemed to ponder that one for a few moments, as though it was a really deep and meaningful point. 'Maybe. Except they don't even need to bite you. A simple touch or look is enough to turn you. And the whole stake-through-the-heart thing? That was real. I read up about this spate of child killings in one area of Romania a few hundred years ago, or maybe it was disappearances, but anyway, the locals naturally blamed vampires for it all...'

Dani could almost hear Brigitta telling the story now, and for the first time felt a wave of paranoia.

'...they began to dig up graves. To make sure the corpses were really dead, they drove stakes into the hearts. Fear spread and people all over started doing this. The problem got so big that the Pope had to declare it a crime to exhume bodies.'

Dani was silent now as her brain rumbled with strange thoughts.

'But do you know the freakiest part?' Easton asked.

'I'm sure you're going to tell me.'

'I am. Modern-day historians are generally accepting that a lot of these things – stories of vampires, ghouls, zombies – all derived from the same issue. Know what?'

'No idea.'

'Premature burial.' He let that one hang. 'Think about it. Four hundred years ago it's not as if everyone had a doctor on their doorstep to properly confirm death. Even today, as police officers we're not technically allowed to do it, we have to have a doctor formally confirm death at every scene, even if it seems bloody obvious. Back in the olden days… well, they got it wrong. Surprisingly often. Just imagine, poor old Grandad is laid out in his coffin in his home, candles all around him, family dressed in black praying and in mourning, and suddenly he lurches up. Talk about being freaked out.'

Easton shivered theatrically.

'One of my worst fears, being buried alive,' he said.

'One of?'

'Don't get me started.'

Dani laughed, and although the conversation trailed off from there, at least Easton's light-hearted talk about Strigoi and vampires had left Dani feeling a little more focused again, even if she did remain on edge. Which wasn't helped by the snow-covered and slushed-up roads that were jam-packed the whole of the journey to Walsall.

When they finally arrived at their destination, Dani found a parking spot on the road a few doors down from Liam Dunne's home, which was on a tightly packed street with modest terraces either side and cars crammed bumper to bumper on both sides of the narrow road. The homes had small front yards, too small for cars to park on, which were generally paved or with tiny and plain-looking gardens. All in all a very similar set-up to the street, and the house, where Clara Dunne's body had been found.

Despite the weed-filled front yard and the obviously cheap plastic windows which were grimy and discoloured, Liam

Dunne's house didn't look particularly out of place on the street, and there were one or two others which Dani noted were in a similar or even worse state – awaiting a property developer with a keen eye and a tight budget who would flip them, making a few thousand pounds in the process.

'I really have no idea what to expect in here,' Easton said as the two of them crunched across an inch of untouched snow to the front door.

Dani didn't answer as she took the keychain from her pocket and first unlocked the mortice deadlock before moving on to the more lightweight cylinder lock. She pushed the door open, some effort needed to prise it far enough to step in, what with the amount of post – largely junk – which had accumulated beyond.

The inside of the house was dark and cold, and there was an awful smell. Dust and mould and something else Dani couldn't put her finger on. She went to flip on the lights. Nothing. Not a surprise. It wasn't as though there was anyone around to pay the bill.

'Leave the door open a minute for some light,' Dani said as she moved through into the front lounge and held her breath as she pulled open the curtains, which caused a swathe of dust to fill the air.

She squinted and hunkered down and brought her arm up to her mouth to breathe before she turned around. The room, although not old in its furnishings, was like some kind of relic; the type of room seen on sci-fi movies when the crew of a spaceship intercepts another which has been lost in space in a time-warp for decades. The two leather sofas might have, at one time, been black or dark brown but were now grey with thick dust. The TV was the same, as was every other object. Black mould climbed the walls all around and reached down from the top corners of the room.

'What shall we do then?' Easton said, coming through the doorway.

'Let's split up. I don't want to stay here any longer than necessary. Look for anything that gives us a clue as to who Liam was, what he was up to in life.'

'Got it.'

'You start down here,' she said to him. 'I'll head upstairs.'

In the hallway the front door was now closed, though there was just enough daylight coming from the lounge to give a good glimpse of the space. But upstairs… it remained pitch black, with all of the curtains drawn. Much like in Brigitta Popescu's house, Dani thought with a shiver.

She took her phone out, torchlight on, as she went up. Flashes of her unsettling trips to Brigitta's house pulsed in her mind. Not to mention the stories Easton had been telling Dani on the trip over here. In the car, with him as company, the stories of vampires and roaming undead corpses had seemed trivial, almost amusing. Now Dani wasn't quite so sure, and there was definitely an added chill as she ascended, which caused her skin to prickle all over.

Dani reached the first bedroom, at the back of the house, and stopped in the doorway to shine the torch around, the unsettling feeling steadily building as she gazed into the dark space.

She took a deep breath then rushed across the room to the windows and hurled the curtains open, then spun back to stare across the room.

A shadow flicked across the far wall, moving towards the door, and Dani's heart lurched as she swept the torchlight to that spot.

Then the shadow crept back again, and she realised it was only coming from the curtain flapping behind her.

She exhaled heavily and muttered under her breath at her own frailty.

The room she was in was mostly bare: an unmade single bed, a basic wardrobe and drawers. A spare room that perhaps had never been used.

Dani only spent a minute or two in there before she went into the next room, at the front of the house. She performed an almost identical routine as before, darting into the room, pulling open the curtains in a quick motion. Except this time, more prepared, the sweeping shadows didn't bother her half as much, at least. And there was still no sign of vampires anywhere.

This room was clearly Liam's, she decided, with pictures on the wall and knick-knacks all over. The double bed still had covers on, the washing basket in the corner was half filled with laundry. Dani felt a wave of sadness as she stared over the space. Whatever had happened to him, whether he was dead or still alive, Liam Dunne's life, as he'd known it, had ended the day he left here. It was as if the house was now in perpetual mourning, a feeling of ingrained misery seeping through every brick and every fabric.

Dani, heart heavy, rummaged through the dusty belongings. She could understand why, five years on, no one had come to properly clean this place out; why the police hadn't carried out a full, forensic-type search. Before now they'd had no reason to do so, but seeing the house like this, with everything in place, was unsettling to say the least.

And to think that Liam's sister had recently been living not far from here, busily searching for her brother, but had never herself been in here to sort through his things. As far as the law was concerned Liam was still alive, and Clara would have had no right of access.

Dani opened the bottom bedside drawer which was half filled with bundled socks and a collection of dead spiders, all shrivelled.

She ignored her squeamishness and dug a gloved hand inside and felt about. She frowned when her fingers brushed against something hard. She grasped the object and took it out. A mobile phone. A pretty antiquated handset at that, certainly from before Liam went missing in 2015, although in reality it was probably only ten years old or so – the industry had moved so swiftly.

Dani held down the power button but it didn't come on. She put the phone into an evidence bag then moved over to a set of drawers. Most were filled with dusty cobweb-covered clothes, plus more dead spiders and insects, though the top one was a clutter of odds and sods. Within it she found what looked like an old-school petty cash container – metal, red, all scratched up from years of use. It was locked, but Dani was sure she'd seen a small key across the room in one of the other bedside drawers.

She went back to get that key and stuck it into the lock and turned. It worked. She placed the box onto the window sill and flipped the lid. Inside was…

A creak outside the room, on the landing. Dani froze and listened. There it was again.

'Easton?' she shouted.

'What? You got something?' His voice carried thinly in the air. He was still somewhere downstairs.

Dani closed the lid on the box and was about to head to the door when her attention was grabbed by movement outside the window, down on the street outside.

She was sure she'd seen a dark shadow scooting between two parked cars. As she stared now, she could see nothing, no one at all.

That same creak again. Dani, trying her best to calm her already wrecked nerves, grabbed the biggest, hardest thing she could – the cash box – and confidently strode for the door.

She jumped out into the hall, box held aloft.

She was left staring ahead, across the landing, into the dark bathroom. The noise came again, this time accompanied by a swathe of cold air. Dani rolled her eyes. The window in the bathroom was either ajar or broken, and the breeze coming in was sufficient to cause the roller blind to flap back and forth against the pane.

Dani sighed, turned and moved back into the bedroom. She placed the box back on the sill, opened it up and took out the picture of Liam Dunne, arm wrapped around the shoulder of a young and striking blonde woman. She flipped the photo over, hoping for something. No. There was no writing there.

Dani stared at the woman's face. Not Ana. Not the dead woman from the van. Did she look Romanian? Eastern European? Slavic?

What was Dani reaching for?

As her brain rumbled, her eyes unconsciously flickered again, looking to the street outside. No, that was no act of her imagination. Nor was it a shadow or a Strigoi or whatever else. Across the road, now hidden at the edge of an alleyway, was a person. Definitely a person. Dressed all in black, head covered by a thick hood. Lurking.

Spying?

It was too big a coincidence to ignore.

Dani dropped the picture.

'Easton!' she shouted, already rushing for the door. 'Get outside, now!'

Chapter 28

Dani hurtled down, was already on the second-to-last stair when Easton bounded out from the back of the house into the hallway.

'What?'

'Someone's spying on us.'

Dani reached the door first, was about to fling it open when she paused. The watcher hadn't spotted her. Had he? So what was the point in charging out there and scaring him off?

She took a deep breath.

'There's an alley about five houses down,' Dani said. 'Some guy, all dark clothes, hood over his head, hiding at the edge.'

She looked over at Easton. She knew well his doubtful face. Did he not believe that she'd seen the watcher at all?

'I thought you'd found a bloody bomb or something.'

'We'll go out calmly, as if we're heading for the car.'

'And then what?'

Dani ignored him. She opened the door and a blast of fresh icy air smacked her in the face and her eyes watered. She took a step out onto the powdery snow and cast her gaze across the road. She didn't have a good view of the alley at all, beyond the parked cars, and could see nothing of the man now.

Easton banged the door shut and Dani stuck her hands in her pockets and casually walked towards the road. At least as casually as she could with her legs twitching with surging adrenaline.

Another problem was that her car was parked in the opposite direction to the alley. Surely the lurker would know as soon as

Dani turned right, rather than left onto the road, that she wasn't heading back to the car, but for them.

Nothing she could do about that. She moved out onto the pavement, headed straight between two parked cars and looked left and right up the road to make sure it was clear before crossing to the other side. A quick glance told her Easton was a few yards behind her. Hardly subtle, the way he was lagging.

Dani reached the pavement on the other side of the road and could now see the head of the alley, though no sign of the person who'd been there. Had they slunk further down, or already scarpered?

Dani picked up her pace a little. Her boots slid on the snowy surface, previous foot traffic having compacted parts of it to thick and glossy ice. Every step she took brought another sliver of the alley into view. Still no sign of the watcher.

Dani pushed her legs a little harder still, not far from a jog now. She reached the edge of the alley, her brain already filling with embarrassment at the thought of how she'd explain not just her jitteriness to Easton, but the fact she was perhaps seeing things too.

No. As she stood at the head of the alley and stared down, there he was. Twenty yards further on. Head down, hands in pockets, steadily walking away. Judging by the clothes, his large frame, and gait, Dani was sure it was a man. And he was just about to turn out of sight. The alley intersected two back-to-back rows of terraces, providing an entrance to the otherwise blocked-off backyards and the man was just reaching the next parallel street.

As he turned off to the right, he glanced back up towards Dani.

Then he ran.

'Easton, go around that way!' Dani shouted, pointing off to her right as she rushed forwards into the alley.

She moved into a sprint, though every other step her foot failed to gain traction and she skidded about, trying to stay on her feet. Rather than falling flat on her face, she pulled back a little, only adding to her frustration as she reached the end of the alley. Her eyes darted across the street she'd come out onto – an almost carbon copy of the one she'd just come from. The guy was thirty yards ahead now, almost at the main road just a few yards further ahead.

Dani had no choice. She gave it everything she'd got. Sprinted as fast as she could. As she passed the next road on her right there was Easton, almost in line with her. She'd hoped they'd be able to intercept the target, but no such luck, and they were soon running side by side down the middle of the road where at least the passing traffic had done a good job of clearing the snow, with two parallel grooves providing snow and ice-free tarmac to tread on.

'This is… nuts,' Easton said through laboured breaths.

Dani said nothing. She just wanted to catch up with this guy. Why was he spying on them at Liam Dunne's house? Could it even be Dunne himself?

They soon reached the intersection with the main road where traffic blasted in both directions. Rows of shops and takeaways and other small businesses lined both sides of the street, and the pavements were dotted with pedestrians.

Dani couldn't see the man anywhere. But there was another side street ten yards down.

'This way,' Dani said.

Picking her moment she darted across the road to the other side and turned into the street and stared down. There he was. Moving more casually again. He thought he'd lost them.

'You go that side,' Dani said, pointing across the street.

Easton nodded and moved to the opposite side of the road and Dani continued right behind the man.

He might have stopped running, but he was still clearly edgy, and it was only a few seconds later when he glanced over his shoulder and spotted Dani who was too slow in her attempt to duck behind a parked van. As soon as the man spotted her he jumped into action again, darting to his left, in between parked cars.

'Easton, he's coming to your side!'

Dani did the same, squeezing between two parked vans. The man was out of sight to her, and as she came into the road she stared down. Couldn't see him at all. Easton was there, the other side of the road, looking similarly bemused.

'You see him?' she said.

Easton shook his head.

'Keep going,' Dani told him.

She carried on along the middle of the road, now moving at a steady pace, though her body was primed and tense, ready to spring into action.

She was sure the man had moved in front of the blue Transit van a few vehicles in front. Was he hiding there?

'Anything?' she mouthed to Easton. Another shake of his head.

She reached the back end of the van and took cautious steps towards the front. Easton was still on the other side of the road, looking up and down.

Dani jumped out past the van's bonnet.

No one there.

'Dani, behind you!'

She swivelled and crouched but had no time to raise a defence as the dark blur rushed towards her. The object – a frozen plank? – smacked into the side of her head. The impact, together with her own momentum, sent her sprawling into the slush.

There was shouting and thudding as Easton raced over to her aid.

Dani shook her head and pulled herself onto her haunches. The man was racing away, back to the main street, Easton right behind him. The man darted left onto the busy road, just as a bus flashed past. Then came a cacophony of horns and tyres screeching and skidding on frozen ground. The man was already out of sight as a car slid into view, swerving viciously… right for Easton.

He jumped back but couldn't move quickly enough and the rear end of the car swiped Easton off his feet and knocked him flat on the ground.

'Easton!' Dani screamed as she hauled herself on to her feet.

The next couple of seconds passed agonisingly slowly as Easton lay unmoving on the ground, Dani hobbling towards him.

Then he flinched and raised his arm in the air. Gingerly, he propped himself up.

'I'm fine,' he groaned as pedestrians and bemused drivers closed in to check on him. 'I'm OK,' he said again as Dani reached him.

Although he didn't sound it, and his face was screwed-up in pain. And even if there was some doubt about Easton, Dani was absolutely sure about one thing: the man was gone.

Chapter 29

One of the many pedestrians at the scene called an ambulance, although the decision was perhaps a little premature, and it didn't arrive until five minutes after the first police squad car arrived from nearby Bloxwich Police Station. By that point it was clear there were no major injuries, and the officers were already in the midst of taking details of what had happened from bystanders and the drivers and passengers of the cars involved in the mêlée – which hadn't just included the vehicle that had side-swiped Easton, but two others which had shunted each other.

To Dani it was a lot of fuss about nothing, even if the scene had drawn quite a crowd of onlookers. But once the ambulance departed – empty – and soon after the squad cars, too, the street quickly returned to normal.

'You were lucky,' Dani said to Easton as he limped alongside her, back to her car.

'You too,' he said.

Her head was throbbing from the blow she'd taken, and they'd bagged the plank that she'd been hit with – a broken piece of a garden fence – as evidence. She had a lump on her forehead the size of a ping-pong ball, but there was no cut and she felt fine, even if she was a little woozy.

Easton would have a hefty bruise on his leg from the impact of the car, and on his arse from when he'd fallen backwards, but together their minor injuries were far less aggravating than the fact that the man they'd chased had got away.

'Who was he?' Dani said, not sure if the question was rhetorical or not.

She shivered as the words passed her lips, the chill this time not because of sinister thoughts, but because her clothes were sopping wet and freezing cold from her having been laid flat out in the slush. How she was desperate for a long, hot bath right now.

'More importantly,' Easton said, 'why was he spying on us? Do you think he was following us? Or already here?'

Dani had no clue, and wasn't even sure which scenario made the most sense.

Both cold and glum, they were soon back outside Liam Dunne's house.

'Had you finished?' Easton asked.

'Not really.' Though the thought of going back inside that place again, particularly now she was so uncomfortable in her cold, wet clothes, didn't exactly fill her with optimism. 'You find anything before?'

'Nothing.'

She thought back to the phone, which was still bagged up inside, and the picture from that red box of Liam with the mystery woman.

'Let's get back in,' she said. She'd just have to push through her discomfort. 'Get this finished, then be on our way.'

Easton nodded. 'Come on then.'

They spent less than twenty minutes more – though it felt far longer than that – before Dani decided she'd had enough. They left with nothing more than the phone, its charger, and the red box with its photograph and other curious tidbits. Bizarrely, they'd found no other photos of the woman anywhere, and it was intriguing that the only other pictures of any type in the house were largely family ones: Liam at various ages, some with parents, grandparents, with Clara. Just two with large groups of friends – all male – which looked to be from a lads' holiday from when Liam was a fresh-faced teenager. Certainly nothing, either by way of photos or other items, that suggested he had a girlfriend or partner.

'What else is in that box then?' Easton asked.

'Just bits and pieces. Nothing much that makes sense. A ring, a bracelet, some old coins. A passport photo of himself. A casino chip. A fridge magnet. A key.'

Easton sniffed.

'What?' Dani asked.

'What was the key for?'

'Haven't a clue.'

'And no sign of a computer or anything like that?'

'No,' Dani said.

'We could bag up more of the stuff in there. Just in case.'

'Just in case what?'

Easton shrugged. 'Feels like we're touching on something here, doesn't it?'

It did. But Dani really didn't know what.

'Let's work on figuring out who this woman is,' she said. 'As it stands we still know so little about Liam's life. She could be the one who breaks his story open.'

Easton didn't look convinced. 'So what now?' he said.

'Let's get back to HQ. Catch-up with the team.'

And get her own thinking back in order. There were so many strands to the investigation now – including figuring out who they'd just chased – that it was making her head permanently spin. Even without the blow she'd taken.

'But let's stop off at home before we do that,' Dani said. She looked Easton up and down. His clothes were as dirty and wet as hers. 'Both our homes.'

'Sounds like a damn good idea,' Easton said.

A damn good idea that they never got to follow through with, because they were still driving out of Walsall, heading back towards Sutton Coldfield, when a call came through on Dani's dashboard. A call from HQ.

Anticipation was already welling as Dani answered. It was DC Mutambe.

'We've managed to do some work on the phone that made the 999 call,' he said, his voice crackling through the car's speakers. 'We've had no luck tracing its current location, presumably because it's not been left on, so real-time GPS tracking has given us nothing so far. But we've had network data back from the phone masts. Old school triangulation.'

'You have a clear address?'

Dani knew from past experience that so-called triangulation was possible to varying degrees of accuracy. Sometimes a few metres, sometimes a few miles if looking at rural areas where there were naturally fewer masts to start with.

'Pretty damn close,' Mutambe said. 'Narrowed down to one of two houses.'

About as good as you could get.

'Local?' Easton asked.

'Wednesbury.'

'Give me the address,' Dani said. Sod the wet clothes. 'We're going there now.'

–

The two houses were all of thirty minutes' drive from where Dani had taken the call. She and Easton weren't the first to arrive. A patrol car plus a dog handler – arranged by Easton – had beaten them to it, though on his request they were waiting on an adjacent street. This wasn't a full-blown raid, but Dani had wanted back-up, just in case. That back-up would remain as nearby as they could while being out of sight, while Dani and Easton approached the houses.

The street, in Wednesbury, was long and twisting. The homes sat prominently on elevated verges either side: a collection of 1960s grey brick detached and semi-detached buildings, quite plain and box-like in their design.

Dani parked her car outside the two adjacent three-storey detached houses, numbers 23 and 25, and kept her eyes busy across the street as she and Easton stepped out.

The road and the pavements were quiet. With the time a little before three p.m., people were still at work and kids were still at school, Dani presumed, though she also got the feeling looking around that more than one of these buildings was unoccupied.

Dani headed up to the path that connected to the front doors for both 23 and 25 – two narrow but tall houses, mirror images of each other. A light was on in the downstairs front window of 23, but 25 had no signs of life at all.

Dani headed to 23 first. Easton hung back, milling.

After a quite lengthy wait, the door was answered at the first time of trying by a doddery man with a zimmer-frame. All of five feet tall he was gaunt and hunched, with tufts of frizzy grey hair and leathery skin and glasses that hung off the end of his nose.

After an introduction that took an age, it was soon apparent that the man, despite his hearing aid, could barely hear a word she said – old age, though, rather than a lifelong problem, she figured, largely because she could hear a radio blaring somewhere within. Dani was soon shouting nearly at the top of her voice to ask him even the most basic of questions: his name. Was he the owner? Did he live alone?

By the time she'd figured out the answers to all of those – which included some off-the-cuff comments about the postman and the weather and the prime minister – she was already sure this wasn't the house.

'Do you know who lives next door?' Dani asked for a third time.

'Next door?' the man said, himself shouting. He shook his head. 'Don't know them. Quiet folk. Never see or hear a thing from them.'

Dani wasn't sure whether to laugh at that or not.

'OK, sorry to trouble you,' she said to the old man.

'Pardon?'

'Thank you for your time,' she shouted.

'Oh. OK. Who were you again?' He looked a little put out now.

Dani sucked up her growing frustration and patiently went through much of the conversation a second time, trying to reassure the man that everything was fine – though was it? – and eventually she managed to convince him that he could go back inside and finish listening to his programme. He sheepishly shut the door and Dani turned to Easton who had a broad smirk plastered on his face.

'Yeah, very funny,' she said.

She moved across the connected path to the neighbouring property. None of the cars parked on the street seemed to belong to either of the houses, and as Dani knocked on the door and waited she stuck her face close to the frosted panes to gaze beyond. She could see no movement inside. Could see nothing much of anything.

There was no answer.

She looked back to Easton who was gazing up at the windows. 'You see anyone?'

He shook his head. Behind him a car was casually driving past. It parked up a few houses further along and Dani kept her eyes on it for a few seconds as Easton came up to her.

'What do you reckon?' he said.

Dani moved over to the front ground-floor window and peered inside. 'It's empty,' she said.

Easton came to her side. Beyond the glass, the room they were looking at – a plain box – was bare except for a cheap and worn carpet.

As Dani turned back around the car that had pulled over further along the street moments before was now steadily moving away into the distance.

Odd. She hadn't heard the car doors open or close to indicate anyone had got in or out. Given events earlier in the day she wasn't sure if her suspicion was warranted or not, but regardless, the car was already too far away to catch the plate, and she wasn't about to send out an alert over something so ambiguous.

'What do you think?' Easton said.

'I think we should get inside,' Dani said. 'As far as I'm concerned we have enough evidence to enter.'

Easton didn't look convinced, but he didn't protest either.

Dani looked around then grabbed a rock from the small and overgrown front garden and moved back over to the front door. She smashed the stone against one of the double-glazed panes. It cracked, but didn't shatter – safety glass. It took a second and then a third hit before the glass had crumbled to granular chunks, though was still held in place. Dani used the rock to knock the whole pane inward and it crunched to the floor.

Dani reached inside and levered down the latch and held her breath as she pushed open the door. No alarm.

She stepped inside.

'Hello. It's the police!' Dani shouted.

Nothing from inside at all. No voices, no creaks or strains.

The narrow hallway Dani was standing in was as bare as the front room, with the same cheap carpet. There were no pictures on the walls, nothing really, not even any sign – a dirty outline – to suggest there ever had been anything on the walls.

But there was a smell. Bleach and cleaner that was doing a lacklustre job of masking a stale and musky odour. Tobacco and weed smoke, Dani thought she could make out too.

'Tell the back-up to get over here,' Dani said. 'They can at least help us sweep this place.'

Dani and Easton had cleared the ground floor by the time the yellow-jacketed officers were walking up the path. They'd found nothing. The downstairs consisted of two plain and empty box-like rooms plus a galley kitchen whose cheap units were worn and battered. No appliances remained. Not a thing in the cupboards. Including dust. It was obvious this place had been cleaned, top to bottom.

The next two floors each contained three bedrooms and a single small and cheaply arranged bathroom.

'What the hell is going on here?' Easton said as they congregated on the top landing. He and Dani had been in and out of each of the rooms, finding absolutely nothing. No furniture, no belongings, no curtains on the windows. Faint indents in the hard carpets gave an impression of the furniture that had previously been in place, but there was nothing here at all now.

'We should at least get Forensics to go from top to bottom,' Easton said.

And Dani agreed with that. Even a solitary fingerprint could prove useful.

What had happened here?

'We need to find out who owns this place, too,' she said. 'Same for next door.'

'The old man?'

'No chances. I'm not saying he's involved, but right now there's every chance that the emergency call came from someone inside that house. A visitor, whatever. Even if they were calling about something that they'd overheard in here.'

'Fair point,' Easton said. 'Are we done here then?'

Standing on the landing, Dani mulled Easton's question as she thought back over each of the basic and drab rooms they'd just been through.

She frowned.

'Come on,' she said.

'We're going?'

'Not quite.'

She moved down the stairs to the middle floor, then over to the bedroom at the back of the house. She stopped at the doorway and stared inside.

'Why's this one different?' Dani said.

Easton shrugged.

Dani's eyes fixed on the carpet. The whole house was decked out in carpets that were a variety of the same theme. Beige or brown, tight and hard short-pile. Hard-wearing, long-lasting for a relatively cheap price, even if they weren't exactly good-looking or sumptuous to the touch. The kind of carpets that landlords used in cheap accommodation. The carpet in this room was exactly the same type. Yet it was also noticeably different.

'You don't see it?' Dani said.

Actually, it looked like he did. He nodded. 'No outlines.'

'Nothing,' Dani said. 'So either there was no furniture in here, it was never used at all—'

'Or the carpet was only put down after this place was cleared out.'

Dani knelt down and yanked the edge of the carpet up. She pulled the edge back a couple of feet to reveal similarly new-looking hardboard beneath, tacked onto the original floorboards. A cheap way of levelling a suspended floor for carpet, but was there another reason here?

'This is the room,' Dani said.

'The room?'

'The room where Jane Doe was killed.'

Chapter 30

Ana knew that Victor, Alex and the others were all downstairs. She could hear their muffled voices, could almost feel the anger vibrating through the fabric of the warehouse. She desperately wanted to know what they were saying. She'd already tried the door, hoping to sneak out into the hall and to the broom cupboard, but it was locked. Was she not even trusted when they were in the same building as her now?

That worried her more than she cared to admit.

She knew something big had happened since Saturday night. Something bad. Bad for Victor at least. Even though he hadn't said anything to her directly, she'd managed to glean some of the details: the fact that Victor's two goons, carrying Maria's body in their van, had been stopped by the police. Even though they'd got away from the scene, they'd left behind their van, together with the body.

From what Ana could tell, Victor was more incensed than he was scared of the possible repercussions of the police closing in. The two goons had now gone into hiding. Apparently they didn't trust their boss not to just slit their throats and send their bodies off to wherever it was Maria had been en route to.

Victor had been in a rage ever since. Together with Jim, there were three men out there whose blood he wanted, plus he was – quite rightly – convinced the police had been tipped off somehow. Which was why that house in Wednesbury had seen not just a deep clean in the murder room, but had been entirely cleaned out since Saturday night.

All because of Ana. And she really wasn't sure how that made her feel. Powerful? Or infinitely small, alone and vulnerable?

There was banging downstairs then thudding footsteps coming up. Ana spread herself out on the sofa and grabbed her book from the coffee table.

She kept her eyes on the pages as the door was unlocked and opened and Victor and then Alex strode in.

'Not to mention the lost customers and the contents of their wallets,' Alex said, mid-sentence. Ana felt she got the gist of what that meant. 'I've already been getting calls from some of our fixers, telling us it's not good enough. That if we've not got the supply back up soon then we're out of the loop for good.'

'If it comes to that then we go back to the start,' Victor said, angry, though strangely untroubled. 'I built this business the hard way. I'm not afraid to do the same again.'

He was speaking with his fists clenched and Ana felt she knew what he meant. Violence. He'd built his business off violence.

'What the fuck are you looking at?' Alex said, glaring at Ana.

Ana shrugged, trying to stay as calm as she could. 'Sounds like you've got problems.'

Victor huffed. 'Problems? And what, my sweet, do you think could be the cause of the problems?'

'A lack of loyalty,' Ana said, glancing from Alex to Victor. 'There's no other explanation, is there?'

Alex shot daggers at her, as though he wasn't sure if she was pinning the blame on him or not. It did intrigue Ana to think who Victor cared more about. Her or Alex.

'Loyalty?' Victor said. 'There's no such thing.'

Alex looked a little put out by that. To be honest, Ana was a bit surprised by the comment too.

'I don't need loyalty,' Victor said. 'All I need is fear. My enemies have to know the price of deceiving me. And believe me, Ana, they will.'

He held her gaze, both of them unblinking until the tension became too unbearable and Ana looked back to her book.

'We might be gone a while,' Victor said.

He grabbed his coat and keys and headed back for the door.

'How long?' Ana said, getting to her feet.

He didn't answer.

'You can't lock me in here all night! There's no food. No toilet!'

Victor said nothing more as he walked out, followed by Alex who slammed the door shut before locking it. Ana ran over, tried the handle, rattled the door, banged on it and shouted out to them. No response as they trudged away. Moments later there was a bang down below as they left the warehouse.

All alone – again – Ana was as scared as she was angry. She paced around the room. What was Victor doing?

Did he already know?

For more than two hours Ana's mind was in turmoil as the warehouse lay silent below. She was tired, thirsty, hungry. There was no food in the room at all. The only drinks were a now empty bottle of Coke and several bottles of spirits.

Eventually it was the Coke bottle she used when she couldn't hold her bladder any longer.

All the while, with her brain rattling away, her eyes would flick back and forth to her neatly folded coat.

Why had she even brought the damn phone here? She should have dumped it the second after she'd made that call on Saturday night. The device was nothing but a noose around her neck now.

With tension rising inexplicably with every tick, she took the clock off the wall. Took out its battery. She didn't even want to know the time. Didn't want to know how long it was, how slowly the seconds and minutes and hours were passing.

Yet tension continued to build with each beat of her heart.

Eventually she'd had enough. She couldn't just sit there forever.

She moved over to her coat. Knelt down, her hands trembling as she laid it out on her lap. She reached into the hole in the seam. Her two fingers felt about, pincering as she tried to grasp the phone. Each time her fingers met, skin on skin, the hole in her chest grew. Yet she continued in vain, because she couldn't bear to face the reality.

The reality. That the stolen phone – her solace as much as it was her death warrant – was no longer there.

In a panic she whipped her fingers out, refolded the coat as her brain erupted with conflicting thoughts. She tried to piece together her movements. When had she last seen the phone? When had she last held it? When had she last felt its form against her side as she walked?

She couldn't clearly find the answers. None of it made any sense.

There was a click and a clunk and the door opened. Ana's heart lurched as she spun around. She hadn't heard them come into the warehouse at all. Had they sneaked in or had she just been too all-consumed?

Victor strode across the room, away from Ana. Alex shut the door behind him then stood across it, arms folded.

'You're back,' Ana said, her eyes not leaving Victor as he walked over to the bookcase.

'Vic?'

He said nothing. Ana's eyes darted around the room. Looking for what? A means of escape. A weapon? What was she supposed to do now?

Victor reached up, stuck his hand between two lever arch files. He pulled out the small black object, a thin lead trailing behind it.

He didn't need to say what it was.

He turned around, the tiny CCTV camera in his hand. His face sullen yet almost sorrowful.

Neither Victor nor Alex said a word. None were needed.

Victor knew. He knew everything. Ana had walked right into this.

She shook her head in despair. 'I'm sorry!' she screamed.
'No,' Alex said. 'But you will be.'
He lurched towards her.

Chapter 31

Dani's head was down, her eyes scanning the screen in front of her so intently that she was barely aware of her surroundings, when the voice grabbed her attention.

'Good morning.'

She shot up to see McNair hovering over her desk.

'Early start, eh?' McNair said before taking a sip from her takeaway coffee.

'Couldn't sleep,' Dani said. She glanced at the clock on the computer screen. Seven fifteen. She'd been in the office since a little after six. The world outside the windows remained pitch black, a newly erected plastic Christmas tree twinkled in front of the glass. Who'd put that there since yesterday morning?

'The trial keeping you up?' McNair asked.

'Not really.' Which was bizarre now that Dani reflected. She'd barely even thought about Damian Curtis or her brother since she'd left court yesterday.

'They're expecting the verdict this morning,' McNair said. For the first time she had Dani's full attention, though her boss looked a little confused. 'I assumed that's why you were in so early. To catch up before you went over there.'

'I will if I can,' Dani said.

McNair frowned and shook her head. 'I was planning to be there myself, to speak to the press as much as anything else, but I'm not sure I've the time now. I'm sure you'll more than comfortably take my place.'

'Of course.' Dani nodded, though she was still only half listening. McNair muttered something as she wandered over to her office.

Dani got back to what she was doing, which was mostly staring at her computer screen, unsure where to go next. There was so much information being thrown into the HOLMES system for the investigation that Dani was struggling to make any sense of it. Forensics, post-mortem, CCTV, background checks, immigration records, interviews, phone records, financial records, the swathes of data were growing exponentially every day. Dani wondered whether perhaps everything they needed to crack the case wide open was right there in front of her, if she could just view it all in the right order.

Before she knew it, with her head down and swimming, the office had steadily filled: Easton, Constable, Grayling, Mutambe; all the key members of the investigation team.

She went to see Constable first.

'Any luck with CCTV?' she asked him as she grabbed a spare chair and scooted over to his desk. He looked a little put out by her accosting him when he was still yet to finish off his pain au raisin and flat white.

He sighed and put down his half-eaten pastry 'There's a lot going on,' he said as he clicked into neatly arranged folders. 'This isn't all in HOLMES yet as I'm still working through it, but I am starting to narrow down some areas of interest.'

He clicked open several video files without playing any of them and then scribbled some nonsensical note onto his pad.

'So, for Clara Dunne's crime scene, the nearest towers we have are two streets away to the east, and the next street along to the west, though actually they're about the same distance from her house. Going east there is a way to get past that camera and then further blackspots that could get you pretty much all the way to the motorway, but someone would have to be seriously prepared—'

'I think we have to assume they were prepared. Given the nature of her death.'

'Well, yeah, but... anyway. On the day of her murder, I've picked up her friend, Mrs Neita, walking past the tower on Bridle Road at nine thirty-eight.' He brought up the video and played the seven-second snapshot. 'I'm pretty sure that's her there. Clothing and basics match.'

Although there wasn't a crystal clear shot of her face, Dani agreed that it certainly looked like Bianca Neita.

'Timing is consistent with her making the 999 call. I didn't see anything else of her approaching Ms Dunne's home within a few days prior to that.'

'So her story seems to stack up then? At least in relation to her going there that morning, and finding the body.'

'I guess so.'

'Anyone else stick out?'

'No one on foot who looked particularly suspicious to me, but then we don't exactly have anything much to work with in that regard.'

Dani huffed. She guessed he was right.

'But I do have this,' Constable said.

He pulled up another file and pressed play. The same CCTV tower, a couple of hours before. A blue van, that looked exactly like—

'The same van we found Jane Doe in?' Dani said, heart racing.

Constable didn't look convinced. 'It is the same type, a Vauxhall Combo, same colour too, but the registration is different. And this registration is legit. Belongs to a guy named Clarence Yardley. From what I found from a quick search he's a local plumber.'

'Have you followed up with him?'

'Not with him directly, but there was a stolen vehicle report for that van two weeks ago, filed by Mr Yardley.'

'So it *was* his van then? That was used to transport Jane Doe?'

Constable turned his hands out. 'We'd have to check VINs but it's possible.'

It was more than possible, Dani thought. It was highly likely. Highly likely that the same people, in the same van, had killed both Clara Dunne and Jane Doe. Or, at least, had been trans-porting Jane Doe's body.

Dani explained about the address in Wednesbury, where the 999 call had come from. 'I need you to track that van, on whichever plate, as much as you can over the last two weeks. Concentrate on every one of our locations of interest. In particular we need to figure out who's been driving it. Also, look further along the A5. Have they been up there before? I don't just want to know where they'd come from that night with Jane Doe, but where they were heading to.'

'You got it.'

'Now you can enjoy your breakfast.'

Dani winked at him then got up. She looked over to Easton's desk. Empty. She checked her watch. She'd expected him in by now.

DC Grayling was in, however, so Dani went over to her next.

'Doing the rounds?' Grayling said with a forced smile.

'Got to keep on top.'

'You want an update on surveillance, I'm guessing?'

'Please.'

'Very little to tell,' Grayling said, her face looking as bored as she sounded. As though she'd been given the rough end of a bad deal. 'It's only been twenty-four hours, though, so what would you expect?'

'Twenty-four hours of information?'

Grayling didn't seem to know how to take that.

'The protocol we've got is that the teams are to call me immediately if they see anything suspicious,' she said. 'But other than that they're to send me a daily written report. Two shifts per day for each location. Six reports, seventy-two hours of information. A lot of reports about not a lot.'

She opened one up – a detailed timeline of events at Victor Nistor's warehouse – and scrolled through it at lightning speed, as if to prove a point of just how long it was, and how dull it was to be reviewing it.

'So give me the highlights of yesterday,' Dani said.

Grayling sighed as though she felt put out. Dani was becoming less and less impressed by the second. Not just because of the attitude but because this was so unlike Grayling. She was normally keen and upbeat.

Everyone had their problems outside of work, Dani mused. Perhaps that was it, though she wouldn't ask. Not straight off the bat, at least.

'There really wasn't much going on.' Grayling took a few seconds now to scan through the file more closely. 'I'm still waiting on the reports from the second shift, but basically… nothing at all happened at Brigitta Popescu's home. The only person who came at all, other than the postman, was the helper. She was in and out within an hour.'

That reminded Dani, she still wanted to catch up with Stef. Though preferably not at Brigitta's house. Dani would avoid ever going back there again if she could.

'Over at Nistor's house, pretty much the same,' Grayling said. 'He and Ana Crisan left at just after ten a.m., together. They arrived at the warehouse an hour later.'

'An hour? It's a ten-minute drive?'

'Maybe they got breakfast?'

Was it worth checking CCTV towers to see if they could trace the movement more fully? Probably not at this stage.

'Nistor remained inside for pretty much the whole day. Plenty of people coming and going. There's full details here. Descriptions of the people, their vehicles, registration numbers.' Grayling sighed. 'A lot of information telling us very little.'

'I think you said that already. So Ana and Victor didn't leave all day?'

'Ana didn't. Victor… well, he did and he didn't.'

'What does that mean?'

'Seems sometime in the afternoon, Crisan and his partner Alexander Stelea, came out of the warehouse but they literally just stood there, had a smoke, then went and sat in Crisan's car, on the forecourt.'

'For how long?'

'A couple of hours.'

'That makes no sense.'

Grayling shrugged. 'I'm just saying what I see.'

'And then what?'

'Then they both went back inside. About thirty minutes later the three of them came back out.'

'With Ana this time?'

'Yeah. They got into Stelea's car and drove off together.'

Dani leaned in to read the record for herself. 'It says she looked hesitant,' Dani said. 'And Victor was holding on to her.'

'Lover's tiff?' Grayling said.

'Did they go home?'

'It's not clear yet. The second shift started about an hour and a half after this.'

'They hadn't returned home by that point?'

'No.'

'Then can you find out when they did?'

Grayling looked at her watch. 'The night shift literally finished half an hour ago.'

'Please can you find out?' Dani said, more sternly now.

Grayling sighed. 'I'll do my best.'

'And if you need help from Constable in tracking Stelea's car, then get it.'

More than a little frustrated with Grayling's attitude, Dani headed back over to her own desk. Just before nine a.m. For some reason McNair's earlier comments were now worming into Dani's mind and as much as she tried to get back into her work, her thoughts had been sidelined.

No. It was no use. She had to know. She had to be there.

Before she left she made a call to Easton. Even if she was tied up for the next couple of hours, there was plenty he could be getting on with, particularly from their outing yesterday. They still had to follow up with Forensics for starters, not to mention making a start on identifying Liam Dunne's mystery woman, and what had happened at the abandoned house in Wednesbury.

The call went straight to voicemail. She left him a message then put the phone away and thought for a few moments. Where the hell was he?

Her dilemma was genuine.

Still, Easton's punctuality problem would have to wait. She needed to go.

She grabbed her coat and flung it on as she strode for the door.

Chapter 32

For the first time after several weeks of the trial, there were TV vans and news crews lining the road outside the Crown Court. Dani kept her head down as she walked past them all. Luckily the reporters and crews were still in the process of getting themselves set up and no one took any notice of her as she edged through. Perhaps on her way out she could find a back entrance. She really didn't want to say anything to the press today, regardless of the verdict.

Dani once again seated herself in the public gallery, which was fuller today than it had been at any point during proceedings to date. No sign of Damian Curtis once again. Dani had been unsure whether perhaps he'd be brought out ceremoniously – or was it unceremoniously – for the verdict. No point, she guessed. The jury had made their minds up now, so his presence here, whatever state he was in, would have no bearing. He'd have to hear about his fate after everyone else. Dani felt a little sorry for him because of that, even if he was a killer. Albeit a killer who she still firmly believed had been grievously coerced into killing.

She would soon find out if the jury agreed.

'Have the members of the jury reached a verdict?' the judge asked the foreman – a middle-aged lady in a headscarf who was on her feet with a piece of paper rattling in her nervous grip.

'Yes.'

'On the charge of aggravated assault and aggravated kidnapping, how do you find the defendant?'

'Guilty.'

The charges against Curtis for his attack on Sophie Blackwood, an entirely innocent victim in what was otherwise a concocted scheme of revenge, were perhaps the most straightforward, and ones which had been barely argued by either side.

'On the chargers of murder, five counts in total, how do you find the defendant?'

'Not guilty.'

There were uneasy murmurs and mutters from around the room now, particularly from those around the CPS team who were looking all the more nervous.

'On the alternative charge of manslaughter by reason of diminished responsibility, five counts in total, how do you find the defendant?'

'Guilty.'

There were ructions from all around Dani now. Family members of the victims perhaps, angry that Curtis had 'got away with it'? Dani noted a strange exchange between Barker and O'Hare too. The two turned to each other and there was a mutual almost nonchalant nod from each of them, as though both were satisfied with the result.

Dani had seen enough. She slunk out. If she was quick, she could make it past the cameras before they even realised the court had been dismissed.

–

Only one TV interviewer, from BBC Midlands, tried to accost Dani as she made her escape. She politely declined to comment, indicating that she was sure DCI McNair would be providing a formal statement shortly. A white lie which had the desired effect of diverting the interviewer's attention back to the doors of the courthouse. How long would she wait there now for McNair to emerge?

Well, it wasn't as if Dani had specifically said that McNair would make her statement – which was sure to follow – from that particular spot, was it?

Dani was soon past the swarm and was able to start to digest what she'd just witnessed. No murder conviction. That was a good thing, wasn't it? Manslaughter by reason of diminished responsibility. Insanity as the press would surely term it. Damian Curtis would almost certainly now spend the foreseeable future, possibly even the rest of his life, in a secure mental facility. Exactly where he belonged, as far as Dani was concerned. Curtis wasn't a good person. He was violent, he was unhinged and Dani hoped he would never be allowed back onto the streets again. But she also still firmly believed that prison was not the right place for him, and even more crucially that he'd been horrifically played into killing. Worked up into a frenzy from which his fragile mind was unable to make sense. The court had heard time and again how Dr Helen Collins was the person who'd done that.

It remained down to Dani now to prove that theory wrong, and finally get the justice that Curtis and his victims deserved.

She took out her phone as she walked. Still no response from Easton, and just the first signs of doubt were creeping into Dani's mind now as to what was going on with him. She sent him a text. She was happy doing this next step alone, but the longer he remained incommunicado, the more annoyed she was becoming, given the crucial point they were at in their investigation.

She walked the short distance across the city to Brindley-place. With the sun out today, and the temperature a balmy four degrees, most of the previous day's snow, particularly in the city, had already melted. Even at mid-morning the Christmas market, which she had to navigate through on her way, was in full swing. The smell of sizzling wurst and steaming glühwein carried through the air with every step.

Maybe she'd make a stop-off on her way back over to HQ later.

The man she was due to meet, Henry Welter, was already waiting for her outside the coffee shop. Short and wiry, he looked jittery and shivery and greeted Dani with a limp hand-shake and a mouthful of overly white teeth.

'Mr Welter? I'm DI Stephens,' Dani said, releasing his clammy hand. 'Sorry I'm a bit late.'

'Actually, I was a little early,' he said, his voice nasal, capping off his geeky appearance perfectly.

'Shall we go inside?'

He nodded and they headed in and Dani bought them both a drink – a black coffee for her and a skinny latte for him. They took a table in the front, by the window looking out onto a fountain which looked bedraggled and sorry for itself, all drained of water for the winter.

'I recognised your name,' Welter said as he took a sip from his milky drink. 'I remember your brother.'

Dani nodded but didn't say anything to that.

'He was so… normal.' Welter's cheeks reddened at his lack-lustre description.

'How long have you worked at Ellis Associates?' Dani asked.

'Oh, many years. Since 2002.'

Which would place him at about forty, if he'd been a graduate then. He didn't look a day over thirty, his hair was neat and thick and full of colour, his skin blemish free. Perhaps some newfangled diet kept him thin as a rake. Dani ought to try it.

'What do you remember of James Alden?' she asked.

Welter looked quizzical. Dani could tell from the shake of his torso that his foot was tapping furiously. Nerves or just a curious habit?

'James was an interesting character,' he said. 'I get a sense of people very quickly.' He said this as though it made him infinitely profound. 'I might be seen as something of an intro-vert, but that doesn't mean I don't understand others. James was a very intriguing proposition.'

'Intriguing how?'

'Ellis is a big company, we get all sorts, from super intellec-tuals to – for want of a better phrase – wide boys. The strange thing is that to some extent, both ends of that spectrum fit perfectly well with consultancy. But with James… the best way to describe it is that he didn't fit. He didn't fit in the sense that I don't think he really wanted to be here. I worked with him closely on Reflow, and it wasn't that he wasn't capable. He was smart and everything else, but he just didn't seem to *need* to be here. If that makes sense?'

'Not massively.'

'Like it was all a play for something else.'

Dani thought back to what she knew of Liam Dunne. The inheritance windfall. Did that explain what Welter was saying?

'Do you know why James left Ellis Associates?' Dani asked.

Welter looked confused. 'Of course. Don't you?'

'Perhaps you could explain what you know.'

'It was because he lied. Simple as that. He lied about his CV. About everything. His education, his past employment. I was part of the disciplinary investigation.'

'And what did you find? About who he really was? Why he lied?'

He shook his head. 'We found nothing. We contacted his school, university, his past employers. No one had ever heard of him, had ever seen his picture even. But he never said a word to us about any of it. We never got an explanation. It was all very bizarre. We did notify HMRC of this, too, obviously, because we were paying taxes for him but God knows if he was even properly registered.'

'You never found that out?'

'That wasn't something I was involved in, to be honest.'

'Do you know how the disciplinary even started?' Dani asked. 'Obviously his CV wasn't checked when he came into the business otherwise he never would have got the job? So what happened?'

'We had a tip-off.'

'A tip-off? From inside the firm or outside?'

Welter looked uncomfortable now. He clearly knew the answer.

'I'm really not sure I can say, it was a confidential matter.'

Dani huffed, shook her head as though she'd never heard anything so ridiculous in her whole life.

'You do realise this is a murder investigation,' Dani said, as hard as she could. 'I'm sure a man as intelligent as you can understand the repercussions of withholding evidence.'

The combination of both attack and flattery seemed to do the trick.

'OK, I mean I'm sure there's no real harm in me saying this to you now, given events since.'

Dani frowned. 'What do you mean?'

'I mean, the tip-off we had, about James Alden lying, about him not being who he said he was. It came from within the team. It came from your brother.'

Chapter 33

'Ben?'

'Yes.'

'Who did he report this to?'

'To me, actually. And I immediately went to Rottweiler... I mean, Harvey. Mr Forster.'

'What did he say exactly?'

'Mr Forster?'

'No, Ben. To you.'

'Exactly? You'd have to check the personnel records. You have those, don't you?'

Dani avoided an eye-roll. 'They're on the way, I'm sure.'

'Oh, right. Well, let me think. Now, don't take this as verbatim, but it was along the lines of, *did you know Alden is lying to us all? He's not even who he says he is. Everything on his CV is a lie. He shouldn't be here.* Something like that, I think. It's been a while, though it was quite a revelation.'

'Ben said this? To you?'

Welter nodded. He looked even more nervous now than before.

'Do you know what prompted that?'

'What prompted it? As in, how did Ben know? Or why did he choose to tell us at that point?'

'Isn't that the same thing? He chose to tell you because he knew, surely.'

Welter looked really uneasy now. Like they were skirting around something and he wasn't sure he was supposed to be talking about it or not.

'Sorry,' Dani said. 'Let's take a step back. Why do you think Ben chose to tell you?'

'I thought... there'd been an incident.'

'Between Ben and James?'

Welter nodded. 'Over a girl. A woman, a woman.'

'They had an argument?'

'Yes.'

'Who was the woman?' Dani fished in her pocket, took out her phone and found the photo she'd taken of the picture of Liam and the blonde woman. 'Her?'

'I've never seen her before.'

'You're sure?'

'Positive. But James was something of a ladies man. You know the type?'

'Try me.'

'OK, look, back in the day, I was younger back then—'

'I think we all were.'

'Believe it or not I was a bit of a party animal, at times—'

Dani didn't believe it in the slightest, but she didn't bother to say it.

'—and we were a close-knit team. Friday nights in the pubs and clubs, sometimes during the week too if we had something to celebrate. James, he had more than one woman come out with him. Tina. Emma.' He looked up as if racking his brain. 'I think those were the names anyway. Maybe others. They came and went.'

'And this was over the course of what? Ten, eleven months?'

'I know, right? That's the way he was. Except this one time, we were having a leaving party. He came alone that night. It was literally the following Monday that Ben came to me. I had to take what happened that night into consideration for the disciplinary, you see?'

Dani couldn't care less about the disciplinary. 'What happened?'

'There was a bit of a... ruckus.'

'Ben and James.'

'Ben and James to start with. A few others got involved too. We all got turfed out of the bar... Gino's or something. About ten of us.'

'But what were they fighting about?'

'You can't just take my word for it, because I was drunk. We all were. And James denied it. Denied it strongly. But...' He scratched his head and frowned as though he couldn't quite recollect properly. 'I saw it. I think. And Ben... we thought we'd lost him for the night, but he reappeared out of nowhere, all in a rage. Not at James, not to start with at least, but at her.'

'Her?'

Welter looked really confused now. As though he couldn't understand why Dani still didn't get it.

'They were all over each other. Her and James. Not just kissing, but I mean, *really* hands on. Up her skirt, over her bra. On the dancefloor. James and—'

Shit. Now Dani got it.

'Gemma?'

Chapter 34

Dani stormed through the Christmas market, which was far busier now than just a short while earlier. She bumped and jostled past the punters too slow to get out of her way. Her phone was plastered to her ear as she went. She'd called Easton two more times since leaving Welter. No answer. Had called Gemma five times now. No answer.

Finally, she did pick up.

'You lied,' Dani said.

'Dani? What's going on?'

'Why the fuck would you do that? You lied to me. Why? To protect Ben?'

'How dare you—'

'Just tell me why. What, were you so embarrassed because you had some guy with his hands all over you on a dancefloor? Was that it?'

Gemma hung up.

'Idiot.'

Dani gritted her teeth in anger. She'd catch up with her sister-in-law soon enough. And maybe it was better if she was calmer when that happened. Yet she still couldn't understand why Gemma had lied to her about not knowing Liam Dunne – or James Alden or whoever the hell he'd been called that week. He and Gemma had kissed. Ben and Liam had got into a fight over her. Did she not realise how serious this investigation was? It was far more important than saving face because of a drunken escapade six years ago, and despite what Dani had initially said to Gemma, it was surely far more likely that that was the reason why she'd lied, than because she was trying to protect Ben.

Ben. Dani needed to see him now. As soon as possible. Ever since she'd first laid eyes on that picture at Clara's house of the Project Reflow team, the picture with Ben in it, Dani had wondered whether his knowing Liam Dunne was more than just coincidence.

She dialled Easton's phone again. Straight to voicemail. Dani growled under her breath. Of all the days for him to do this…

Her phone vibrated in her hand. She fully expected it to be Easton and was ready to give him a piece of her mind. No, it was HQ.

'DI Stephens?' she said as she answered.

'It's Claire.' DC Grayling. 'I managed to get the reports from the night-shift surveillance.'

'Thank you,' Dani said, even if she didn't really sound thankful, but that wasn't Grayling's fault. Much.

'It's not… I don't know if this is a problem or not. But Ana Crisan never arrived home last night.'

'How do you mean?'

'The car that she and Nistor and Stelea left the warehouse in, it did turn up last night, back at Nistor's house. About ten p.m. But Ana wasn't with them. And she hasn't been seen since.'

Dani felt an ominous lump in her throat. The startling news was all she needed to help push her anger aside. An unwelcome tonic. 'We need to find her. Get whatever help you need. Find out where that car went after leaving the warehouse.'

'I'm on it.'

'I'll be back with you in a couple of minutes.'

Dani ended the call. From what she knew of Ana and Victor, this was seriously bad news. They had to find Ana.

She turned onto Colmore Row. HQ was just the other end of the road. Her phone vibrated again. Easton, finally.

'About bloody time,' she said to herself before she answered. 'Where the hell are you?'

'Erm, is this DI Stephens?' came a nervy-sounding male voice she didn't recognise.

That same ominous lump in her throat was back, although this time it was almost choking.

'Yes.'

'I'm afraid there's been an incident. With DS Easton. You need to get here right away.'

Chapter 35

There's been an incident… you need to get here right away.

Every day of her working life – and many days in her private life too – Dani dealt with violence, with death, sometimes with the macabre. So what was she supposed to think when she heard those words?

Had Victor attacked? Had Curtis somehow escaped his secure hospital and restarted his vengeful rampage?

Was Ben somehow behind whatever had happened?

Dani couldn't bear the thought of any of those scenarios. Easton wasn't just a colleague, he was the closest thing to a friend she had, and on hearing those words come through the phone, from Easton's number, she'd fully expected the worst. Her legs had gone weak. She'd barely been able to speak.

Thankfully, at least the officer using Easton's phone was more with it, and had succinctly explained the situation as best he could before the call ended.

Still, Dani had immediately rushed for her car and blasted down the Aston Expressway towards Sutton Coldfield. Thankfully she was already feeling less distressed when she turned on to Easton's street to see the flashing blue lights of two police cars outside his house, and a small number of curious bystanders, as ever when there were emergency vehicles on call.

Dani parked her car at the bumper of one of the patrol cars and an officer came to greet her as she stepped out.

'DI Stephens?' he said.

'Yes.' She held out her hand to him.

'PC Banks. We spoke on the phone.'

'Where is he?'

'Easton? Or the other one?'

'Both.'

'Easton's in the back of my car, over there. The other guy, Wesley or something, has already been shipped off to A&E.'

'Let me speak to Easton.'

Banks didn't look too sure about that. 'I don't know how this should work. I mean, I called you because he kept insisting, and I know who you are and everything, but right now he's under caution for—'

'Then I'll speak to him under caution.'

Dani didn't wait for another response. She strode over to the car. She could see Easton, sullen-faced, head down, in the back seat. Another officer was standing guard on the outside. Dani moved around to the far side and indicated for Banks to unlock the car. Dani opened the door and sank down into the seat next to her colleague.

He wouldn't meet her eye. His head remained bowed, his hands cuffed behind him.

'Some mess,' Dani said.

Easton huffed.

'Give it to me straight. No bullshit.'

'She can go fuck herself. I'm done with her.'

'Sod your feelings towards your sister, Easton, just tell me what happened, so I can see if I can sort this crap out.'

He glanced at her briefly before looking out of his window. His left eye was swollen and turning black, and there was blood caked in his nostrils.

'She's in there now. Lording it as though it's her place. As though she has some right to it. She thinks she can do what she wants.'

'Are you going to tell me or not?' Dani's impatience was clear.

'You know what it's been like,' Easton said, looking back to her. 'I've pretty much been Dad to those kids the last few months while she's out living some sort of party-hard Z-list celebrity fantasy life.'

'That still doesn't explain why you're sitting in the back of a patrol car with your hands cuffed and your face smashed up.'

'She brought this bloke home. Night before last.'

'Wesley?'

He looked a little surprised that Dani knew the name. 'She's known him for years. Wouldn't even surprise me if he's the dad to one of those kids. Not that he'd give a damn about that.' He paused. 'It's my house, Dani. I'm not going to have my house, my life turned upside down by people like that.'

'You got in a fight with him?'

'He was shouting at Jasmin. Screaming at her for taking too long in the bathroom. That's what kicked it off. Emily took *his* side. Can you believe it? Both of them having a go at an eleven-year-old girl, nearly frothing at the mouth. This was last night. I told them both to leave. They did. Then they turned up drunk, falling all over the place this morning. About seven a.m. Woke me and the kids up. They were arguing with each other.'

He shook his head in disgust.

'And then?'

'The shouting, the screaming, the swearing, got worse and worse. When I came down he had his hands around Em's throat. So I grabbed him and turfed him out. Spent the next two hours – in between getting the kids to school – trying to console her, trying to tell her it was all right, that she needed to ditch arseholes like that. Obviously she's having none of it, thinks I overreacted, that I shouldn't interfere. Then Wesley comes back, banging on the door. Demanding to see her. And...' He shrugged. 'That's when it happened.'

'What happened, exactly?'

'She opened the door to him. He stormed in, all in a rage again. He grabbed her again. I went to get him off her. And... it's my house, Dani.'

'You beat the crap out of him.'

He humphed. 'He hit me first. Even if no one else believes me, that's the way it was.'

Dani held his gaze for a few moments now. Yes, she did believe him.

'Let me go and see what I can do,' Dani said.

She stepped back out and after a brief interlude with Banks she headed inside to see Easton's sister, who was on the sofa being consoled by a female PC. Dani introduced herself as a detective but didn't make a point of saying she was Easton's colleague, then spent a few minutes getting Emily's version of events.

Which was much like Easton's, except for the fact that she was a bit more cagey about Wesley's role in the whole thing. No mention of him ranting and raging. No mention of him grabbing her by the throat, although her neck was definitely reddened. No mention of Wesley returning and storming in. Just that the two men had got into a fight. But she didn't throw Easton under the bus completely. Perhaps because she knew if she did, then Easton would turf her out for good. She couldn't afford to ruin the good thing she had going living here rent-free.

What a piece of work she was. Dani felt all the more sorry for Easton after having spent only a few minutes with his sister. He'd been taking her crap every day for months.

Dani was soon back outside. She found Banks still milling by his car.

'The other guy, Wesley...'

'Aaron Wesley,' Banks said.

'He was under arrest too?'

'He was accompanied to the hospital. His nose was smashed. Blood everywhere. Possible fractured arm.'

'Was that a yes or a no?'

'Please make sure the officer with him reads him his rights ASAP. Breach of the peace. Assault. Actual bodily harm. Once he's been cleared by A&E, I want him in for questioning.'

Banks didn't look too sure about that.

'Yes?' Dani said.

'OK,' he said.

'And please release DS Easton. I need him.'

He looked even less sure about that.

'It's not like he's going to do a runner, is it?' Dani said. 'You've already got his version of events. He acted in self-defence, tackling an intruder in his own home. If you need him again, just give me a call.'

'I should really check—'

'You don't need to check with anyone,' Dani said. 'This is my decision, my problem. Now, please, get those cuffs off my colleague so that we can both get back to my murder investigation.'

He chewed on that for a few beats, looking as sulky as he was pissed off. Apparently he didn't like his authority challenged, but Dani wasn't backing down here.

'So?' she said.

Banks reached for the key. 'Yes, Ma'am.'

Chapter 36

'I'm sorry,' Easton said.

Dani said nothing as she kept her eyes on the road ahead.

'Dani, I said I'm sorry.'

'Why are you telling me?'

'Because I've put you in the shit. The investigation too.'

'You've put yourself in the shit.' She looked over at him. 'What were you thinking? You broke his arm!'

'Come on, Dani, you know me. The guy's twice my size and he was acting like a maniac. What was I supposed to do?'

'Call 999. Run. I don't know. But putting him in hospital…'

'I acted on instinct. It wasn't just me I was protecting.'

'Yeah, I think your sister is really appreciative of everything you did for her.'

That comment got her a sour look. 'I meant the kids. You know you could be—'

'Let's not worry about me,' Dani said. 'If I get hauled over hot coals for taking you away from there then so be it. I do have more important things on my mind than a lovers' tiff gone wrong.'

'Lovers' tiff? You know as well as I do how domestic violence escalates.'

It was true. A scarily large number of the murders they investigated were rage-filled domestics. She shouldn't have been so flippant about the situation. For all she knew Wesley had been hellbent on punishing Emily without mercy. Easton could well have saved her life, but Dani had probably still jumped the gun by taking Easton away from there so hastily. At the very least she was in for a bollocking from McNair. At worst… Dani didn't want to think about that right now.

Talk about acting on instinct, though.

'Let me fill you in,' she said.

She explained about her already event-filled morning. The court verdict. The trip to see Welter, and his revelation about the scrape between Ben and Liam Dunne. On the phone earlier she'd already set Mutambe up to further investigate that incident, contacting the bar where it happened to see if there was CCTV footage remaining, or if any of the current staff knew anything about the incident. Perhaps unlikely given that they were talking about an event six years ago, but it was worth a try. She went on to discuss the surveillance reports and her fears over Ana.

'Which explains why we're heading over to Tipton, then, I guess,' Easton said.

'We need to make a visit to Long Lartin too,' Dani said. 'If not today then definitely tomorrow.'

'I thought you never wanted to go back there? Not to see Ben at least?'

'What choice do I have?'

Easton didn't say anything to that.

—

An hour later and it was already apparent that they'd almost certainly have to wait until tomorrow to make the visit to the prison. They'd already made a brief stop at Victor Nistor's home address, where they'd initially had a brief chat with the two officers on surveillance duty. No sign of Nistor or Stelea since the morning, and Dani's knocking at the door had been fruitless. It was after three p.m. when they arrived outside the warehouse. The unmarked police car was across the street, about twenty yards away from the warehouse gates. Dani parked up a few yards behind them, then they walked over.

'Hardly inconspicuous, are they?' Easton said.

'No, they're not.' Though it wasn't exactly their fault. They were only acting off instruction. It wasn't as if the investigation team had the time or resources to acquire space in a nearby building, or anything else more sophisticated and less obvious.

Dani introduced herself to the officers in the car. They were plain-clothed, but they reeked of copper. Victor Nistor would have to be an idiot to not realise he was under watch. Not the worst position to be in. He wouldn't like the heat, that was for sure.

'Anything?' Dani said.

'Quiet day. Nistor and Stelea were in earlier but they left about an hour ago. Together. No one around since.'

'No sign of Ana Crisan?'

He shook his head. 'Nothing.'

Dani thanked him and she and Easton continued on through the open warehouse gates and up to the side door next to the loading area.

'World's worst haulage business,' Easton said. 'Never anything to haul, or anything to haul it with.'

'I'm sure Victor would say that's because they're so busy, every vehicle they have is always on the road.'

Easton rolled his eyes.

Dani knocked on the door.

'Why are we even bothering?' Easton asked.

'We have to,' Dani said.

But just as she expected, there was no answer. Which only added both to her frustration at not being able to face-off with Victor, and to her worry over Ana's whereabouts.

'So what next?' Easton said. 'We break the door down?'

Dani thought he was joking, though actually she'd already been pondering whether she could later justify doing so.

No. She didn't believe she could. Not yet. And she was likely already in enough trouble today.

'Come on,' she said. 'We've still one more place to try.'

With darkness quickly descending, Dani was already regretting leaving Brigitta Popescu's house as her last stop on the whistle-stop tour of Tipton. Still, at least she had Easton to keep her company this time.

The Surveillance team outside Brigitta's house had likewise seen nothing of Ana all day. In fact, Brigitta hadn't had any visitors at all. Was there even any point in doing this? Dani thought as they headed up the drive to the front door.

Yes, there was. And they were here now so why not?

Dani knocked on the door. She was well prepared for no answer. At least not at the first time of trying. So she was quite shocked when barely three seconds after knocking she heard locks release, before the door opened slightly.

Two bleary eyes peeked out of the narrow gap.

'I expected you would come back,' Brigitta croaked.

The door creaked open a few more inches and Dani peered in to see Brigitta shuffling down the darkened corridor towards the lounge.

'I guess we're invited in then,' Easton said.

Dani didn't say anything. Just took a deep breath, then stepped inside.

Five minutes later normal business had resumed. Easton and Dani were seated next to one another on a sofa in the badly lit lounge. Across the room Brigitta was seated next to the shrine, her face and withered body partly cloaked in darkness.

'Death and darkness follows you,' Brigitta said, her eyes steely as she stared at Dani. 'I saw it the first time we met.'

She shook her head as though disgusted. Dani shivered.

'Sorry, what do you mean?' Easton said.

Dani was speechless. She felt like Brigitta was about to accuse Dani of being a Strigoi or something, though really she was massively offended. What had she done to Brigitta?

Or was it Dani's near-death experience that Brigitta could somehow sense…? No, that was crazy thinking.

'You found another one,' Brigitta said. 'Another body.'

Dani and Easton shared a look. Did she mean the Jane Doe?

'Did you know her?' Dani asked.

Brigitta shook her head.

'But you knew about the body?'

'The news.'

'You're sure you don't know who she is?' Easton asked.

Brigitta didn't say anything as she stared over at them.

'Do you know Ana?' Dani asked. 'Ana Crisan. She's a good friend of Victor's.'

Brigitta still didn't say anything, though her hard gaze was fixed wholly on Dani now. It wasn't long before the unsettling feeling grew too uncomfortable and Dani looked away.

'Mrs Popescu,' Easton said. 'Ana Crisan. Do you know her? We're looking for her.'

'Another one gone,' she said, shaking her head solemnly.

'Do you know where she is?' Dani said, more sternly.

In silence, Brigitta stared her out again. Dani looked to Easton, giving him a 'what the hell?' look. He leaned over.

'Let me have a word with her. You go make a drink.'

Had he sensed how on edge Dani was?

'Mrs Popescu, would you like me to make you a cup of tea?' Dani asked.

She received nothing but the same cold stare as she got to her feet. She paused, waiting for an answer. Finally, Brigitta gave a single nod.

Dani sighed, relieved, as she stepped out of the room and made for the kitchen.

She flipped on the lights, though somehow they did little to properly illuminate the space, as though even they struggled to penetrate the ever-present darkness that enveloped the house. Back in the lounge Easton and Brigitta's voices carried thinly through the air.

Dani found three mugs, then stood staring through the dark window to the pitch-black garden outside as she waited for the kettle to boil. Her reflection stared back at her, though the glass somehow made her face look misshapen and cracked.

The kettle rumbled and Dani looked down from the window. As she did so she caught a fleeting glimpse of a shadow in the glass, the reflection of something swooshing somewhere behind her, out in the hallway. A cold draught tickled the skin on her neck and she whipped around, the teaspoon rattling in her trembling hand.

There was nothing there.

Of course there was nothing there! What the hell was she expecting?

Though her heart nearly jumped right up her throat and out of her wide-open mouth when the front door creaked and then opened.

In walked Stef.

'Brigitta!' she shouted, carefree, followed by a roll of Romanian words that meant nothing to Dani. 'Oh, it's you,' she said much more sourly when she clocked Dani, spoon in hand.

'You want one?' Dani said.

Stef grumbled and strode forwards, rolling her eyes when she looked into the lounge. She carried on to the kitchen and angrily plonked two bags of shopping onto the battered pine dining table. She glared over at Dani.

'You're doing it all wrong,' she said. She moved over and snapped the spoon from Dani's hand. 'She doesn't like it like this.'

'OK?'

'Why don't you go and sit. I'll bring the drinks through.'

'Sure. Thank you. Just milk for me. A sugar for DS Easton.'

'She doesn't have any sugar.'

'No problem. However it comes.'

Another eye-roll.

Although the truth was that Dani was pleased that Stef had turned up out of the blue – again – as she did want to ask her some questions too. She decided though that it was probably best to give her a minute, so politely excused herself and headed back to the lounge – where she frowned when she saw Easton's empty seat. She gazed across the room. Easton was on his haunches, right by Brigitta's side, the old lady wittering away to him quietly. Easton the charmer. Who knew?

'Dani?' Easton said, when Brigitta finally stopped talking and glared over. They both looked at Dani like she'd just interrupted something intimate. 'Brigitta was just telling me about when she was first married. And about when Nic was a boy in Romania.'

'Sounds interesting,' Dani said. She took her seat. 'Don't mind me.'

Brigitta was staring her out again, and the mood in the room flattened. The uncomfortable moment seemed to last an age, though Dani didn't look away this time. The corners of Brigitta's mouth ever so slowly turned up into a sinister and knowing smile. Dani was sure it was. Or perhaps it was just a trick of the dim light.

No, that was no trick.

Then a blood-curdling scream from the kitchen broke the ever-thickening silence.

Chapter 37

Dani was already on her feet, rushing for the lounge door, when a crashing sound rattled in her ears. She sped into the hall, then the kitchen. Stef was standing, staring into the darkness beyond the kitchen window.

'What happened?' Dani said, pulling to a stop a couple of steps from Stef. Her eyes fell to the mess of tea-covered crockery on the floor. 'Stef?'

Stef turned around, her face ashen. She opened and closed her mouth but said nothing – too shocked to speak?

'Stef?'

'What's going on?' Easton said, coming up behind Dani and sounding less receptive than she was. Dani held her arm out to hold him back.

'Stef, what did you see?'

Still nothing from Stef.

'Someone in the garden?' Dani asked.

The slightest of nods. At least Dani thought that was the silent reaction she saw from Stef. She strode for the back door. Turned the key and pulled it open and a whoosh of icy air barrelled in.

Dani rushed outside, into the near pitch-dark space. There was no security light, no illumination at all except the light seeping from the kitchen, and it took Dani's eyes several seconds to adjust as she tentatively edged further into the black. Shadows swirled all around her.

Or was that just the effect of her warm breath in the freezing air?

'Dani?'

Easton's voice right behind her made her jump. She stopped moving, heart pounding against her ribs. She whipped her eyes left and right across the modest space. A sliver of lawn. Some crazy paving. Fences on three sides. No sign of a person. Dani rummaged for her phone, took it out and shone the paltry torch about.

'There's no one out here,' Easton said.

Had there ever been?

Or had Stef actually been spooked by the reflection of someone – something? – in the house? Dani shivered at the thought.

She turned and stomped back inside.

There was no sign of Brigitta in the kitchen. Was she even aware of the commotion? Stef was crouched down with a dustpan and brush, sweeping up the dripping mess of broken crockery.

'What did you see, Stef?' Dani asked.

Stef carried on what she was doing.

'Stef, tell me what happened,' Dani said. More of a demand now. The harder tone caused Stef to pause. She straightened up and turned to face Dani, brush in hand.

'Nothing,' she said. 'It was just a cat, or a fox.'

'You sure about that?' Easton asked. 'You seem a bit rattled to me.'

Stef gave the silent treatment once more.

'Why don't you go and make sure Brigitta is OK,' Dani said to Easton.

He hesitated but then relented, shutting and locking the back door before he disappeared off. Dani gave Stef a few more moments to compose herself. The young woman finished clearing the mess from the floor, putting the broken pieces of cup into the bin and wiping the floor clean with a cloth.

'What do you want me to say?' Stef said, quite sternly, when she'd finished. She was facing Dani, arms folded.

'Just talk to me. I can see you're on edge. Why?'

Dani always felt that way in this house. Was Stef the same?

But had there really been someone out there? The same person who'd spied on Dani and Easton at Liam Dunne's house perhaps?

'There's nothing wrong,' Stef said. 'I thought I saw something in the dark. That's all. I wasn't expecting it.'

'A little jump, I could expect. But that was a hell of a scream.'

Stef ignored that comment and set about boiling the kettle again.

'Why don't you leave that?' Dani suggested. 'Come and sit down. I want to talk to you.'

She indicated the small, battered table, with its floral plastic cover which was scratched and permanently stained in places from many years of use.

Stef seemed unsure of Dani's proposition but eventually relented. They took seats opposite each other, both sitting back on their hard chairs, Stef with her arms folded, her now calmer face hard and defiant.

'Every time I come here... I get this odd feeling,' Dani said, blushing a little at her lame and somewhat inarticulate words. 'Brigitta is—'

'Brigitta is amazing,' Stef said. 'But she lives in the past.'

'Her stories of Strigoi...'

Stef rolled her eyes. 'Fairy tales. I used to believe them too. You have to understand the world was different in the old days. Especially where we came from. Where Brigitta came from. It was nothing like England today. Our world was so much more... our own. Small. Contained. Problems were dealt with by us, we...'

She seemed to lose her train of thought.

'Were self-sufficient?'

'Not so much in my day, maybe, but yes in Brigitta's time, of course. And so when something happened which couldn't be explained... that's where witches and Strigoi and superstition come from.'

'Brigitta is certain Strigoi stole her daughter.'

'Who knows what happened to her?' Stef said shaking her head. 'Or her granddaughter.'

'Her granddaughter?'

Stef waved the question away. 'Family problems.'

'You're sure?'

Stef said nothing.

'Brigitta seems convinced that women are still going missing. Here, now, in England. And that—'

'What are you trying to tell me?' Stef said, anger evident. 'That you believe the crazy words of an old lady? Vampires and werewolves, and whatever?'

'No,' Dani said. 'I'm not trying to tell you that at all.' Even if she couldn't escape the feeling of a malicious presence in this house. Was Stef's overreaction moments earlier not further demonstration that something wasn't right here? 'But I am telling you that we have more than one unexplained death we're investigating. I also have Brigitta telling me there may be more bodies. A place filled with bones. Does that mean anything to you?'

'I have no idea what you are talking about,' Stef said, and the confusion and doubt on her face seemed genuine enough.

The conversation took a pause as Dani tried to gather her thoughts. She couldn't escape the idea of her being watched, and her eyes flicked to the dark window every few beats. Was someone out there still?

'I've looked into you,' Dani said.

Stef looked disgusted. 'Why? Were you hoping you'd find something bad? Something so you could send me back to Romania?'

'Where does your animosity come from?' Dani said. 'Is it just against me? The police?'

Stef tutted. 'You don't know what it's like for us here. So unwelcome. This town is my home. It has been for years, but every day I'm made to feel like I don't belong. It's the same for us all.'

'I've never done that to you.'

'No? Then why are you here? Again. You won't leave us alone. You'll do anything to prove your point. That there's something bad about us. That we're all criminals.'

'I've never accused you of anything.'

'Not to my face. Yet here we are again. And you've been spying on me, behind my back. So what did you find?'

Was now the wrong time to say that Dani had found out that Stef *had* lied to her? But was it a lie or just withholding information?

'I'm not saying you've done anything wrong,' Dani said. 'But I do think that people you know have. Your brother included.'

That shut her up.

'Believe me,' Dani said. 'I know how easy it is to get tarred because of the actions of a sibling.'

Stef clearly didn't have a clue what Dani meant by that. A refreshing change for someone to not know of her and her brother's notoriety.

'I barely even speak to Alex any more,' Stef said.

Alex Stelea. Her older brother. Victor Crisan's accomplice.

'And why's that?' Dani asked.

Stef scoffed.

'I'm just trying to understand,' Dani said. 'Understand you. Him. What's happening here.'

Stef kept her mouth shut.

'You came to England very young,' Dani said. 'You were only nineteen, weren't you?'

'Yes.'

'You came alone?'

'I travelled alone. I came here to stay with Brigitta.'

'And Nic?'

Stef paused for a moment, as if she believed answering the question might incriminate her somehow, simply by associa-tion.

'Nic was here then, too, yes. But only for a few months before he was sent to prison. And before you ask, I know nothing about what he did or why. That's not my life, and it all happened before I even arrived.'

'How do you know his family?'

'Our families are close back home. That's all there is to it. I used to call Brigitta my aunt. She was a kind lady who everyone looked up to. We respected her. I still do.'

'So you came over here, on your own. And then what? Alex followed?'

'About two years after me.'

'To work with Victor?'

'Yes.'

'And how does Victor fit into this? The family dynamic.'

'He doesn't. Victor is just someone Nic worked for here. Then Alex worked for him too.'

'Nic worked *for* Victor?'

'Yes.'

Dani was a little surprised by that, for some reason. The impression she'd always had was that Nic had been the more senior, but was that simply because he was older?

'And what exactly is it that Victor and Alex do?' Dani asked.

'They own a transport business,' Stef said, face deadpan.

Dani said nothing. Over the next few seconds of silence Stef became more and more fidgety.

'What?' Stef said.

'Sorry, I was waiting for you to answer my question.'

'I did.'

'Not properly.'

'What are you talking about?'

'You know exactly what I'm talking about. You don't need to bullshit me. Victor and Alex are crooks. My best guess is they run prostitutes. Young Romanians and other foreign girls who are easy to coerce. Drugs, extortion, too, usually go hand-in-hand with these types. I will get to the bottom of everything they're doing.'

'Whatever it is you think they do, it's not my business.'

'I don't doubt that. But if you know anything—'

'I already told you that I don't.'

Yet Dani didn't believe a word of it. One thing she knew for sure was that Stef was bright, and she was no shrinking violet. There wasn't a chance that she'd never at least suspected her brother and his business partner of criminality. Would she not admit to it because she was afraid, or was it due to complicity?

'I asked you before about Clara Dunne, and her brother Liam.'

'And I told you I don't know them.'

'You did. But do you know this woman?'

Dani reached out with her phone, the screen lit up with the photograph of Liam Dunne and the mystery woman. Dani was sure there was a twinkle of recognition in Stef's eyes.

'Stef?'

'I don't know her.'

'Bullshit.'

Stef flicked a glare Dani's way. 'I don't know her.'

Dani stared right back, waiting to see if Stef would change her answer, or at least add to it. She didn't.

'Tell me about Ana,' Dani said.

The curveball threw Stef for a moment.

'You do know Ana Crisan, don't you?' Dani asked.

'I know her, yes.'

'She's Victor's girlfriend?'

Stef scoffed once again.

'I get the impression that you don't like Victor much?' Dani asked.

'Do you?'

Dani held back a slight smile at that. Whatever Stef's motives for her not opening up, there was something about her that Dani liked.

'What's the deal with Ana?' Dani asked.

'The deal?'

'She's young, intelligent. Like yourself. Yet here you are working away, earning a living, while Ana… she seems tied to Victor's side, and I'm not sure it's by choice.'

'Victor gets what he wants. And he wants Ana.'

'What if he wanted you?'

Dani could tell Stef was now clenching her jaw. Disgust?

'Would you run away to another city too?' Dani asked. 'Like Ana did?'

'I'd run further.'

Both of them smiled at that.

'But there is a problem,' Dani said.

That wiped the short-lived smile from Stef's face.

'Ana is missing.'

Stef said nothing.

'We've had surveillance on Victor and Alex—'

'Pretty obvious,' Stef said. 'They were hardly well hidden.'

'No. Maybe not. Yet Ana has still gone missing.' Dani paused to let that sink in. 'She was last seen leaving Victor's warehouse last night, with both Victor and Alex. They got into Alex's car. Later in the night when that car arrived back at Victor's house, Ana wasn't in it.'

Stef was looking more and more worried now.

'She didn't run away,' Dani said. 'Not this time.'

Stef said nothing.

'Do you have any idea at all what's happened to her? Where they took her. Why?'

'No, I don't,' Stef said, shaking her head. She looked far more solemn now than before. 'I honestly don't know.'

And the worst thing was, this time Dani believed her.

Chapter 38

The risks had always been clear in Ana's mind. Not just in taking the phone, but in using it. Not just in using it, but in using it to call the police in order to try and help them ensnare Victor.

She'd known the risks, yet she'd done it all anyway.

What did that say about her? About how desperate she was?

Yet there was no doubt that she'd still been in absolute, almost paralysed shock back in the warehouse when she realised Victor had rumbled her secret. Had been so scared, so numb, that she hadn't attempted to escape, to fight either physically or verbally. She'd simply acquiesced, and walked fatefully out of there with Alex and Victor, both of them keeping close watch as if even they were surprised by her lack of overt reaction.

Had there been any other choice?

At the time she'd thought not. Now? In this place? She wished she'd fought back with every ounce of strength and resolve. She should have done whatever it took, because she surely wouldn't get another chance now.

'Do you know Alex tried to talk me out of it,' Victor said as he paced up and down in front of Ana. Alex was resting on the workbench behind. Ana was in the middle of the grotty and damp room. Rope tied her hands behind her, and to the bolted-down chair she was sitting on. 'Perhaps it was a little unnecessary. Setting up the camera. Waiting for you to reach for that fucking thing. But I wanted to see. I wanted to see your deceit for myself.'

Without even thinking, Ana was pleading and begging. She'd wanted to stay strong, to show no weakness, but how could she do that now?

'Shut up,' Alex said. Not loud, but stern enough to cause Ana's pleadings to die down to a feeble whimper.

'I just want you to tell me why,' Victor said.

He stopped pacing and looked down to Ana. She tried to avoid his eye but after a few seconds of awful silence she found her gaze slowly lifting until it met his. He wasn't angry. Not now. That was the strangest thing to Ana. Victor wasn't angry at all. He looked hurt. Almost defeated. Like her treachery had really broken him. Despite everything, she even felt bad because of that.

'Why, Ana?' he said. 'After everything I did for you.'

She wanted to retort to that, but thought better of it. Everything he'd done? Kidnap, rape, abuse. What had he done that was actually *good*? Did she really not see it?

'Tell me why!' he boomed. His sudden outburst was enough to cause Ana's whole body to flinch and then tense. She held her breath.

Then spoke.

'Because I hate you,' she said, barely louder than a whisper. 'You disgust me.'

Now he wasn't broken. Now he wasn't defeated. He was absolutely livid. Even as he remained rooted to the spot, Ana could tell that anger seeped through every pore.

'Victor, it's time for you to go,' Alex said, straightening up from his perch, and glaring down to Ana like she was nothing but a piece of dog muck stuck to the bottom of his most expensive shoes.

'Goodbye, Ana,' Victor said through clenched teeth.

Then he turned and stomped past her. She craned her neck as far as she could. Saw him opening the thick metal door in the corner of the room. A moment later it clattered shut behind him. The force made the whole room vibrate, the sensation reached ominously up through Ana's bones.

Silence followed. Ana soon found herself staring to Alex who glared back at her with sinister relish. But he said nothing. Barely even moved.

'Now it's just you and me,' Alex said eventually, as a horrible grin spread across his face.

He took a step towards Ana. Once again she held her breath. She was frozen. Too scared to even breathe. As his face was caught under the orange light hanging above them, there was a devilish twinkle in his eye.

'He really loves you,' Alex said. 'I've never seen a man so weak because of a woman.'

'He loves me? Then why am I here!'

Her sudden defiance only added to Alex's menace and amusement.

'You think Victor is strong. But he loves you so much he couldn't go through with this himself. He couldn't even bear to watch. But *I* can do it. I'll do it gladly.'

'Please,' Ana said, but her voice was now weak and pathetic.

'It could have been so different for us. I would have treated you like a queen. You would never have wanted anything more.'

She screwed up her face at the thought. Alex revolted her. Even more so than Victor did. Yet she'd always known that Alex had liked her. How could she not have noticed the way he looked at her. The way he forever eyed her up and down, tongue practically dragging on the floor at times.

She'd even teased him over it in the past.

Why had she done that?

He laughed. 'I know what you're thinking now. *If only.* If only you'd been nicer to me. If only you hadn't been such a bitch. Maybe you wouldn't be here. Maybe I wouldn't make you suffer the way I'm going to.'

He turned to the table behind him and unrolled a utility belt. The metal tools inside clinked and clanked as he did so. The sound alone made Ana's insides curdle.

He turned back to face her. A gleaming metal object now in his hand. What was that? Pliers? Cutters?

Ana swallowed down bile as grim thoughts swirled.

'And believe me, my dear Ana, I *will* make you suffer.'

She could do nothing but cower down and cry out desperately as he came towards her.

Chapter 39

It had been many months since Dani had last made the trip to this part of Worcestershire. The population of the sleepy village known as South Littleton was barely twice that of the nearby Category A prison – Long Lartin – a sprawling and depressingly bland 1970s construction. Unfortunately, it was to the prison that Dani and Easton were headed.

Dani parked up her car, shut down the engine then took a deep breath before she stepped out.

'Don't look so worried,' Easton said to her as they closed their doors.

Dani didn't respond. Why was she feeling so anxious anyway? It wasn't like she hadn't been here to see Ben before. Though this was the first time since she'd tried and failed to find the evidence that would prove that he was behind Damian Curtis's killing spree, and the first time since Curtis's trial had started.

Was it because of what she saw as her own failure that she felt so daunted now? Knowing Ben he certainly wouldn't pass up the opportunity to taunt her.

Not that Curtis was top of the agenda for today.

There'd been a fresh smattering of snow overnight, though the freezing temperature had turned the thin layer into ice. Dani carefully crunched across it as they headed through the car park to the visitor entrance. She checked her phone on the way, noting the missed call from McNair. Dani was holding off speaking to the boss as long as she could. Undoubtedly, she was in for a reprimand – at the least – over her decision to hastily pull

Easton away from the mess at his home the day before. She'd already had the update from him in the car that Wesley had been charged – while still in hospital – with assault and breach of the peace, but had since been discharged and was now out on bail. Easton would still have to answer questions about his role in the events, and Dani couldn't stop the big machine if it was determined that he too should be charged, but for now she wanted him by her side.

'I feel bad coming here,' Dani said.

'I already said, you—'

'I don't mean because I'm apprehensive about seeing Ben. I mean because I'm worried about Ana. The more time that passes—'

'We've a whole team back at HQ following up, trying to find her.'

True enough. Though that still didn't make Dani feel any better. Any delay could prove disastrous for Ana.

Perhaps they were already too late.

Dani hadn't expected they'd be meeting with Ben alone. Not after everything that had happened. So it was no surprise when the prison guard opened the door to the interview room and Ben was sitting behind the table in the middle of the room with his slimy lawyer Gregory Daley by his side. Daley was dressed immaculately, as always, even down to the finer details including his designer glasses, gleaming cufflinks and tie-pin. Though he was also now sporting a goatee beard that Dani hadn't seen before and which added at least a decade to his age and didn't suit his rounded face at all.

Ben... well, he looked older too, his hair wiry and almost entirely grey, his face more lined than before, his cheekbones more jagged from loss of weight. The ageing hadn't come across properly when she'd seen him at distance on the video link the other day, but every time Dani saw Ben up close and in the flesh he seemed to have aged several years, as though the prison was in a time-warp where the days, weeks, months and years passed by more quickly than on the outside.

Not that she felt sorry for him at all.

'How've you been, Dani?' Ben said with a warm smile as she and Easton took the seats opposite Ben and Daley. The interview-room door was shut and locked behind them.

'All the better for not seeing you,' she said, though she chastised herself for her churlish response, which only added to Ben's smile.

'We weren't given much notice for this meeting,' Daley said. 'So you can appreciate if we're under-prepared, but I'm assuming this is going to be related to Damian Curtis?'

Dani set her hard glare on Daley. 'You assume? Why would you assume we came here to discuss Damian Curtis? Is that because you believe your client has something more to tell us regarding Curtis's crimes?'

Daley held his tongue.

'It was a nice performance, though,' Dani said to Ben. 'Your little cameo in court.'

'I'd asked to go in person, but—'

'But you're a dangerous murderer, so a day out wasn't on the cards.'

Ben shrugged. 'I thought I saw you on the link,' he said.

'Detective Stephens, if this has to do with my client's testimony—'

'We didn't come here to discuss Damian Curtis,' Dani said. 'Or the trial. Or the little show that Ben put on the other day with that sudden recollection of events related to Dr Collins that he'd never before mentioned to anyone.'

Daley gave a 'so what' look. 'The evidence was there to find, it's not our—'

'Yes. It's my job, the police's job, to find evidence. The CPS to present that. And believe me, I *will* get to the bottom of what happened between you and Curtis and make sure you get what you deserve.'

Dani held Ben's gaze for a few moments. Each second that passed, a sliver of his confidence seemed to disappear. He looked away first, to his lawyer. Daley said nothing.

'Anyway,' Dani said. 'Enough of that. Like I said, we're not here today to talk about Curtis. Something very different, in fact.'

'Which is?' Daley said. He looked a little uneasy now.

Dani nodded to Easton and he slapped the picture onto the table then pushed it across the desk to Ben.

'Can you tell us if you recognise the people in this picture?' Easton said to him.

Ben made a macho point of staring out Easton for a couple of seconds before he reached for the photograph with his cuffed hands and brought it closer to him.

'Would you care to explain the purpose of this?' Daley said.

'If you're patient, we will,' Dani said, never taking her eyes of Ben. 'So?'

'Well, of course I recognise myself,' he said with a smug smile, though it only lasted until his eyes briefly met Dani's. He looked back down to the photo. 'It's a team photo from when I worked at Ellis Associates.'

He sat back in his chair. Nonchalant.

'You know the names of all the people it shows?' Easton asked.

'I'd have to have a good think, but I certainly did know them, at the time. When was this? Five, six years ago?'

'Close,' Dani said.

'We're particularly interested in what you remember of this man.' Easton reached forwards and put his finger on Liam Dunne's face.

'James?' Ben said, looking perplexed. 'James Alden?'

'That's the one,' Dani said. 'Except his real name was Liam Dunne.'

'Have you heard of that name?' Easton asked.

'I have,' Ben said.

'How?' Easton asked.

Ben looked to his lawyer before he answered, though Daley didn't even flinch. It was clear this was all news to him.

'I don't remember the exact details, but it was found out that James – or Dunne or whatever he was called – had lied about who he was. I don't know why. But I do know it got him the sack.'

'You don't remember how *you* found out?' Dani asked.

'No,' Ben said with a carefree shrug.

'Do you remember how your employer found out?'

According to Henry Welter it had been Ben who blew the whistle.

'I don't know,' Ben said.

At least one of them was lying then, and Dani was far more inclined to believe it was Ben than Welter. But why?

'What was your relationship with Dunne?' Dani asked.

'Relationship? We worked for the same company. On the same project team for a few months. Until he left. That was it. There was no relationship.'

'What was his relationship with your wife?' Dani said.

Ben's face screwed up in anger 'Excuse me?'

'We were alerted to an altercation between yourself and Liam Dunne,' Easton said. 'This altercation took place at a nightclub in Birmingham, called Gino's back in 2014. A—'

'Detective,' Daley said, 'I really think you should cut to the chase here. You're asking—'

'I was trying to get to the point until you interrupted,' Easton said. That shut the lawyer up. 'Can you explain what happened that night?' Easton asked Ben.

'I'm presuming you already think you know the answers to that,' Ben said.

'Give us your version then,' Dani said.

'From what I remember it was a drunken argument. Nothing more.'

'Over Gemma?'

Ben paused for a moment. 'I really don't remember the spark. I was drunk. So was he. I took offence to something. When I brought him up on it, he got in my face.'

'So what? You punched him?'

'There was a scuffle. As I recall neither of us was hurt. Though our whole party was thrown out of the club. We all went home. End of story.'

'Is it?'

'What?'

'Is that the end of the story?'

'I just said so.'

'So you and Gemma were fine after that?'

'As far as I recall.'

'And you never took your disagreement with Dunne any further?'

'It was a drunken argument, that's all.'

'So you weren't the person, who, two days after that disagreement, told your employer about Dunne's duplicity?'

'Is that...' Ben stopped and seemed to mull over whatever he'd been about to say. 'OK. Yes. That was me.'

'Wow, Ben. I'm impressed. I didn't even have to force that truth out of you. So how did you find out?'

Ben looked to Daley again. The lawyer leaned over and whispered into Ben's ear. Likely telling him not to answer the question, for whatever reason.

Dani sighed, sensing Daley wasn't going to like where this was going and deciding she was better just getting there. 'Why don't I speed up this process a bit, rather than us dithering on your patchy recollection of your own actions.'

'I agree that would be most helpful,' Daley said.

'Liam Dunne has been missing since 2015.'

Ben didn't react at all to that.

'We don't know where he went, or if he is still alive,' Dani said. 'We do know he went missing just a few months after he lost his job at Ellis Associates. Because of you.'

Daley couldn't help himself. 'If you're suggesting—'

'I'm not suggesting anything,' Dani said. 'Did you know Liam was missing?'

Ben shook his head, though he looked a little more worried now than before.

'Do you know this woman?' Dani said, taking the copy of the photo of Liam and the mystery woman from Easton's pile, and sliding it across the desk.

Ben glanced at it for only a couple of seconds before he looked up and shook his head.

'You're sure?' Dani asked. 'You don't remember Liam having a girlfriend, or ever bringing a date along to one of your nights out?'

'Never.'

Perhaps the woman was a dead end, but Dani wanted to hold onto the hope that she was of significance, if only she could figure out who she was.

'Now, this is where the story gets really murky,' Dani said. 'Because last week, we found Clara Dunne, Liam's sister, dead in her home. We're treating her death as murder, and we have strong evidence that before her death she was performing a personal investigation into her brother's disappearance.'

She let that one hang but neither Daley nor Ben said a word.

'In relation to Clara's death, and Liam's disappearance, we are currently investigating the activities of a gang believed to be involved in various criminal activities including prostitution, drugs and extortion. The gang are all Romanian nationals.'

Dani indicated to Easton.

'Do you know any of these men?' he said, placing three more photos onto the table – one each of Victor Nistor, Alex Stelea and Nicolae Popescu.

'You don't have to answer that,' Daley said, looking as anxious as he sounded now.

'I don't know them,' Ben said.

'You don't? Because where I'm sitting the circumstantial evidence is looking very strong indeed.'

'What evidence?' Daley said. 'And evidence of what?'

'You were convicted of the murder of your first wife, Alice,' Dani said. 'Correct?'

'Correct,' Ben said through gritted teeth.

'Though my client has never admitted guilt,' Daley decided to point out, as though that had any bearing. 'And you are probably aware we are currently in the process of considering grounds for appeal.'

Dani ignored him. 'And, through your association with a prominent local gangster, known as Callum O'Brady, who you also later killed, you were able to cover up Alice's murder for a number of years.'

O'Brady. An Irish gangster who Ben had become indebted to. Who Ben, after killing Alice in a crime of passion, turned to for help in covering up her murder. That had worked. Until years later when Ben's life, and his mental health, began to spiral out of control. In the end he'd killed O'Brady along with several members of his gang to try to break free from their grip, and had tried to kill both Gemma and Dani when they'd discovered the truth about Alice.

'Ben?'

'My client is hardly going to admit to these ludicrous statements,' Daley said. 'He has already been tried in relation to the deaths of both Alice—'

'I'm well aware of his trial, thank you,' Dani said. 'Given I was one of the people Ben tried to kill. My point is, the circumstances are startlingly similar, don't you think?'

The room was silent for a few moments.

'You killed Alice,' Dani said. 'For revenge, I might add, because she wanted to leave you. You then used Callum O'Brady to cover up her death to make it look like a home invasion gone wrong. Fast-forward a few years. You knew Liam Dunne. You had a falling out with him. Over his hands-on nature with your wife.'

Ben was getting seriously riled. Every mention of Gemma made him angrier. Which was exactly where Dani wanted him.

'So you had reason to want revenge on Dunne too. Then... pouf. He disappears. Now, years later, we realise not only is there a link between him and you, but we're able to link the death of his sister – who was desperately searching for her brother – to another local gang. This one run by Victor Nistor.'

Dani tapped the head of Victor on the picture on the table as she spoke.

'So, let me ask you very clearly. How do you know Victor Nistor?'

'I don't know him.'

'Did you kill Liam Dunne?'

'I—'

'Do not say another word,' Daley said, slamming his hand onto the table. 'Detectives, as you are very well aware, my client is speaking to you today of his own volition, and not under caution. Unless you are intending to charge him, then this meeting is over.'

Nobody said a word as Dani considered that proposition.

'So?' Daley said.

Dani kept her eyes on her brother, though the return of his smug expression said it all. 'Ben?'

He shook his head.

'We're done here,' Daley said, getting to his feet.

Chapter 40

'You don't really believe Ben had anything to do with Liam Dunne's disappearance, do you?' Easton asked as Dani started the engine and pulled out of the parking space.

'Why not?' she said.

'Because it's...'

'It's what? A coincidence? It's ridiculous?'

'Both.'

'I would have said the same thing years ago. How could I ever have imagined that my own twin brother would kill Alice, kill O'Brady and the others. Could have tried to kill Gemma and me. But he did. The simple fact is that Ben isn't like you and me.'

Though Dani shivered at that thought because not for the first time it brought her back to the same old question: why was Ben, her twin, a killer? Did the same defects of mind that he suffered from affect her too?

'I'm just saying,' Easton said, 'I think you're taking a leap. Don't bite my head off when I say this, but it's almost as if you're forcing things to fit. Curtis. Now Dunne. Anything that goes wrong anywhere near your brother and you try to make—'

'But why do things keep going so wrong around Ben? To me it all being down to coincidence is far more *unlikely*.'

She glanced over to Easton and could tell he was wholly unconvinced.

'Ben's got form for this. Seeking revenge. Getting dirty people to do his dirty work. It doesn't change the fact that we 'still believe Victor and his gang are neck-deep in this too. But I can't not properly explore Ben's role.'

Despite her words, though, Easton had done a good job of throwing some doubt into her mind. Was she blinkered when it came to Ben? Desperate to find blame in him, however tenuous, and regardless of what evidence and logic were telling her?

She was still pondering that when a call came through to her phone. She recognised the number. The morgue. She clicked on the dashboard to accept the call.

'Detective Stephens, it's Jack Ledford,' came the grainy voice through the car's speakers.

'Morning, Jack.'

'I have Saad Tariq with me here too.'

'OK?'

'We were going over the results of the PM for your Jane Doe, and, well, you'll probably want to get yourselves over here.'

-

The brief call had left Dani as perplexed as she was intrigued. The morgue was hardly the usual place to find Tariq, an FSI, who was more usually locked away in a lab. But then this case was hardly usual.

As ever the concoction of bleach and death stuck in Dani's nose as soon as she'd entered the building, and the nauseating mix intensified with each step that she and Easton took towards the theatre.

'I wish I had somewhere else to be,' Easton said.

Dani didn't say anything, though she kind of agreed. There were two parts of her job she really didn't like, and both involved standing over dead bodies: murder scenes, and post-mortems.

Dani knocked on the door to the theatre then stepped inside to see Ledford and Tariq across the room, standing by a gurney which had a white sheet over the top.

They both turned around.

'That was quick,' Ledford said as he pushed his glasses further up his nose.

'You said it was important.'

He raised an eyebrow. 'I'm not sure I exactly did, but I'm sure it is.'

Dani frowned at that comment, but didn't say anything. Why was he always so obtuse?

'I actually completed the PM yesterday evening,' Ledford said, 'but I wanted to run a couple of things past Tariq before I came back to you.'

Ledford reached out for the sheet and was about to pull it down to reveal Jane Doe's mutilated corpse when Dani held her hand up to stop him.

'Actually, rather than the PM, I'm more interested in what Tariq has found.'

Ledford looked a little put out by that. 'Very well.'

'Though we will still need to see the body, I'm afraid,' Tariq said.

On cue Ledford pulled the sheet back and Dani instinctively glanced to the washed-out body before looking back to Tariq. Even the short glimpse filled her with a sense of torment at seeing the remains of the young woman, so vulnerable.

'We went over the van she was found inside in painstaking detail,' Tariq said, 'but you also asked us to consider the body too. As you know, we can get residue transfer onto skin, so we were looking in particular for any foreign fibres, substances or prints. Surprisingly, we actually found quite a few fingerprint fragments around her body. Mostly around her genitals, her breasts and her hips.'

Dani squirmed at the connotations of what that meant. 'But we also found fingerprint fragments around here...' He reached out with a gloved hand and pulled up Jane Doe's right arm to reveal her armpit.

'The same fingerprints all over?' Dani asked.

'Unfortunately we're only talking about fragments, but I don't think so. The ones around her body were more developed, and given their locations…'

He handed Dani a sheet of paper with a diagram of Jane Doe's body with red circles to highlight the areas of interest.

'It would seem to me they were probably transferred during a sexual encounter,' Ledford said, filling in the obvious blank. 'Which is also consistent with the fact that semen traces were found on her hand and her breasts,' Ledford said.

Dani's insides twisted.

'But the ones under the arm, well—'

'It was from the body being moved,' Dani said. 'But you didn't see anything like that on her ankles?' Dani could picture the scene. The two burly men from the van, one holding her ankles, one holding her under the arms as they tossed her onto the plastic sheet to roll her up.

'We didn't, but—'

'Latex?'

'There is residue on her ankles, not from latex gloves, but perhaps from a well-worn leather glove. Nothing unique enough that we can trace with any accuracy, but it at least gives us a glimpse of what happened to her.'

'What about the semen and prints?' Dani said. 'Any matches?'

'No to the semen. No to the prints from her apparent sexual encounter,' Tariq said, 'and a kind of a no on the other.'

'Kind of?'

'They are only partials, but…' He paused as he flicked through his papers. He pulled out two sheets and put his clipboard down.

'If you remember from Clara Dunne's home, we had partials there too,' Tariq said.

'Yes,' Dani said. 'Transferred from a glove, we thought.'

'These partials don't directly match those. Which could be for more than one reason. Obviously it could be different

278

people, or it could be different fingers. Or even just different parts of the same finger. And if you look at them like this…'

He moved over to Dani and held the two sheets out for her, before drawing one over the other to give a faint superimposition.

'If you look at the lines, it's possible this is the same finger,' he said. 'A thumb, more precisely, given the apparent shape, if you carry on the pattern.'

'So we can link trace evidence at Clara's home directly to Jane Doe?' Easton said.

'It's certainly a possibility. And there are clothing fibres in the van which are a very close match to those found at Clara's home,' Tariq said.

Everyone went silent for a few moments, Dani trying to think over the revelation. It was a huge finding, one which provided further clear evidence that the two men who had been transporting Jane Doe's body had also been in Clara Dunne's home.

But had those men actually killed Jane Doe? And Clara?

Dani looked over to the body again, and as much as she didn't want to, she tried to imagine the woman's final moments.

'Nothing was found in the house in Wednesbury, though?' Dani said.

'No trace of Jane Doe,' Tariq said. 'The room you highlighted there to me had been sanitised really quite significantly. There was nothing of anything in there.'

Dani nodded. 'OK. So here's what I think happened,' she said. 'We've already hypothesised that our victim was likely a sex worker. Probably against her will. And there would have been others in that house, too, who we still need to find. For whatever reason, Jane Doe was attacked. Perhaps in a violent encounter with a punter. She died at his hands.' She looked to Ledford. 'Blunt force trauma or strangulation?'

He raised an eyebrow, as if unsure how she'd known. 'She suffered both, as well as some horrible cuts to her body from a knife of some sort, but asphyxiation was the cause of death.'

He seemed a little disappointed that Dani had determined that without him even getting a chance to go through his PM findings.

'The two men in the van were called to collect the body, and dispose of it,' Dani said. 'This can't be the first time something like this has happened. The men are professionals, of a sort. Have you run that partial? The superimposed version?'

'Of course,' Tariq said. He reached for another piece of paper. 'And there is a certain amount of guesswork that goes into this, as I'm sure you can appreciate, not just in terms of the orientation of the two fragments, but which finger, on which hand they belong to.'

'Just tell me. Have you got a match?'

'But that's the thing. We have, potentially. But we have more than one possibility. Four people, in the database, to be precise, who the amalgamated print could belong to. And of course, it could even belong to someone who isn't on record.'

He held the paper out for Dani. She took it and stared down at the basic profiles for each of the four. Name, date of birth, last known address. Her first reaction was disappointment. No Victor Nistor. No Alex Stelea. No name at all that she recognised. But then on second glance her eyes stopped on one of the names. She didn't know it, but it was the only one that clearly wasn't anglicised. Silviu Grigore.

She looked to Easton.

'We need to find this guy. Now.'

Chapter 41

Dani wasn't taking any chances. Not this time. Luckily both McNair and Fairclough – from Organised Crime– had agreed. The two men who'd been found with Jane Doe's body had already escaped the police once, had done so through the use of force and violence, and Dani was determined to make sure they wouldn't get such a chance again. The operation had there-fore taken a couple of hours longer to organise than it would otherwise have done, but they were now ready to go with a team that included half a dozen Tactical Response officers with their heavy duty semi-automatic assault weapons. At least that's what Dani thought the guns were – she had zero experience of firearms herself.

Those six armed officers were in the back of a van a few cars away from Dani's, all out of sight from the target location – the last known address of Silviu Grigore – on the next street along. At least for now. A plethora of uniforms were in other vehicles dotted around the vicinity. Just in case. Now they were assembled, they needed to act quickly, before suspicions were aroused. They'd had eyes on the terraced property in Willenhall, on the outskirts of Walsall, for the last thirty minutes, though had seen no one come and go and they had no idea how many people were inside.

Time to find out.

'OK, let's get this moving,' Dani said into her radio.

Easton started the car and they followed the unmarked van with the armed officers as it took the right turn up ahead, onto the similarly quiet residential street.

'Are you sure this is how you want to play it?' Easton asked her.

She was damn sure. 'I'm not changing my mind now.'

The street had double yellow lines all down one side, the opposite side was crammed with parked cars. The van pulled over onto the double yellows three houses away from number 51. Easton carried on past it, parking two houses up on the other side.

'Everyone in position?' Dani said.

She got a series of affirmatives, including from the van with four uniforms that was now stationed along the back alley behind the terraces should anyone make a run in that direction.

'We could just send the big boys in straight off,' Easton said, the engine still idling. 'Surely it's safer that way?'

'We are the big boys,' Dani said as she reached for the door.

She pushed it open and stepped out into the cold. She shut the door just as Easton switched off the engine. She didn't wait for him as she moved towards the house. No delay now. Not with the two vehicles parked so obviously and obtrusively outside. Dani nodded over to the driver of the van. The armed officers would remain in the back until they got word. Dani's decision. Everyone was ready to move, but she didn't want guns on the street unless it was absolutely necessary. Perhaps it was more risky for her and Easton this way, but it was far less risky for pedestrians and everyone else.

Easton caught up with Dani just as she reached the door to 51. She took one more glance at the van before she rapped on the wood with her knuckles.

Then she waited.

And waited.

She looked left and right. Across the street. Passersby, people at windows, were already taking notice. It wasn't hard to see that Dani, Easton, and the surreptitiously plonked car and van were out of place.

Dani knocked once more. Waited again. Nothing.

'Anything at the back?' Dani said into her radio.

'Nothing.'

'Shit. OK, get the big red key.'

The big red key. A sixteen-kilo handheld battering ram that could apply more than three tonnes of impact force. Seconds later two uniformed officers, riot helmets on, visors down, appeared from nowhere lugging the enforcer. Dani and Easton stepped back as the burlier of the two men swung the enforcer with venom and smashed it against the door lock. Wood splintered and the door opened first go. The other officer kicked the broken door further open then rushed inside, his friend close behind, Easton and Dani more tentatively following.

They needn't have bothered being tentative. It only took a few moments to realise the house was empty.

—

Dani and Easton remained inside for little more than thirty minutes, by which point all of the officers, armed and unarmed, had moved on, except for a sole PC and the team of FSIs now working through the inside. Dani couldn't shake her disappointment. Her frustration. Even her embarrassment. This felt like a recurring theme now. Get a lead. Follow lead. Run slapbang into a solid concrete wall.

'What do you reckon?' Easton said to her as they traipsed back to the car.

'Someone was definitely living there very recently,' she said. 'Furniture. Clothes. TV. Food. All in place.'

'In-date milk still in the fridge.'

'In-date, but it's not even three days since Grigore and his pal attacked the police and fled the scene, so that doesn't really tell us much.'

The scene in Brownhills. A few minutes' drive from where they now were. It all fitted. So where was Grigore?

'Maybe he never came back here,' Easton said. 'He's gone on the run. Hiding. Maybe with Victor's help.'

'Possibly,' Dani said. 'Or maybe he's not running from us at all. But from Victor.'

Was that a better answer? Potentially. After all, how did the saying go? An enemy of my enemy is my friend.

If they could find Grigore and his mystery accomplice...

'Shall I drive?' Easton asked.

'Why not,' Dani said. Her head was too busy to concentrate on the roads.

'Where to?'

She really didn't know. It was already six p.m. Already dark. But...

'HQ first,' Dani said.

Easton didn't look particularly impressed with that idea, but he didn't protest.

They'd only moved half a mile when Dani blurted, 'Stop!'

Easton did exactly as he was asked. He thumped the brake and the wheels locked and the car rocked to a halt, sending both occupants shooting forwards in their seats. There was a couple of moments of awkward silence. Easton was wide-eyed, staring at Dani.

'What?' he said.

Dani laughed. 'I didn't mean for you to take me so literally. Pull over.'

Easton did so as the cars behind flashed and honked their annoyance at Easton's erratic manoeuvre.

'Think about it,' Dani said, trying to get her thoughts into shape. 'Grigore is on the run.'

'You said that already.'

'He's hiding from his big boss, not the police. When he ran from us the other night, he probably thought we wouldn't ID him. It's only because of those fingerprint fragments. Secondary transfer that he might not even have thought about. The police aren't his number one concern, even if he is going to be seriously wary of us.'

'I'm not sure I get the difference.'

'The difference is in how he reacts after he runs. When they were stopped in the van, they had nothing on them. No ID, no money, no phones. For the very reason that they were transporting a dead body. They were careful. Planned.'

'And?'

'And how on earth do you run away with absolutely nothing but the clothes you're wearing?'

'Are you going to tell me or do I really have to guess?'

'I'll tell you. You don't.'

'You don't?'

'You can't. At least not without first coming home. Home, or wherever else it is you've stashed your money. Your phone. Whatever else.'

'Emergency grab bag?'

'Maybe. But there is another possibility too.'

'There is?'

'Let's get back there.'

It took all of two minutes to return to the house. The FSIs were still busy doing their thing and Dani called Tariq over to give him the news.

'You can get cleared up and out of here.'

'We can? We've still got—'

'I know, you're not finished. But I'll take the risk. We don't need to go the whole hog—'

'But I thought that was exactly what you told me we did need to do?'

'Just trust me,' Dani said.

Ten minutes later only Dani and Easton remained. Dani roamed. And found exactly what she was looking for. Loose floorboard. Under the sofa.

'I think that's called old school,' Easton said as he and Dani looked down at the rolls of bank notes. The switched-off mobile phone – a burner, no doubt. The two passports. The picture in both was of the same bull-nosed man, though only one bore the name Silviu Grigore.

Dani looked up to Easton, trying not to appear smug.

'Maybe he never came back at all,' he said. 'If his stuff is still here.'

'No. He's been back. I'd bet anything. And I think it's even better than I first thought. He's been back more than once.'

'How on earth can you—'

'Come with me.'

She headed out and into the kitchen at the back of the house.

'Open the door,' Dani said.

Easton walked over and pulled the handle on the back door but it was locked.

He frowned and looked around, searching for the key.

'How did the FSIs get out earlier?' he asked.

'They had to walk around the road to the alley,' Dani said. She pointed to the empty key hook above the work surface a yard from the door. 'No key in the lock. No key on the hook. Because?'

Easton shrugged.

'He's been back already. And's he's now using the back door because he doesn't trust coming in the front, in case Victor has eyes on this place.'

Easton looked really dubious now. Though it was obvious what Dani was saying, even if to him it was perhaps all too simple, and convenient.

'That doesn't mean he's going to come back again,' Easton said.

'Maybe. Maybe not. But there's one way to find out.'

Chapter 42

Dani hadn't been on a stake-out like this for years, and even after three hours in the cold she felt sure it would be worthwhile. Most criminals weren't geniuses, and very few knew how to properly run and hide for any length of time, particularly when exactly what they needed – money, shelter, clothes – remained in one place. Home.

Perhaps Grigore thought he was being clever. Hiding from Victor in plain sight. Or perhaps he just saw no other way. Most likely the majority of people he knew also knew Victor Nistor. Grigore – if he was hiding from the boss – was unlikely to have many allies. He needed somewhere to stay, food, clothes, but he couldn't run the risk of using bank accounts or credit cards, because of the chance that the police too had ID'd him, and would see the activity. He was unlikely to want to burn his limited cash resource on hotels and new clothes and the rest unless absolutely necessary.

Dani was sure she would be proved right. Eventually.

But how long could they wait?

She knew Easton, who was currently in the car, on the street at the opposite end of the back alley, remained less than convinced. And a little agitated that his evening was being slowly eaten into.

At least he wasn't standing out in the cold. Not right now, anyway.

A chill breeze stung her cheeks and Dani hunkered further into her coat and pulled herself closer to the wall behind her as she spied around the lamppost, down the alley to the barbed-wire-topped wall at the back of 51, nearly a hundred yards in the distance. Technically the alley she was in served the houses on the same road, but there was a cross street halfway between her and 51, cutting the alley in two. Easton was a couple of hundred yards further on the other side.

'I can literally hear your teeth chattering from here,' Easton said, his voice just audible through Dani's radio which was set to its lowest possible volume.

'Very funny,' she whispered.

'I'm not joking. If I have to cover you because you've given yourself pneumonia…'

'Shh,' she said, whipping her head around when she heard the faintest of sounds behind her.

This had always been the risk. Not only being outside, and more exposed than Easton in the car, but being between two quieter back streets than he was. She'd hoped – if Grigore was coming back at all – that he'd come up the cross street in front of her to enter the alley, but fifty yards away in the other direction, a lone figure had stepped out from the street.

Head down, hands in pockets, the person was moving her way with a measured stride. Whoever it was, there was no indication they knew Dani was there, lurking in the shadows. Within moments, though, they'd be walking right by her. Even with no streetlights here, they would surely spot her in the thin haze of moonlight.

Of course, there was nothing to say this person was Grigore at all, even if there hadn't been a single other soul walking down here in the last two hours.

But it *could* be, which was why Dani's heart was already dancing. Dani kept her eyes on the figure as they neared. The size, the shape. Most likely a man. Dani was certain this wasn't random. Which was why she was already reaching up with her radio when the man lifted his head, pointing in Dani's direction.

A split-second later, he turned and ran.

So did Dani.

'Easton, get around here, now! Brookville Road.'

'I'm on it.'

'And call back-up. Just in case. White male. Six foot two. Black hooded coat.'

Dani was already out of breath as she spoke the words. The man – Grigore? – was nearing the end of the alley.

'Stop! Police!' Dani shouted.

Her call did nothing to deter the runner.

A flash of the foot-chase from Oldbury, two days ago, burst into Dani's mind. She'd lost out that time against the mystery man. Had that been Grigore too? But why?

'He's gone left,' she said into the radio. 'Towards Stratford Road.'

She heard the piqued revs of the engine before she saw the car. Easton sped past her just as she reached the end of the alley. She rushed out, her momentum preventing her from turning the corner sharply enough and causing her to veer across the pavement and out into the road behind the car.

Perhaps that was the same problem the runner had. Or had he simply thought he could make it across to the other side in time before Easton passed?

Either way, Dani watched in shock as the man lurched into the road. Easton's brake lights flicked on, tyres squealed on the cold ground, but he could do nothing to slow the vehicle in time and there was a thudding impact which sent the burly figure up into the air. He crashed across the bonnet, onto the roof and then smacked back onto the tarmac behind the car, landing in an awkward heap.

Dani raced up to him, already fearing the worst. Easton jumped from the car.

The man was writhing and groaning in pain, clutching his leg which was all twisted. Not a nice sight, but he certainly wasn't dead, at least.

In the process of the crash, the man's hood had come down, revealing his meaty face that was now creased in both pain and anger.

Even in the dark, Dani recognised him.

'Silviu Grigore? I'm arresting you on suspicion of murder.'

Chapter 43

Dani's endless, tiring day was finally over. Midnight had long passed as she headed away from HQ and along the Aston Expressway towards Sutton Coldfield, the traffic on the roads as light as Dani was weary. She'd spent the best part of the last two hours with Easton in an interview room with Silviu Grigore. Easton had left the office some forty-five minutes ago, while Dani tried in vain to think of anything else she could usefully do before heading home. The time spent with Grigore had been next to useless. Grigore was giving nothing away. Had answered everything put to him either with 'no comment', or by pretending that he didn't even understand the question. In the morning Dani would source a translator so that next time around he wouldn't have that excuse.

For now, though, they were at an impasse. Dani was sure they had enough evidence to charge Grigore with murder. Both in relation to Jane Doe and Clara Dunne, the circumstantial evidence was strong. But that wasn't good enough for Dani. She wanted to know the full truth. What had happened to the two women? What had happened to Liam Dunne? What was the involvement of Victor Nistor and Alex Stelea and Nicolae Popescu and the second man that Grigore had been with the night he'd been stopped with Jane Doe's mutilated body in the back of his van?

And perhaps the most troubling unanswered question in Dani's mind: what was Ben's role in it all?

As Dani passed over a junction her eyes fell on a sign for Good Hope Hospital, the largest hospital in the North

Birmingham area. Not the hospital that Jason was at, but spotting the sign still led to a knot tightening in her stomach. Stuck in the thick of an ever-changing investigation, she'd barely seen Jason since the weekend, and when she had seen him, it had mostly been late at night or at a horrendously early hour in the morning when he'd still been asleep.

Her tiredness now made the situation feel all the worse. Friday was supposed to be the first of their home 'trials', where Jason would stay the night, just the two of them. A normal couple, doing normal coupley things, if only for a day or two. For months Dani had longed for that moment to arrive. Now it felt like it was too much too soon, a burden almost, and she hated herself for thinking that way.

Unfortunately, with the melancholy thoughts taking hold, Dani could think of little else for the remainder of the drive. She'd been intending to get home, strip off her work clothes and dive straight into bed, rather than faffing with sorting out work clothes for tomorrow and heading back to the hospital to see Jason. But now she wasn't so sure, despite the late hour.

Her street was deserted. Not a soul in sight, no lights visible inside most of the properties except for the odd one where the security-conscious owners had left a porch or hall light on to deter burglars.

Dani's house was encased in darkness, not just because of the lack of interior lighting, but as a result of the layout of the street's lampposts which meant there wasn't one within thirty yards of her home, creating something of a black void around hers and her neighbours' properties. It was only when she turned onto the drive, and her headlights lit up the brickwork, that she was able to confirm that indeed her house remained standing.

She shut down the engine and the lights flicked off and she was plunged into darkness once more. Dani tensed. Her eyes darted nervously as she stepped from the car. She trod carefully through the dark towards the front door, because she couldn't see the path at all, and also due to the rapidly forming frost making the surface treacherous.

The street was silent, except for a gentle breeze rattling the bare branches in the trees. But then a faint scraping sound behind Dani, back towards the road, caused her to jerk and she whipped her head around to stare back at the street, nearly losing her footing in the process.

Of course there was no one there. The noise was mostly likely to be a cat or a fox or even just a frozen twig blown from a tree.

What the hell was she expecting to see anyway? A bloody vampire or something?

She carried on to the door, already shivering from the cold, but not helped by the dark thoughts now swirling in her mind.

Did she really want to stay here alone tonight?

She unlocked the door and took a half step into the porch and quickly reached out for the light switch before she'd even taken the key from the lock. The two spotlights overhead flicked on and Dani stepped fully into the porch as she pulled out the key.

That sound again.

Definitely not a twig.

Dani spun around. One hand on the door, ready to slam it shut.

That was her intention at least.

Except she hadn't expected to be paralysed by fright when she saw the blacked-out figure standing just a few yards from her.

Dani gasped, but she couldn't move. Brigitta Popescu's ominous words rattled in Dani's mind. Bodies, bones, Strigoi.

The figure, dark clothing, hood shadowing their face, took a step forward. Dani could see only a glimpse of skin and it glistened from the porch lights. Glistened red.

Blood.

Another step and the figure pulled down the hood.

Dani was left wide-eyed and open-mouthed.

'Ana?'

Chapter 44

'Please... help me.'

Dani reached out and grabbed Ana's arm. The young woman flinched but then acquiesced as Dani pulled at her and coerced her into the porch. Dani quickly opened the porch door and flicked on the hall lights and soon she and Ana were both safely inside with both the front door and the porch door closed and locked behind them.

Yet Dani wouldn't feel relief yet. Was the house really empty?

'Ana, whose blood is that?'

Dani looked her up and down. The red on her face and her neck and her hands was dried and cracking. The black puffer coat she was wearing – surely too big to be hers – also had several large patches on it where the material looked duller than the rest – stained?

Ana didn't answer the question but a tear rolled down her cheek.

'You have to help me,' she said.

'I will help. But you need to talk to me. Are you hurt?'

Another tear escaped and Ana shook her head, but the shake slowly turned into a nod.

'It wasn't my fault,' she said. 'I had no choice.'

'Had no choice? Ana, what's happened?'

'Alex. I think... I think he's dead. I think I killed him.'

–

What was Dani supposed to do in that situation? Perhaps the sensible thing would have been to arrest Ana and take her to the

294

local station, and then sleep on it. Or even to call the cavalry in and get them to take over while Dani gathered her thoughts and waited to brief Easton, McNair, Jason – whoever – in the morning.

Dani hadn't done any of that. The simple fact was that Ana, for some reason, had sought out Dani in her hour of need. Whatever she'd done and for whatever reason, she hadn't run away, she hadn't gone to anyone else, she'd come to Dani for help. And Dani would give it, because Ana could be the key to the police unravelling everything.

–

The clock on the dashboard flicked over to two a.m. Ana, in the passenger seat next to Dani, was still shivering, despite the multiple layers of clothes that Dani had given her after her quick shower to remove the dried blood. But not before Dani had taken swabs of the blood, along with the bloodied clothing, which she'd packaged away to give to the Forensics team when she caught up with them.

Dani still didn't know for sure whose blood it was, or what injuries Ana herself was suffering from. Her face was bruised, she had a thick and cracked lip, and her right eye was black and badly swollen. Plus she had hobbled through the house like she was several decades older than she really was, clearly in pain with each step, but she was still yet to explain to Dani exactly what had happened. Although she had given enough. Which explained why they were now on the road.

Not that Dani was doing this completely gung-ho. She'd already called for back-up, and they'd be meeting with them sooner or later. The car Ana had arrived in remained on Dani's street. Alex's car, apparently. The FSIs would get their chance to comb over that. But not yet. Dani had a bigger priority.

'How did you know where I lived?' Dani said. A question which had been bugging her since the moment she saw Ana.

'Alex. There was a message on his phone from Victor. Victor was finding out about you. I think because he knows you're investigating him.'

That made sense. Though it did also worry Dani. She was a target of Victor's now too.

They rattled along the A5 dual carriageway at speed. She didn't have lights or sirens but the roads were dead and she wouldn't waste time sticking to the speed limits now, despite the many speed cameras.

'You came this way?' Dani asked.

'I… I think so,' Ana said. 'It's hard to remember. I was… I was too scared to think properly.'

With Ana remaining scatty, so far Dani was working largely off instinct. Ana had said she'd driven for about half an hour. Had followed signs for Sutton Coldfield. She'd claimed the road signs she'd seen along the way – on the main roads at least – also included Lichfield, Birmingham. Had remembered that the nearly full moon, big and bright on a night with intermittent cloud, was up in the sky to her right.

That was enough for Dani to figure the basics. Ana had travelled from the north and west of Sutton Coldfield. A pretty vague area still, although it was consistent with the location, between Brownhills and Cannock, where Silviu Grigore and his as-yet-unknown accomplice had been stopped three days previously, on their way to dispose of Jane Doe's body.

That spot was only a mile ahead of them now.

'What else can you remember?' Dani said to Ana without taking her eyes from the road. 'Tell me from the beginning. Whatever you can.'

'It was… underground. I think. Or at least inside the ground. Like in the hill.'

'A cave?'

'No. Maybe. A bunker? The entrance was tiny. Wet and cold. A tunnel.'

'A tunnel? But of earth, mud? Or brick? Concrete?'

'Not brick. But hard. Concrete, I think.'

'And when you came out into the open?'

'I had to squeeze through the branches. It was dark. I just remember trees, everywhere. I followed a path.'

'Tarmac? A hard path?'

'I don't think so. It brought me to the car. Alex's car.'

'Were there other cars?'

'There was space for others. But it wasn't a car park.'

'Just a clearing in the woods?'

'I... think so.'

'And then what?'

Ana shook with terror. Dani frowned.

'That was when I saw him. It.'

'Who?'

'There was a hill. Off to my right when I came to the car. A figure standing right at the top, looking down on me.'

'But you didn't see his face?'

'It was too dark. He was too far. All I saw were his clothes, moving in the wind.'

'Clothes? Like what, a scarf?'

Ana looked confused. As though she couldn't explain what she'd thought she'd seen. Or at least not without sounding like a lunatic.

But what had she seen?

'I just knew I had to escape.'

'Then you got onto a road?' Dani said. 'What did you see first?'

As Dani asked the question they passed over the spot where Jane Doe's body had been recovered.

'Some signs. But I can't remember where to. I wasn't thinking properly. Then there were houses. But not for long.'

'What about this road we're on now?' Dani said. 'Do you recognise it?'

She slowed down. Past the spot they'd recovered Jane Doe's body, they were now entering the unknown, and Dani didn't want to risk making a wrong turn and throwing the whole search off-course.

'I don't think… wait, yes!' Ana said, pointing into the distance. 'That roundabout. I came from that way. I saw that pub.'

Dani turned right at the roundabout. The small village of Norton Canes lay ahead of them. The start of the sprawling Cannock Chase was only a few miles further ahead – twenty-six square miles of rugged countryside and forest. Ana's description thus far, and the fact that Silivu Grigore and his accomplice had been carting Jane Doe's body in this direction, convinced Dani that they were on the right track. But would Ana remember enough to get them to the exact spot? If not, how on earth were they going to find what they were looking for in such a vast area?

Unfortunately for Dani, she was left with that exact issue a little over ten minutes later as she pulled the car over to the side of the A460, one of several roads which bisected the Chase. Dark forest surrounded the unlit road, the car's headlights struggling to make an impression.

'Ana?' Dani said.

'I'm sorry. I just don't know.'

Dani thought for a few moments. Ana said nothing more. Dani sighed, then took out her phone to make the call.

Chapter 45

An hour later the area was slowly being overrun by blue lights. Three police cars, a dog van. Ana remained in the car while Dani organised the troops and set them off on their search. The dogs were the best bet, Dani believed, though only if they were somewhere near where Ana had come from so that they'd be able to find a scent trail to follow.

With the help of a little-used OS map, which Dani had in the car, she'd identified two areas not far from where she had pulled over which she believed could be the hill Ana said she'd seen, even though there was no indication on the map of any buildings nearby – whether old or new, or even remnants of something from days gone by like mines, bunkers, quarries, whatever.

Still, Dani wasn't giving up easily. And after travelling another mile to a spot equidistant between the two hills, where the other officers had met them, she'd now set them on their way. The officers would do their best to search in the dark. Come daylight, if they hadn't found the trail, Dani would bring in extra bodies. As many as it took until they'd scoured all twenty-six square miles of Cannock Chase.

As soon as she was able to, she'd also set up the team back at HQ to scour CCTV to retrace Ana's journey. The team would be back online within six hours, though Dani was more than tempted to ring them all and get them into the office in the middle of the night.

She held off for now.

With the late-night help all busy with their tasks, Dani headed back to the car where Ana was sitting shivering. Cold or scared or a combination of both?

'We've got some time on our hands,' Dani said. 'Unless you want to go out there into the cold and dark forest, perhaps you can start telling me what's actually going on.'

She looked over at Ana whose face twisted a little with apprehension. Perhaps Dani's tone had been slightly harder than she'd intended, but so what? Ana needed to start talking. Not just about what had happened tonight, but about everything she knew of Victor and Alex and their dirty deeds.

'We'll find where they took you,' Dani said. 'We'll find Alex, Victor too. What I want to know is why?'

Ana looked even more unsure now. Her shivering had turned to trembling. 'Alex was… he would have killed me.'

'But why, Ana?'

'Because! Because I called the police. About Maria.'

'Maria?'

'She was only eighteen.'

'She was the body we found—'

'I made that call,' Ana said. 'I couldn't sit and watch any longer.'

'Who killed her? Silviu?'

Ana frowned. 'Who's Silviu?' She paused. Looked even more scared now.

'Ana, who killed Maria? We tried to catch the men transporting her body. One was called Silviu Grigore. We've arrested him now.'

'I'm sorry. I really don't know him. But those men… they didn't kill her. They just…'

'Took the bodies away?'

Ana closed her eyes and kept them closed, even as she started to speak. 'You must know what that house is. I know the police were there. You traced the call I made.'

'A brothel?'

Ana shook her head, not in disagreement, Dani thought, but in disgust.

'I don't know who killed Maria,' Ana said. 'A man who came to see her. She wasn't the first, but I told myself she had to be the last.'

'What about Clara Dunne? She wasn't a prostitute.'

'I don't know anything about her.'

'Really?'

'I don't! You must believe me.'

'And Liam Dunne?'

'I'm sorry. Victor doesn't tell me anything. If you're saying Victor killed them… maybe it's true, but I don't know anything about it. I only know what I see.'

'Which is what?'

'The women. They bring them into the country all the time. Force them into work. I have to…' She trailed off and clenched her fists. 'I have to help, make them feel comfortable and safe. Even as I'm taking away their passports, their phones, their freedom. Their lives.'

'How many women? We need to find them. To make them safe.'

'I don't know. A hundred. Two hundred, since I've been here. But Victor and Alex send them all over the country to other handlers. It's not just for them.'

A transport business. Dani shivered.

'So there are other houses like the one in Wednesbury? Others that you know of?'

She hung her head. 'Yes.'

'I need the addresses.'

Ana flinched as Dani reached over and opened the glovebox. She dug around and found a pen and a scrap of paper.

'Please?'

Ana hesitated but then took the pen and paper and began to scribble.

'The place where Alex and Victor took you, did you know about it before?'

Ana stopped writing.

'Ana?'

'I knew there was a place. A way to… deal with problems.'

'Problems? As in dead bodies?' Dani said, her revulsion clear. 'Is that what that place is? Somewhere to dispose of bodies?'

Ana nodded. Dani could hardly believe what she was hearing now.

'How many?'

'I have no idea!'

'Then think. Think about what you've seen, what you've heard.'

Ana didn't say anything for a good while. Then, 'I'm so sorry.' She was sobbing now, and Dani was torn as to whether she should feel sympathy or not. Could Ana have done more, sooner?

'Where's Victor now?' Dani asked.

'I don't know.'

Dani sighed. Word from the surveillance teams was that they'd seen nothing of Victor, Alex or Ana all night. Clearly there was good reason for the last two. But what about Victor? Did he know Ana had escaped? Was he in hiding now?

Dani was at a sticking point. Yes, they'd made some headway in figuring out who Jane Doe – Maria – was, and they had Silviu Grigore in custody, but there was still so much that she didn't know.

'You said you saw someone on a hill, watching you. Do you think it was Victor?'

Ana closed her eyes again for a few moments. 'I know it sounds crazy,' she said, looking back to Dani. 'But maybe it wasn't a man at all. Maybe it was a…'

Dani gave her the time, but she didn't finish the sentence. 'A what?'

Ana looked out of her window to the dark forest beyond. 'No, you'll think I'm insane.'

'What did you think it was, Ana?'

Dani jumped when there was a knock on the window. Heart racing she turned around and heaved a sigh when she saw the bright yellow jacket and a face she recognised – Michael Robinson, the sergeant she'd left in charge of the search.

She stepped from the car.

'Anything?' she asked, although his stoic face already indicated the answer.

'The dogs have found nothing. Not even a whiff for them to start tracking. And we've gone all around the two hills you noted, and there's literally nothing there but trees and grass. No buildings or caves or anything of the sort.'

Dani sighed and looked at her watch. They hadn't been searching that long. She could ask them to continue looking. But was that fair when they might not even be in the right place? Perhaps it was better to call them off, and re-organise a more widespread search in the daylight.

'What do you want to do?' Robinson asked.

Dani thought. She slumped. 'Call it a night,' she said, reluctantly. 'You've done what you can.'

He nodded and headed off. Dani got back into the car. Ana's face was creased with concern.

'They didn't find it,' she said.

Dani shook her head.

'But you do believe me?'

Dani thought that was a strange question. Had she somehow suggested otherwise? Why on earth would Ana not be telling the truth?

'Yes, I believe you,' Dani said, despite the doubt that Ana had herself placed.

'So what now?'

Dani thought about that for a few moments. She stared straight ahead, out of the windscreen, watching as the collection of officers, cold and sullen – though likely relieved that their night-time traipsing was over with – got themselves ready to clear out.

They were likely relieved. Dani was the opposite.

'I really don't know,' Dani said.

They waited another ten minutes. Until the taillights of the last of the patrol cars, no blue lights now, had faded into the distance.

'We aren't going too?' Ana said.

'Are you sure you've told me everything?' Dani said, turning to glare at Ana, who looked a little unsettled by the accusatory tone.

'Why would I lie?'

A good question. But Dani really didn't know what to think or to believe any more.

'I'm not lying to you!' Ana said, her voice raised. 'Why would I lie about being out here? About them bringing me here. About attacking Alex?'

'But how did you manage to attack him? How did you escape?'

Ana looked even more worried now. 'I told you. I managed to untie my wrists. When he got close I surprised him. I got to the knife before he did. It was luck more than anything. And I didn't even mean to... to hurt him. Not like that. My only thought was to get out of there.'

The two women stared each other out for several seconds.

'It's the truth!' Ana said.

Dani said nothing. She started up the car and was about to turn around to head back the way they'd initially come, but then had an alternative thought. Yes, it was ridiculously late, she was ridiculously tired, and wanted nothing more than to crash out in bed, but a few more minutes wouldn't hurt now. So instead she pulled onto the road and carried on going straight ahead, heading further north, before she looped west, moving even further away from home.

'Where are we going?' Ana said, as though picking up on the fact that they weren't yet going back, and sounding all the more worried for it.

Dani didn't answer. Her mind was too busy working over-time.

'When we came off the A5, through Norton Canes, you said you recognised the pub. But you didn't remember specifically going through that village?'

'No... but...'

'But you did say there were houses, not long after you'd come out of the forest in the car.'

'Yes.'

'And there was a hill, with a man, or *something* at least.'

'Yes,' Ana said.

Dani didn't say anything more after that. She carried on, snaking along the edge of the Chase, several miles until they came to the western edge and the A34, deep within the terri-tory of Staffordshire Police now. Dani wouldn't let that deter her tonight.

Dani turned onto the A34, heading south, back towards Cannock.

She glanced over to Ana, the bemused look on her face slowly clearing.

'Wait... I—'

'You recognise it?' Dani said.

'That's the pub,' Ana said, pointing to the building a couple of hundred yards in the distance. 'The same one from earlier?'

'No. It's not the same one. But it is a similar set-up. Dual carriageway. Roundabout. Pub.'

'Down there. Yes, this is it!' Ana said, more animated now. 'I remember that building too.' She pointed to a small industrial unit. It was pretty nondescript but Ana seemed sure enough.

'It's left here!' Ana shouted.

Dani slammed the brakes and took the left. She hadn't even seen the junction in the dark, the road was so obscured by foliage. They found themselves on a twisting country lane. Dani slowed the car, giving Ana the time to properly look around, though the featureless and unlit road could have been anywhere. They drove on for more than a mile, without any indication of life, yet Dani's satnav showed that the town of Cannock was still only a couple of miles off to their right, and within a mile they'd be entering its outer suburban reach. The entire area off to the left of the screen was blacked out. Wilderness.

Dani slowed further. Then a flicker of movement caught her eye, somewhere up front, in the sky. She stared at the space beyond the glass but couldn't catch it again.

Yet she was sure she'd seen something.

After another few hundred yards, with the orange glow from the ever-nearing houses continuing to build in the sky in the near distance, Dani pulled the car over into a lay by.

'What are you doing?' Ana said.

'Just trust me.'

Ana looked really unsure about that, but Dani opened her door and stepped out. A moment later Ana had done the same from the passenger side.

'What do you see?' Dani said. 'Anything?'

Ana looked around, then shook her head. 'I don't know. It's so dark.'

Dani reached in through the open car door and turned off the headlights. She was sure Ana gasped in panic as she did so, as though she didn't trust Dani's intentions, but Dani had done it for both of their benefit. It took a while, but slowly her eyes adjusted to the darkness. She kept her eyes fixed on the spot where she was sure she'd detected movement moments earlier.

Sure enough, when the clouds above them parted, and a bluish-white light from the moon swept over the area, Dani caught a glimpse of it again.

A prominent hill, a few hundred yards in the distance. And at the top of the hill…

Dani looked to Ana, whose face said it all.

'I was sure it was a... I thought I was being watched. You don't even want to know *what* I thought was watching me.'

What *had* she thought? Strigoi? It's certainly what had come to Dani's mind.

'It's fine,' Dani said.

'It's just a flagpole,' Ana said, laughing as if in disbelief.

'I think so,' Dani said, as her eyes fell on the faraway object, the tall pole, the fabric wrapped around it flapping in the breeze.

'We found it,' Ana said, now sounding horrified by the fact.

'Not yet,' Dani said. She closed her door. 'Come on, this way.'

Before she could talk herself out of it, she turned and headed across the ditch by the side of the road, and into the pitch-black woods.

Chapter 46

Dani clicked her torch on and shone the wide arc of white light left and right. Despite the beam's power, it did next to nothing to help, as all Dani could see in front, all around, was the thick trunks of trees. She couldn't even see the top of the hill, or the flagpole upon it any more, though she still had a good idea where it was.

'Why are we doing this?' Ana said, her voice quaking. She was already two or three steps behind Dani who slowed slightly to let her catch up.

'When you came out into the woods, and first thought you were being watched, where exactly was the hill?'

'It was on my right.'

Dani waited for her to add to that description. She didn't. 'But how far away? Can you remember where the moon was?'

Despite Dani's apparent rashness at heading out in the dark, she really didn't want to be rambling aimlessly for hours, and if they could at least narrow down the search area even slightly, it would be of great benefit.

'Ana?'

'I don't know the distance. A hundred metres maybe. Two hundred even. And I'm sure the moon was right behind it, lighting it up from behind, because the figure... the flag, its shadow, was reaching right down towards me.'

Dani glanced to Ana and even in the thin moonlight could see the look of terror in her eyes as she recalled her escape.

'The moon's right in front of us now,' Dani said, 'but it must have moved a fair bit in the last couple of hours, so we probably need to bear left from here.'

Ana looked unsure, but she didn't protest as Dani veered left. So far they'd not found any semblance of a track, and Dani had no clue how far away they were from one. The ground underfoot was soft and wet, but not particularly muddy, largely being made up of piles of discarded leaves and pine needles all soggy from the cold and damp autumn and winter.

'Stop!' Ana said, her voice quiet though intense.

'What?' Dani whispered.

'I thought I heard a noise.'

Ana was hunched down, looking back in the direction they'd come from. Dani shone the torch that way, but it looked exactly the same as everywhere else. Trees. No life.

'It was probably an animal or something,' Dani said, trying her best to sound calm and confident, even though she'd been in much the same position as Ana now was, back at her house earlier, when she'd heard a noise, hoping it to be innocuous, moments before having the fright of her life.

But there was no one else there now. Dani was sure of it.

'Come on, let's keep moving,' she said when the eeriness of the situation got the better of her.

She pulled on Ana's arm and the two of them were moving again, albeit more slowly and more cautiously and more silently than before, as though both of them were now straining every sense that little bit more.

'If you see anything at all that you recognise, just shout,' Dani said.

'This wasn't it,' Ana said, shaking her head. 'It was more of a trail than this. This is…'

She didn't finish the sentence, and Dani wondered what she'd been about to say. This is pointless? This is hopeless? This is stupid?

A part of Dani agreed with each of those options, though it was a part which she was managing to keep pushed somewhere to the back of her mind for now.

Soon they'd been walking for more than fifteen minutes with no identifying features in the landscape at all. Cloud had once again covered the moon, meaning they couldn't even use that to help pinpoint their direction, and Dani was becoming more and more disorientated, unsure if they were moving in a straight line or not. If they had been, then they surely should have come to the edge of the hill by now, yet they were still on the flat.

She dipped the torch down and took out her phone, but there was no signal and without one the map app was useless. 'Shit.'

'What?'

'Nothing.'

She put the phone away.

Should they turn around and head back? Dani was becoming more tempted by the second to do just that. Yes, they both had decent coats on, but they were hardly equipped to be spending the next five hours out in the freezing cold, before morning came, roaming around relying on hope to see them through.

But they didn't stop and turn back. Dani marched them on. Right up until they finally came to a track. Or a semblance of a trail at least. Dani shone the torch up and down, eking the path out from the darkness as best she could. The narrow strip of hard-trodden mud was all of three feet wide and formed a twisted route between the trees and undergrowth.

'Could this be it?' Dani said.

'I... I don't know.'

Dani sighed, which received a petulant glare from Ana.

'Come on, this way,' Dani said, heading off to the right.

The trail twisted for a couple of hundred yards, and Dani's sense of direction was soon thrown. Yet she kept on, trying to remain undeterred. Then the torch light captured something up ahead, sending back a bright flash of light. A metallic reflection.

Dani twisted the torch, trying to hit the same spot again as she moved. There it was again. She squinted in the darkness, trying to figure out what she was looking at. She glanced over to Ana, whose keen stare suggested she'd seen it too.

'What is that?' Ana said.

Dani didn't answer, just kept on walking. They were all of ten yards away when she figured out the answer.

'A fence?' Ana said.

A metal fence, more precisely. Six feet tall with spiked prongs at the top. A security fence, although it had certainly seen better days. The structure was mangled and had fallen in on itself in places, and was covered in evergreen growth, largely ivy, in others.

Dani shone the torch along the ground and saw that the trail snaked alongside the fence as far as they could see.

'You must have seen this before?' Dani said, her tone almost accusatory.

'No. I didn't. I mean… perhaps I did pass here, but I don't remember a fence. I didn't have a torch though.'

Fair point.

They'd only moved ten yards alongside the fence when Dani stopped again. She stepped right up to the fence, a spot where the metal was almost entirely lost behind twisting green growth. She was sure she'd seen something poking out from underneath. She reached her hand out and dug into the intertwined stems, and her hand disappeared into the unknown. Her mind flashed with a scene from an *Indiana Jones* movie. The one where the heroine pushes her hand into a crevice filled with giant cockroaches and writhing centipedes, looking for the switch to release Indiana from a death trap. Dani shivered at the thought of those monstrous creepy-crawlies, but had soon cleared away the growth to reveal nothing but a rusted and dented and faded sign.

'Danger. Keep Out. Unstable ground,' Ana read.

'A mine?' Dani said. It had to be. Or a quarry perhaps, although there were no markings on the maps she'd seen to suggest either. Unless they were completely off-track.

'Come on,' Dani said, moving again.

'I don't like this,' Ana said. 'I really don't.'

'We must be getting close.'

'But I didn't even see any of this! This isn't the right…'

She stopped mid-sentence. Had stopped walking too. Dani was sure she knew why. Up ahead, there was a section of the fence that had caved in, about five feet wide, though the metalwork was almost entirely lost under a tangle of ivy that was congruous with everything around it.

They both moved towards the spot, side by side, passed over the broken fence in unison, pushed through undergrowth for several yards. The form of the hill was now visible in front of them. The ground rose steeply into the distance.

Then Dani spotted it. Right at the base of the rise, disguised by yet more twisted branches and creepers, was what looked like a hollow in the rock. All of five feet tall, barely more than three wide.

'We found it,' Ana said, absolute terror in her voice.

Chapter 47

Dani tried her phone again. Still no signal. What the hell should she do? She'd much rather have a team to support her here, but how long would that take? First she and Ana would have to traipse nearly back to the car to even get a signal, then sit and wait, then make the whole journey back through the forest again.

As much as she'd rather have other officers with her now, she really didn't want to go through any of that.

And anyway, if Alex was already dead inside here, then what was the worst that could happen?

Dani crept up to the entrance, shone the torch inside, but it was so black and featureless beyond that the torchlight did little to help show what they were facing.

Dani turned to Ana, but as she did so the torchlight flicked into the near distance and Dani paused as she stared across the ground surrounding them. Just like everywhere else there was a thick layer of leaves and other debris scattered all over, but it was clear the ground around here was undulating with small mounds. A horrific thought wormed into Dani's mind but she pushed it away.

'How far inside?' Dani asked.

'I don't know. Not far. But... I can't go back in there.'

Ana was shaking as she spoke, and Dani didn't believe it was from the cold.

'You'd rather stay out here on your own?' Dani said.

'I'd rather be in a foamy bath in the suite of a five-star hotel.'

'Tell me about it.'

Dani turned and ducked and headed in. She was confident Ana would soon follow. Three steps inside she glanced over her shoulder to see Ana right there.

The cramped space was dank and musty. Water pooled underfoot and Dani's feet splashed through it sending mucky liquid up against the bottom of her trousers with each step. She kept the torchlight focused up ahead and soon she could see a junction of sorts where the tunnel split into two.

'Which way?' Dani said to Ana.

'I don't know.'

Dani shone the torch to the left. The tunnel carried on that way as far as the light could reach, sloping downwards as it went, no end visible. To the right the ground remained more level, and Dani was sure there was an end in sight that way. Which was why she chose that path.

Sure enough, after a few more steps, the form of a doorway took shape.

'This must be it,' Dani said as much to herself as to Ana.

Every step now was more fraught than the last. How Dani longed to be somewhere else. The five-star room Ana had mentioned. Dani could imagine it now. The warmth, the comfort, the smells and the feel. That picture of serenity couldn't be any further from her reality.

By the time Dani was five yards from the open doorway, she could make out some of the room that lay beyond. Shelving. Workbenches. She flicked the torch down to the ground, kept the light focused on the unidentifiable, crumpled mound on the floor just past the threshold.

She edged forwards ever so slowly. Her heart raced. Her legs were shaking from surging adrenaline. Pure fight or flight. But Dani wasn't about to turn and run. Not now.

She reached the doorway.

'There was a light,' Ana said. 'I don't remember turning it off.'

Dani, torch shining into the space, didn't take her eyes off the heap on the floor as she reached around the doorway. She felt for the switch. Found it. She flicked it and the strip light overhead in the room sputtered into life, achingly slowly. Only when the flickering had stopped did Dani turn off her torch light. She took another half step forward, her eyes still on the heap on the floor right in front of her, spatters of red all around. Most of it still wet.

She'd expected to see the form of a man in the heap. To see skin, a face. Alex, to be precise. But all she saw was a discarded pile of blood-drenched clothes.

The room was empty.

Alex was gone.

Chapter 48

'I don't understand,' Ana said, as Dani prodded the pile of bloodied fabrics with her toe, as if she expected it to come to life.

It didn't.

'Did you check he was dead?' Dani said.

'No! I only wanted to get out. But I stabbed him. In the chest, in the back. He wasn't moving. He *must* have been dead.'

'Except he's not here now.'

Dani saw a flicker of doubt in Ana's eyes.

'You don't believe me?'

'Where's the knife?' Dani asked.

Ana glanced around the room. 'I don't know.'

'Did you drop it? Take it with you?'

'I don't remember!'

Dani bit her tongue. She scanned the room. First she looked to the chair in the middle. Just a plain old wooden chair, although it was bolted to the ground. Why? There was no sign of the rope that Ana had claimed had tied her to it. Next Dani looked over to the workbenches. There were no tools laid out now, like Ana had claimed. Tools which Ana had believed Alex was about to use to torture her with.

What was going on?

Was Ana lying?

'What is this place?' Dani said.

She didn't get an answer from Ana, nor had she expected one. She was thinking out loud. She moved over to the dusty metal shelving unit in the far corner, where there were several similarly dusty cardboard boxes. Dani reached out and flipped the lid on one of them. Discs for an angle-grinder. They looked ancient. She moved to the next box. This one was more curious. Not tooling at all. She reached in and her hand came back out clutching onto a swatch of leather, all ragged at the ends like it had been cut or torn from a bigger piece.

'How did Victor and Alex even know this place existed?'

Once again she got no answer from Ana. Dani put the leather to one side, then reached into the box once more, and this time pulled out a pendant necklace.

What the hell?

'Ana, what—'

Dani looked over her shoulder. Then spun around abruptly, her eyes fixing on Ana's petrified and teary face. She was still standing right by the door.

Except now she wasn't alone.

Dani hadn't heard the newcomer at all. How on earth had they moved so stealthily?

Dani's gaze moved first from Ana's terrified eyes to the glint of metal held up against her neck, then traced across the thick gloved hand, the black-coated arm and along – until she was staring into two dark eyes behind Ana.

Two dark eyes in a bulbous face that Dani immediately recognised, even though she'd only ever seen him before in photographs.

Nicolae Popescu.

Chapter 49

'You've been looking for me,' he said, his voice as growly as his accent was thick.

'Put the knife down,' Dani said.

Was that the best she could think of?

Popescu grinned evilly.

'I have a whole team of officers coming this way,' Dani said. 'Don't do anything stupid.'

Popescu snorted. 'No. You don't. You two are all alone.'

'Where's Alex?' Dani asked.

Popescu flicked his gaze over his shoulder. Dani took her chance and shuffled forward a half step. Ana's eyes went even wider than they already were, as if warning Dani to stay put.

'I finished him off,' Popescu said.

Ana moaned and squirmed.

'She did a good job, but he wasn't dead. Not quite.'

Why would Popescu kill Alex?

Then Dani got it.

'You're running from Victor,' Dani said.

Popescu looked disgusted.

'You and Silviu were both running. Because we stopped you with that body. You know we arrested Silviu earlier tonight?'

He didn't react at all to that. Had he already known?

'She was called Maria,' Dani said. 'You were coming here, right? To dispose of her. This is the place you always come to dispose of bodies, whenever Victor asks. But you were caught by the police. And now you're a risk to Victor. He wants you de—'

'Shut your face, you stupid bitch,' Popescu snarled, flicking the knife towards Dani.

The angry reaction was undoubtedly supposed to intimidate Dani. But Popescu had made a mistake. Even though he'd seen Ana's previous handiwork, he'd still underestimated her. With the knife away from her throat, Dani knew what was coming.

She wouldn't pass up on the opportunity either.

Dani raced forwards. She reached out and grabbed out, toward the workbench. Grabbed what she could. A wooden stump – a broken handle? A weapon of sorts, at least.

Ana stamped on Popescu's foot, grabbed hold of his knife arm with both her hands. She tried to wrestle the blade further away from her. But Popescu towered over her, and was thick and muscly to boot. Ana was nowhere near a match for his size and strength.

Popescu threw his fist into Ana's side. She squirmed and he pulled his arm free and lifted the knife to drive it down into her neck.

'Ana, move!' Dani screamed.

Ana did her best. She pulled to the side. The knife slashed across the flesh of her shoulder. She cried in pain. Dani swung the wood in an arc towards Popescu's face. He didn't see it coming. There was a crunch as wood hit bone and he stumbled a half step back. Dani wound up to hit him again. She never saw the meaty fist winging towards her face.

Popescu's thick knuckles smashed into her nose. Blood spurted and Dani reeled back and lost her footing. She was on her way down as Popescu delivered the same hammer-like blow to Ana. Her head snapped to the side, and the blow sent her crashing into the shelving. The side of her skull cracked horrifically against the metal, and she plummeted awkwardly to the concrete floor, smacking down a fraction of a second after Dani.

Dani lay on the floor. Dazed, nearly out of it. She tried to shake her head. Blinked a few times to clear her fogging vision. She couldn't lose consciousness. Not now. Not like this. She fought against it with everything she had. Across the way, Ana was crumpled on the floor, unmoving, as a line of blood dribbled down her face from her hairline.

Dani glanced up. Popescu was hovering right over her now, one thick boot either side of her torso. He used the heel of one to turn Dani onto her back. She groaned and writhed but her world was swimming, her body distant, and she didn't have the strength to fight back, however much she willed herself to try.

Popescu dropped down. His hefty weight crushed Dani's chest, knocking the air from her lungs. Her head spun all the more and she once again fought to stave off unconsciousness.

Popescu pinned her arms with his knees. He looked down on her with hatred and disgust.

'You shouldn't have come after me,' he snarled.

Dani didn't say anything. She could barely breathe, let alone speak.

'If it hadn't been for his stupid sister…'

His sister.

His sister. Clara Dunne?

Dani's brain fired now, his words exactly what she needed to find clarity. Dani bucked and writhed. Not that she intended to throw him off, but she needed an inch to breathe properly. To think properly. To talk, and keep him talking, before he thrust that knife down into her heart, or her neck, which he could do at any second if he wanted.

'*You* killed Clara,' Dani said, her words still choked, though at least she'd got them out. His distraction was exactly what she needed. 'You killed Clara because she knew the truth.'

Popescu clenched his teeth. 'She had to go.'

'But you didn't bring her here. Not like the others. Why?'

'Because… I hate this place.'

'How many people have you killed? How many have you brought here?'

Popescu shook his head. He was looking more and more angry. Surely that wasn't a good thing.

'You still don't know a thing,' he said.

'Then tell me. Why did you kill Liam?'

He shook his head. 'You really don't know anything.'

He looked almost disappointed.

That was when he lifted the knife, and plunged it down into Dani's flesh.

Chapter 50

The blade sank effortlessly into the flesh of Dani's shoulder. She screamed in pain, her eyes welled. She gritted her teeth and fought through it as Popescu slowly drew the knife free. Blood dripped off the end of the blade. Dani was woozy, delirious from the agony.

'You really don't know?' Popescu said. 'You don't know who Dunne was?'

Popescu dropped down to face Dani. The stab wound was sufficient to make sure she didn't take the opportunity to fight back. She flinched when his free hand fell down to her hip. He patted about her side and drew her phone from her pocket.

'Open it,' he said to her, pushing the phone down to the ground, next to her hand.

Dani grimaced as she stretched out to press her thumb onto the screen. Popescu flicked for a couple of seconds before he turned the phone to Dani.

The screen was blindingly bright and it took Dani's eyes a couple of seconds to properly focus. She was left staring at the picture of Liam Dunne and the blonde woman.

'My sister,' Popescu said.

'I don't...'

Dani had been about to say, 'I don't understand.' But then, perhaps she did after all.

'What *is* this place?' Dani said as a tear fell from her eye.

Popescu snorted in disgust. Revulsion. 'This is where *he* brought them. All of them. My sister too.'

And now it all made sense.

'Liam Dunne killed your sister.'

An open secret. Stef had known it too, no doubt. Who else had? Victor? Brigitta? Not even two days ago Stef had looked at that picture in Brigitta's house and had sworn she didn't know either Liam or the woman. She'd lied. Because she did know Popescu's sister. She'd said so herself; that not just Brigitta's daughter, but her granddaughter had gone missing too. Brigitta's daughter many years ago, in Romania. But her granddaughter...

'And believe me,' Popescu said. 'I showed that bastard just how bad that decision was.'

Pure hatred dripped with every word.

Finally, Dani could make sense of it all. Liam Dunne had murdered Popescu's sister. Had brought her here. Had likely brought others here before her. He'd paid the ultimate price. Both Dani and Clara Dunne, Liam's own sister, had been searching for the truth. The truth of Liam's disappearance. They'd both believed him to be a victim.

But Liam Dunne hadn't been a victim. He was a sick murderer.

Popescu held the knife aloft.

'And now, Detective, I'm very sorry but—'

Thwack.

The blistering impact halted Popescu mid-sentence. Dani had seen it coming. He hadn't. The wood smacked into the side of his face. Blood spurted, a tooth flew from his mouth.

Ana didn't let up.

She whacked him again on the top of his skull with her elbow. Dani reached forwards and grabbed his knife hand. Much the same attack as the two women had tried moments earlier. This time they had to make it count. Dani bucked and managed to worm her way out from underneath Popescu, even as she continued to hold his arm at bay. Ana hit him a third, then a fourth time in the head. Dani launched her knee up and dug and ground it into Popescu's groin. He groaned in pain.

Ana hit him again, and as Dani twisted his wrist the knife came free.

The next second Popescu pulled out from Dani's grip. Ana hit him in the head again. Popescu went to haul himself up. But Ana was like an animal. She grabbed his leg, just below the knee, and sent him crashing back down to the floor. His head smacked against the back of the chair in the middle of the room. Ana landed on top of him, snarling. She reached out to the side and grabbed the knife…

'No!' Dani shouted.

Too late. Ana thrust her arm towards him and four inches of the blade disappeared into Popescu's neck. She wrenched the knife free. Blood spurted and poured as Popescu's body twitched. He desperately gargled for breath.

Dani watched on helplessly, too shocked to move.

Within seconds Popescu's movements slowed. Soon, the blood flow reduced to a tame trickle.

After that, Popescu lay entirely still.

Chapter 51

The huge spotlight flicked on and Dani winced from the strength of the ultra-bright beam. Then she cringed with pain as the needle was pushed into her skin once more.

'Last one, I promise,' the paramedic said, his face as apologetic as his words.

Dani looked back across the clearing that was now filled with ambulances and police cars, their strobes of blue doing a good job of lighting up the forest surrounding them. As Dani glanced across to the flagpole on the hill in front of them, she could see the first daylight peeking over as the sun made its slow rise. Within an hour there'd be no need for the hastily erected spotlights at all. At least not on the outside.

In the mine, however...

'All done?' Dani said when the paramedic turned away.

'All done. Though I really do think you should—'

'I'm not resting now,' Dani said as she jumped off the end of the ambulance.

She headed back towards the gap in the fence. But then veered to her left when she spotted Ana sitting in the back of one of the many police cars. She headed over and crouched down by the open door. Ana was shaking despite the hot drink in her hand and the silver blanket wrapped around her.

'What will happen to me?' Ana said, solemn and more than a little concerned now. After all, an hour ago she'd stabbed a man in the throat in full view of a detective.

'You're going to be fine,' Dani said. 'I'll make sure of it. You saved both of us tonight.' She put her hand onto Ana's shoulder. 'Thank you.'

Ana gave a meek smile. Dani turned and headed away. She moved beyond the gap in the fence, the trail now lit up brightly the whole way. She passed several white-suited FSIs before she came to the smaller clearing by the cave entrance where there were close to a dozen FSIs, together with digging equipment, large piles of freshly dug mud all around.

Dani paused and watched them for a few moments.

'What have we got?' Dani shouted when one of the FSIs looked her way.

'Definitely human remains,' she shouted back. 'At least five so far. Hard to say how long they've been here. Some are definitely older than others.'

Dani sighed then headed back into the cave. If it was possible, the bright lights in here made the narrow space all the more oppressive. At the junction, Dani's eyes followed the tunnel downwards to the left. She could hear voices that way. She already knew that that was where Alex's body had been found. Along with a jumbled pile of other bones.

Brigitta Popescu's words rattled in Dani's minds. *Bones... so many bones.*

Had she always known the truth about her granddaughter, and about Liam Dunne too?

Dani carried on to the storage room. Or was it a workshop of sorts? Whatever it had been when this place was a working mine, it was now overshadowed by the room's use for the macabre, which had started with Liam Dunne, though certainly hadn't finished with him.

Dani found Easton in there, along with Tariq and another FSI.

'Some job you've given us, DI Stephens,' Tariq said, sounding quite jolly, despite his words, like this was all a big adventure. 'I've had to call in help from Staffordshire, too, as we didn't have enough bodies available, and this is technically their turf anyway.'

Dani winced at the use of the word 'bodies'. Tariq didn't seem to get his faux pas.

'Anything I should know about yet?' Dani said.

He sighed. 'This room alone is going to take considerable time to sort through, but a few initial checks with the blacklight and with Luminol suggests we have blood traces all over. Who it's from could be the difficult part to figure out.'

'And we also found this,' Easton said, as he moved over and unrolled a utility belt across the worktop. A whole host of ghastly-looking tools lay inside. At least they were ghastly if taken in the context of what Dani now believed they'd been used for. 'Apparently, further down the shaft they've found a load more boxes, probably cleared out of here at some point. Some of them contain personal items. Jewellery. Shoes. Clothing. Photos.'

Dani shook her head in disbelief. 'Trophies.'

'It's possible, right?'

'All along we were looking for Liam Dunne as though he was the victim of some horrible crime. When all along he was a monster. Perhaps he got exactly what he deserved.'

Easton didn't say anything to that. Dani heard a crackle of radio static from outside the room. She turned and saw a yellow-jacketed officer heading her way.

'Damn reception,' he said as he shook the radio in his hand. He looked up and spotted Dani. 'Ma'am, DCI McNair wants to speak to you.'

Dani slumped. 'I'd best go take this.'

–

Dani did eventually manage to get the radio working, though the conversation with McNair was short. Something along the lines of, 'Get over here now.'

Which was why, forty-five minutes later, Easton was pulling up to the entrance of the underground car park to HQ. As much as Dani had wanted to leave him at the scene, there was no way she could have driven herself on so little sleep, and with the knife wound in her shoulder. Though the high-strength pain killers the paramedic had given her together with her still-surging adrenaline was certainly something of a potent combination. The come down, when it hit, was going to be brutal.

Dani thanked Easton before he shot off back to Cannock. She could only hope she'd get the chance to rejoin him soon, though the fact McNair had called her here made that prospect seem unlikely.

The time was a few minutes shy of eight thirty. McNair had been at work for all of an hour, having been rudely awoken by Dani. On the other hand, Dani had been working for more than twenty-four hours straight now. Still, she wasn't sure she was going to be getting a friendly reception, despite all of her efforts.

She found McNair in her office, busy typing away on her keyboard. She looked up from what she was doing, an unimpressed frown on her face.

'Do you know how many national papers I've had to bat back since I spoke to you last?' She didn't even give Dani the chance to answer. 'How did they even find out?'

'How do they always?' Dani said.

'Hmm,' McNair said. 'Anyway, you can only imagine the morning I've got ahead of me, fending them all off. So let's make this quick. Short story. What's happened?'

Short story? Was there even a short way to explain this?

'To get to the point, I think Liam Dunne, our missing person, was actually a killer.'

McNair said nothing as she stared at Dani. Did she not have anything to say to that revelation?

328

'It makes sense with what we know,' Dani said. 'Name changes, location changes for one thing, trying to cover his tracks, but likely also in the victims he chose.'

'Meaning?'

'Meaning Liam Dunne's unintentional links to Victor and his gang. My thinking is that he targeted vulnerable women who wouldn't be missed: prostitutes, drug abusers. Loners. But he never stayed in the same place long enough to arouse too much suspicion, changed his name several times. Still, they're exactly the type of women Victor runs. The type of women who, I'm very sorry to say, don't exactly set alarm bells ringing when they disappear, which is why most likely we were never alerted to his existence as a killer. Except Dunne made a mistake. Somehow he got involved with the sister of Nicolae Popescu.'

'Nicolae Popescu being?'

'Something of a henchman for Victor Nistor. Dunne then killed Popescu's sister. When Popescu found out... well, I'm guessing he took Dunne to that mine. The place Dunne likely killed Popescu's sister, among others. And Popescu let his dark side loose.'

Dani's skin prickled at the thought. Not just of what Dunne had done to his poor victims, but what Popescu had done to Dunne. Would the police ever figure the full story?

'But Popescu's sister wasn't a prostitute?'

'I can't say for sure, but it would seem unlikely, given who he is. The fact we found a photo of her and Dunne together, though, suggests maybe they were something of an item.'

'Yet he still killed her?'

Dani thought about that. In the end she could only shrug.

'We'll figure this out as best we can.' Though with Dunne already long dead, perhaps that was easier said than done. 'Since Dunne was killed I think that place has been used as a convenient dumping ground for Nistor and his gang whenever they have a problem. Overdose. Prostitute bludgeoned. Gang rival to take care of.'

McNair looked even more dubious. About which part, Dani didn't know.

'Clara Dunne has been searching for her brother for years,' Dani said. 'Somehow she figured out the link to Popescu. And she was silenced because of it.'

McNair didn't say a word for several seconds. 'What about the body? Jane Doe? That wasn't Dunne.'

'Maria? I think she was something of a red herring. A prostitute killed in a rage by an angry punter. Popescu and Grigore were the henchmen tasked with disposing of her body. They took her to a place where they knew they could safely dump a corpse.'

'Except this time it wasn't safe. We caught up with them.'

'We did. Then we have Ana. Who tried her best to blow the whistle on Victor Nistor's operations. But she got caught too. And Alex Stelea was tasked with disposing of her. Again, the place of choice was the same.'

McNair shook her head in disbelief.

'Which brings us nicely back to Nistor,' she said. 'Where is he?'

'Something we need to find out.'

'We have a national alert out for him. We'll get Interpol on the case, too, on the off chance he's already managed to skip out of the UK.'

'I'll do everything I can—'

'No. You won't,' McNair said.

The room fell silent. Dani gritted her teeth. She didn't like the look on McNair's face.

'You're injured, and you've been through a hell of an ordeal,' McNair said. 'I'm recommending you take some time off.'

'Ma'am, I really don't want—'

'And don't forget we haven't even got around to discussing that incident with DS Easton the other day. Have we?'

Dani slumped. 'No. We haven't.'

'So, like I said, I'm recommending you take some time off. You've broken this case, and I and everyone else is very grateful, as always, for your efforts.'

'Am I suspended?'

'Just go home,' McNair said. 'I'll be in touch.'

Dani said nothing more. She should have felt triumphant right now, but she felt the exact opposite. Could McNair not at least have let her enjoy the moment?

Perhaps after some much needed rest, she'd see the bright side.

Tail between her legs, Dani turned and walked out of the door.

Chapter 52

Ten days later

Easton pulled the car over to the side of the road outside Dani's house.

'I guess I'll see you around then,' he said.

'Merry Christmas,' Dani replied.

'And a Happy New Year.'

'Let's hope so.' Dani opened her door and stepped out, but then leaned back in before she shut the door again. 'And make sure you—'

'You'll know everything. Don't worry.'

'Thanks.'

Dani closed the door then waited a couple of seconds as Easton headed away. She looked to her house; the lights in the Christmas tree in the bay window twinkled away. She took a deep breath, then headed up the driveway.

She opened the front door, then the porch, and did a double-take when she saw Jason standing there in the hall, his coat, hat and gloves on, crutch in one hand, his other helping to prop him up against the wall.

'Finally,' he said. 'Longest coffee ever. Come on, we don't have much time.'

He hobbled across to the wheelchair and plonked himself down. It then took a few goes and plenty of scrapes against the wall to get the chair out of the house. Dani had previously suggested it would be easier to take the chair out first, but proud

Jason didn't like the idea of the neighbours seeing him hobble about ungracefully.

'Not too much longer and we won't have to bother with this rigmarole at all,' he said as Dani closed the door and locked up.

'I'll keep you to that.'

Over the last few days they'd already started looking at houses in the area to buy, at first only considering ones that were step-free and wheelchair accessible. Jason had pulled his face at every single one. As he'd put it himself, 'Why take such a defeatist attitude? I'm not going to be in this wheelchair forever.'

Of course whether that was true or not was still up for debate, and to a large extent out of their hands, though Dani could understand his need to stay positive and focused, even if it turned out to be false hope.

'So, go on then, fill me in,' Jason said as Dani wheeled him onto the pavement, heading off down the road towards the church. It was a chilly evening, though the atmosphere on the road was purely festive with sparkling Christmas lights all over.

'They're not going to charge Easton over the fight. So that's done and dusted. He can move on.'

'What about for you?'

She sighed. 'We won't hear now until after the new year, but from what Easton's gleaned, the top brass aren't showing much inclination to pursue anything more than a reprimand. Perhaps helped by the press around the Dunne case.'

For which Dani's name, and comments on her bravery and outstanding commitment, had been plastered all over the news – both local and national – even if she had taken a back seat over the last few days. Not of her volition. At least not initially.

'So what about the case?' Jason said.

'You mean you haven't taken enough from the internet and the six o'clock news?'

'Ha, no fake news for me, please. I want it straight from the horse's mouth.'

'Wow, you have such a way with flattery. So I'm a horse?'

'Horses are beautiful. Graceful.'

'OK, Casanova. The good news is that yesterday Victor Nistor was charged with Clara Dunne's murder. With Ana's attempted murder, too, among a whole host of other things, from people trafficking to sexual assault.'

'And he won't get away with it,' Jason said.

'Not if I've got anything to do with it.'

'Which I'm sure you will.'

'Eventually.'

And as much as she now realised that this brief period of mental and physical recuperation was probably a good thing for her, she remained hugely disappointed, and more than a little aggrieved, that she hadn't been there the day they'd caught up with Nistor at Dover, and hauled him into a cell. She'd have loved to see his face.

'Grigore has also been charged with Clara's murder,' Dani said. 'And good for us, he's not keeping as tight-lipped as Nistor. It sounds like his lawyer thinks Grigore can get some favours by going against the boss, and with his intel we've already managed to break into the trafficking operation.' *We've*. Like Dani had been a part of it. 'We've found more than two dozen young women Nistor and Stelea were controlling.'

'Bloody hell. And Liam Dunne?'

Dani shook her head and sighed. 'Too early still. They have identified remains which they believe to be his, but Easton reckons it's going to take months more, at least, to piece together his crimes. Forensics believe there are the remains of at least twelve people at the mine, and judging by the state of the remains the majority of those were there since before Dunne disappeared.' Dani gulped.

She didn't add what Easton had told her about the clear evidence that the bodies had all been hacked apart – whether pre- or post-death, they weren't yet sure.

'On Dunne's phone the pictures and details of four women were found. We've traced two of them to Missing Persons. One of Romanian origin, one Hungarian. But we think there are more. Easton has searched Missing Persons cases going back years, but it's going to be near impossible to put all the pieces together. Dunne chose these women – young, vulnerable, possibly illegal immigrants – for a reason. Questions weren't asked when they went missing. That mine could be just the start. We're still working with the other forces to look at the other places Dunne lived.'

'But nothing so far?'

'Nothing.'

They took a left turn and the looming Victorian church came into view a hundred yards ahead. Crowds were milling outside as people filtered in for the Christmas Eve carol service.

'Just be happy that this time Ben really didn't have anything to do with it all,' Jason said.

Dani was glad that it was dark out, and that Jason was in front of her and couldn't see her face, otherwise he'd have realised she was blushing with embarrassment at the thought that, a couple of weeks ago, she'd been getting set to bring Ben right into the heart of her investigation. Just like she'd been accused of doing, unjustifiably, with the Curtis investigation. This time around she'd been saved by Ana's intervention. If she hadn't escaped, and hadn't tracked down Dani, then maybe right now Dani would have still been full throttle trying to pin the crimes on Ben.

What did that say about her? That no matter where her life and her work took her, all roads still led to Ben?

She cringed at the thought.

'The appeal was lodged yesterday,' Dani said.

'Best not to think about it.'

'How can I not?'

'Ben was always going to appeal, one way or another. Daley wouldn't have it any other way. The whole thing with Curtis and Collins only gives them more focused ammunition.'

'Ammunition? For God's sake! Ben could get his murder conviction overturned if they convince a jury that Collins's testimony at his original trial was tainted, and if they get another expert to convince them that Ben is insane.'

Jason didn't say anything to that, saved by them arriving at the church. Dani was left feeling seriously disgruntled that they'd ended the conversation on a downer. Talk of Ben still had that effect on her. Dani had a brief reminder of her strange conversations with Brigitta Popescu about Strigoi. The old lady had claimed she could sense death and darkness in Dani. Perhaps Ben was like a Strigoi to her, sapping her of all energy and hope, ever since he'd attacked her.

But her apprehension – her fear about the idea of Ben one day being a free man – wasn't irrational. The threat of him getting out of jail on a technicality was real, and Dani felt powerless as to how to help the situation.

There must still be a way to prove Ben's involvement in Curtis's killing spree. But how?

Dani was still focused on that even as she wheeled Jason through the waiting crowd, the churchgoers kind enough to make way for the wheelchair user.

They got the perfect position inside, right in front of the altar and the attendant choir. Candles burned brightly everywhere. A twelve-foot-tall tree dazzled. Dani tried her best to enjoy it all, to soak in the atmosphere. The church was bustling and soon filled.

The vicar took the pulpit and opened with a well-rehearsed speech, though Dani struggled to listen initially. Unfortunately, despite the festive setting, her mind was still too busy thinking about Ben. Plus, even though they were here in church now, it was hardly as if either of them was deeply religious. Tonight was more about them enjoying some sense of normality: reminiscing about good times, family times, getting into the Christmas spirit. After all, only a few weeks ago they hadn't even been sure if Jason would be out of hospital by now. Yet, as the vicar carried on, Dani's attention slowly focused more and more on his words.

'...Christmas is also a time to be thankful,' the vicar said. 'Thankful for what we have, and always mindful of those who are less fortunate than we are. We all face challenges in life, and we all know what it is like to suffer, or to see loved ones suffering...'

Jason reached out and put his hand onto Dani's.

'And as we come to the end of this year, we should look back at all of the good, and the bad, the struggles and the triumphs alike, of the year that's now coming to an end.'

Jason squeezed Dani's hand. She didn't react. She was too busy trying to keep her welling tears from escaping.

'At times we all suffer with regret. Could we have been kinder? Could we have done more? Should we have felt happier? But regret is not a barrier. Regret is an opportunity. An opportunity to do things differently next time, to learn from our mistakes. And as we look forward to welcoming in the new year, we should all strive, with all the energy and enthusiasm we can muster, to take hold of that opportunity, and to make it our reality.'

And Dani couldn't agree more with those words.

Next year. Next year would surely be her year. The year where she'd finally lay all her demons to rest, once and for all. Her's and Jason's both.

A Letter From Rob

Thank you for reading *Echoes of Guilt*, and I really do hope you have enjoyed DI Dani Stephens's latest adventures and trials! I also want to say a big thank you to everyone at Hera, Canelo and Darley Anderson who helped to get this book from concept to final product.

Dani is a character who continues to intrigue me, and I've had a lot of fun developing her over the last few books, even if she would probably not describe the experience as 'fun' for herself! People often ask me how I come up with my ideas for characters and plots, and a lot of the time I find it really hard to answer, because the reality for me is that a character or book rarely comes in one single eureka moment. Rather, I'll have multiple sparks over a period of time, which I slowly play with in my head until I feel I have the sufficient bare bones of a book to make a start on drafting.

Often those bare bones are very bare indeed, sometimes they're a little more fleshed out. *Echoes of Guilt*, though, was a little different for me, because I can very firmly pinpoint where I had the conceptual idea.

With two young sons, me and my wife rarely get holidays just for the two of us anymore, but last autumn we managed a much needed childfree break to Bucharest in Romania. Neither of us had ever been to Romania before, and the few days we spent there were absolutely fascinating, both in terms of the people we met and the place and its incredible history (particularly the rise and fall of communism, the relative recency of which is still such a big and relevant event in the country's history).

It was on that holiday that I decided I wanted to bring a bit of Romania into my next Dani book, and while sitting in the hotel lounge one afternoon I began to develop the plot for Echoes of Guilt while I read up on Dracula. Now, of course everyone knows of Dracula, but I wanted to bring this element out in a crime thriller without it descending into schlock horror, without it descending into the overtly supernatural. I hope you enjoyed these elements of the story, and that you found them as creepy as I tried to make them – and if you did, then you've got our trip to Romania, and the multiple measures of Romanian plum schnapps I had there to thank for the inspiration!

Once again, thank you for taking the time to read my work (and this letter). I'm always grateful for reviews, if you could spare a few minutes to write and post one online. I also welcome direct comments and feedback, and you can reach me via my website (where you can also sign up to my newsletter), and on social media, links as follows:

Website: www.robsinclairauthor.com
Twitter: @rsinclairauthor
Facebook: fb.me/robsinclairauthor

All the best
Rob Sinclair

Books By Rob Sinclair

The Sleeper series:
Sleeper 13
Fugitive 13
Imposter 13

The Enemy series:
Dance with the Enemy
Rise of the Enemy
Hunt for the Enemy

The James Ryker series:
The Red Cobra
The Black Hornet
The Silver Wolf
The Green Viper
The White Scorpion

The Dani Stephens series:
The Essence of Evil
The Rules of Murder
Echoes of Guilt

Others:
Dark Fragments